Wedding Season

Also by Katie Fforde

Wedding Season

KATIE FFORDE

St. Martin's Press   New York

WEDDING SEASON. Copyright © 2008 by Katie Fforde Ltd. All rights reserved. Printed in the United States of America. For information, address St. Martin's Press, 175 Fifth Avenue, New York, N.Y. 10010.

www.stmartins.com

Library of Congress Cataloging-in-Publication Data

Fforde, Katie.
   Wedding season / Katie Fforde. — 1st U.S. ed.
      p. cm.
   ISBN 978-0-312-60017-4
   1. Weddings—Planning—Fiction. I. Title.
PR6056.F54W43 2010
823'.914—dc22

2009040238

First published in Great Britain by Century, a division of The Random House Group Limited

First U.S. Edition: March 2010

10   9   8   7   6   5   4   3   2   1

To Desmond, our wedding was the first he'd ever been to and he didn't mess it up, then or now. With love.

Acknowledgements

Weddings always involve lots of people and in doing the research for my book, I met a lot of them and I hope I haven't left anyone out of my thank yous. However, a couple of people are responsible for me writing the book in the first place. And yes, you are going to be named and shamed!

Firstly, Jema Hewitt for inspiring the whole idea and nearly teaching my daughter and me to make a corset. It was so much fun.

Secondly, Debbie Evans, friend, neighbour and hairdresser. Not only does she do my hair at a moment's notice, at all hours of the day or night, but she made me realise that no book about weddings was complete without a hairdresser.

These are the two responsible for the whole idea but others had a hand in it too.

Sue Trevaskis from Colour Me Beautiful who wasn't bossy but has inspired in me a desire to bounce up to people and say, 'You really need to have your colours done.' Most of us do, actually!

To Kate Cobb, wedding planner for real. Major respect to you!

Amanda Grange, author of *Mr Darcy's Diary* and others, for her advice with regard to costume. Very generously, she didn't say, 'Do your own research.'

To Christine Gaunt, artist and dressmaker who shared her knowledge in the Curves changing room with great generosity.

To Cassie Winters-Pilcher, personal trainer and cake expert. Without her, that cake would never have been made.

To my personal trainer David 'Mac' McKinnon who not only knows everything there is to know about diet and exercise, he also has an encyclopaedic (and worrying?) knowledge of hen nights.

A book, like a wedding, is the product of many people. Without a wedding there would be no bride, and without an author there would be no book. But the bride would look a bit lonely standing at the altar without very many other people.

My publishers are the bridegroom to my bride. They are inspiring, inspired, hard working, patient, and incredibly supportive. When I despair they tell me the answers and are so nice about it. They never say, 'That's your job, Katie.' They are nearly too numerous to mention but here goes.

In editorial there are Kate Elton, Georgina Hawtrey-Woore, and others who work so hard but never get to go out to lunch with The Author. Charlotte Bush and Amelia Harvell, who spoil me so shamelessly and keep me smiling through thick and thin. (Mostly thick, sadly.) Mike Morgan, who takes me on road trips every year. Rob Waddington, Oliver Malcolm, Jay Cochrane and Trish Slattery who force my books on the public so successfully. Claire Round and Louisa Gibbs in marketing. And Richard Ogle and the art department who produce such lovely covers.

To patient, long suffering Richenda Todd, without whom the egg on my face would be truly awful.

To all at AM Heath, Sara Fisher, lovely Sarah Molloy, Bill Hamilton and the rest of the team. Thank you!

Time for confetti now!

Chapter One

Sarah stood by the lych-gate and surveyed the perfection of the summer morning. It was June and the sun was shining with the promise of a perfect day. The church was an early English gem, surrounded by closely mown, dew-spangled grass, ancient lichen-covered gravestones and clipped yews. She'd already seen Sukie, the florist, who'd been there since dawn, and now some of her anxiety left her. Two years of work had come to fruition. It was all going to be all right.

Then she screamed as someone appeared from behind a tombstone. 'Agh! Hugo! You brute! You gave me such a fright!' As her beating heart caught up with her brain and she realised she wasn't being attacked, by a stranger at least, she went on: 'You had me thinking it was Halloween for a moment there.'

Hugo, tall, blond and rumpled, always gave Sarah the impression that he'd just got out of bed – and not his own.

'Sarah, you're so sweet, I should give you up for Lent,' he drawled in reply.

Sarah smiled. Hugo was one of the best photographers she dealt with and they always exchanged sallies and insults, but she had deliberately never got to know him as a friend – she felt it was more sensible to keep the relationship strictly professional. 'We both seem to have got our seasons mixed up.'

'As long as we've got the day right. Perfect for it, huh?'

Sarah nodded. 'And you'll love the bride. She's really beautiful.'

'Bridesmaids?'

'Darling. Two little sweeties – we won't call them angels until we know how they behave – and one big one to keep them in order. Heavenly dresses.'

'Second families to worry about? Bride and groom's parents still married to each other and pitching up?'

'Yup. Marriage does work for some people, apparently.' She smiled again slightly, pretending she was joking.

Hugo rumbled his amusement. 'Don't you believe in "happy ever after" then?'

'Not very often. Which is why I think it's important that the wedding is as wonderful as it can possibly be.' She gestured to the scene of perfection before them. 'It might be the only happy memory.'

Hugo inspected the dew that had gathered on his perfect shiny shoe. 'Honestly, Sarah, if the people who pay you to organise all this knew how you feel . . .'

'They don't need to know about my feelings, only about my ability to find the perfect venue and a personable photographer who makes everyone look fabulous.'

He chuckled again, taking the hint that she needed to get on, along with the compliment. 'So, anything I need to know?'

Sarah considered. 'I don't think you should have any trouble. The bride's mother has put an awful lot of energy into this and is very anxious that nothing happens to spoil that, but she's got a great hat. I'm sure she'll succumb to your ready charm.'

Sarah could never understand why she was the only one who realised Hugo's ready charm was part of his stock-in-trade as a photographer, but she admitted that, for a wedding planner, she did have more than the usual amount of cynicism. And for good reason: she hadn't been in the business more than a couple of years and already two of the perfect weddings she had organised had broken up, one barely eight months after the happy pair drove off in a cloud of dried delphinium petals. Five of the six girls from her school who had got married the moment they hit twenty-five had since separated. There was also her sister's debacle of a marriage, not to mention (and Sarah never did) her own heartbreak, recovered from but not forgotten. No, in Sarah's eyes, happy-ever-after was the rare exception that proved the rule.

'Well, I'll just prowl around a bit more,' said Hugo, unaware of Sarah's thoughts. 'Find somewhere really picturesque to take the less formal shots.'

'Try to avoid grass stains on the dresses, if you can. Please! I always get complaints.'

He tipped his head and closed his already heavy-lidded eyes, indicating that while he heard her request, he wasn't necessarily going to concede to it.

'It's all right for you, no one ever moans to you!'

'Because I'm the best,' he said simply.

And because he was, and they both knew it, she just said, 'I'd better get back to the hotel to make sure everyone's there who should be, and not too many people who shouldn't.' She frowned. 'I'm still not convinced it wouldn't have been better to have the reception at the bride's home – it's fabulous, but they decided it was less upheaval to have it at a hotel. It is a very good hotel, of course. But the money!' She raised her hands in a gesture of amazement. 'Now, I must get on.'

She turned away, aware of his sleepy gaze on her back. She hoped he wouldn't get the bridesmaids to lean against lichen-covered gravestones and thus ruin their dresses for ever, but accepted that for him getting the right shot was vital and nothing much else came into consideration. She was good at managing people and she usually got what she wanted out of them, but she was never convinced that Hugo took any notice of her at all.

As she walked back to her car she wondered if Ashlyn was the sort of bride who would encourage people to open the champagne before the wedding and turn what should be a morning of solid preparation into an extension of the hen party. But her mother would probably put a stop to anything like that. A glass for everyone during the final hair and make-up session was fine, but only one!

She arrived at the hotel to a diorama of potential tragedy. Everyone was more or less static when they should have been calmly getting on with dressing the bride.

Instead, Ashlyn was sitting at the dressing table in a chemise, stockings and French knickers, with her mobile phone in her hand, tears of rage adding the wrong sort of sparkle to her eyes. Elsa, the dressmaker, waiting to help her into the dress now hanging on the back of the door, stood awkwardly inspecting her nails and picking bits of fluff off her black trousers.

Bron, in charge of hair and make-up, had also stepped back. Ashlyn's long and slippery tresses were half up, half down, and her frantic texting had threatened her French manicure. The perfect make-up already needed reapplying.

'What's happened?' demanded Sarah, instantly aware she was witnessing an unfolding calamity.

There was a moment's tense silence and then the bride answered: 'My fucking bridesmaid has decided not to come!'

Shock settled round the room like dust after an explosion. Sarah had never heard Ashlyn use language like that before. A moment's reflection made her feel it was justified.

'Oh no,' said Sarah, her eyes shut, wondering how on earth two enchanting three-year-olds could possibly manage without an accompanying adult bridesmaid.

'Oh yes.' Ashlyn bit out the words between her newly whitened teeth. 'She's decided that a weekend away with her new boyfriend would be more fun than attending her best friend's wedding!'

'That's so out of order,' murmured Bron, wondering when she could carry on doing the bride's hair.

'And to think I paid for that bitch's weekend at Barnstable Spa, which is not exactly cheap!' Ashlyn went on. 'And Mummy paid for her dress – another small fortune.' Elsa, who'd also made the bridesmaid's outfit, winced. 'Well, at least I can change her disgusting wedding present for something decent!'

Sensing that the bride was beginning to move on from this disaster, Bron stepped forward with her comb and pins, preparing to carry on defying gravity with Ashlyn's water-smooth hair. Elsa's shoulders relaxed and Sarah said, 'We can manage perfectly well without her. Poppy should be able to take your bouquet from you and we can ask your sister-in-law to take it from her. Don't worry.'

Ashlyn gave a huge sigh. 'I should have known not to trust her. She sat on my guinea pig when we were little and I've never forgiven her.'

There was a tiny pause, showing respect for the dead guinea pig, and then Bron said bravely, 'OK, if I can just get back to doing your hair. We haven't got all day.'

As Bron laughed, a little awkwardly, Sarah wondered if there was a bit of puffiness around her eyes this morning, or if she'd imagined it. She didn't know Bron very well, perhaps she always looked like that.

Elsa stopped picking at her trousers and seemed calm, waiting for the moment when her dressmaking skills might be needed. Ashlyn's mother had insisted that she attended, principally so she could make final adjustments to the chief bridesmaid's dress, as she'd missed her final fitting. Most probably she would only be required to hook up Ashlyn's dress at the back and break it to the bride that the dress would look better if it wasn't worn over the French knickers she'd had such fun buying, but over nothing at all. She had a thong in her bag if Ashlyn preferred that option.

Then the door opened and the bride's mother walked in. 'Everything all right, darling?'

There was a moment's silence. No one wanted to be the messenger that turned the bride's mother's big day into a disaster. Then Ashlyn bit the bullet. 'Fulvia's backed out. She's going to Paris with her boyfriend instead.'

Mrs Lennox-Featherstone screamed, not loudly, but loud enough to alarm her husband who called anxiously through the door.

'Is everything all right in there?'

'No it is not!' hissed his wife. 'That – trollop – whom we've taken with us skiing, for God's sake, has backed out!'

Sarah realised this was probably the moment when she really earned her money as a wedding planner and co-ordinator. 'It's all right, Mrs Lennox-Featherstone, we can manage perfectly well without her.'

'I've paid for that dress,' said her client's mother. 'Over two thousand pounds – and it's not spending the wedding in a plastic bag!'

Elsa jumped. It was not her fault the dress was not going to be worn or that the enormous amount of hand-beading had taken her so long to do – it was time-consuming. But she couldn't throw off her feelings of guilt.

'That's all right,' said Ashlyn, calm now her mother was having conniptions, 'Elsa can wear it. She and Fulvia are the same size and, unlike Fulvia, she's been a real friend.'

Elsa gasped loudly. 'Ashlyn, I—'

'Yes you have,' persisted Ashlyn, as if it was their friendship that Elsa had been about to deny. 'You sorted me out when Bobby and I had that huge row and we've had such fun together! That lovely day looking at fabric. And you haven't forgotten that time at—'

'Stand up and let me look at you,' snapped Mrs Lennox-Featherstone, obviously feeling there wasn't time for reminiscing just now. 'Why do you persist in wearing black? It's absolutely the wrong colour for you. Drains you. Well, put on the dress and let's see what you look like. It's all right, Donald,' she called through the door. 'You can go away now. It's all going to be fine.'

'Um, I can't wear the dress,' said Elsa.

'Why not? We know it fits,' said Ashlyn's mother.

'Because I'd feel a fraud, not being Ashlyn's real bridesmaid,' said Elsa, sending Sarah a look that told her she needed help.

'It might be a bit awkward with – er – Fulvia's parents coming to the wedding.' Sarah had already wondered if she could leave them seated so near the top table and decided that she had to.

'I don't suppose they know about their little tart's defection,' snapped Mrs Lennox-Featherstone. 'Although they should have guessed, sending her to that awful school. None of the pupils leaves without an A level in bitchiness.'

'OK,' said Sarah, taking charge. 'It is a shame that Fulvia has backed out but, as I say, we don't really need her.'

'Oh yes we do,' said Ashlyn and her mother simultaneously.

'Not only did the dress cost a fortune,' went on Mrs Lennox-Featherstone, 'but the photographs will be unbalanced without a big bridesmaid.'

'Hugo is an excellent photographer,' said Sarah. 'I can assure you that—'

'I want Elsa,' said Ashlyn, like a child on the verge of a tantrum. 'I like her a lot more than fu—' She glanced at her mother and went on to use her ex-best-friend's name without the alliterative expletive. 'Fulvia.'

'So you simply must be her bridesmaid, dear,' said Mrs Lennox-Featherstone. 'What the bride wants, she must have.' She gave a tight smile and glanced at her daughter.

'I can't!' persisted Elsa, feeling more and more uncomfortable.

'You don't want to spoil Ashlyn's big day by being selfish, do you?'

'Of course not,' said Elsa. 'But being a bridesmaid is a really big thing. It should be someone who's known Ashlyn all her life not someone she's only met—'

'I've known you nearly two years,' said Ashlyn. 'I like you – *and* you haven't killed any of my pets!'

Elsa tried to laugh at this attempt at lightheartedness. 'No, but . . .'

'Please!' said Ashlyn. 'I really want you to.'

'I can't,' said Elsa, finding some determination at last.

'Why not?' demanded Ashlyn's mother, who wouldn't take no for an answer without a very good explanation.

'Seriously, I can't!'

'But why not?' demanded Ashlyn, who took after her mother and was curious as well as demanding.

'My armpits!' she said desperately and with all the firmness she could muster – given the word she was being firm with.

'What about your armpits?' said Ashlyn, a frown disturbing her perfectly shaped eyebrows.

'I haven't shaved them. At least, not for a few days . . .' Elsa faltered, anxiously regarding the women who were all looking back at her, appearing to condemn her for slovenly, unhygienic habits.

'Not a problem,' said Bron smoothly, having kept out of the fraught discussion until now. 'I have disposable razors in my kit.'

Mrs Lennox-Featherstone, who, like the others, had perched on the edge of the double bed, stood up and came across to Elsa. 'I realise that as a family we're asking an awful lot of you, but this is Ashlyn's special day; we've been preparing for over two years. Please help us out.'

Elsa regarded her client. She knew as well as anyone

how long this wedding had been in preparation as she had been thinking about, designing and eventually making the dresses for it. It had been her first really big contract and she'd put into it not only the expected blood, sweat and tears, but a good chunk of her soul too.

'We would all be so grateful.' The older woman put her hand on Elsa's shoulder, and Elsa realised she'd never seen her vulnerable before. Bullying, Elsa might have stood up to, but not this heartfelt plea.

'OK,' she said, really wishing she could find it in herself to refuse, but conceding that she was finally beaten. 'On the condition that Ashlyn doesn't wear those knickers,' she added. That was something she wouldn't budge on.

'What's wrong with my knickers?' said Ashlyn indignantly. 'They're silk chiffon and Bobby's going to love them!'

'I'm sure he is, but they'll show through your dress where it glides over your thighs. It'll spoil the line. I've got a thong if you don't want to go knickerless.'

Distracted from Elsa for a moment, Ashlyn's mother turned to her daughter. 'Darling, I really do think you'd better wear something. You can't go to church without pants on.'

'Whatever,' said Ashlyn, 'as long as Elsa agrees to be my bridesmaid.'

Sarah, aware the room seemed very crowded all of a sudden, took charge once more. 'Elsa, you go to the bathroom and have a shower and a shave – sorry, that sounds a bit weird! Mrs Lennox-Featherstone, you go to your room and get dressed. Bron will want to do your hair soon. And Ashlyn, you sit still so Bron can finish yours and then she'll touch up your make-up.'

'Let's open a bottle of champagne,' said Ashlyn when her mother had left the room and Elsa had been sent to the bathroom with a razor and an exfoliating scrub. 'I put a couple of bottles in the mini-bar fridge.'

Sarah really wanted to say no. She knew it was fatal for people to start losing control at this stage but she was weakened by events. She wouldn't have any herself but she really appreciated how welcome it would be to the others. 'OK then, if you must.'

'Can you open it for us then, Sarah?' The bride fluttered her eyelashes just a little and Sarah sighed.

'Get the glasses, Bron, there's a dear,' she said.

Everyone had a glass, and Sarah realised it had been a good idea after all. Just seeing the champagne pour creamily into the flutes had a calming effect.

Chapter Two

Elsa realised she shouldn't have washed her hair just after the shower hit the top of her head, but it felt so good, standing under the pounding water. The hotel had provided very pleasant-smelling and luxurious toiletries and Elsa thought she might as well make the most of them. She also deserved them. It was going to take far more effort to do this than anyone realised. Going home with soft and gently perfumed skin was, she felt, a justified perk. Besides, the shower in her converted loft and workroom wasn't that good. She stayed under the water for as long as she thought she'd get away with.

Eventually she went back into the bedroom feeling clean and shiny with armpits dewy, hairless and fit to be seen. 'I probably shouldn't have washed my hair,' she said apologetically.

Bron, who had been checking Ashlyn's hair, which was swept into a chignon that enhanced her blonde beauty, looked up briefly and said, 'It's OK,' before turning back to the delicate diamond tiara sitting on the top of the shining gold base, making sure that no pins were visible, and nothing less than a hurricane was likely to dislodge it.

'Happy?' Bron asked the bride in the mirror.

'Magic,' said Ashlyn, seeing herself as a proper bride for the first time. 'I look quite like Claudia Schiffer, don't I?'

'Even more gorgeous,' said Sarah, laughing gently. 'Now, if you don't mind going somewhere and keeping very still, we'd better let Bron get on with Elsa.'

Elsa, seated in front of the mirror, draped in a gown,

peeked at herself through her hair. She really hated having it done and recently had taken to cutting the ends off herself with her dressmaking scissors – but not too often in case it permanently blunted them. It wasn't so much that she minded the end result, she just hated spending all that much time looking at herself in the mirror.

Bron stood behind her, holding Elsa's hair and moving it this way and that. 'It's a lovely colour,' she said.

'Thanks,' muttered Elsa.

'And in great condition. I'm just thinking . . . We haven't got a lot of time to put it up, what do you think about a restyle?'

'Won't that take longer than just putting it in a bun?' said Elsa. She'd already had enough excitement for one day.

Bron shook her head and shuddered at the same time. 'Definitely not. Up-dos take ages. A cut and a blow-dry will be much quicker and I think it'll look fab.'

'What about the headdress?' said Ashlyn from her seat by the window, as she idly flicked through a magazine. 'She has to wear it.'

'Not a problem. What do you think, Elsa?'

Elsa didn't want to think. 'I'll shut my eyes,' she said. 'You do what you think is best.'

'Excellent,' said Bron softly, and picked up her comb.

Elsa sat at the dressing table, trying not to look at her reflection. She spent her working life coaxing beautiful fabrics into graceful shapes to make young women's bridal dreams come true but she really hated getting dressed up herself. Her wardrobe consisted of several pairs of black trousers and several black tops. She felt safest in black.

Bron's gentle fingers raised her head or moved it every now and then. She combed, she cut, and Elsa still didn't look. As with using the bath products, having a haircut would make the torture that was to come useful, if possibly unbearable.

Elsa had never liked being the centre of attention and would do anything to avoid it. It went back to her schooldays when she blushed terribly easy and everyone used to tease her. She still blushed – although not quite as much – but the habit of never doing anything that made people look at her stuck.

Bron chatted gently to Elsa as she worked, commenting on the wonderful condition of her hair. 'And as I said, it's a lovely colour.'

'You don't think I should have some highlights in it or something?'

'No, it's a lovely rich brown, and so shiny. Highlights would spoil it.'

'Oh.' Elsa sat in silence for a while as Bron continued to comb and chop.

'Right,' said Bron, 'now for the make-up. You can shut your eyes quite legitimately now.'

'So did you train to do make-up as well as hairdressing?' Elsa asked, to make conversation as much as anything.

'Not really. I worked as a hairdresser for a television company for about five minutes before I went freelance. One day the make-up artist didn't turn up so I did it. I'd seen it done lots of times and sort of picked it up. It makes you more employable if you can do both.'

'So you're freelance, are you? I thought you worked in a salon.'

'I do, nowadays. I'd like to go freelance again, but it's a money thing.' And a boyfriend thing, thought Bron, but she didn't share this with Elsa, who was technically now a client. 'Right, have a look,' she said a little while later.

'Oh my God! A fringe!'

'I know I should have asked, but you might have said no.'

'I hardly recognise myself! My eyes look huge! Is it the make-up?'

Bron shook her head. 'I haven't put much on, just a touch here and there.'

Elsa stared at the stranger who stared back. She looked younger and yet more sophisticated at the same time.

'Wow!' said Sarah, looking up from her clipboard to inspect the new bridesmaid. 'That looks amazing. Look at your cheekbones.'

'You do look lovely,' said Ashlyn. 'Just as well you're a brunette or I'd be jealous.'

'It's amazing what the right haircut will do,' said Bron. 'Now, the headdress. Did you make these?'

'A friend of mine did. I can make them but quite honestly I had so much to do with the dresses, I asked her to do them for me.'

'How do you fix it? Oh, I see, little combs. I hope it'll stay on. Your hair is so shiny, I might need some clips.' She stood back. 'Oh! It looks adorable.'

Elsa hadn't been referred to as adorable since she was three, but she had to admit that she did look better. Her usual beauty routine of toothbrushing and moisturiser didn't involve looking in the mirror. Seeing her features emphasised with make-up was a shock. Her eyes really were quite large, with thick lashes; her skin glowed and her lips looked fuller. 'Wow, I look amazing – and only a little bit like a deer caught in the headlights. Thank you so much.'

Bron laughed. 'If you want to be a dear, put the dress on! It's getting late. I can see Sarah looking at her watch.'

Elsa hadn't been to many weddings and none as a main part. She had been thoroughly briefed by Sarah, Ashlyn and Ashlyn's mother, and they had all given her quite different instructions. Now she sat in the back of one of the wedding cars, a vintage taxi, with the two little brides-maids and one of them's mother. As she was wearing the big dress, she was sitting on the bench seat next to the smallest bridesmaid, while the other two sat opposite.

'I love your dress,' said the mother, who Elsa thought was called Pam. 'Did you make it?'

'Yes, I did all the dresses.'

Pam sighed. 'It's heaven.'

Elsa smiled, not sure if she should take the credit for her creation or be modest about her appearance. The dress was a picture. It was a slightly simplified version of the bride's, in the palest pistachio with very occasional cerise detailing.

The bodice was boned, a process which took hours of very precise cutting and seaming. It had been a real stroke of luck at the time that Fulvia, the errant bridesmaid, had shared Elsa's dimensions, because she was never available for fittings. Elsa had made a model of her own body, aided by a giggling friend and a bottle of wine, when she was a student, so she could fit the dress perfectly. On top of the boned bodice was embroidery enhanced by crystals. It would have been perfectly suitable as a wedding dress, she had thought, wondering at the extravagance and generosity of the bride's family.

'It must have cost a fortune,' said Pam.

Elsa took a breath. 'It did, and not a small one, but it also took hours and hours of hand-stitching – almost as much as the bride's. Poppy and Amanda's dresses didn't take so long.' She smiled at the little girls who were now admiring their ballerina-length dresses with broad sashes. They had simple wreaths of fresh flowers on their heads, which (fortunately) had not been Elsa's responsibility. A lovely girl called Sukie wearing dungarees and a broad grin had delivered them at a ridiculous hour before she had dashed off to the church.

'Looks like we're off at last,' said Pam. 'There's Ashlyn getting in the car with her father. He'll be able to keep her calm, I hope. Did you dress Vanessa, too?'

'Mm. That was quite difficult.' It was a silk suit of the most heavenly fabric that Mrs Lennox-Featherstone had bought in Singapore and had been hell on earth to sew.

'So they paid you thousands, as a family?'

Elsa took a breath. It was a lot of money, but if you counted up the hours of time and labour, and the fact that the money was spread over two years, it didn't make her a rich woman. 'Yup.'

'So you don't mind being a bridesmaid then? At least you're getting to wear one of your creations.'

'Mm,' said Elsa. 'I'm actually happier in my black trousers.'

'Great hair, by the way.'

Elsa blushed.

Elsa had a long time to admire the back of Ashlyn's dress, which had been super-complicated to make. All those folds and gathers, beading and ribbons, had at first seemed a bit over the top to Elsa. But Ashlyn had insisted, and combined with a bit of tactful toning down on Elsa's part, the effect was gorgeous.

The whole wedding was gorgeous, she had to admit. Sarah had done wonders. There was even a local choir so that the hymns had harmonies, and the fact that most people didn't know them didn't show.

Yet she was still anxious. She didn't feel right wearing a client's dress, even if she had tried it on a couple of times. But was it, she wondered, trying to distract herself from the minefield of the reception and the photographs that lay ahead, like staying in your own spare room? Magazines suggested that if you had a spare room you should sleep in it yourself to make sure it was comfortable. Maybe wearing one of her own creations would reveal any little flaws that might only come to light with wear. Call it research, she told herself, and shivered.

At last the ceremony was over. Widor's Toccata boomed out from the organ and eventually it was time for the bridesmaids to process out after the bride. Just concentrate on the little sweeties, Elsa silently ordered the congregation, don't look at me.

But fate wasn't listening. It was only Elsa who processed, the little ones had been caught up by their loving parents, abandoning Elsa to a walk of, if not shame, definitely embarrassment. She stiffened her back and tried to look natural. Why had she never realised how difficult these darn dresses were to walk in?

There had been no video in the church but now the still photographs were to be taken. Elsa wasn't sure what she should do. Would they really want her in the photos? Mrs Lennox-Featherstone had said she did, but surely you wouldn't want a virtual stranger appearing next to beloved little nieces and old family friends? Having her photograph taken was something else she hated, ever since she'd been caught with her mouth open, looking completely gormless, as a child. Her parents' gentle teasing about this photograph hadn't helped.

'Er – chief bridesmaid – what's your name? I've got Fulvia down here, but somehow I don't think that's right.' Hugo the photographer smiled his lazy but scarily efficient smile in her direction.

'I'm not really a bridesmaid,' began Elsa, 'I'm only—'

'Yes you are,' said Mrs Lennox-Featherstone. 'For all intents and purposes, you're the chief bridesmaid. Tell Hugo your name, dear.'

Elsa longed to rebel, to stalk off across the churchyard and not let herself be captured on film, all dressed up like a dog's dinner, feeling a complete idiot, but for one thing she didn't have the courage, and for a second, she didn't want to spoil anyone's day.

'I'm Elsa,' she said to Hugo.

'Well, I'm glad to find that out,' said a male voice from behind her. 'I'm Laurence, your partner in crime.'

Elsa shot round. She felt guilty enough already without people saying things like that to her.

'The best man?' said a tall, faintly smiling man who wasn't exactly good-looking, but seemed well made and confident. He wasn't standing in for anyone else, obviously.

'Oh, hi. I'm not really the bridesmaid,' she said for what felt like the hundredth time. 'I'm just wearing the dress.'

'And a very lovely dress it is,' said Hugo. 'Now, if you'd just stop crushing yourself against that buttress so we can see you and it, I'd like one of the pair of you . . .'

Elsa gave up. She'd told everyone she wasn't the real bridesmaid and they didn't seem to care, so she decided to just go along with what anyone wanted her to do, as long as it didn't involve dancing or kissing or arcane practices like that. She stood next to Ashlyn, as requested, and then took a paper cup of chilled orange juice that Sarah had arranged to be served.

'This is all very civilised,' said Laurence. 'I was a best man last year and it was absolutely baking. We had to stand around for hours having our photographs taken and someone fainted from the heat.'

Sarah, who was nearby, a golden Labrador at her heels, making sure that she'd ordered enough juice, heard this and said, 'It also makes people less likely to fall on the alcohol the moment they get to the reception if they're not dying of thirst. Oh, I'd better get out of the way.'

Hugo had made everyone laugh and had been very brisk and organised about getting the right people into groups. Even the dog had posed appropriately. Elsa was surprised. Hugo had such a laid-back appearance but behind the lazy smile was obviously someone who got things done.

'That's a wrap for now,' said Hugo and everyone relaxed. Then he took another photograph.

'Rotter!' said Ashlyn. 'I had my mouth open!'

'But your teeth are lovely. Now, on to the reception, everyone. I'm afraid I'll be asking for more posing there, but you love it, so that's all right.'

Elsa saw Ashlyn pouting prettily and wished she could

pout. It was obviously something you were born either able to do or not, like curling your tongue.

'Come with me,' said Laurence, taking her arm. 'I'll drive you to the reception.'

'I'm sure you should be looking after someone else,' Elsa protested. 'After all, I'm here on false pretences.'

'Not at all. You're my responsibility. Believe me, I know,' he went on, when Elsa still hesitated. 'I've been a best man lots of times.'

'Oh? Why is that? Were you the most popular boy at school or something?'

'Not at all. It's just that I don't drink and the brides always make their bridegrooms pick me even if they hardly know me. I'm guaranteed not to lose the ring, allow the groom to get too drunk the night before, or, worse, strip him naked and tie him to a lamppost.'

Elsa giggled. 'And presumably you're guaranteed not to goose the bridesmaids?'

'Actually, the brides don't usually care about that. It stops the groom doing it, after all.'

'So you're saying I might not be safe in your car?'

'You will be, absolutely safe. I'm known as Laurence the Dependable.'

'Well, that's nice.'

'No it's not, it's boring as hell, but it's what I seem to be stuck with. Shall we go?'

When Elsa saw Laurence's car she wondered if his title was really accurate. It was an ancient-looking Morgan and barely had room in it for Laurence, let alone Elsa and her dress.

'I think I might have to take a taxi,' said Elsa.

'Not at all. I'm an expert at squeezing meringues into my car.'

'This is not a meringue!' Elsa was stung. 'It's a beautifully crafted, elegant creation and cost a fortune.'

'So is my car. Trust me.'

By following his instructions, Elsa did find that she and the dress could both be squeezed into the Morgan quite neatly.

'You are practised at this,' she said, making sure she hadn't trapped any of the precious material in the door.

'Oh yes. It's the only stipulation I made today. Sometimes the family wants me to drive their car so I can take a bevy of aunts.'

'Is a bevy the proper collective noun for aunts?'

'It was in one particular case. I had to drive them to the station afterwards – they were drunk as skunks. Not a happy experience. At least it wasn't my car.'

Elsa laughed. 'You should get paid. You could hire yourself out. Sarah – she's the wedding organiser – she'd get you work.'

Laurence gave her a look that told her this suggestion didn't find favour with him and started the car. 'I do have a life, you know.'

'Sorry! I didn't mean to offend you.'

'It's all right. I know you didn't. But the thought of doing all this for people I really didn't know is fairly dreadful.'

'Oh.' Elsa subsided, feeling crushed in spirit as well as in hand-beaded organza. Now she felt like a burden.

Laurence looked left before turning out into the road and patted her knee. 'Don't worry, I'm not quite as good-natured as people think. I don't do anything I don't want to.'

Chapter Three

'OK,' said Ashlyn, when they had got out of their respective modes of transport and were all in the hotel's exceptionally grand foyer, 'which one of you two is going to help me in the loo?'

Sarah looked at Elsa. Her short but intensive career as a wedding planner had not previously required her to take on this duty. Sometimes it seemed as if her clients needed everything doing for them but it hadn't gone this far before. 'It's definitely the bridesmaid's job.'

'But . . .' Elsa looked around for Laurence for support. He wasn't visible; he was probably in the Gents, unencumbered by several miles of tulle.

'Darling, I'd do it of course,' said Mrs Lennox-Featherstone, 'but about a million people are about to arrive and we need to arrange the receiving line . . . God, they're here already,' she muttered. 'I thought knowing the way gave us a good fifteen minutes' grace. Ah, Daphne. How lovely you could come. What a blissful hat. The bride's not quite ready to say hello – needs the lav, poor girl.'

'Well, I can't go into the Ladies,' said Bobby, playing with the gloves that went with his hired outfit. The bride's mother had insisted on all the men wearing morning suits. 'Or I'd willingly hold your dress up while you pee.'

'Oh, for God's sake! I'm bursting here.' Ashlyn gathered up her skirts and rustled purposefully towards the Ladies. Elsa, who'd covered the dress every night after she'd finished working on it and did not want it to be trailed along a dirty floor at this stage, hurried after it. She had to kick off Fulvia's shoes, which were at least two sizes too big, and throw her own, shorter train over her arm in order to keep up.

Sarah, aware that it really wasn't Elsa's job to hold the bride's skirt while she answered the call of nature, hastened after them, clutching Elsa's discarded shoes. If Elsa had been the real bridesmaid she'd have left her to it, but Elsa had helped them all out of a spot, she deserved support now.

In the Ladies, Ashlyn, a strong-minded woman whose need was great, took charge. She looked at the cubicle which seemed extremely narrow and said, 'Here, catch.'

To Elsa's immense relief, she did not actually throw her long train, but Elsa caught it quickly all the same.

'Pick it right up and drape it over the wall to the next cubicle,' went on Ashlyn. 'Why they have to make these stalls so damn narrow I have no idea. They do weddings all the time. I'm going to complain about it.'

Sarah, glad *she* wasn't going to have to write a letter explaining in polite language that the dimensions of the toilets made it difficult for brides to relieve themselves, helped Elsa gather up Ashlyn's train. Ashlyn would undoubtedly be far more down to earth in her use of words than she could allow herself to be.

'Here,' Sarah said now, 'I'll climb on the loo next door, you hand all that you can of it up to me so we can drape it over the partition.'

Elsa, carrying the bulk of it, squeezed in beside Ashlyn and between them they hauled the spangled train up the side of one cubicle wall and Sarah supported it as it came over the other side.

'If I'd known my creations would suffer these indignities . . .' Elsa began.

'What?' said the others. Sarah was about to avert her gaze and Ashlyn was about to pull down her thong. They both stopped to look at Elsa.

'I don't know! I just never think of them having to be peed in. Or squashed into ancient sports cars.'

Ashlyn giggled. 'Did Laurence bring you in his Morgan? It's fun, isn't it? And Laurence is nice. Not dashing but jolly dependable. Now look away, girls, I don't think shutting the door is an option.'

'I think you could—' began Sarah.

'Too late,' said Ashlyn. 'Oh, that feels better.'

'I did warn you against the champagne,' said Sarah, keeping her gaze averted.

'It wasn't the champagne,' said Ashlyn, pulling up her thong with a snap. 'It was the water you made me drink afterwards to stop me getting a hangover. Anyway, all's well now. Let's get back to the party.'

'Er, hang on!' said Elsa. 'I need to go too and my train's nearly as long. Now that we've mastered the technique . . . I promise to shut the door,' she added.

As Elsa sat at the top table a couple of hours later, she began to stop feeling like a fraud. She'd already confessed to Laurence, the best man, the bride's parents knew already, and the groom's parents didn't much care. The speeches were nearly over and her tension was beginning to ease.

'That was a brilliant speech,' she said when Laurence had sat down again. 'You didn't seem nervous at all.'

'Well, you get used to people looking at you after the first few weddings,' he said, filling her glass. For someone who didn't drink, he was very prompt with the wine bottle.

Elsa considered this. 'Do you? I don't think I ever would, although my mother tells me being shy is an affectation, an assumption that people are looking at me when, of course, they aren't.'

He laughed gently. 'She hadn't ever been a bridesmaid and sat at the top table, then?'

Elsa shook her head. 'Don't think so. I'll ask her next time she says it.'

'Do you see her often?'

Elsa nodded. 'Quite often. I live in a corner of my workshop, and if I need a bit more comfort, or a garden to lie in, I go home. They also feed me up occasionally. They're only a few minutes away.' She frowned, wondering if this made her seem pathetic, constantly running home to mummy and daddy.

'There's nothing to be embarrassed about.'

She turned to him, about to deny being any such thing but thought better of it. She sighed. 'It does seem a bit sad, a woman of my age going home to play in the garden.'

'You're not exactly ancient! What, twenty-three?'

'Twenty-six, actually,' she said with dignity.

He seemed surprised. 'Oh. It's just that fringe makes you look much younger.' Then, possibly seeing Elsa blush, he went on, 'So tell me about living on the job.'

Elsa relaxed a bit. 'Well, I couldn't afford to rent two places, so my dad helped me convert a corner of this warehouse – well a floor of one – into a little bedroom, kitchen and sitting room. There's a teeny shower room, too.'

'Does it feel cramped?'

'Not really. I can open the sitting room out on to the workroom if I want to. My parents say it would be a great place for a party.'

'Have you ever had one?'

'No. I'm not really a party girl. I think maybe it's because I'm an only child and got used to my own company.'

'Were you lonely?'

She considered. 'I don't think so. I don't ever remember being bored. But it means that now I don't like trying to talk to people in big echoey spaces – more than just a couple of people, anyway.'

'I know what you mean. I'd always prefer to talk to just a few people than a whole braying crowd.'

'So you're not keen on large donkey sanctuaries then?'

He laughed and gave his head a little shake. 'No. Like you, I prefer one donkey at a time.'

Elsa sipped her wine. She liked Laurence, she decided. He got her jokes and didn't interrogate her – well, not too much. He was fun and she found him very easy to talk to.

Then he said, 'Did you know that guests who don't know the people on their table, or who aren't getting on with them, make up stories about the people on the top table?'

'That's a bit horrifying! But how do *you* know that? I thought you were always the best man at weddings?'

He laughed. 'Not absolutely every time. This is only my third appearance as the groom's right-hand man.'

'Always the best man, never the groom, eh?'

Elsa said this as a throwaway line – she hadn't expected a little sigh before he said, 'Yes.'

She felt instantly remorseful. She put her hand on his sleeve. 'I'm so sorry. I didn't mean to step on your toes – it was just a sort of joke.'

Gallantly, he laughed. 'Stepping on my toes comes later, when we dance. But the last wedding where I was best man the bride was my ex.' He looked down at her, smiling ruefully. 'I told you it was the brides who chose me as best man, didn't I?'

Elsa's heart was touched. 'God, that's awful! How utterly tactless. How could she do that to you? And how could you do it?'

He shrugged. 'It did hurt, obviously, as I was still in love with her at the time, but that was why I did it. She asked me to.'

Elsa felt her throat constrict with tears of sympathy. 'That's so sweet.' She knew if she wasn't careful she'd actually cry. She was either over-tired or had had too much to drink.

Laurence said briskly, 'No need to get sentimental, I'm pretty much over her now.'

'I'm so glad!' His eyebrow went up a little and his mouth twitched. Trying to backtrack she said, 'I mean, I'm glad for you. I don't care personally.' She paused and sipped some water.

'It's all right,' he said, still gently amused by her discomfiture. 'I know exactly what you mean.' He paused. 'So, what about you? Is this your first time? Or have you followed lots of your girlfriends down the aisle?'

She shook her head and found that her fringe went into her eyes. She flicked it away. 'No. I've never been a bridesmaid before and they didn't give me long to learn my part.'

'So you don't really know Ashlyn, then?'

'Well, I do, actually. We got to know each other quite well when we were doing fittings, choosing fabrics and things.'

'So you're here because the bride begged you to be,' said Laurence firmly. 'And quite right and proper too. Now, can you dance?'

'Dance? What do you mean?' She was horrified. Did he want her to dance a rapid quickstep, backwards and in heels, like Ginger Rogers? Somehow she didn't think he meant disco dancing.

'Sorry, I didn't realise that was a hard question. I'm asking you if you can waltz at all. I'm not talking proper ballroom here, but when Ashlyn and Bobby have had their first romantic number, we have to join them. Now, if you can waltz, I can too. If not, you can just hang on and I'll steer.'

'That doesn't sound very romantic.'

'It's not supposed to sound romantic. I'm the prosaic best man being frank.'

'I thought you said your name was Laurence?' She smiled.

He frowned and shook his head. 'I must have given you too much to drink.'

'Well, you did but don't worry about it. I was only being flippant and everyone says I take life far too seriously, so it's probably a good thing.' Elsa sighed, wishing she could be bright and outgoing without having to be slightly drunk.

'They say that about me too.'

She didn't really believe him – he had a very frivolous car after all – but she didn't want to argue. 'Then we're well matched. That's good!'

He nodded. 'It also makes me believe in the power of coincidence.'

'What do you mean?'

'Nothing, really.' He paused before going on. 'The brides, having chosen me as best man, are not usually terribly considerate in their choice of chief bridesmaid.'

This made Elsa laugh. 'I'm sure you'd have loved Fulvia! She's a real goer. Well, obviously, she's gone to Paris, after all.'

'I know Fulvia,' he said mock seriously, 'and while she is definitely a goer, she's not much fun.'

'No?'

'No. Lovely to look at but absolutely no brain. Not much sense of humour either.'

It was somewhat of a surprise to Elsa that a man should feel like this. She'd always assumed that a good figure and pretty face were what was important. Although she saw his point; in her work she often dealt with brides who were extremely pretty but weren't easy to communicate with. Ashlyn had been a lovely exception – demanding, but fun, and able to be clear about what she wanted. 'Oh. Well, I hope I'm not too disappointing.'

He smiled. 'Not at all.'

'Hm,' said Elsa. 'You're very polite, aren't you?'

'Very. Famous for it. So, can you dance?'

She wondered briefly if dancing round her studio on her own counted as dancing. 'A bit. But steering me might be the best option.'

'It will be a pleasure.'

Elsa considered. 'I suppose having such an ancient car makes you good at steering.'

He nodded, really smiling now. 'It does. Now, let's see if Ashlyn can get down from the dais and on to the dance floor in those shoes.'

'Oh God, my shoes. They're about ten sizes too big.'

'Really?'

'Well, a couple, anyway. I can't dance in them. You'll have to find someone else.'

'Ditch the shoes. So Fulvia has big feet, has she?'

'No,' said Elsa, 'I have small ones. It's one of my few virtues.'

Laurence looked at her sideways. 'Oh, I wouldn't say that.'

'No you wouldn't, because as I said, you're very polite. I'm honest.'

'Honest but deluded,' said Laurence.

Suspecting she was being paid a compliment and unsure how to react, Elsa ignored this. She'd never learnt how to flirt.

Just then, Ashlyn and Bobby shuffled past them. The band was playing their specially selected 'first dance' number and they were heading for the dance floor.

Elsa watched the bride and groom dance together with awe. They must have practised. That dress was not designed to move in, and yet they glided over the floor with grace and harmony. At the end, everyone applauded, not just because it was expected, but because they were really very good at it.

'Wow,' said Elsa. 'I'd love to be able to dance like that.'

'Well, now's your chance,' said Laurence, helping her to her feet.

'It won't be like that,' she muttered under her breath, but he either didn't hear or chose to ignore her.

Elsa left her shoes under the table, and this emphasised

the already noticeable height difference between her and her partner. The first few steps were a disaster. Her feet felt so vulnerable next to his huge, shiny black shoes, she would only move them backwards.

'I'm sorry, I really can't do this,' she said. 'Please find someone else. There are lots of girls here who'd love to dance with you.'

'But I want to dance with you. Come on, you can do it.'

Three more staggering steps proved that Elsa couldn't.

'Tell you what, put your dress over your arm. Good, now put your feet on mine. We'll dance together.' Then he put his arm firmly round her, lifting her slightly. Elsa surrendered and put her feet on his, trusting that his shoes wouldn't allow her feet to crush his.

It felt magical! He moved gracefully round the floor, and because he did, so did she. When the dance was over she forgot that she was shy and inhibited, flung her arms round his neck and kissed his cheek. 'Thank you, that was fantastic! I loved it!'

'Mm,' said Laurence, 'so did I. Maybe you should have some lessons, so you can dance on your own two feet instead of mine.'

'Maybe I should!' She sighed, yearning to be able to glide, as if on wheels, like Ashlyn and Bobby had.

Laurence chuckled. 'Now it's your turn to show me up. I'm hopeless at bopping about. I feel silly and I look silly.'

'I'm sure you don't!' said Elsa, indignant for him. But a few moments later, she had to admit – privately, of course – that he was right. He couldn't dance for toffee.

Chapter Four

Sarah eased her shoes off under the table. The reception was fine – so far. No one had grumbled about where they were sitting. The food had arrived in an organised fashion, and only one table had to wait any length of time. Spotting this, Sarah had appeared with a bottle of champagne and given everyone another glass.

Then she had produced a large china plate and a special pen. 'This is for you all to sign and write messages on. If you go first, you'll have more space.'

'Won't the writing wash off?' asked one girl, who had taken the pen and was now chewing the end of it, wondering what to say.

'No, you bake the plate and the writing is fixed. Lovely idea, I think, don't you? But please don't write too much!' Ashlyn had wanted a plate per table and so have a set of dinner plates, but Bobby, who'd wanted a different sort of china, had said two plates, maximum, although it would mean people would have to express themselves in very small writing.

Everything else had gone smoothly. Unlike at many weddings she had worked on, the Lennox-Featherstones had insisted that Sarah was catered for as if she were a guest. She had agreed only because there was room for a little table on its own from which she could leap up if the need arose.

It was a very stylish, lavish do, she had to admit, and a lot of the credit was down to her. Now she had leisure to look about her, she could admire the details. The size of the budget had definitely helped.

The flowers were superb. Sukie, her florist of choice, had done a wonderful job. The tables all had a glass cube packed with one sort of fragrant flower. Sarah had caught the whiff of freesias, fat-stemmed hyacinths and roses, as she'd moved from table to table before everyone sat down, checking everything was as it should be.

There was a long, low, sophisticated floral runner on the top table. In this the varieties of flowers went in waves, a patch of roses, followed by one of sweet peas, then one of delphiniums, and so on. Sukie had told Sarah she was creating a herbaceous border effect, to reflect the bride's mother's love of country gardens.

Ashlyn had a simple bouquet of lilies of the valley. Like many simple things, it had been fantastically expensive because, Sukie had told Sarah, it had taken 250 stems to make it really lavish. Elsa had a trailing bouquet that also included lilies of the valley, but not quite so many, and the little bridesmaids had simple posies of all the flowers represented, tiny, but very fragrant. Sukie had taken a lot of time finding out exactly what was required and Mrs Lennox-Featherstone had already told Sarah how beautiful the flowers were.

'I'll write to her myself, of course, but if I don't get round to it straightaway, do tell Sukie how pleased we are. You are clever to have found her.' Sarah had sighed with satisfaction. Having people she could rely on made her job so much easier.

The few little misunderstandings about waiting and bar staff had been sorted out and now all she had to do was check that everything was all right at the end and make sure that anyone who needed to be paid, was. Sarah had a worryingly fat wad of notes she wore under her clothes in a travel wallet.

'Here,' said a voice.

She jumped and turned to see a glass of champagne held by Hugo.

'Hello.' As she didn't need to ask him anything at the moment, she didn't know what else to say.

'Drink?'

'No thanks. I'm working. And so are you,' she added with mock severity.

'It takes more than a couple of glasses of champagne to fuddle my head and I haven't had one yet. Here, drink it up and stop being bossy.'

She was about to protest at the 'bossy' but realised that she was, because her job demanded it. Whether the job or the bossiness came first she didn't care to speculate.

She smiled a thank you. 'Why are you still here?' she said, having taken a welcome sip. 'I'd have thought you'd have had somewhere else to go.'

'There're the going-away shots, and all sorts I haven't taken yet. Besides, I'm staying over – my sister and her family live not too far from here and I need to see my nephew.'

'Need?'

'Oh yes. He's just painted a really good dinosaur. I need to see it.'

'Oh.' This surprised Sarah. She didn't see Hugo as an adored uncle, being scrambled over by little children and enjoying it.

'And just now, I want to share a quiet drink with you.'

This was rather a surprise. 'Why me? Wasn't there another unattached female you could find?'

The corner of his large, humorous mouth lifted. 'Weddings are full of unattached females. I chose you because while you're possibly unattached, you're not noticeably needy.'

Sarah laughed. 'I'm not needy at all! I don't need a man to complete me as a woman, thank you very much. The idea!'

'I wouldn't dream of suggesting that you did, Ms Spiky,' he said.

Sarah looked sideways at him. She suspected that Hugo was far too adept at flirting and far too used to getting his own way with women for anyone's good. But was he flirting now? If he was, she could think up a suitable put-down, but if he wasn't, and she said something emasculating, he would realise she thought he had been flirting. And then he would probably think he wanted her to flirt with him. She took a gulp of champagne that made her choke. He patted her on the back while she snorted into her handkerchief.

'Are you all right?' he said, when she had finally recovered.

'I just choked, all that spluttering wasn't an expression of my feelings, you know. It was just the bubbles going down the wrong way.'

'That's OK then.'

The next sip was very small and very carefully drunk. She put her glass down.

'So, fancy a dance?' Hugo asked in a way that made Sarah wonder if he was expecting her to say yes or no.

Actually, Sarah's feet had been twitching under the tablecloth and she longed to confound him by accepting. But she wasn't a guest, it would be inappropriate. 'Better not. I'm working.'

He must have noticed her silent sigh. 'I'm quite sure no one would mind if you took a few moments off to enjoy yourself. Although I suspect you don't do that much, even when you're not on duty.'

'You really have no idea what I'm like when I'm not working, Hugo. And you shouldn't speculate, either.'

'Oh, I don't think you can stop people speculating if they want to.'

Sarah thought she detected a slight edge to his voice, but perhaps she had imagined it. 'Of course not, but you can hope they have the manners to keep their speculations to themselves.' She made a careless gesture. She and Hugo

33

had worked together often but they didn't get a chance to chat and she realised she didn't know him very well at all.

'Hope springs eternal, obviously,' he drawled now, 'but be prepared to be disappointed.'

'I am always prepared to be disappointed,' said Sarah, 'and I am never—' She stopped abruptly, aware that somehow he'd backed her into a very stupid corner. She bit her lip to hide her smile.

'You're never disappointed in your disappointment?'

'No! People are always disappointing, that's all.' She shrugged.

'What, all people, all the time? Hell, I knew you were cynical but surely you have *some* faith in human nature?'

She let slip an exasperated sigh. 'I have infinite faith in *human* nature, it's just . . .' She shook her head, searching for a way of expressing herself clearly.

'What? Dogs? Cats? . . . Men?' he added more softly.

'Yes, if you must know.' If he could be direct, so could she.

'So tell me, how many times has your heart been broken?'

This was not territory she was prepared to put even a toe on. 'I'm not speaking personally – at least, not me, personally. But I've known – do know – lots of women who've been very let down by men.'

'And these women were perfect, were they?'

'Well no, but – no one's perfect, obviously.'

'Except you, of course.'

Although she was used to their banter she was not sure if he was still teasing her. 'I'm not claiming to be perfect, of course I'm not,' she said. 'But I am good at my job.' It was only after she heard the words that she realised it sounded as if she were justifying herself.

'And I'm not?'

'No, that's not what I meant. Of course you're good at

your job. I just think I'm better.' He laughed. At her, not with her, she was certain. 'Oh shut up,' she muttered. 'Go away and annoy some other poor woman.'

'I'll go away and get you another drink. You seriously need to lighten up, Sarah. And then, we're having that dance.' He headed over to the bar.

Sarah decided there must be something that required her immediate attention somewhere. It had to be a real task, or she'd just look pathetic. While she was thinking, Mrs Lennox-Featherstone came up on the arm of her husband.

'Darling Sarah!' She was obviously just a little bit drunk. 'I do hope you're enjoying yourself. I know you're working but you must have some fun too. It's all going so well. Oh, Hugo!' She kissed him. 'Are you looking after Sarah? Not that she needs looking after but she does need a little break.'

'Just what I was telling her, Vanessa,' said Hugo, handing Sarah another glass of champagne.

'I am on duty,' said Sarah firmly.

'But you haven't got to drive anywhere afterwards! I've booked you a room, remember. I'm sure it'll be a broom cupboard, but as we've taken over the entire hotel they were perfectly happy to let us have it for half nothing.' She kissed Hugo again. 'Come on, Donald. When we've checked everyone's enjoying themselves I'm going to get you on that dance floor.'

'Oh, Nessie, must you?' muttered the bride's father.

'Deffo,' said Vanessa and led her husband away.

'So you're staying over?' said Hugo, when Donald and Vanessa had gone.

'Yes. It's lovely of Vanessa to do that. I have to check everything is in order at the end and it saves me having to drive home too late. As she said, the hotel were quite happy as they could hardly put someone not involved with the wedding in it.'

'Is it a broom cupboard?'

Sarah shrugged. 'Well, it was probably a powder room or something once upon a time. It's quite narrow and definitely only a single. The bathroom's nice though. Slightly bigger.'

Hugo chuckled. 'I haven't been to see my room yet. I'm sure it's fine. It's handy for me as it's quite a way from where I live to my sister's and this is halfway.'

'Have you lots of nieces and nephews?'

'One of each, but the niece is tiny. Jack and I are sticking together, boys against the girls.'

Sarah laughed; it was nice hearing him talk about his family like this, but she found his use of language significant. She doubted the girls would win.

'So, come on. Let's dance.'

As they approached the dance floor she realised it was a slow dance and everyone on the floor was clinging to their partners, resting their heads on shoulders wherever possible. Never mind, she thought, it'll change in a minute, and if I back out now it'll look like I'm scared to wander round in Hugo's arms for a few minutes. Which would be the truth, she added. She liked him as a friend, but attractive though he was she didn't dare even consider him as anything else.

It had been a long time since she'd been this close to a man. Hugo smelt of party: a little alcohol, a touch of tobacco and, underneath that, some very luxurious aftershave. Sarah wished she could dislike it but was grateful she didn't. He held her firmly to him, one hand on her back, the other holding her hand. She put her own free hand on his shoulder and they danced.

Once she thought she felt his cheek on her hair but then dismissed the idea. Why would he do that? But the thought made something in her respond. It was probably because she was a healthy young woman who hadn't been in a relationship for a long time. Her body was bound to respond to a man who held her close. Once she'd sorted this out she relaxed into the dance, and even closed her eyes. This was nice!

'Hey! Can I cut in?' A large and determined uncle (Sarah recognised him) prised her from Hugo's arms and set off with her forcefully, leaving an amused Hugo behind. 'Didn't know you were part of the party,' he said into her ear. 'Thought you were staff. Damn glad you're not.'

'Oh, I am staff!' insisted Sarah, delighted that this might make him let her go.

'No,' said the uncle firmly. 'The precedent's been set. You're on the floor, you're dancing.'

For the remaining minutes of the dance Sarah realised that in spite of being a healthy young woman who hadn't had a relationship for ages, she was not responding to this man clamping her to him. Entirely the reverse, in fact.

Sarah didn't accept any more dances. She worked for the rest of the evening. Now, at nearly midnight, all the wedding party had left and the family had all gone up to their rooms. She was having a final trawl through the room, looking for anything left behind, when Hugo joined her.

'When do you clock off?'

'Not until I've made sure there are no abandoned handbags or shawls or shoes, even. I've nearly finished now, though.' She was about to add that she was longing for her bed but stopped herself in time. It would have resulted in a lot of unnecessary banter and it was too late at night for that.

'Good. The barman is still there and prepared to give us brandy. I think you need it. I know I do.'

Sarah had not kept herself out of relationships for more than four years without knowing how to do it, but her technique relied heavily on 'having to get back', 'not wanting to drink and drive' – simple logistics, in fact. But

Hugo already knew she didn't have to go anywhere and he was only offering her a friendly drink. She couldn't deny she'd finished her work and the thought of a brandy was very tempting. Her will power, so necessary to keep a calm and efficient head when on duty, was all spent.

'Oh, OK,' she muttered.

'It's all right, no need to sound grateful,' said Hugo, laughing, and steered her towards the bar.

There was a small sofa in the window embrasure with a little table in front of it and a view of the garden beyond. Hugo directed Sarah there and went to the bar.

The barman was Sarah's last hope. If he wanted to go off-duty – and he surely must – Sarah could say so. She could just drink up her brandy and go to bed – she'd sleep like a top.

She sat back and looked at the garden which was lit with occasional flares, making it look exotic, almost foreign. She felt content. The day had gone brilliantly. There was quite a lot of post-wedding administration to do tomorrow, but she could handle that. She didn't have to sort out any major upsets. This was the biggest wedding she'd done so far and she felt very satisfied with herself.

Then Hugo put a bottle of brandy on the table. 'Don't worry, it's nearly empty. I thought it was easier to just buy the lot. Then when the barman's finished setting up for tomorrow he can go to bed.'

'Oh. I'm quite tired too,' said Sarah, managing not to say the 'b' word.

'I expect you're completely shattered. Here, drink this. It'll help you unwind.'

Sarah sighed and then sipped the liquid. It felt like molten gold running down her throat. She settled back into the cushions of the sofa.

Hugo sat next to her and sipped from his own glass.

'That is truly delicious brandy,' murmured Sarah sleepily. 'Thank you very much.'

'It's a pleasure. Have some more.' He tipped some more into her glass.

They settled into the sofa, not talking. The garden in front of them was beautiful and in the distance, from some other room, came some jazz, sensuous and poignant, just perfect. Sarah savoured the stillness after a long day full of bustle and noise. Then her glance caught Hugo's. She couldn't quite read his expression in the soft lighting and for a tiny moment she was confused. And then he smiled. In spite of all her personal barricades, she felt a flutter of anticipation.

He took her glass out of her hand and put it on the table, and then he turned her head and brought his mouth down to hers.

Sarah let herself go. It was just a kiss – and yet what a kiss! Hugo's lips held hers with just the right degree of firmness and later, gently opened her mouth. Brandy, tiredness, relief from stress and possibly years of abstinence caused Sarah to respond to everything his mouth demanded. It went on for ever; dawn could have broken while it continued and Sarah wouldn't have noticed. At last Hugo broke free.

Sarah's eyes opened and at the same moment she realised how very much she had enjoyed kissing him. A long sigh went through her and she cleared her throat. 'I think I'd better go to bed now,' she whispered. Reluctantly, the sensible part of her took charge once more.

Hugo sighed too. 'It's probably wise. There's no need to rush things, after all. I'll take you up.'

Sarah protested, but he took no notice. At the door of her room he kissed her again. Sarah chided herself for letting this happen again and then she thought: Why not? A kiss is just a kiss, after all.

Chapter Five

Bron drove home slowly, not really wanting to arrive. She had so enjoyed getting everyone ready for the wedding, especially Elsa. She really had felt like a fairy godmother cutting her hair and putting her make-up on, and even helping with that lovely dress. The end result was fantastic. The fringe had made Elsa look wonderfully waif-like. That, and the make-up, had made a woman who was pleasant and attractive into one who was almost stunning. And she was leaving all that girly fun behind.

There would be a row or possibly a sulk. Roger was a better sulker than he was a fast bowler, or whatever his specialty was, and a row would be almost preferable, except it would end in tears, her tears, as it had when she had left that morning.

The trouble was, he hated her working at weekends, and weekends were when she could do freelance work, in particular for weddings. He hated her doing freelance work too. He liked her to work regular hours, at the local salon, so she could be at home when he needed her to be. It was fair enough, she realised. Most women would grumble if their husbands worked all week and then freelanced at the weekends, but as Roger played so much cricket, Bron felt she might as well be working. Except that he wanted her to watch him play, and it bored her stupid.

And she hated her day job. She didn't get on with the owner of the salon, which meant she did more hairwashing and less cutting and styling than by rights she should have done. And although she'd told Roger this, explained why she wanted to leave and try her luck as a mobile hairdresser, he just said she should learn to stand up for herself. People often told other people to stand up for themselves, Bron reflected, although they'd be horrified if they stood up to the person telling them to do just that.

Now she pulled her shoulders back as she locked the car and checked her watch. It was four o'clock. She should have a couple of hours before he was home and perhaps, if he'd done really well, he might have forgiven her for not being there to watch him play. She would have to wash his whites, but that was nothing new.

There was a note on the kitchen table that was still covered with the remains of his cooked breakfast: *You were on the tea rota. You owe Edna a haircut.*

Bron sighed. It wasn't that she particularly minded doing Edna's hair for nothing, it just seemed rather heavy payment for standing in for her tea duty. Unlike Bron, Edna lived for cricket. Even without the need to make sandwiches and bake cakes she would have been there, watching the chaps, clapping at the right time, knowing what the score was.

As Bron collected the dishes and put them in the dishwasher she wondered how she could have not realised that getting involved with Roger meant giving up her weekends to cricket. He'd asked her to go and watch him on their second date, and he'd looked so utterly wonderful in his whites that she had fallen in love with him – or maybe, in hindsight, it was just in lust. Either way they had both faded into habit and convenience now.

As she had got into her white Rolls-Royce to go to the church, Ashlyn had added her pleas to her mother's and begged Elsa to stay on for the wedding. Sarah had to be there anyway, Elsa too, now she'd been promoted from dressmaker to bridesmaid; it seemed a shame, Ashlyn had said, for her to be left out. 'Besides, my lip-gloss may need reapplying after a few glasses of fizz.'

Bron had told Ashlyn she was perfectly capable of reapplying her own lip-gloss and sadly waved the bridal car away.

Bron would have much preferred to stay at the wedding. She had worked very hard to help everyone look beautiful and she got on well with Sarah and Elsa, although she hadn't known them long. Bron had done the hair for a couple of weddings organised by Sarah, and because Bron was reliable, Sarah said she would always encourage brides who didn't have a favourite hairdresser to use her.

But could she be reliable when her freelance work caused such trouble at home? She sighed, and thought back to a little incident that had happened just as she was leaving. She had put her last box into her car and was about to close the boot and go home when a large golden Labrador bounded up to her.

'Major!' a male voice had said. 'Here!'

The voice appeared from behind the side of the house. It belonged to a tall man wearing a suit that didn't really fit him. There was a thinner, longer dog of indefinable breed close to the man's heel. The yellow dog bounced away from Bron like a ball ricocheting off a wall and landed by the man.

'He didn't frighten you, did he?' he asked as he came within earshot.

'Oh no,' said Bron, glad of the diversion. She didn't want to go home; any little delay was welcome. 'He's lovely. Hello, Major.' As the dog was by her side again and she was rubbing his chest, it seemed only polite to use his name.

'Ashlyn wanted him to come to the wedding and wear a blue bow round his neck,' the man explained. 'But everyone agreed it would be hopeless unless he was well and truly worn out first. I've been walking him since dawn, more or less. I'm the gardener,' he explained. 'I'm now going to find the blue bow and be ready to greet the wedding party when they come out of church so he can be in the photos.'

'Lovely!' said Bron.

'Aren't you going to the wedding?' the man went on.

'No, I'm just the hairdresser.'

'I can't believe Vanessa – Mrs Lennox-Featherstone – didn't invite you.'

'Yes she did, but, sadly, I can't come. I must get home.'

The man had smiled. 'Shame.'

Bron had thought it was a shame too.

Roger came home at about ten, when his favourite shepherd's pie looked less golden-brown and more dried-up. Bron had made it as a peace offering although her tired bones would have much preferred to slump in front of the television with a glass of wine and a bowl of pasta. She'd had to get up incredibly early to be with Ashlyn on time. 'Hi, darling! How did it go?' she asked, trying to show some enthusiasm.

'Great! We won. You should have been there.' He looked at her under his eyebrows, the double meaning clear. 'Don't bother to dirty a plate, I'll eat it out of the dish. I'm starving. Mm. This is great!'

No kiss for her then, but he'd stopped greeting her affectionately a long time ago.

Pleased, though, that she'd got this right at least, Bron pulled out a chair and sat down to watch him eat. He didn't seem to want to talk and, as she was tired too, neither did she. When he'd finally finished, he threw his fork down and said, 'We're going to Mum and Dad's for lunch tomorrow, did I tell you? I think Mum wants her hair doing.'

As Sunday lunch with his parents was an almost weekly

43

ritual she hadn't unpacked her car. She didn't mind doing Roger's mother's hair, but she did wonder if Roger, an accountant, would have spent every weekend doing someone's books for free.

She had a bath and went to bed. Why was it that Roger was so free with her services as a hairdresser, but when she wanted to work for herself, to actually get paid, he didn't like it? Somehow along the way the balance of their relationship had gone wrong. They were no longer equal partners.

Lying as near to the edge of the bed as she could get without actually falling off, she realised that they never had been, really. She and Roger had moved in together too early in their relationship; mostly, she realised, because her parents had been moving to Spain and she had nowhere else to live. She'd never lived on her own or with girlfriends – getting together with Roger seemed a natural progression.

Now she was a bit stuck. It was Roger's house and although she had some savings, she would find it hard financially to live on her own. Hairdressers' wages were not good unless you worked at a top city salon. She couldn't even apply for jobs in somewhere like London or Birmingham without a lot of lying, and then supposing they didn't want her?

No, it was probably better to hope this was just a phase they were going through and to try to work on the relationship – at least until she had a chunk of money behind her. Running-away money, people called it.

To her huge relief, Roger didn't reach for her when he finally came to bed. She wouldn't have refused him, she didn't hate him, but his lovemaking didn't do for her what it had in the beginning. He still pressed the same buttons, went through the same routine, but for her it had stopped working. Once he had turned her insides to melted chocolate just by looking at her, now his kneecaps tended to bang into her shins in a way that not even the most dedicated masochist would appreciate. She sighed and eventually went to sleep herself.

The following morning, when she had put stain remover on all the patches of grass on Roger's whites before putting them to soak, and was checking that she had Roger's mother's favourite semi-permanent hair dye in her kit, her mobile rang. It was Elsa.

After the 'Hi! How are you!'s Elsa said, 'They were thrilled with how it all went, and I totally love my hair! I can't stop running my fingers through it. Ashlyn's mother told me what a sweet girl you were and what a shame you couldn't come to the wedding. It was good you managed to fit in a quick comb-out for her, when she wasn't on the list.'

'I'm so glad it was all a success.'

'But I must give you back your clips that you used to keep the headdress on with.'

'Oh, you don't need to worry about that!'

'No, I want to.'

'Well, if you'd like to pop over this evening, I'd love to hear all the details.' Bron didn't often invite her friends over – she could never quite forget it was Roger's house – but she felt it was OK to do so sometimes. Roger surely wouldn't object to Elsa – she was young and pretty and didn't laugh too loudly or anything likely to make him wince. And she did want to hear about the wedding. She gave Elsa the details and then told Roger.

'A friend of mine is coming over for a drink this evening.'

'Oh? One of your hairdresser friends? You want to discuss the latest edition of *Frizz*, or whatever? Well, that's OK as long as I can watch that film.'

'We'll go in the conservatory, or the kitchen,' said Bron, hoping Roger wouldn't be rude to Elsa. He could be quite sarcastic.

She waited on the doorstep for him, so she could lock

up. 'Are you wearing that?' Roger asked when he came out to the car.

'Apparently not,' said Bron and went back into the house to change out of her clean jeans and into a skirt that had a mark on it, but would be more in keeping with Roger's idea of Sunday clothes.

At least doing Roger's mother's hair took them both away from the tedium of what passed for entertainment in that house. Roger and his father liked to watch sport on Sunday afternoons. This was punctuated by Roger's father commenting on items in the paper. Bron almost always disagreed with his opinions, which weren't so much right wing as fascist, but had learnt to say nothing after the time she had suggested politely that England would really suffer if every immigrant who had arrived since the War was repatriated. The discussion turned into an argument and only just stopped short of a row.

Early on, Pat, Roger's mother, had retired to the kitchen to do the washing up. At the time, all fired up with the injustices of the world, Bron had longed to demand that the men of the family cleared up. A couple of months later she discovered that Roger's father's contribution to Sunday lunch was opening and pouring a bottle of wine.

She liked Pat and felt a loyalty to her. Pat did whatever her husband Vince wanted without argument, probably because argument was futile. In spite of this doormat imitation, when she was on her own Pat was fun in a gentle way and the two women got on well.

Really, Bron should have realised Roger wasn't a long-term prospect the moment she met his dad, but she had still been blinded by love and thought the similarity between father and son was only superficial. Now, she and his mother had got into a routine. After the men had gone off to the sitting room, they cleared the table, stacked the dishwasher and put the tins into soak. Then they went up to the bedroom for the hair appointment.

'Tell me about the wedding,' said Pat when Bron had finished pouring jugs of water over her head at the ensuite sink and was gently towel-drying her hair. 'I love hearing about all the clothes and things.'

'It was lovely. A bit of a panic at the last minute though, because the chief bridesmaid backed out.' Bron squeezed a dollop of serum into the palm of her hand and then pulled it through Pat's wet curls.

'Really? How rude!'

'I know! And the bride and her mother insisted that Elsa, the girl who made the dresses, stand in for her. I had to do her hair. I cut it and gave her a fringe. It looked wonderful! I did the bride's mother's too, only that was just a quick comb-through and make-up, really.' She looked at her client and friend in the mirror, wondering if it was time for a restyle. She took out her scissors. Their familiarity in her hand was comforting and restorative.

Pat wasn't so interested in her hair as in the wedding. 'So tell me what everyone wore. And was the bridegroom handsome?'

'I didn't see the bridegroom, but the dresses were heaven!'

There was a short pause and then Pat said, 'Don't worry, dear, I'm sure Roger will get round to asking you to marry him eventually. Took his dad five years.'

Bron exhaled quietly and snipped a little bit off the back of Pat's hair. Was that what she wanted, really? If she and Roger were married, would she feel more secure, confident, and less put upon? It was hard to say. She might do, but she wasn't in love with him any more, she knew that. But did it matter? Wasn't being 'in love' only a matter of hormones anyway? Wasn't it some chemical that wore off after a while? Maybe it would be OK to be married to someone familiar but not exciting. Excitement was probably very over-rated.

Chapter Six

Early that evening Elsa had walked out of the town to where a small estate of new houses had been built near the river. A couple of rungs up from starter homes, they seemed mostly to be lived in by young families. She could hear someone mowing a lawn out of sight; a car was being washed by an enthusiastic father with his two small sons, all getting very wet and soapy; and two young mothers watched their toddlers play in a paddling pool while they chatted. It was very domestic and happy, very Sunday afternoon, and she wondered if Bron was thinking of starting a family. It would be the perfect place to live if she was because there would be a ready-made network of friends. Elsa sighed, thinking of the group of friends she'd known at college – none of them lived within easy reach and because of the nature of her work and her shy personality, she hadn't built another one.

She heard the ding-dong of the bell and saw a shape appear behind the glass of the front door. When Bron opened it, Elsa thought she looked a little fraught.

'Hello, come in,' Bron said, smiling slightly. 'I've got a bottle of wine on the go. Would you like some?'

'Oh yes, why not,' said Elsa, 'I walked here.'

A tall, good-looking man appeared in the hallway. 'Elsa, this is Roger,' said Bron.

The man regarded Elsa with speculative eyes. 'Hello, Elsa, are you one of Bron's crimper pals?'

Elsa had to think what he meant for a minute. 'No, I'm a dressmaker. I did the wedding dress for Ashlyn's wedding. You know? The one Bron did all the hair for? Yesterday?'

'Oh yes. So you drive some poor bugger mad by spending every weekend doing some wedding or other too, do you?' He smiled, to take the sting out of this statement, but Elsa sensed he actually meant what he'd said.

Elsa blinked. 'No, only sometimes.' She didn't bother to add that there was no 'poor bugger' in her life to be driven mad.

'Bron's always off, leaving me to fend for myself on a Saturday. Missed your tea duty yesterday, didn't you, Muffin?'

Bron raised her eyebrows apologetically. 'I'm afraid I did. I should have remembered to swap. You don't really want to miss paid work to make a mountain of sandwiches and jam sponges.'

'But you're actually quite good at cakes,' went on Roger, ignoring the reference to paid work. 'She made a really excellent one for my parents' anniversary. No one believed it wasn't made by a professional.'

'Really? You're multi-talented then,' said Elsa.

Bron shrugged, apparently not wanting to admit to anything.

Roger didn't give her time to speak anyway. 'Are you going to offer Elsa a glass of wine? There's a nice bottle in the cupboard she might like. There's something I want to watch before supper so you've got half an hour.'

'I really just came to give Bron her hairclips—'

'Do stay,' said Bron. 'Just for a minute.'

'OK then, but I won't be long. I'm on my way to my parents.'

Elsa followed Bron into the house. 'Come with me to the kitchen while I pour us some wine,' she said. 'I've got some Pinot Grigio in the fridge. I don't know why Roger always assumes I like sweet wine. I think it goes back to one of the first times we visited his parents and his father had opened some Liebfraumilch. I said it was lovely. It wasn't.'

Elsa felt glad she lived alone, with her work, and not with a difficult man. How awful to come back from a hard day on your feet and have to tend to someone who wanted looking after all the time. The odd twinge of loneliness must be better than that. She hoped her relief didn't show on her face.

Bron poured the wine and then led the way to the tiny conservatory at the back of the house.

'This is nice,' said Elsa.

'I expect you're wondering why there are no plants here,' said Bron. 'Roger doesn't like plants, they make a mess.'

'Oh. I hadn't wondered actually,' she said. 'I'm hopeless with plants myself. My mother gardens.' Elsa settled herself on a cane chair. 'So you make cakes as well as work miracles with scissors?'

Bron made the same self-deprecating gesture she had before. 'Only as a hobby, really, but I've done quite a few wedding cakes for friends of friends, people like that. I don't charge for them, then they can't sue me if they're ill after eating them.' She smiled apologetically.

Elsa, struggling to make Bron feel better, laughed. 'I'm sure there's never been a case of someone being ill after eating a fruit cake.'

Bron sipped her wine and seemed to relax a little. 'Well, maybe not. Now, more importantly, tell me about the wedding.'

Elsa adjusted the cushion behind her and searched her mind for details. 'Well, the service went OK although I thought I'd die of embarrassment. I just had to keep reminding myself that they were all looking at Ashlyn, not me. And her dress looked fantastic! I thought it would be too much when she wanted beading, embroidery *and* lace, but it wasn't. It was rich, but not over the top. Everyone looked fab. It was a very stylish wedding, I must say.'

'I'd love to see the photos, but I don't often get to, sadly. It's OK if the bride is a client of mine, but if we've only met once or twice, for the practice session and then the wedding, they don't usually remember.'

'Well, we can ask Sarah. She's bound to get a look at them. Anyway, it all went really well except there was a bit of an incident with a dog in the churchyard – it was lovely but completely mad. It knocked over one of the little bridesmaids. Just as well she didn't cry, and then someone nearly tripped on the ribbon that had been round its neck.'

'Oh, was the dog called Major by any chance?' asked Bron.

'I have no idea. Why do you ask? He was a golden Labrador.'

'That must be him. I was just packing up to go when he arrived with this man. Apparently he had had to walk him all morning so he wouldn't be too hyper for the wedding.'

Elsa laughed. 'He obviously didn't walk him for long enough then!'

'Tell me more about the wedding,' said Bron. 'I did an amazing makeover on you, I want to know all the details.'

Elsa sighed. 'OK, I suppose that's only fair.'

'And don't miss anything out!' said Bron.

'OK, after the service we got to the reception and Ashlyn needed the loo.' Elsa sipped her wine. 'I tell you, Bron, I had no idea how difficult those dresses were to pee in.'

'But you do now?'

Elsa rolled her eyes. 'Oh yes! Still, we managed. I had to go too.' Elsa suddenly realised she'd got into territory she really didn't want to.

'Go on then.'

'I had to sit at the top table which was *so* embarrassing. But the best man was really nice to me, very polite.'

'And did you dance?'

'Sort of.' Just for a second Elsa allowed herself to

remember the tall, kind man who had let her dance on his feet but she pushed away the image. It had developed a dreamlike quality since and she'd probably imagined half of it. She snapped herself back to the present. 'Oh, by the way, I think Sarah and the photographer had a bit of a thing.' Sliding over her own experiences, Elsa rather guiltily changed the subject by dumping her friend right in it.

'No!' Bron said, instantly distracted. 'How amazing! Why do you think that?'

'Well, they didn't seem to speak much when the photos were being taken, and the only time I caught them together she seemed quite – how should I put it – brisk.'

'Go on,' said Bron eagerly.

'Did you know she was staying over in the hotel?' Elsa asked.

'Oh yes, she did say.' Bron nodded encouragingly.

'Well, as I left, I was sure I saw them slow dancing together!'

'Really? But she always seems so . . . well, not frigid exactly, but sort of – buttoned up.'

'Well, I dare say she'd had the odd glass of champagne by that time – it would have been perfectly under-standable, the reception had gone like a breeze – and they were sort of locked in each other's arms.'

'You can't know for sure,' said Bron.

'Of course not.'

'But it would be good! I don't know Sarah all that well but she never seems to go out for fun. It's always just work with her. And she and Hugo seem to get on well.' Bron fiddled with her glass. 'She muttered something about a wedding next Saturday, so maybe I'll ask her.'

Elsa stayed silent for a minute before changing the subject. Bron really didn't seem herself tonight. 'I've got to take the bridesmaid's dress back to Mrs Lennox-Featherstone,' she said brightly.

'Oh, a bit scary. But she's really nice underneath all that posh voice and stuff, isn't she?'

'Yes,' agreed Elsa, 'it's just a bit daunting, that's all.'

'I'd offer to come with you but I'll probably be working, I'm afraid.'

'It'll be OK. I'll ring up and find a good time.'

'Do you like working for yourself, Elsa?' asked Bron, refilling the glasses. 'I've wondered about going freelance again myself.'

'Well, in lots of ways I love it. I don't have to get dressed to go to work—'

'Sorry?'

Elsa laughed. 'I live on the job. I rented a floor of a warehouse and me and my dad made a little flat in the corner. I just wander out from my sitting room into my workshop. I'm very strict with myself about not bringing my toast and marmalade though.'

Bron giggled and then looked a bit anxious.

'Are you all right? You don't need to go and make Roger's supper or anything?'

'Oh no – we had a huge lunch and then tea with his parents. I'll make him cheese on toast at about half-nine and he'll be fine.'

Elsa didn't speak. She was afraid that if she did she'd say something very uncomplimentary about Bron's partner. Even if Bron didn't seem entirely happy with the situation, it wasn't for Elsa to comment.

'So,' went on Bron, 'what are the downsides?'

'Loneliness, obviously. There's no one to bounce ideas off, unless I get someone in to help me with the handwork. And I do work stupid hours sometimes. But basically, I love my work, so that's OK. I go round to my parents for a proper bath from time to time. I'm very lucky.'

'But no boyfriend?'

Elsa shook her head. 'Nope. Not all that much social life, either. None of the friends I knew as a child still live round here – they've all gone and got careers elsewhere. Finchcombe isn't really a big enough town to employ too many people.'

'No,' Bron agreed.

'I really don't mind though,' Elsa went on. 'My mother thinks I waste my life stuck in my workroom but I'm fine with it.' She caught sight of Bron trying discreetly to look at her watch and got up. 'I'd better be off. Oh, I nearly forgot, here are the clips.' She stuffed her hand in the pocket of her jeans and produced them. 'You look tired, Bron.'

'Mm. Maybe a little.' Bron smiled as she stood to walk Elsa to the door.

Elsa set off towards her parents' house in the older part of the town. They would need details of the wedding too, and her mother would have to see her new hair sooner or later. Her mother would give her supper too. On reflection, she didn't really want to ring Ashlyn's mother on a Sunday night. She would still be tired from the wedding and, more to the point, Elsa had drunk nearly half a bottle of wine. She didn't want to risk slurring her words – she'd ring in the morning.

As she walked, Elsa thought about Bron. Roger seemed rather domineering. He certainly had Bron firmly under his thumb and presumably wanted it to stay that way. Far better to be single than to be attached to a man like that, but then who was she to comment on someone else's relationship? Maybe he had had a bad day.

The next morning, having called Mrs Lennox-Featherstone, who'd said come straight over, Elsa dressed very carefully. As a gesture to the beautiful, early summer morning, she wore string-coloured linen trousers instead of her uniform black, but with a black fitted T-shirt, so as not to stray too far from her comfort zone. Her new hairstyle shone with health and she put on make-up in honour of the occasion.

The house was a little way away from the town and Elsa admired it as she drove slowly up the drive, putting off the shy-making moment as long as possible.

It was a house worthy of admiration, with classic, Queen Anne proportions. Small for a manor house, it was huge by any other standards, with two storeys over a basement and tall sash windows. There was a flight of steps up to the front door. Going by the size of the stone walls that surrounded the property, it also had a huge garden.

Eventually Elsa had to stop the car and get out. She had steamed the dress and inspected it closely for marks or signs of wear. Only the keenest eye would recognise that it had been worn, and it definitely qualified as having had 'one careful lady owner' in the best tradition of second-hand cars. She still felt terribly nervous although logically she knew she had no reason to be.

The dress was in a special bag hung over her arm, the train caught up so it couldn't trail on the ground by mistake. Elsa took a breath and pulled at the bell-pull; she heard the bell ring through the house. So as not to appear too anxious, she turned to admire the perfect lawns and the roses that lined the distant wall and rambled up into neighbouring trees. When she heard footsteps, she turned back and took another calming breath.

A young woman wearing an apron over her slacks and polo shirt opened the door. 'Miss Ashcombe? Mrs Vanessa is expecting you.' She had a middle-European accent and a friendly smile. 'Follow me.'

Elsa, holding the dress high, followed the maid through parqueted corridors until they reached a large, sunny room, with French doors open to the garden. Mrs Lennox-Featherstone was on the telephone and waved an arm towards a table and two chairs that were over by the windows, looking out into the garden. Elsa went in their direction but stayed standing, holding the dress so it wouldn't crumple on the floor, trying not to look as if she could hear every word an increasingly irate Mrs Lennox-Featherstone was saying.

'That's just too irritating for words!' said Mrs Lennox-Featherstone into the telephone. And then, 'How am I expected to do that? It's ridiculous!' She put down the phone abruptly.

'It's maddening! Bloody insurance won't cover an empty property.'

'Won't they?' asked Elsa politely.

'Apparently not. We've got a little cottage nearby that we're getting done up in the autumn, but if it burns down between now and then, we'll get nothing! Just because it's empty! Surely it's more likely to catch fire if there's someone in it?'

'I would have thought so,' said Elsa.

'Hm, well, if you hear of anyone who needs somewhere to live for a couple of months, let me know. Really, that's far too short a let for anyone and it's not fit for holiday accommodation.' Elsa's hostess gave a final huff and then turned her full attention to her guest.

'Where should I put the dress?' said Elsa, feeling rather self-conscious under the spotlight of Mrs Lennox-Featherstone's enquiring gaze. 'It should be hung up, really.'

'Oh I'll take that.' The bag was draped over a chair without quite sufficient reverence for Elsa's sensibilities. 'Now, let's have a look at you . . . I knew it,' declared Mrs Lennox-Featherstone after a moment's critical scrutiny of Elsa's face. 'Black really is quite the wrong colour for you. I think you might be a summer person, but we'd need to check. Sit down.'

Obediently, Elsa sat at the indicated chair, wondering if her hostess was speaking in tongues.

Mrs Lennox-Featherstone took the other chair. 'You really are a lovely girl. That fringe is adorable – very Audrey Hepburn. That hairdresser was really talented.'

'Yes she is,' said Elsa, glad of an opportunity to say something. 'She's a friend of mine.' After last night, she felt this was true.

'Is she? Does she do much freelance work? I have an idea to take a party of my old ladies – one of my charities – to the theatre. I think it would be great fun to give them all a mini-makeover first, so they feel pampered and special. She'd need to bring a colleague,' she added thoughtfully. 'Have you got a number for her? Or better still, a card?'

'I haven't a card, but I've got her mobile number in my phone. I'm not sure if she's actually doing much outside her normal working hours, apart from weddings.' While Bron had hinted that she would like to do more, Elsa didn't want to push her into something she wasn't ready for.

'Pop it down there for me.' Elsa was handed a pad and a little gold pen. 'Ah, here's Olga with the drinks. Lemon green tea all right for you? It has anti-cancer properties. You could have water, if you'd rather.'

Olga set the tray down on the little table and Elsa saw there were glasses and a bottle of water on it as well as a pot of tea and two china cups and saucers.

'Oh, the tea will be fine, thank you, Mrs Lennox-Featherstone,' said Elsa, wanting to please her hostess; it seemed safer.

'Oh, call me Vanessa, do. My name always makes me think someone's taken a bite out of a pillow and it's gone down the wrong way.'

Elsa smiled. This did pretty much sum up her hostess's surname.

'Good girl,' said Vanessa. She picked up the teapot and began to pour. 'Now, I want to give you a present. No, don't protest, you deserve something for standing in for that little cow at the last moment, but I'm afraid I'm going to be frightfully bossy and tell you what you should have. There's your tea.'

Elsa took the cup, aware that she'd hardly opened her

mouth and yet unable to think of anything to say that would be worth the agony of saying it. Mrs Lennox-Featherstone was flitting from one topic to another like a demented butterfly.

'I want you to have your colours done.'

'I'm sorry?'

'A wonderful woman I know will tell you what colours work for you and which ones don't – clothes, make-up, that sort of thing. I'll come with you, so you won't be on your own. It'll be huge fun. I'll set it up and let you know the date.'

'Really, it's extremely kind of you . . .' Elsa protested. It sounded like another form of torture and anyway, what was wrong with black?

'No, dear, don't thank me. It's a bit of a mission. I'm like it with underwear too. Not that you need help on that score. Your bra has obviously been properly fitted. But if you knew how many women are ignorant of the fact that the nipple should be halfway between the top of the shoulder and the elbow. You see more nipples at elbow height than you can shake a stick at.'

Elsa, struck by the combination of shaking sticks and nipples wanted to giggle. It was partly nerves, she knew, and took a couple of deep breaths to help her relax.

'You mustn't mind me, darling,' said Vanessa, 'I do get bees in my bonnet about things. I'm a woman with a mission. I should have been at the top of a multi-national company really, but I gave it all up for love.' She smiled. 'How are you liking the tea?'

'It's fine – lovely.'

'I know one can get quite hung up on health kicks and superfoods but I do think green tea is worth drinking.'

'It's very pleasant,' repeated Elsa. She took a couple of large sips. Just as soon as she was finished she could leave. She'd stayed the polite amount of time, after all.

Just then the telephone rang again, and while Vanessa got up to answer it, Elsa finished her tea in one.

'Can't talk now, darling, I've got a guest,' said Vanessa. 'I'll call you later.'

Feeling churlish for gulping her tea, Elsa got to her feet. 'It's been lovely, Mrs . . . um . . . thank you so much. You've been very kind,' she said quickly, in case she was interrupted.

Her hostess smiled warmly. 'It's been a pleasure, and I'll be on to you as soon as I've arranged for my friend to sort out your colours. Oh, by the way . . .'

'Yes?' It was uncharacteristic of Vanessa to pause, which made it significant.

'Laurence Gentle, the best man, asked me for your telephone number. I said I had to check with you that it was all right to give it to him.'

'Oh.' Why on earth would he want her telephone number? Unless of course his sister wanted one of her dresses – if he had a sister that is. 'Yes, I suppose it's all right.'

'He is a really nice man, I can assure you of that.'

'Yes. He seemed nice.' He had.

'By nice I mean decent, in the old-fashioned way. Bit set in his ways, of course, but he is a bachelor and that can happen.'

'Can it?'

'Of course. If men aren't gay and don't have partners they can get quite odd. But I'll give him your number then. Oh, and thank you for bringing back the dress. Not sure what I'll do with it.'

'You could sell it on eBay,' suggested Elsa.

'Oh, darling, I really don't think I could do that. No, I'll think of something.'

As Elsa drove away she decided that whatever else Vanessa did with the bridesmaid's dress, she wouldn't put it in a bag and hang it in a cupboard until it turned to dust.

Chapter Seven

When Sarah had woken that Sunday morning, she'd been instantly, uncomfortably aware that she had not slept well. She rarely did after a big event, and Ashlyn's wedding was definitely that. Her head tended to take a while to stop seeing table plans, floral arrangements and potentially inefficient staff. But this morning she had an extra reason to feel as if she'd been up all night – Hugo.

She'd gone off to sleep all right but then she'd kept waking up. It was nothing to do with the room. It might have been tiny, but it was a good hotel: the sheets were silky, the towels were fluffy and the mattress was just right. No, it was what nearly happened that disturbed her.

She really shouldn't have let Hugo kiss her. The drink and the dance were all right. That would have been fine. But it should have stopped there.

As it was still only seven o'clock when she woke, she turned on her back and considered why it had happened. She sighed. It didn't take much brainpower to work it out. Hugo was extremely attractive, and she had been tired, a tiny bit drunk and forgot to be her usual professional self. She and Hugo had worked so well together up until now, it would be an awful shame if she'd spoilt it by getting carried away by the moment.

She gave a shuddering sigh, forcing her mind away from those lovely kisses, hoping they weren't addictive and that she could go back to her everyday, sensible life without difficulty. She sat up and rubbed her eyes. Of course she could! She wasn't in love with him, after all, and as long as she never let it happen again, she'd be fine.

Inevitably her mind went back to Bruce, the man she'd thought was the love of her life. She saw him at the first Freshers' do at university and thought he was the most attractive boy she had ever seen apart from on a movie screen. Somehow, magically, Bruce had seen her too and was attracted to the quieter, more sensible girl she was, rather than the giddy hordes of excited teenagers around her. They had become a couple almost immediately. She'd fallen head over heels in love with him and they'd planned their future together: where they'd live, how many children they'd have and how they'd be celebrating their Golden Wedding anniversary still very much in love. She'd trusted Bruce implicitly. And although every girl on campus fancied the pants off him, it was to Sarah's side he was glued.

Until he wasn't. Walking into his flat to find the love of her life in bed with another girl had knocked her so badly she had sworn she would never make herself a hostage to love again. It had felt as if her heart had been ripped out – a man she'd thought she would spend the rest of her life with had betrayed her, cruelly. It was not as if she hadn't had enough to cope with, either. Her mother had died shortly before she went to university, she needed to keep an eye out for her father, and, of course, there was Lily, her younger and very vulnerable sister. Working through heartbreak at the same time as doing her college work and supporting her grieving family had been utter hell. If it hadn't been for her family and her friends she didn't know how she would have survived. She had vowed to herself that she would never take that risk, ever again. Not even after all this time. After all, she had a business to run now, and Lily still needed her big sister. And she owed it to herself.

She shook herself out of her remembered pain. Kissing Hugo had been lovely, she had to admit, but she couldn't afford to let it go any further. Anyway, he probably hadn't given it another thought; she'd heard the odd rumour about him, after all. She resolved to put it firmly behind her. And at least they hadn't arranged to have breakfast together or anything ghastly like that, she thought as she picked up the phone and asked if she could have some toast in her room. Thanking goodness for posh hotels with high standards of room service, she was driving away within twenty minutes, keen to get home where life was ordinary and normal.

Not quite as normal as all that; her sister was sitting on the doorstep. Four years younger than Sarah, Lily had the air of a schoolgirl dressed in adult clothes, except that the clothes weren't all that adult, consisting of, in this instance, a baby-doll pyjama top over a pair of pink jeans studded with diamanté. Her blonde hair was caught up here and there with sparkly clips and more pink and diamond beads circled her neck and wrists. She could have been a tall six-year-old at a dressing-up party. She looked, thought Sarah, divinely pretty and a little unhinged. Not for the first time, Sarah marvelled how two sisters could be so different.

Lily was clutching a carrier bag and looking sheepish and excited at the same time. She leapt to her feet when she saw her sister.

'Sares! Why did you have your phone off? And where have you been? Not with a man, surely?'

'Hello.' Fondly, Sarah enfolded her sister in her arms, thinking, as she always did, how tiny she was and choosing to ignore her teasing. 'What are you doing out of bed at this hour? A bit unheard-of, isn't it?'

'Sarah! I'm a grown-up now. Please let us in, I'm dying for the loo. And I've got such an ace plan!'

Sarah laughed. 'Keep your legs crossed while I unlock the door then. Here, you'd better take the flat key. I've got stuff to unload from the car.'

Sarah's flat was on the first floor of a very nice converted chapel. It had everything she needed: one big bedroom she used as an office; a smaller second bedroom where she slept; and a large living room with a kitchen at one end where she did everything else. The bathroom was small but for a single person it was more than adequate. Sarah loved it.

By the time she had unloaded the car, Lily had used the bathroom and was rummaging through Sarah's cupboards for breakfast cereal.

'Sarah! You've got such healthy eating habits! Haven't you got anything here with any sugar in it?'

'Here, try this. It's got dried berries. It looks pretty and if you don't think it's sweet enough you can always add sugar. Tea or coffee?'

'Tea please! Oh.' Lily put down the empty milk carton she had just upended. 'Have I used the last of the milk?'

'Yup, but don't worry. I want coffee and I want it black.'

'I'll have a fruit tea then.' Lily shovelled a spoon of cereal into her mouth, getting a bit of milk on her chin. 'I've got such good news! I wish you'd sit down.'

Sarah was making coffee, rinsing out her thermos flask that she always took with her to weddings, filled with an emergency supply of peppermint tea, and generally settling back home. However, as she had once complained that Lily danced around the place like an animated children's illustration, she took the point and seated herself next to her sister at the breakfast bar. Lily was now drinking the last of the milk from her cereal bowl.

'If it's that good, why haven't you told me already? Why have breakfast first?'

'Because I need to have you calm and sitting down.' Lily patted Sarah's hand and got up.

'I am calm and I'm sitting down. Unlike you.'

Lily laughed. 'Those stools are so uncomfortable.' She went into the sitting part of the room and bounced on to the sofa. 'Oh Sarah, I can't believe it. I'm so happy!'

Sarah was used to Lily's sudden bursts of energy, so this emotion wasn't instantly transferable. She got up more slowly and followed her sister to the sofa. 'Great!' She tried to match her sister's enthusiasm. 'Why?'

'I'm engaged! We're engaged, I mean, Dirk and me.'

Sarah put down her coffee mug and flung her arms round Lily's neck, this time with genuine fervour. 'Oh, Lily! That's brilliant. I'm so happy for you.' She hadn't met Dirk often but he'd struck her as just the sort of steady young man Lily needed in her life.

'I can't believe how happy I am!' said Lily, beaming at Sarah.

Sarah sat back and thought for a moment. She didn't want to upset Lily but she felt she had to bring it up. The older sister part of her that she tried (and sometimes failed) to control said, 'I hate to say this, but are you sure this time? We have been here before.'

Lily got up from the sofa. 'I knew you'd be worried, but it's not like last time, I promise you. Dirk is kind and caring – not at all like Rex.' She turned to her sister who was struggling to keep the concern from her face. 'What I did with him was silly and childish. We shouldn't have run away like that and you were right about him being a pig. But I know it's different this time. I can feel it.'

Sarah managed a smile. Watching her sister's heartbreak had been only marginally easier than suffering her own. Neither of them had been particularly lucky in love, she thought ruefully.

'Honestly, Sares, it's not at all like before. We're not eloping. We're having a proper wedding, and I want you to organise it.'

Lily said this with an expansive sweep of her arms, as if she were conferring a great favour on her sister, forgetting that planning weddings was her job. And while Sarah wouldn't have dreamt of accepting money for doing it, even if Lily had dreamt of offering it, it would take up a lot of time. But she realised that Lily was asking for her approval, as well as her help; having Sarah arrange the wedding would be like her conferring her blessing. Lily had always looked up to Sarah, and since their mother's death and their father's remarriage, Sarah had been more like a mother to her than a sister. And Sarah felt very protective towards her baby sister.

She took a deep breath and brushed aside any misgivings she might have: after all, Dirk was nothing like Rex. 'Of course I'll help you,' she said. 'I'll tell you anything you need to know, but I'm not sure I'll have time to actually organise it all.'

'You won't need to do much!' More arm flinging from Lily. 'We're going to a wedding fair. We can find out everything we need there!'

Sarah was tired, in spite of the strong coffee, and she started to laugh. Trust her darling sister to think that all you needed was a few brochures and some free samples. All her experience and knowledge were as nothing to a huge and crowded event where myriad people tried to sell you things – mostly things you didn't want. But this was just like Lily and it was always easier to give in. 'When are we going to this fair?'

'Now. It's today. That's why I had to come round so early.'

'I have got a lot—'

'Oh, don't be such a spoilsport! You're always so boring!' Lily bounced up and settled nearer her sister, and took hold of her arm.

Suspecting that Lily wasn't the only person who felt this, and Hugo coming sharply to mind, Sarah sighed. 'OK, OK, I'll come. Where is it?'

'Never mind that. Before we go anywhere I thought I'd show you this.' Lily found her carrier bag and took from it a faintly familiar scrapbook.

'My goodness! I can't believe you've still got that,' said Sarah. 'You used to cut out pictures from magazines and all your old birthday cards, and little notes from your friends.'

'I stopped doing that when I was ten,' announced Lily proudly. 'This is a new one.' She opened the scrapbook somewhere in the middle and plonked it on Sarah's knees. 'Start there.'

Sarah began to turn the pages. There were pages and pages of wedding dresses, beautiful designer gowns from the sleekest silk sheath with sequins at the hem to dresses with skirts made entirely from frills – tiny ones at the top round the bottom of the bodice getting larger as they reached the ground. Sarah looked more closely. This particular one had spangles round the edge of each frill. She was well used to wedding dresses, and knew the magazines these fantastic creations had been cut from. What made her stare was the fact that her sister had cut out her own face from photographs and stuck it over the models' faces.

'Lily, I can't believe you've done that! It must have taken ages.'

'Well, I wanted to see if the dresses would suit me.' She leant over and flicked through a couple of pages and then she plonked a finger down on one with a long ruched bodice to the hips, with a skirt caught up with huge knots of fabric roses. It had a long train with more ruching and more roses – the love child of a flamenco costume and a meringue. 'That's my favourite.'

Sarah peered at it for a few seconds. 'Not a penny less than five grand, possibly more. What's your budget?'

Lily flicked her hand in irritation. 'Oh, typical you to spoil it all by talking about money!'

'It does have to be talked about. But I expect Dad'll make a contribution. Have you told him yet? I'm sure he'll be really happy for you.'

'I wanted you to be first and, anyway, I don't want Her

putting her oar in.' Lily made a face. Unlike Sarah, she had never got on with their stepmother.

'She won't! Kay has never interfered in our lives. Although they won't have much money to spare, not with the boys.'

Lily sighed with irritation.

'It's all too easy to let a fortune slip through your fingers,' said Sarah. 'Let me show you some of the weddings I've done, to give you an idea of how much things can cost.'

Sarah went to her office to find her photograph album. This was the record she kept for her own purposes, of flowers, cars, venues etc. She placed it on Lily's crossed legs and put the kettle on again.

Lily turned over the pages. 'That dress! Gross. Oh, sweet bridesmaids. If Kay had had little girls instead of boys, I'd have them as flower girls or something.' Then she paused. 'Who's this? Bit gorgeous!'

Sarah went over to see whom Lily was referring to. 'Oh. That's Hugo,' she said as nonchalantly as she could. 'He's a photographer. He was setting up a shot elsewhere so I couldn't ask him to move.'

'He's lush!' She peered more closely at the photo. 'And so like Bruce!'

Just hearing his name gave Sarah a small shock. 'Is he?' She joined her sister on the sofa and looked at the photo again. 'Oh. I see what you mean.' God, he was very like Bruce – the same charming smile and laid-back, easy manner. Was that why, although he was undoubtedly attractive, a part of her had instinctively always been so resistant to him? He definitely looked like the boy who'd broken her heart so many years before. And all the more reason to keep things strictly professional between them from now on, she told herself.

'So, Lily,' she said now, trying to think how to change the subject without looking as if she was, 'show me your ring!'

Although it was a ploy, Sarah realised it was quite a useful one. The engagement ring would give her some clue as to the budget. If Dirk could afford to give Lily a socking great rock, he maybe could afford to give Lily the wedding of her dreams.

'Oh, it's so sweet!' she enthused. It was a genuinely very pretty ring. Obviously antique, it was a small ruby with goldwork round it to make it look like a scarlet pimpernel. But it didn't seem to Sarah to represent the small fortune that Lily probably wanted to spend on her wedding. 'I love it,' Sarah said. 'You've got such delicate fingers. Not many people could make a ring like that look so pretty.'

'It is lovely, isn't it? Dirk just produced it from his pocket one morning while we were going for a cappuccino. It fitted perfectly.' She admired her hand for a few moments. 'Apparently he'd taken one of my junk jewellery rings and kept trying rings until he found one that was the same size.'

'Oh, that's so romantic. So much less conventional than selecting rings in a price bracket and getting you to choose.' Sarah was impressed that Dirk, who had struck her as slightly lacking in imagination, had managed to give her sister a ring that she really loved, in a romantic way.

Lily closed her scrapbook, put it back in her carrier bag and said, 'So, let's go to this fair. You don't mind driving, do you? It's in Swansea.'

Sarah was horrified. 'But that's miles! The other side of the Severn Bridge.'

'It's why we need to get a shift on!'

'This is the sort of thing I'd have done with Mum, if she'd still been alive,' said Lily, painting her nails as they travelled down the motorway.

Sarah heard her sister's voice crack and felt sudden compassion. Their mother had been dead for over ten years and both girls still felt the loss. Of course a girl would expect her mother to help her with her wedding. But their mother would have been far more likely to accompany Lily to an agricultural show than a wedding fair.

'Well, she might have,' acknowledged Sarah, 'but she wasn't really into girly things, was she? She was a practical, outdoors type.'

Lily giggled, which Sarah thought was a good sign. 'S'pose so. Do you remember that time we went camping? She was the only one who liked it.'

Sarah joined in with the giggling. 'And the family opposite who had the boys? They both fell madly in love with you.'

'Yes, they did, didn't they.' Lily had always been so sure of her charms, even as a little girl.

'No, I expect I'd have had to go with you to wedding fairs anyway,' said Sarah.

'If I got on better with Kay, I might have asked her.'

Sarah was getting fed up with Lily moaning about their stepmother. 'Come on, Lily, be fair, she's fine. She and Dad get on really well. You're always so hard on her. Anyway, she's got the boys to look after. She's really busy!'

Lily sighed. She hadn't really enjoyed having her place as the youngest member of the family usurped by a couple of rumbustious lads who were now five and seven. 'We just don't see eye to eye on artistic matters.'

Sarah snorted.

Lily blew on her nails and looked reproachfully at her sister. 'And are you going to tell me they have to be page-boys?'

Sarah nodded. 'Well, you have to ask them. If they, or Dad and Kay, really hate the idea, you're off the hook. Otherwise, you have to think of what you'd like them to wear.'

'Reins!' said Lily defiantly.

'Silly!'

'Well, you know how naughty they are. By the way, did I tell you, we want to get married quite soon?'

'That doesn't surprise me. You were never much good at deferring your pleasures.'

'What does that mean?' asked Lily, pouting.

'You know perfectly well. You always want everything immediately.'

'Well, you can't say that about me this time.'

'No? You were pretty insistent that we set off to this fair immediately!'

'Well, I have got a reason to hurry . . .'

'Which is?'

'I'm pregnant.'

Sarah's hands tightened on the steering wheel and she nearly swerved. 'Oh,' she said after a frantic second. 'That's very exciting.' It crossed her mind to wonder why Lily had announced her engagement before she told her she was pregnant, but her sister was always a bit of a mystery to her so she didn't waste time on it.

'That's why we want to get married so quickly.'

'But Lily, people don't worry about these things nowadays – there's no need to rush. You could get married after you've had the baby.' It was not ideal, but relatively common. She pictured the flowing gown that Lily might want the baby to wear to go nicely with her own dress. Maybe they could have the baby christened at the same time, and save money.

Lily was shaking her head worriedly. 'Dirk's parents will go mad. If they find out—'

'Oh, for goodness' sake! It's the twenty-first century!'

'Not in their land. They're very strict. They don't believe in sex before marriage.'

Without ever having met them, Sarah was already very fed up with these people. 'But they must know you were married before – if only for a very short time.'

'We told them it was annulled.'

'Oh, so getting your wedding annulled instead of being divorced somehow restores your anatomy to its original state?'

'Oh well, they know I'm not a virgin in the actual sense . . .'

'Is there another way?'

'They're just from a different planet! They didn't have sex before they were married and don't think anyone else should.'

'But, sweetie, they'll find out you're pregnant sooner or later.'

'Please, let it be later! I'll die of embarrassment having to tell them!'

Sarah chuckled. 'You mean, you have to admit to having sex?'

'Yes! Nightmare!'

'Why doesn't Dirk stand up to them? Tell them you're pregnant and you want to have the wedding at your leisure.'

There was a pause. 'But I don't want to. I want a proper white wedding, and so does Dirk.'

'Lily, lots of vicars won't marry you in a church if you've been married before.'

'It's all right,' said Lily quietly. 'Dirk's parents have already booked the church.'

'What!' This really did shock Sarah. 'How come?'

'The moment we told them they were on the phone. The vicar's an old friend of theirs, has known Dirk since he was tiny, and he's all right about me being divorced.'

'That's good then! When is it?'

'The eighteenth of August.'

'Oh, quite soon.' She didn't currently have much going on in August but still . . . 'It gives us – what? – end of June, July – a couple of months. It's cutting it fine, love.'

'I know, but I promise you, Dirk's mother must have

suspected something because she was on that phone before you could say butter.' Sarah smiled. Lily's mixed metaphors were always funny.

'I think you mean before you could put a knife through butter.'

Lily shrugged. It wasn't important.

'And you will have to tell them. Otherwise they'll be writing to the tabloids about a three-month pregnancy ending in a ten-pound baby.'

'We will tell them, but not until it's too late for them to make a fuss. As I said, I think she may have an inkling but can't bear to face the truth.'

Grateful that she didn't have to find a church and persuade the vicar to marry a divorced woman in the middle of the wedding season, Sarah tackled another tricky subject. 'I know you don't want to think about it, but before we get to the fair and get dazzled by all the options, we do need to think about the budget. How much can you afford to spend?' She asked the same question in two ways to force her sister to think about the answer.

'Ah – that is rather a pain.'

After her sister's pause had gone on quite a long time, Sarah broke in. 'You mean you haven't got any money? But you still want a traditional white wedding with all the trimmings?'

'Don't be cross!' pleaded her sister. 'I know it's stupid but I want to sweep down the aisle in a fabulous dress.'

Sarah reflected that when Lily had got married before, she and her intended had rushed off to Gretna Green. Lily had confided later that it wasn't at all romantic; in fact, it had been rather sordid, and the marriage had started to go wrong almost before the ceremony had been performed. Sarah had kept her thoughts to herself about Lily's first choice of husband and was glad she had. Lily had learnt her lesson the hard way and was entitled to a proper wedding now.

'And it's not just that,' her sister went on.

'What is it, Lily?' Sarah was good at being firm but fair – her job gave her a lot of practice and she had learnt her skills on her sister.

'His parents gave Dirk quite a bit of money a while ago and they're assuming he's still got it and can spend it on the wedding.'

'Well, that's totally unreasonable! He probably used it for a deposit on his flat or something.'

'No he didn't. He used it to settle a massive credit-card bill that he ran up while he was a student. He's really sensible with money now. But he didn't tell his parents. But as he did tell them how he'd saved to get the deposit for his flat, they think he's still got the money.' Lily sighed and Sarah felt a stab of sympathy. 'When they asked about it, he didn't have an answer ready so they assumed – and he was too chicken to say it wasn't true – that he still had it. So' – Lily sighed again – 'we've got to have a big posh wedding on hardly any money when really we should be saving up for things for the baby.'

If Sarah had felt sympathetic before, she felt even more so now. 'Oh, poor you. That's awful, having to spend your money on wedding cake and personalised confetti when you really want a cot and a good pushchair.'

'Personalised confetti? What are you talking about?'

'I was only joking. It's fantastically expensive and rather naff, in my opinion, to have your picture on every little fake rose petal your friends throw at you.'

'Is that really possible?'

'Anything is possible if you're prepared to pay, but you're not. Your guests can buy their own, bio-degradable confetti,' she stated crisply, hoping to end that topic of conversation.

'Yes,' said Lily meekly. 'What about the dress? I know we should be saving but now it's happening I want it all to be so special.'

'I know, Lily, and it will be. But listen, the average amount people spend on their dress is just under a thousand pounds, while the ones you had in your scrapbook – as I said, five grand minimum.' There was a hiccup and Sarah guessed that Lily was deciding whether or not to cry. 'But there are all sorts of ways round that. You could go to a sample sale, for example, if there are any on at this time of year. Or hire one? Have a second-hand dress?'

'No! I don't want to go down the aisle in a dress someone else has worn before. It would be unlucky.'

'Oh,' said Sarah. 'So does that put my other suggestion out of the question?'

'What do you mean?'

'That you wear Mum's dress? I've got it, in a box. You could have it altered to fit you, and update it.'

'Mum's dress.'

Sarah couldn't quite tell from her voice how she'd reacted to this. 'Well, think about it. But don't worry, Lily, I can organise you a really cheap – I mean economical – wedding, as long as you're prepared to compromise.'

'I am. I'll have to.'

'Then it will all be fine. Now tell me about me becoming an aunt.'

'Oh, the baby! Well, it's very small, Sarah. Hardly bigger than a tadpole.'

For a tadpole, it was creating an awful lot of fuss.

Chapter Eight

The wedding fair was in a castle of white stone, converted into a huge hotel. It was, Sarah recognised, the perfect location for a large wedding, and she hoped Lily didn't suddenly yearn for it. The hotel had probably thought, reasonably enough, that once inside its spacious and undoubtedly romantic rooms, many of the attendees would fall in love with the setting and want their wedding there. Experience told her this would only be possible for those planning a long engagement. As a wedding venue, it would be booked up for at least two years.

The fine weather that had blessed Ashlyn's wedding continued and the festive mood of the day was enhanced as couples, groups of young women, and the occasional mother-and-daughter combination entered the building, full of plans and ideas.

Champagne or orange juice greeted everyone as they entered. There was a tray of chocolates too. Sarah took an orange juice, biting her tongue on her anxiety about Lily opting for the champagne. However much it went against the grain, she mustn't be a killjoy today.

'Isn't this exciting!' Lily said, skipping a little. 'It's like actually being at a wedding already!'

Sarah smiled slightly. When she'd first started out in business, she'd taken stands at wedding fairs, but for a while now word of mouth and her website had got her all her custom. This was a relief. The amount of talking that went on during the long day didn't equate to enough brides needing her services to make it worth the effort.

For a moment, Lily hovered in the reception area, undecided where to start, then she pulled Sarah's arm. 'Chocolate fountains! Come on!'

Just the thought of liquid chocolate and wedding dresses in the same room made Sarah's heart quiver with apprehension but she didn't comment as Lily led the way.

'Look at all that chocolate!' said Lily ecstatically. 'Isn't it heaven? It reminds me of when we melted down all our Easter eggs and ate them with a spoon.'

Sarah chuckled. 'You were sick.'

'So I was!' Lily remembered happily. 'Sick as a canary!'

The woman in charge of this liquid heaven seemed confused by this image for a moment, then she handed them both strawberries. 'Have a taste,' she said.

'Oh, Sarah, this is so gorgeous! I must have this!'

'It might be better at the hen night,' said Sarah. 'As a bride, you shouldn't get near it, it would be awful if you got it on your dress.'

'True,' said Lily, taking another generous strawberry's worth. 'And Dirk's mother wouldn't approve.'

At last Sarah was able to lead her sister away, but only after she'd tried every fruit, sweet and biscuit, coated in chocolate.

'The chocolate's really nice,' said Lily gaily while they were still in earshot. 'I thought it might be a bit like that chocolate they sell in sex shops.'

Sarah was about to ask how Lily knew about such things but then decided she'd rather not know. 'Well, the woman did tell us it was only as good as the chocolate you used.'

They got past the painted stones as place names, the harpist (although Sarah was tempted), any amount of personalised helium balloons, several florists and a false nail stand unscathed, except by leaflets and cards. But when Lily saw a rack of wedding dresses, she escaped from Sarah's vice-like grip and sprinted towards them.

'Aren't these the most heavenly dresses you have ever

seen in your entire life?' asked Lily, when Sarah at last caught up with her.

Sarah, who'd seen many more wedding dresses than Lily, said, 'Mm.'

'If you'd like to try any on,' said the smiling assistant, 'please let me help you.'

'Oh yes, please!' said Lily enthusiastically. 'Can I try that one? I'm a size ten.'

Sarah cleared her throat. 'At the risk of sounding like our dear departed mother, I think you should go and wash your hands.'

Lily looked at her hands. 'Oh my God! So sorry! Covered in chocolate! I'll be back!'

Lily had many skills, and one of them was being able to find a Ladies in a completely strange place without needing to ask. It was as if she was tuned in to the smell of handwash and hot-air driers, and could track them down, like a bee scenting its hive.

While she was gone, Sarah perched on a little sofa, resting her feet that were still aching a bit from Ashlyn's wedding. She didn't want to engage with the woman in charge of the dresses because she knew Lily wasn't going to buy one, however much she might want to.

Lily skipped back a few minutes later smelling of something floral. 'There was a woman selling personalised perfumes,' she explained. 'Couldn't resist. Right, dresses. Can I try that one, please?'

'Perfect,' said the woman, handing it to her. 'This dress only looks really good on more slender brides. Call me when you need help with the buttons. Oh, and there's a zip at the side, too.'

Sarah stayed sitting while Lily was in the changing room, putting her perfect but pregnant size ten into a garment which was so fitted, even a fairy cake would show if you ate one, let alone a five-month pregnancy.

How, Sarah wondered, had a woman with her history

got to be a wedding planner when she was so cynical about marriage? She didn't often have time to ask herself this rather important question, but while twenty pearl buttons were hiking in her sister's tiny waist with the aid of at least two other women, it seemed the perfect opportunity.

Her own utter disillusion formed her attitude to marriage, that was straightforward enough. But why encourage other women to commit to men who probably wouldn't commit back? It really went back to that holiday job she'd had as a waitress, working for a friend of her mother. She'd only been expected to hand round trays of nibbles, but the lack of organisation in the kitchen had maddened her. There was an industrial dishwasher, but none of the women was willing to work out how it operated except her. Then she had to organise a system of plates in, plates out. Her bossy streak emerged.

Later, after university, she got a job in public relations and events management and one thing led to another. She found she had a flair for wedding planning and, ironically, helping to create the special day for others took her mind off her own heartache until it became only an unpleasant memory – although it had obviously scarred her for life in terms of ever daring to love again. She decided, when she had her first set of business cards printed, that while she couldn't do anything about the happy-ever-after aspect of weddings, she could create a dream day for every bride. It wasn't long before she realised dreams were a lot harder to create than anyone might think, but it was still her aim, and when it all went perfectly, she found it enormously satisfying. Now she only hoped she could help her sister's dream along towards perfection.

When Lily finally emerged, there was practically a round of applause from the other assistants and the few soon-to-be brides who were there. She looked stunning, there was no getting away from it.

'Oh!' said the assistant. 'I've gone all teary. You look so lovely!'

'Well, Sarah?' said Lily. 'Isn't the dress for me?'

She swallowed. Lily did look beautiful but Sarah's practical side came to the fore. She bit her lip and summoned all the tact she was famous for. 'Well,' she said cautiously. 'If you waited until next year to get married you could have that dress. It would look gorgeous.'

'Why won't it look gorgeous now?' asked Lily, frowning a little as she turned this way and that in front of the glass. 'It's probably the shoes.' She waggled a bare foot. 'I need some heels.'

'It's not that,' said Sarah quickly. 'It looks wonderful now, of course it does, but . . .' She paused, not wishing to announce her sister's condition to the world. 'It might look better next year, that's all.'

Lily got the point. 'Oh! You mean because I'm pregnant, I shouldn't have this style?'

Sarah caught the eye of the saleswoman, who giggled. 'Well, I wasn't going to say that, but it's what I meant.'

'The baby is only tiny! Just a few centimetres!' protested Lily.

'But unless you're getting married tomorrow, you won't manage in anything as sleek as this,' put in the sales-woman. 'An empire line would be more suitable.'

'But I've always had such a tiny waist! I want to show it off!' Lily protested again.

'Well, you can,' said Sarah, 'but you have to have the baby first!' She didn't suggest that her sister's waist might not be quite so tiny after she'd had the baby because (a) it was cruel and (b) her sister was the sort of woman whose figure would more than likely just ping back into shape a day after her milk came in. Maddening, but true.

Lily shook her head. 'Not possible. I'd better get out of this. I am so disappointed!' She scowled at Sarah as if it were somehow her sister's fault she was pregnant. She stomped back to the changing room, fiddling with the buttons as she went.

When Lily re-emerged later, some of her sunniness had returned, especially when Sarah said, 'Honestly, there are lots of fabulous styles that not only hide the fact you're pregnant, but look heavenly as well.'

Secretly, Sarah wasn't as certain about this as she sounded, but there was no point in spoiling all Lily's pleasure in her wedding preparations. After her first dismal attempt at matrimony, when Lily had worn jeans and wild flowers in her hair and it had all gone horribly wrong, the girl was allowed her dreams. And no one had been more delighted than Sarah when Lily had introduced her to Dirk.

'Let's get some more champagne,' said Lily, all smiles now. 'I'm thirsty!'

'You really shouldn't be drinking, you're pregnant,' said Sarah, but she said it to herself.

At lunchtime, which they ate in the conservatory that must have been tacked on to the castle long before anyone ever tried to stop anachronistic additions, Lily produced a book.

'Look, it tells us here when you have to do everything. It's a timetable.'

Sarah nibbled a cucumber sandwich. 'I actually do know all that stuff. It's my job.'

Lily took no notice. 'I think I'm quite well ahead. We've got the venue, after all.'

'It's a church, Lils, I think you should call it that.'

'And Dirk's mother wants a marquee in the garden for the reception. I'd much rather go to a hotel . . .' She glanced up at her sister, who shook her head. 'OK, I'll go with the marquee. Did they have one in *Four Weddings and a Funeral*?'

'I'm sure they did.' As this film was so often mentioned to Sarah she realised she should probably watch it, but since its hero bore more than a passing resemblance to her ex, she'd always avoided Hugh Grant films.

'Ooh, it's also got a place for the budget. How much do you think I should spend on my dress?'

'Depends. You still haven't told me how much your total budget is. There's no point in allocating a thousand pounds if that's all you've got for the whole thing.'

'Mm.' It was Lily's turn to be pensive now. 'Actually, I think that may be our budget. I should ask Dirk.'

'You should definitely ask Dirk. But don't worry too much. As I said, I'm sure Dad'll contribute something. And I'll do everything I can to keep costs down.'

'Fireworks!' said Lily, sounding a bit like one. 'They're on the list!'

'It doesn't mean you have to have them. Look, read it carefully. It also mentions chocolate fountains, and we've decided you could have that at the hen night. Everyone can chip in for that so it won't cost you much.'

'Children's entertainer,' mused Lily. 'That sounds a nice idea. I don't actually know anyone with children yet, but there are bound to be one or two.'

'If there are only one or two, you won't need an entertainer. You have to cut your cloak according to your cloth,' Sarah said gently.

'A cloak? Will I need one? It's not on the list.'

'Oh, Lily! It's just an expression!'

Lily threw down her vol-au-vent. 'Oh. I really want one now.'

Sarah sighed and extracted the book from her sister's hands. 'You don't need that silly list! I can tell you everything you need, and if you want a cloak, you can have it. But it won't be all that cold in August – we hope. We'll need to save money where we can.'

Lily collapsed like a deflated doll. 'Oh God, this is all so difficult! I want a lovely fairy-tale wedding and I can't have one because we haven't got enough money.'

'You can have a fairy-tale wedding, you just have to be careful, and clever with how you spend your money. I've done one or two weddings on a shoestring and they were brilliant. All it really needs is for you to look lovely, and you will, even if you wear a bin-liner – no, I'm not suggesting that – and for Dirk to look handsome. And you're both such a good-looking couple, you're bound to do that.'

Although Sarah said a lot of this to cheer Lily up, she did genuinely mean it. 'I bet you have a beautiful baby, too.'

'And will you babysit sometimes? I can't bear the thought of never being able to go out.'

'Of course I will. I'll love it. I'll spoil it to death.'

'Does that mean you'll buy it a pram and stuff like that? Then we can spend a bit more on the wedding.'

'Lily, go and talk to Dad about all this. In the old days the bride's parents paid for everything. Although money is tight I'm sure he's got a savings account or something for just this sort of thing. He didn't pay for your last wedding, after all.'

'No he didn't,' said Lily.

'And of course, I'll chip in too. You don't have to have imported flowers, smoked salmon, or unlimited champagne. I'll draw up a proper list and we can talk it through. We'll make it wonderful, don't you worry.'

Lily smiled beatifically. 'All right, I won't.'

A moment later Sarah realised by telling Lily not to worry, she'd just have to worry herself instead. But then that was what she was there for – and always had been.

'Shall we go and look at honeymoons now?' suggested Lily.

'That time of year, it'll have to be Europe – all the exotic places have hurricanes in August. Another way to save money.'

When Sarah had left Lily at the railway station at Finchcombe, just in time for the only train that would take her back on a Sunday, she drove home considering a career in funeral management. She was weddinged out. She never wanted to see another piece of tulle, a flower arrangement, a bit of confetti, or a hand-engraved champagne flute. No, she said to herself, a career in the very opposite direction was what she wanted now. She realised she would have to talk to her father about a contribution to Lily's wedding but that wouldn't be hard. Although she'd have to help Lily a lot with regard to suppliers and how to make economies, with any luck she wouldn't actually have to plan it.

Later that evening she washed away the cares of a very long day. The shower pouring over her head and body was blissful. Every time she used it she blessed the business that allowed her to put one in. Maybe she did like weddings after all, and funeral directors (she thought as she squirted shampoo into her hand) worked very unsocial hours sometimes.

The phone ringing penetrated her aquatic bliss. She turned off the shower and found a towel, half hoping the answerphone would kick in. Sunday evenings should be sacrosanct, shouldn't they?

Her answerphone obviously felt the same and refused to operate. She got to the telephone, clutching her towel, hoping it was Lily or someone she didn't have to be professional for.

'Hi,' said a female voice. 'Is that Sarah Stratford? The wedding planner?'

Oh. Definitely work. She hitched up the towel, wondering how anyone could ever want a videophone. 'Yes.' Did she want to admit that? Still, too late now.

'I'm Mandy Joseph, Carrie Condy's assistant.'

Sarah trawled through her mental checklist of names she should instinctively know. Mandy Joseph had said it as if it was one she expected to be recognised. 'Wow,' Sarah replied, to buy herself more time.

'You'll have read that she's just got engaged?'

'Oh yes! Yes.' Now Sarah spoke with more confidence. The American actress, of course. She had read that Carrie Condy had become engaged to an equally beautiful and up-and-coming young actor. 'Oh wow!' she said once more, with feeling this time.

'Well, she heard about you from a friend, and wants you to arrange the wedding.'

'Wow!' said Sarah for the third time. 'That's fantastic! Who did she hear about me from?' Which of her clients could possibly know Carrie Condy? she asked herself frantically.

'Someone who was at the wedding you handled on Saturday.'

'Oh. Well, it was a lovely wedding.' The budget a young star who'd been nominated for an Oscar might have floated around in Sarah's head like a happy pink bubble. Suddenly she was happy with weddings – she loved weddings!

'So we heard. Are you available?'

'Oh, I'm sure I am. What date did you have in mind? To get the best venue, we need to book early.'

'August.'

'That's fine, but next year? Or the year after?'

'This year. August this year. Carrie wants to get married as soon as possible.'

Chapter Nine

'But that's only two months away,' said Sarah, her heart in overdrive.

'We have a very small window. In fact, shall I tell you the date now?'

Sarah nodded and then realised that wouldn't work on the telephone. A sixth sense told her what she was about to hear. 'Yes please,' she breathed.

'The eighteenth. It's a Saturday.'

'I know,' said Sarah. Her mouth had gone dry.

'Is that all right for you? If not, I have a whole list of names here, I could try one of them?' Mandy Joseph didn't sound threatening, she sounded sympathetic, as if she could stop bothering Sarah at any moment.

'No!' It was a squeak. 'No, that's fine.' Still clutching the towel Sarah groped for the bottle of water that was on her desk, opened the top and had a swig. She cleared her throat. 'So, what sort of wedding did Carrie have in mind?' Should she have said Carrie – or Miss Condy?

Carrie was obviously fine because Mandy Joseph didn't miss a beat. 'Oh, pretty traditional. Like the one you did for Ashlyn.'

Sarah slopped some water into a glass. If all the moisture from her mouth was going to keep evaporating like this, she needed to be able to replace it quickly. 'That took two years to organise, not two months.'

'Why so long?'

Sarah cleared her throat. 'Most good venues – not to mention churches – are booked up that far in advance, especially if you want a Saturday. If you were to change—'

'Saturday's the traditional day, right?'

Sarah spotted a glimmer of opportunity. 'Not necessarily. If you – if Miss Condy – got married in London, weekdays are traditional.' This would make it so much easier to arrange. It should just about be possible to find a good hotel in London available on a weekday with two months' notice. Don't say Carrie Condy was pregnant as well as Lily? That would be a coincidence too far, surely?

'Oh no. Carrie definitely wants a country wedding. The church with the little house thing over the gate – just like Ashlyn.'

'That's going to be really difficult. There aren't many—'

'Carrie doesn't mind where in England she gets married, just as long as it's really pretty.' There was a pause, and Sarah used it to sip more water. 'As I said, we can find another planner if you think you can't do this. We were recommended you, but—'

'May I ask who recommended me?' Ashlyn's wedding had only been the day before. Who on earth could have been there and passed on her name to such a high-grade client and so quickly?

'Oh yes, it was Hugo. Hugo Marsters'

'Hugo!' The image of the two of them last night flashed into her mind, but she hurriedly dismissed it.

'Yes, I've been a friend of his sister since for ever, and I was visiting with her earlier today. He showed me some *wonderful* photographs of the wedding on his digital camera. I know that is just what Carrie is looking for. So can you do it?'

Sarah wouldn't have refused this job whoever she'd been recommended by, but the fact that it was Hugo gave her an extra incentive; if he thought she was good enough to do this, she must do it, and brilliantly. Just to prove how professional she was. 'Of course I can do it,' she said, trying to banish all traces of desperation from her voice. 'I was just pointing out the potential problems, but if Carrie's happy to get married anywhere, I can find a church, I'm sure.' In fact, she wasn't at all sure, but she had discovered that if she sounded confident her determination and refusal to be beaten usually got her what she wanted. With luck the vicar concerned could be bribed with a huge contribution to his tower-restoration fund and allow a starlet to be married outside her own parish – which was probably in America anyway.

After answering some key questions, Mandy, unaware of Sarah's false confidence, said, 'So what's the deal?'

When Sarah finally got off the phone she collapsed on the bed for several minutes before getting some clothes on. Wedding planner to the stars. It did sound wonderful, but could she do it? With a proper amount of time, of course she could. With a deadline as tight as that, maybe not, especially as her sister was getting married the same day.

As she pulled on a pair of knickers she remembered that she'd put clean knickers on in the hotel that morning. Two lifetimes had passed since then. It was strange that her body was still much the same: the same healing spot, the same little chip in her toenail varnish. She found her favourite fleecy joggers and a T-shirt. Summer it may have been, but she'd got cold talking on the telephone half-naked – she needed comfort clothes.

The discussion Sarah had had with Mandy gave her the information that not only did Carrie Condy want a very elaborate and yet traditional wedding, she would not be around much. Hearing this, Sarah had suggested she go to a top wedding dress shop and buy a dress off the peg. She explained that it would be made to fit and look as if it had been made exclusively for Carrie, but Mandy was insistent. Carrie wanted a couture gown, 'made to measure and everything like Ashlyn'. Sarah didn't ask how Carrie had got to know about Ashlyn's dress because the answer would probably have been Hugo. Hugo was definitely the sort of man who would know which wedding dresses were handmade and which were only 'prêt-à-porter'. She didn't know if this was a point in his favour, or against him.

At her desk, she created another file on her computer, and an actual file. On the actual file she wrote Carrie Condy in bold letters and wondered if the project was too much for her, and if she should ring back and suggest Carrie go to one of the big wedding-planning firms.

But apart from the fact that Sarah really enjoyed a challenge, and wanted this important client, the answer was quite likely to be that Carrie wanted the same planner that Ashlyn had had. Briefly Sarah wondered if she could convince both Carrie and Ashlyn that Carrie should wear Ashlyn's actual dress. It would save so much time. But even if Sarah were willing to ring Cannes and ask Ashlyn, she was by now fairly sure that Carrie would want a dress exactly the same as Ashlyn's but different. Sarah wrote Elsa's name down in both files. She would ring her later as toiles and boned and beaded gowns took a long time to make, but her first priority was the venue. She took down her book of churches – a fragile Collins Guide – and her file of all the churches she had used so far, which listed all their attributes, including things like the availability of loos and parking. Her heart sank. There was no way the church that Ashlyn got married in would be available.

It was nine o'clock at night, and Sarah still hadn't eaten. She went to the kitchen end of her sitting room and poured some cereal into a bowl. It was all she wanted, a nice bowl of cornflakes. Then she remembered there was no milk and seriously considered crying. 'Get a grip!' she told herself loudly. 'You've just got the most fantastic contract! The fact that she wants the same date as Lily is a bit of a problem. But man is a problem-solving animal! It'll be fine!'

She was chewing a lump of cheese, having no energy to

turn it into a sandwich, when her mobile rung. Hugo's name flashed up and she switched it off. No way would she speak to Hugo until she was a bit more together about Carrie's wedding. She would need all her wits about her for this event. It strengthened her resolve. Not only did she not want to risk another man getting anywhere near her heart, she couldn't afford any distractions, not if she was going to pull off the wedding of the year at such short notice. The whole kissing episode would have to be faced sometime – she couldn't avoid Hugo for ever; they worked in the same business – but just now, Sarah wasn't fit for either a professional or a personal conversation. He could leave a message.

She fell into bed without brushing her teeth.

The next morning Sarah made what felt like a hundred telephone calls, to find no church either able or willing to do a wedding in two months' time. The worst part was the disbelief expressed by whoever answered the phone that anyone could be so naïve as to think that a really picturesque church would be available on a summer Saturday. Sarah got fed up explaining that it wasn't her who was so ignorant, it was her client. She had also decided that as the chances of whatever church they did get having a lych-gate were so small that she would have one made by some people she knew of who made stage sets. The only other way she could get a summer Saturday and a lych-gate would be to find the right sort of church and then poison the bride who'd already booked it, she thought. She was a professional, she could do that.

She was hunting through the church book again when the phone rang. It was Hugo. He was very persistent. Sarah let the answerphone pick up again.

The following day Sarah drove to the hotel where Ashlyn's wedding had taken place. She was anxious.

Although she was here in part to thank all the staff concerned in the wedding again, and to clarify arrangements for another wedding which was thankfully not due until early in the new year, she was also meeting Hugo.

They usually met up after a wedding they'd both been on duty at to go through the photographs. In the excitement of the last couple of days she'd temporarily forgotten this fact, especially as there had been no hurry this time. But Hugo had been insistent, and now she would have to face him. Since she hadn't been answering her phone, they had made today's arrangement by text – it had taken several of them to persuade her – which was unusual for Sarah, but after everything that had gone on she had been just too tired for proper conversation. That was her excuse and she was sticking to it.

In fact, the faint prickle of sweat under her hairline and the butterflies in her stomach told her there was a quite different reason for her sudden mania for texting. They told her it was because Sarah was terrified of speaking to Hugo again after how they had parted, but she ignored the signs. She was determined to keep it all very professional.

As she parked the car, however, and set off to the front door, she was forced to smile at herself. The previous night she had told herself that as a professional she should be able to murder a bride who had a venue she wanted. Now she felt about as professional as a cast member of a school Nativity play performing opera at Covent Garden. Somehow she'd have to brace up, face Hugo, work with him, all as if nothing had happened.

She had convinced herself that he probably wouldn't be feeling like she was. From what little she knew of him, he would probably feel that he'd ended a successful day with a bit of a snog with a colleague. What was wrong with that? If they'd gone to bed together he would probably define it as a 'friendly fuck' and carry on regardless.

But Hugo didn't have her relationship history; she didn't (as far as she knew) look like someone who'd broken his heart, very badly. He might well want to carry on where they'd left off. She'd have to be very firm indeed.

Fortunately for her, she was there first and ordered a bottle of cold fizzy water. She put her files on the table and created a working atmosphere. All she had to do was wait for him.

She took a sip of water to calm herself. Just as she did so, she looked up and saw Hugo arriving, smiling and obviously pleased to see her. A bubble caught the back of her throat. As she coughed and banged her chest and he came up behind her and thumped her back and handed her a napkin she realised it would be very difficult to remain professional now. This was the second time she'd nearly choked in his presence.

'Hello, Hugo,' she said croakily a few moments later.

'Here, have another sip, but slowly this time.' He handed her a glass. 'OK now?'

'Fine thanks. Sorry about all that. Right, down to business.'

Hugo pulled out a chair and sat down opposite her, his head on one side in an enquiring manner. 'Hello, Sarah, lovely to see you too. What's up?' He reached over to take her hand but she moved it swiftly on to her lap.

'Nothing. Now, let's see the photos,' she said as calmly as she could.

'Forgive me, but I'd expected a slightly warmer reception than this. Have we nothing to talk about except business?'

She shot him an appealing look. 'Really, no.'

He raised a sceptical eyebrow. 'I was hoping, after Saturday night . . .' He suddenly seemed as nervous as she was. 'I wanted to ask you to have dinner with me. I'd like to get to know you properly. I think we'd be good together.'

Sarah looked at her hands, took a deep breath and said, 'Really, Hugo, we can't . . . We have to work together – quite a lot – so it would be better if we kept things entirely professional between us, don't you agree?' She looked up at him and allowed herself to relax a little. That had come out very well, even if she was shaking inside.

'What do you mean? We can do both. I've never let my private life interfere with my work,' he said, rather defensively.

'Quite.' She felt a little stronger now. 'You're a lovely man, Hugo, but I just haven't got time for dinner let alone a relationship right now. We're a good team, a professional team.' She saw the look of disappointment that briefly flashed across his face and dismissed it: he probably wasn't used to being turned down.

'I like you, Sarah. You're beautiful, funny, smart . . .' Sarah tried to block out his compliments, reminding herself that he was used to charming the birds off the trees. He was almost certainly on script now, even if a part of her was just a little bit flattered. '. . . nothing I can say or do will make you change your mind?' she heard him say.

Squaring her shoulders and looking him straight in the eye and holding the memory of all her past heartache before her as a reminder of what happened when you took a risk, she said: 'No.'

'You're a strange woman in some ways, Sarah,' said Hugo, defeated.

'But I am very good at my job!' She couldn't deny the 'strange', not unless she was prepared to tell him about the boy who broke her heart at university, who looked just like him and whom it had taken her ages and ages to get over. And she wasn't. 'So, let's have a look at the photos. Have you made your choice? Then we must think about getting them up on the website so people can order them.'

A waiter appeared. Hugo looked at him, back at Sarah

and sighed. 'Coffee please. Very strong and black. Thanks.'

As Sarah drove home she felt very pleased with herself. She'd very nearly been her cool, calm, professional self. And if her insides had clenched a bit when she let her glance drift towards his hands, or at the dimple that formed in his left cheek when he almost smiled, she was certain she hadn't let him see. He had seemed quite upset when she'd turned him down but he'd get over it. She'd probably only dented his ego, after all. And with any luck they wouldn't have to work together again for a bit, although the photos were fantastic. She had to admit he really was very good: she'd have to recommend him to Mandy. As she'd told him, she wouldn't let her feelings get in the way of business. Unless Carrie had her own photographer, and with any luck she would have, she'd have to use Hugo – he was one of the best in the business.

It was only then she remembered. She'd been so intent on keeping things cool between them, that she had completely forgotten to thank him for passing on her name to Mandy.

Never mind, she could text him or email him when she got home. She really did wish Hugo weren't so attractive – or rather that he hadn't made her see how attractive he was. They'd worked perfectly well together before; now it was going to be really difficult.

'Men!' she said out loud. 'Who'd have anything to do with them!'

Chapter Ten

Bron walked down the High Street looking for the wine bar. Roger had not been thrilled about the idea of her going out midweek, but she'd cooked him a very good fish pie and there was sport on television and so she had been firm about going. He was grumpy because the meeting was about another wedding, not really because he wanted her company.

Then she saw Elsa and hurried towards her.

'Isn't this exciting!' said Elsa as they entered the wine bar. 'Sarah didn't say much on the phone. Did she tell you what it was all about?'

'She sounded very businesslike,' said Bron. 'Apparently it's another wedding for a mega client.'

'Oh good. I've got work for the next couple of months, but then I've got a bit of a dry spell.'

'Let's sit here,' said Bron. 'We can really spread ourselves out. Shall we order drinks while we wait?'

'Definitely.'

Bron picked up the menu. 'We might as well have a bottle. House white OK for you?' Elsa nodded. 'Better get some water too.'

When both women were settled with drinks and olives, Bron said, 'So, Elsa, while I've got you on your own, I really want to ask you some more about what it's like working for yourself. I know we talked about it briefly the other night but I wanted to pick your brains properly. I've been giving it a lot of thought recently and I keep wondering if I should go freelance again.'

'Do you really not like working at the salon? One of the things I regret about my job is the amount of time I spend on my own. I think it would be fun to work with jolly people. I worked in a dry-cleaner's as a Saturday job and I loved the other women. They used to get me to do the mending because I had "nimble fingers".'

Bron, fiddling with the menu, considered her answer. 'I'd like the salon more if I liked the people I worked with, but my boss is only a bit older than I am and is pretty vile, one way and another. The other girls are younger and tend to stick together. I'm a bit on my own, apart from the clients.'

Elsa sipped her wine, allowing Bron to talk.

'Take today, for example, one of my regulars – a lovely woman in her fifties – wanted something a bit different. We were going through colour charts and discussing what would go with her skin tones – all that stuff – when Sasha came over, took the chart out of my hands, and said, "That's the colour you should have, Mrs Aldroyd."' Bron took a sip from her glass. 'And suggested something that would have been absolutely minging!'

Elsa laughed. 'What colour was it?'

'Oh God, nearly grey! It would have made Mrs Aldroyd look about a hundred and twenty.' Bron gave a little giggle. 'We had to wait until Sasha had gone away before we could work out what was best. Then' – Bron's indignation escalated – 'she came back, saw we hadn't done what she'd suggested and went ape!' She took another gulp of wine and sighed. 'Mrs Aldroyd would definitely become a client if I went freelance. Sasha was practically telling her off for not wanting grey lowlights!'

'My mother's in her fifties. She wouldn't want grey lowlights.'

'Well, no!'

Elsa chuckled sympathetically. 'What does Roger think about you going freelance? You have talked it over with him?' Having seen, albeit briefly, how Bron and Roger were together made Elsa wonder about them.

'He thinks I'm mad even to think of going it alone. He's an accountant and the insecurity worries him. He'd insist on doing my books, I know he would, he is a bit of a control freak, and then he'd tell me how little money I was earning.' She made a face. 'I'd hate to be a kept woman. At least now I pay my way.'

'It would only be for a while, I'm sure you'd soon build up a client base and earn more than you did before. There's much more work for hairdressers than dress-makers, surely? Most women go at least every six weeks – they'll have a dress made once in their lifetime.'

'I never thought of it like that. Of course you're right.' Bron selected an olive. 'But I don't know if I could convince Roger.' Delicately, she removed the olive stone and picked up the menu again. 'And also, I don't think he likes the idea of me doing so many weddings. It means I'm not always there for the cricket.'

'That seems a bit unreasonable.'

Bron put the menu down. 'Oh no, it's fine! I always knew he was a cricketer. And he doesn't play it all weekend. And only in summer.'

'So what do you do on Sundays? Picnics, walks – things like that?' Elsa heard the wistfulness in her voice but hoped that Bron hadn't.

'We have lunch with his parents. I really like his mother. She and I get on like a house on fire,' said Bron quickly. 'Can I top you up?'

'Oh, go on. I'm not driving. And you needn't either, really. Where you live, you could take a taxi home.'

'Are you trying to lead me astray?' asked Bron, filling up her glass as she said it. She didn't get many opportunities to go out with friends; she should make the most of it.

'Yes,' said Elsa simply.

Just then, Sarah came rushing in. 'I am so sorry! I got

horribly held up. I wouldn't have been quite so late if I didn't know Bron was with you, Elsa.' She kissed both women and then collapsed on to a chair.

'White wine OK? Plate of pasta?' said Elsa, laughing.

Sarah nodded. 'You'd better get some water as well.'

'We have already,' said Elsa.

'Oh God, do I sound like a head girl? I'm sorry!' Sarah took a sip from someone else's glass as a gesture of surrender of her role as boss woman.

A few minutes later, when they'd ordered more wine, water and food, Elsa said, 'So what kept you?'

Sarah sighed. 'My darling sister. I love her, I really do, but she's chosen to get married the exact same day as my major new client – who I'm going to tell you about in just a mo.' She took the glass that Bron handed her. 'Actually, Lily picked the date first, to be fair, but I can hardly ask my client to move her date.'

'So? Who's the client? You've been so mysterious about it we know it must be someone amazing,' said Elsa.

Sarah looked quickly around, leant in and whispered, 'Carrie Condy.'

'Oh. My. God!' said Bron slowly. 'That's amazing! I was reading about her being engaged in a magazine only today.'

'No wonder your boss is on your case if you read magazines all day,' said Elsa.

Bron stuck her tongue out. 'That truly is amazing! Well done, Sarah!'

'It is amazing, but sadly, she wants it now. And she wants exactly what Ashlyn had: ancient church, summer day, same dressmaker – everything.'

'What do you mean, now?' said Bron and Elsa together.

'Virtually now. In two months. Any chance you can make a wedding dress like Ashlyn's in two months, Elsa?'

Elsa gulped. 'Just about, but it'll be tight. Ashlyn's dress took two years to do!'

Sarah flapped her hand dismissively. 'But only because she had two years,' she said. 'How long did it take from when you knew what you were doing?'

Elsa sighed. 'About six weeks, with fittings, and with doing the bridesmaids' dresses as well. Is, um, "Carrie" having bridesmaids?'

'She hasn't mentioned them, or at least, she hasn't told her PA about them. Carrie's out of the country at the moment and will be a lot. Which'll make fittings difficult.'

'I made that wretched Fulvia's dress without any fittings at all!'

'But she was the same size as you,' Bron reminded her. 'It probably made it easier.'

Elsa shook her head. 'Not really. It meant I knew her measurements, but you can't really try on clothes you're making.'

'Oh, I don't know,' said Sarah. 'I've been known to iron a skirt without taking it off, but maybe I'm an extreme case.'

The other two looked at her.

'OK! It was ages ago. But going back to this wedding: Elsa, you'll be able to charge top whack for this. I know you gave Mrs Lennox-Featherstone a bit of a discount for quantity, but Carrie can pay the full price.'

'Fab!' said Elsa.

'And she's going to want almost the same as Ashlyn's – which I know had lots of hand-beading and stuff, but at least you'll have been there before.'

Elsa nodded. 'I can get someone in if necessary. I know a really nice woman who's happy to help with that sort of thing if I need it.'

'And, Bron, I'll suggest Carrie uses you but she might want her own hairdresser and stylist.'

Bron nodded understandingly. 'Of course. I wouldn't expect to deal with a celebrity like Carrie. It's lovely just to be part of things now.'

Sarah went on, 'But if she really wants everything just

like Ashlyn had, she'll need you. And I definitely want you in on all the planning. After Ashlyn's wedding, which was the biggest thing we ever did together, I think we're a team. We bounce ideas off each other.'

'Talking of teams,' said Elsa, 'what about Hugo?'

Sarah froze for a moment. 'What about Hugo?'

'Well,' Elsa went on. 'He's part of the team too, isn't he?'

'Oh well, not really. She's bound to have her favourite photographer. Some really swanky people use fashion photographers to do their wedding shots.'

Bron and Elsa exchanged glances. 'I can't imagine a fashion photographer dealing with all those people,' said Elsa. 'Not to mention the dog. Anyway, Hugo was – is – really swanky. He does very grand events.'

'How do you know that?' asked Sarah abruptly, causing Elsa and Bron to look at her questioningly.

'I overheard someone saying so at the wedding,' explained Elsa, 'and while we're on the subject of the wedding – Ashlyn's wedding,' Elsa went on, 'did I see you and Hugo slow dancing as I left?'

Sarah felt herself blush scarlet. She gulped down some water. 'Blimey, it's hot in here!'

'Well?' demanded Bron, when Sarah had finished fanning herself, pouring more water, and generally trying to cause a diversion.

'Yes,' Sarah whispered. She sipped again, wine this time. 'But that was all.' This was a lie, but a white and very necessary one, she felt. 'I was very tired and it seemed less effort to hang my arms round his neck than to hold myself up.'

'Oh,' said Elsa.

There was a small silence. Sarah was forcing memories of their kissing out of her mind so she could concentrate fully. Was she destined to be constantly reminded of that evening?

'So,' said Bron, sensing Sarah's discomfort and moving

swiftly on in a tactful way. 'What was the hotel like? Elsa told me you had a room. I bet it was lovely. I love hotels! All the freebies, the lovely sheets.' She sighed. 'Roger and I had a lovely weekend away when we were first together. Maybe I should suggest another one.'

'That's sounds like a good idea,' said Sarah. 'But my room was very small, really. Heavenly bathroom though, with all the extras. Loads of towels, a robe, face flannel, sewing kit.' If a couple of kisses can threaten to make me lose focus, what would a full-blown date do? she asked herself. Luckily she'd nipped that one in the bud. She must not have any more contact with Hugo than she absolutely had to. Then she wouldn't get remotely distracted. If she couldn't actually see his dimples she would be able to focus completely on the job at hand. Otherwise it could make her seriously drop the ball and she couldn't afford to do that.

Elsa sighed. 'It sounds heaven. And was the bed comfortable?'

It took Sarah a few seconds to remember Elsa was talking about the hotel room and not anything to do with Hugo. For a moment she wondered if Elsa suspected something and was prodding her for details, but then she dismissed the idea. Elsa was too nice and innocent for that. 'Oh yes. Mind you, the floor would have been comfortable, I was so tired.'

There was a moment's sympathetic silence, then Bron said, 'I still don't see why you won't ask Hugo to do this wedding, if Carrie wants everything to be the same as Ashlyn's.' Bron hoped so much that Carrie's desire for a clone of Ashlyn's wedding would include her. If she could say she'd had a top celebrity as a client it would help her if she ever did manage to go freelance full-time. Even Roger might be impressed.

'Yes, why not?' agreed Elsa. 'He's so good. He made everyone at their ease – even me.'

'Any half-decent photographer will do that,' said Sarah. 'It's their stock-in-trade to be charming. Now I must go to the loo. When will our food get here, I wonder? I'm starving.'

While she was out of the way Elsa said, 'Do you think it's funny she's not asking Hugo?'

'Definitely. And I think there must be some reason. She's usually so ready to recommend him.'

'Maybe she's embarrassed that she danced with him because she shouldn't have while she was on duty,' Elsa suggested.

'Oh that's so silly,' said Bron, waving her glass about in a precarious manner. She felt wonderfully relaxed now. 'She's a workaholic. Anyway, I think we should ask Hugo. After all, Carrie's wedding is going to be really important for us all – well, I hope me – it's mad not to have the best photographer for it.'

'How would we get in touch with him?' asked Elsa.

'There's her phone. He's bound to be in there,' said Bron.

'Do you dare?' Elsa giggled.

Bron took a breath and, emboldened by the wine, she said, 'Of course. This is for the team. It's not like we're setting Sarah up or anything.'

'Go on then,' Elsa urged before they lost their nerve.

Bron picked up Sarah's mobile and negotiated the phone book, squinting at the numbers. They were both giggling now, like a couple of naughty schoolgirls. 'He's there.'

'Ring him then. Before she comes back.' Elsa glanced nervously at the door to the Ladies.

A moment later, in as composed a way as she could, considering the two large glasses of wine she'd drunk already, Bron said, 'Hi Hugo, we're at the Number Nine Wine Bar in the High Street, having a summit meeting about a big celeb. wedding. We definitely need you. Can you come?'

'You got voicemail?' said Elsa.

Bron nodded. 'I never know what to say to answering machines. He won't come. I left out all sorts of details.'

'Yes, like which town we're in. I dare say he could work it out. But never mind, we did our best. Oh, here's Sarah.'

They were on to their third bottle of wine and halfway through large plates of pasta when Bron suddenly kicked Elsa under the table. Her mouth was full at the time so she could only nod and gesture.

Elsa turned and saw Hugo through the window of the restaurant. She took a breath. 'Sarah, we didn't say anything before because we thought he wouldn't come, but here's Hugo!'

Chapter Eleven

'Oh God!' muttered Sarah, sounding anguished. 'What's he doing here!'

'We asked him to come!' said Elsa out of the corner of her mouth, wondering, too late, if they'd done the wrong thing by ringing him. What if there was a perfectly understandable reason for Sarah not to ask Hugo and they'd only made things worse? 'We thought he should be here. What's the matter?'

Hugo had reached the door of the wine bar, seen the women and pushed open the door.

'It's just that I never wanted to see Hugo again if I could avoid it,' said Sarah softly, but just loud enough to be heard.

'Why?'

'Oh God,' she breathed. 'Too late, he's coming over.'

'Good evening!' Hugo said, arriving at the table. 'How nice to see you all.' He looked pointedly at Sarah. 'What's all this about a summit meeting?'

Feeling guilty for getting Hugo to come to the wine bar without clearing it with Sarah first, Elsa said, 'A really important client wants to get married in about five minutes flat and, er, we thought . . .'

'I know,' said Hugo.

'How do you know? I thought it was all highly confidential!' said Bron.

'Didn't Sarah say?' He looked at Sarah again, enquiringly this time. She could only stare at her hand, clutching her wine glass.

Feeling chastised, she turned to Bron and said, 'It was through Hugo I got the contact.'

'Why didn't you say!' said Elsa. She glanced at Bron. Had they made things completely impossible for Sarah now, or what? Catching the glance, Bron made an I-haven't-a-clue face.

'I would have told you,' said Sarah, feeling defensive, 'if I'd had a chance. We've hardly begun to discuss it.'

'So why didn't you invite me to the meeting?' he asked. She couldn't tell if he was teasing her or not. This was going to be harder than she thought.

'I would have done,' she said. 'This was just a preliminary chat. For girls.'

He raised his eyes. 'Oh, for girls! I'd better get another bottle then, and be an honorary one.'

'I'm not sure you'd make a very convincing girl, Hugo,' said Sarah quietly, glad that they were on safer ground once more, but uncertain as to whether he was still suffering from wounded pride or not.

'No? You wait and see.' Now his look was frankly challenging.

And as she watched him get up and go to the bar, she realised he *was* a bit offended with her. Surely he hadn't really minded her turning him down? It was a shame if he had, but it couldn't be helped. Sarah took herself to the Ladies again. Once there she splashed her face with water before daring to look. Not good! Although she hadn't had much, it was obvious she'd been drinking, and what make-up she'd put on that morning had long since disappeared. Her hair had started to turn feral. She exhaled deeply, gave herself a quick lecture involving 'getting a grip' and 'don't be such a wuss' and then searched her handbag for some emergency kit. If only Hugo weren't so attractive, she'd be fine. She delivered the lecture again. She'd be fine, she kept repeating to herself. She was a professional. She'd been taken by surprise, that was all. She was calmer now and back to her professional self. He was a good photographer, they were colleagues, and he need never know what effect he had on her.

Hoping she hadn't spent a noticeably long time doing repairs, Sarah went back to the others, holding her head up. Be dignified, she told herself. Be cool!

'It's all right,' said Elsa, seeing Sarah's anxious and slightly disapproving face as she surveyed the number of bottles on the table, 'Hugo's going to drive you and Bron home.'

'And you,' said Hugo. 'However near you live, you're not walking. back at this time of night. Sit down, Sarah, you're not going yet.'

Sarah squeezed herself in next to Hugo, thinking at least she had a chance of getting to the door before he did, should she need to make a run for it. She could pick up a taxi easily enough.

'So.' Sarah decided to take control. 'Have you met Carrie Condy herself?'

'Yes,' said Hugo modestly. 'Once or twice, through friends of friends. I thought you'd be perfect when Mandy mentioned Carrie was looking for a wedding planner.' He smiled at her.

Oh God – the curl at the corner of his mouth, the crinkle of his eyes . . . but she must stay in control. 'And I do appreciate it, but you know she wants everything exactly the same as Ashlyn's wedding, *including the bloody lych-gate*! And it's your fault!' That's it, you can do this, she told herself. Keep it professional and lighthearted. He's a colleague. Just because they'd crossed the line once, it didn't have to affect their working relationship.

Hugo chuckled unrepentantly. 'I know, but I thought if anyone could do it, you could. Anyway, you could always get one mocked up.'

Sarah nodded. 'I've thought of that already, it's the church that's going to knock the whole thing on the head.

Carrie just doesn't seem to realise that pretty churches are booked up even if you set aside the whole inconvenient thing about having to have some connection with it, like living in the parish, or it being the groom's parish, or whatever.'

She put her elbow on the table and rested her head in her hand. She suddenly felt overwhelmed by it all.

'I might just be able to help you there,' said Hugo.

She straightened up again. 'How? Tell me. I've been going mad.' She wanted to remind him again that he'd got her into this mess, it was up to him to get her out, but she knew that wasn't true or fair. It was an amazing favour he'd done her, giving Mandy her name.

Hugo seemed reluctant. 'It might not work, though. Maybe I shouldn't have mentioned it.'

'Well, nothing much else is likely to work,' said Sarah.

'Is getting a venue really so difficult?' asked Elsa.

'Picturesque ones at very short notice are. And not only do you have to have the right sort of church, you have to have an accommodating vicar. There are rules about who can get married where.' Sarah sighed. 'It's not that I'm not grateful for the contact, Hugo, because I really am. But it's going to be jolly hard to do. Especially as Carrie happens to have chosen the same date as my sister. She only told me she was getting married last weekend.' Sarah closed her eyes. That's the real reason why I'm so stressed, she told herself, it's nothing to do with Hugo.

'Poor girl,' said Hugo, filling Sarah's glass, and sounding almost tender. 'And you can't persuade your sister to change the date?'

'Not really. The church is booked and she's pregnant.' Her hand flew to her mouth. 'I shouldn't have said that. I've probably had too much to drink.' She took another sip of wine anyway.

'We won't tell anyone,' said Bron. 'Are you excited at becoming an aunt?'

Sarah bit her lip. 'Well, yes, I will be nearer the time, but I think I've had a bit too much excitement recently.' Too late she wished she hadn't said that and really hoped that Hugo, sitting next to her, wouldn't think that he was part of the 'too much excitement'. He definitely was.

He didn't put his hand reassuringly on her arm as he might once have done, before the 'kiss', and Sarah suddenly yearned for him to. Why was it that those little gestures, which are so disgusting when done by the wrong person, are so lovely when done by the right person. Things like that should be neutral; you should either like the pressure or not. She glanced round the table quickly, hoping no one could discern her weird thought processes.

'So, Elsa,' said Hugo smoothly, as if he were not sitting next to a madwoman. 'How did you enjoy being a bridesmaid at the last minute? I must say, you looked lovely.'

Elsa blushed at the compliment and it occurred to Sarah once again what a very pretty girl she was. Why was she single? she wondered. After all, she wasn't a hardened spinster like Sarah.

'I got into it eventually,' said Elsa.

'That hairstyle is perfect. It really suits you,' said Hugo.

Sarah realised how charming he could be and part of her regretted that she'd been so adamant, but then she remembered how charming Bruce had been. Better safe than sorry.

'And you're up for making a wedding dress just like Ashlyn's?' asked Hugo.

Elsa shrugged. 'I did think it would be a good idea if we could persuade Carrie to actually wear Ashlyn's dress.'

'I'd rather ask Ashlyn if Carrie could wear her dress than ask Carrie if she'd contemplate having her big celebrity wedding in a "pre-loved" one,' said Bron.

Everyone laughed. Sarah said, 'Even my sister, who's on a really tight budget, although she won't admit it, won't wear a second-hand one. I thought I might get her to wear our mother's wedding dress, but I don't think she will. It's bound to be really dated by now anyway.'

'I could probably adapt it for her, if she'd like me to,' said Elsa. 'That's how I started out, making things over for people.'

'Really? That's interesting,' said Hugo. By the way he looked at Elsa Sarah could tell he really was interested. He was very good at all this and Sarah wondered if it was because of his sister; from what he'd said they seemed quite close.

'Yes. I had a Saturday job in a dry-cleaner's. I did the mending. Then I went to college.'

'What about you, Bron?'

'I went to college too.' She seemed to Sarah to sound a little defensive. 'I see hairdressing and beauty therapy as a bit of a vocation.'

'Oh?' Again, Hugo's attention was total. This seemed to give Bron confidence.

'Yes,' she explained. 'Lots of people think that hair-dressing is only for people who couldn't do anything else. I could have done lots of things, but I wanted to do hairdressing. There's a lot more to it than people realise.' Bron picked up her glass and luckily the waitress arrived at that moment with a large plate of tortellini.

'Ah, here's your food,' said Elsa to Hugo. 'Shall we look at the pudding menu, girls?'

'Oh yes,' agreed Sarah. 'I always look at it. I don't often let myself have one, but I love to read about them.'

'We could share one,' said Bron. 'What about chocolate tart with a trio of ice creams and fudge sauce?'

'Oh yes,' said Elsa.

'Why don't you have one each?' asked Hugo. 'If you like that sort of thing.'

'Not nearly as much fun,' explained Sarah. 'And we'd be sick.'

'And fat,' put in Bron. 'Men don't like sharing their food. Roger gets terribly annoyed if I pinch a chip or ask for a spoonful of pudding.'

'He's probably an only child,' said Sarah.

'Well, yes, he is,' said Bron. 'But so am I. I don't mind people sharing my meal. I think it's friendly.'

'I'm an only child too,' said Elsa. 'I'm also pretty relaxed about food. Mind you, my dad has always stolen my chips. I got used to it very young.'

'I'll order the pudding,' said Sarah. 'Hugo, is there anything you'd like?'

He shook his head. 'I'm happy with this, thank you, but please feel free to share it if you want to.'

'We wouldn't do that, Hugo,' said Bron. 'That would be very unfair.'

They chatted easily for the rest of the evening, and Sarah finally relaxed. Hugo was good company and regaled them all with amusing anecdotes about some of the weddings he'd been to that Sarah hadn't organised. Finally, as the waitresses began stacking chairs, they felt they really should leave.

Everyone squashed into Hugo's car, laughing and joking. Elsa and Bron got in the back before Sarah could nab a place there.

'I hope you don't mind being a chauffeur, Hugo,' she said, suddenly feeling guilty for taking advantage of his good nature.

'I don't mind,' said Hugo. 'I have been a chauffeur in my time.'

As they drove in silence through the night she realised there was a lot about him she didn't know. Part of her yearned to find out more about him as a person, but she knew she mustn't do or say anything that might risk drifting away from their professional relationship. They'd managed to establish their old easy relationship – well, perhaps not entirely, but time would help that.

When he'd dropped off the other girls, they had both given him a peck on the cheek when they said goodbye. Feeling horrible awkward about the whole thing she did the same, a quick rushed peck that was more like a stab, really.

'Goodbye, Hugo, thank you very much for the lift.'

'You are entirely welcome, Sarah,' he said.

She walked up to the door of her building feeling wistful. He probably was as nice and as trustworthy as he seemed – he was certainly as sexy. It was a real shame she couldn't trust anybody.

Chapter Twelve

About ten days after their jolly evening at the wine bar, Elsa got out of bed and put the kettle on. This done, she went into her workroom while she was still bleary-eyed and sleepy, wearing the big sloppy T-shirt she'd slept in.

One of the things she really liked about living on the premises was being able to go straight to work if she wanted to, even on a Sunday, without having to shower, or dress, or travel. She liked having her first-thing-in-the-morning mind, as yet uncluttered by the daily grind, to apply to her creative process.

Later, she might visit her parents, have lunch or tea or go for a walk. They never minded her being casual about these things – if they weren't in they weren't in. Now she had got a prom dress and a beaded corset off her hands, she had a slot to really think about Carrie Condy's wedding dress.

She knew that Carrie Condy wanted everything about her wedding to be the same as Ashlyn's, but she also knew that even brides who weren't celebrities wanted to be uniquely beautiful on their wedding day. Another inconvenient fact was that she couldn't really make any proper plans, apart from drawings, without speaking to Carrie. She could produce fabric samples galore, but until Carrie made her choice, she couldn't do a thing. Sarah was going to ring her the moment she heard anything.

She wasted a few moments thinking about Ashlyn's wedding and her role in it. Had she secretly enjoyed being part of the action in a beautiful dress? Or was she really and truly happier in her usual black? On balance she felt she was a backroom girl at heart. She was the one who made things happen for other people, rather like Bron was. Let the limelight be for others.

Maybe she was just too scared to come out from behind her black clothes, her tape measure and her pins? Although she had enjoyed actually wearing the dress, there was no denying that. And it had been good research, knowing what they felt like to wear for a whole evening.

Now she got out her original *Englishwoman's Domestic Magazine* that dated from Victorian times and had beautifully produced prints. Her mother had tracked down this volume when Elsa first declared she wanted to be a dressmaker and it had been one of her favourite sources of information ever since. So many copies of these books had been broken up for the fashion plates, but hers was complete and she loved it.

She had sheets of grey sugar paper already torn into large rectangles and her old box of pastels near by. She had already studied a pile of magazines so she knew what Carrie looked like and her general style. Picking up a crayon at random, she began to draw.

She discarded the first few drafts without even looking at them, but eventually an idea began to form in her mind. She didn't know if Carrie had artificially enhanced breasts or not, but if she had, it was important, Elsa felt, to avoid any styles that might make this too apparent.

Usually with clients, there'd be a meeting when Elsa would talk about fabrics, details, their favourite flowers, favourite paintings, films, costume dramas – anything that would indicate what dream the bride-to-be had in mind for herself. Every girl wanted to be a princess on her wedding day – or if she didn't, she didn't come to Elsa for her wedding dress.

But with Carrie it was different – a great deal more

difficult. There'd be no time for a cosy, girly session in Elsa's workshop, when Elsa turned up the heat, produced tea and chocolate biscuits and the bride could take off her clothes and start dressing up.

Because of Carrie's busy schedule, Elsa would have to have lots of drawings and fabric samples to send her, so her client could at least reject the ones she didn't like. Sarah had hinted that Elsa might have to visit Carrie wherever she happened to be in the world if she wanted to guarantee a decision from her. Sarah was only too aware that time was short, and under two months to make a gown as elaborate as Ashlyn's was putting a lot of pressure on Elsa – she had other projects on, after all. Still, Elsa liked a challenge as much as Sarah did and she felt reasonably confident that she could get it done in the time, provided nothing untoward happened.

She finished her third design – her favourite so far, one that managed to be sexy and yet demure enough for a bride. Elsa felt that no bride should expose too much flesh if she was getting married in a church and was adept at creating dresses with sleeves and backs that detached, so the bride could display all the St Tropez or fake-bake she wanted to at the reception. She was drawing arrows and details of how this happened on the sketch when her mobile rang.

She was startled. She was so involved in her drawing that she could hardly remember what that funny little noise indicated. The phone had stopped tinkling by the time she retrieved it from her bag. She checked to see who had called her and it was a strange number. She frowned. Not Sarah then. She went back to her drawing, noting as she did so that her T-shirt was covered in smudges from her pastels. And it was nearly ten o'clock – far too late to be wandering about without knickers, even for a Sunday. She stretched and filled the kettle again before going into the tiny bathroom.

The phone rang again when she had just poured boiling water on a tea bag, still wearing her towel. She nearly ignored it but in case her parents had fallen down a crevasse and needed her to call the emergency services, she answered it.

'Is that Elsa?' said a voice she recognised but couldn't put a name to. 'It's Laurence. Remember? From Ashlyn's wedding?'

She jumped. When Mrs Lennox-Featherstone had said he wanted her number she hadn't thought he'd actually ring her.

'Oh, yes,' she said carefully. If his sister or his niece wanted a wedding dress it would have to be for next year now.

'I wondered if we could meet for a drink or something sometime.'

'Oh.' Elsa wasn't used to being asked out – not by men anyway – and she presumed this was a date. The last time she'd gone out with a man he'd been the son of friends of her parents. Both sets of parents were worrying about their single children and tried to match them up. It hadn't been a success. But Laurence had been nice – kind and funny. Perhaps he was just being friendly.

He pressed on. 'So, would that be possible? Do you think?'

'Er – yes.' A bit late, Elsa remembered her social skills. 'I don't see why not. When did you have in mind?'

'What about this evening? It is very short notice, I know, but it's Sunday and there's nothing on television.' She could hear the chuckle in his voice. 'The programme about cars is having a break.'

This made her laugh and remember their banter at the wedding. 'You mean if you could watch grown men behaving like teenagers you would?' she asked, feigning indignation. 'As you can't you're asking me for a drink?' He wasn't the only one who liked that programme, although she wasn't going to say so.

He laughed too. 'Exactly. How about it? I have a favour I want to ask and I'd rather do it in person.'

'When you've dulled my senses with strong drink?'

'You're reading my mind.'

Elsa giggled. Yes, she had enjoyed the wedding, but mostly because Laurence had been so nice to her and fun to be with. 'Well, if you need a dress for someone, unless it's for next year, there's no chance.'

'This is nothing to do with dresses,' said Laurence, trying to sound offended and not quite making it, 'or at least, only indirectly.'

'OK then,' said Elsa, after a moment's teetering indecision. Nothing ventured, nothing gained, as her mother would say. 'I'll meet you for a drink. What time?'

He was silent for a bit and then said, 'Could it be earlyish?'

'Yes. Why do you ask?'

'Because if we meet early, we can make it dinner if we like each other.'

'I see where you're going with this. But supposing one of us likes the other and the other doesn't.' Elsa didn't often get an opportunity to tease like this and she found she enjoyed it.

'That doesn't make any sense,' said Laurence firmly.

'It makes perfect sense,' insisted Elsa. 'Supposing one of us was really bored. How would they get up and say, "So sorry, got to go," if the other person was having a brilliant time and had already decided it might be dinner?'

'Tell you what,' said Laurence after a moment's unravelling, 'let's be bold and make it dinner. If we're miserable, we can skip pudding and coffee.'

Elsa smiled and shook her head. 'OK. I'll be bold. Where would you like us to meet?'

'I'll pick you up from your flat then you don't have to worry about your car.' He paused. 'If you don't want to be driven home by me you can always take a taxi.'

'Now you're reading my mind,' said Elsa, although she was fairly sure that she wouldn't mind Laurence driving her home. After all, he didn't drink and she knew he was a good driver.

'So what's your address?'

Elsa considered a moment. 'Actually, could you pick me up from my parents' house? I usually go over there on Sundays.' She didn't want him coming to her workroom just yet. She liked to know people quite well before she let them go there.

'Oh. Is that so they can check me over before I take their daughter away in my antique sports car?'

Why hadn't she anticipated he'd think this? 'No! I'm nearly thirty, you don't have to convince my father of your good intentions.' Elsa laughed, amused by this idea.

'I wouldn't be worried about that,' said Laurence, 'but I am glad of an opportunity to check out what your mother looks like.'

'Why?' Elsa was baffled.

'Because all women end up looking like their mothers.'

'It's only dinner, Laurence,' she explained patiently, smiling to herself. 'Even if we have pudding and coffee, it's not going to take that long.'

Elsa could hear the laugh in Laurence's voice. 'Give me the address. I'll pick you up at eight.'

Her mother was lying on the sofa with her feet on the arm when Elsa called round. Elsa'd worked all day and, having nothing much to eat at her house, wanted a snack to keep her going before Laurence picked her up. She didn't want to drink on a completely empty stomach and her mother's fridge would have something she could raid. She went into the sitting room first. 'Hi, Mum. Cup of tea?'

'Glass of wine. Your father walked the legs off me.'

'It's good for you. You don't get enough exercise,' said

Elsa's father from behind the newspaper. 'I'd like a glass of wine too. There's a bottle open.'

Elsa brought her parents their wine and some pistachio nuts in a wooden dish and then said, 'Can I make myself a snack? I've got a date tonight.'

Her mother's legs shot off the arm of the sofa and she sat upright. 'Nice.'

Elsa was not deceived. Every fibre of her mother's being was concentrated on not getting over-excited, or being too curious, or making it plain that this was an unusual occurrence. Her daughter wasn't remotely fooled. 'Mm,' said Elsa. 'Actually, maybe I'll have a glass of wine too.'

Before she left the room to fetch it, she saw her mother's lips clamp down on her anxieties about drinking and driving. Elsa smiled to herself in the kitchen; her mother was going to love Laurence. She made a quick sandwich and took it with a glass of wine through to her parents. Her mother was desperate for her to find a boyfriend and equally desperate for Elsa not to know this, but, sadly, Elsa was too good at reading her mother's body language to be in any doubt on the matter.

Elsa perched on the now vacant sofa arm. 'Yes. Actually it's the man I met at Ashlyn's wedding.'

'The man you danced with, who had the Morgan?'

Elsa nodded. 'You did file every detail, didn't you?'

Her mother made a dismissive gesture. 'Well, you don't go to so many posh weddings, do you? I'm bound to remember.'

'Anyway, he's picking me up at eight.'

'Eight! That's less than an hour! I'd better tidy up and put something decent on. And what are you going to wear?'

'It's all right, don't panic, not this. I've brought something to change into.'

'Let me see.'

Elsa produced the rucksack with her change of clothes

folded neatly in it. 'Hm,' said her mother, no longer so neutral.

'I don't suppose there's any danger of getting any supper, is there?' said Elsa's father, unaware of the sartorial discussion, still struggling with the crossword.

'There are some nice sausages if you peel the potatoes,' said Elsa's mother, taking out the T-shirt that her daughter thought quite smart enough for a casual date, even a first one.

'I suppose you want me to cook them, too?'

'That's right,' said both of his womenfolk in unison.

'Seriously, darling, have you really not got anything that isn't black?' said Elsa's mother.

'This is a lovely T-shirt. Quite new. There's nothing wrong with it.' She remembered that Ashlyn's mother had told her she shouldn't wear black and wondered if she was right. She had also told her she was going to make her get her colours done – but with luck she'd forgotten all about it. She was a very busy woman.

'Really, darling . . .' Elsa's mother began, and then stopped herself. 'OK, well, have a look at my jewellery and see if you can find something to jolly it up with . . .' She paused, determined to be as encouraging as possible. 'I'm loving that fringe!'

Elsa made a face at her mother's slang, as she was supposed to, and then her mother said, 'Right, I'm going to hoover.'

'It's Sunday evening, Mum!'

'But there are people coming!'

'Only one and he won't cross the threshold,' said Elsa to her mother's departing back. 'If I'd known it would cause all this fuss, he could have picked me up from mine.'

In spite of a natural desire to ignore her mother's advice, Elsa ran her fingers over the array of necklaces and beads that hung from a rack by her dressing table. Her mother loved big, ethnic, statement accessories, dating back, she insisted, to days when she made her own decorations with melon seeds dyed with cochineal and earrings with beads from her own mother's hoard.

Elsa took a moment to fluff up the fringe and realised she loved it too. Then she held up one necklace after another until she found a simple pendant on a cord. It was turquoise and silver and went with a pair of earrings that Elsa had. It wasn't exactly making a big statement about her artistic tastes, but it looked pleasant enough. She didn't show herself to her mother until five to eight, so her mother couldn't sigh, and almost audibly wish that her daughter let herself go a bit more.

Laurence arrived promptly at eight. Elsa opened the door and almost didn't recognise him. The last time she'd seen him he'd been wearing a morning suit. Now he had on a casual shirt tucked loosely into jeans. He kissed her cheek.

'I'm so glad you didn't dress up,' he said, 'I thought I'd take you to a place I know with a garden. Great food, too.'

As Elsa had dressed up, her smile wasn't all that warm. She noticed her mother hovering in the hallway. 'This is my mother. Mum, this is Laurence.'

'Hello, Mrs Ashcombe, lovely to meet you,' said Laurence, 'and I'm Gentle.'

'Glad to hear it,' said Mrs Ashcombe, her eyebrows raised.

'No, it's my name. I'm Laurence Gentle.'

'Hello, how nice to meet you,' went on Elsa's mother with a grace her daughter envied. 'Would you like to come in and have a drink or do you want to get off?'

'I think we'd better get off, thank you.'

'Bye, Mum, thanks for tea. I'll see you soon.' Elsa kissed her mother's cheek, then called, 'Bye, Dad!'

Mrs Ashcombe stood in the doorway as they went down the path. 'Oh, is that your car? Better not let Elsa's father see it or you'll never get away.'

'Another time I'd be delighted for him to have a look if he's interested.'

'How kind. That would be fun but don't hang around now if you've got a table booked. Have a lovely time.'

Elsa waved.

Laurence was good company. He guided her to a table in the garden and organised drinks and menus with the calm efficiency that made him such a good best man.

'Now, what would you like?' he said as a large glass of white wine was set down on the table by her. 'The fish is very good here. What do you fancy?'

The menu was more sophisticated than the relaxed garden atmosphere implied. 'I'll have to read it properly. There are so many lovely things.'

'How hungry are you? The pâté is particularly delicious.'

'Mm, but maybe I'll just have something light . . .' she said, having eaten a cheese sandwich less than an hour earlier.

'And follow it up with the steak and chips. Good idea, I think I'll join you.'

'I hadn't decided on that but maybe—'

'Hand-cut chips, who can resist?'

She put her head on one side enquiringly. 'Are you softening me up for something?' she asked him suspiciously.

He nodded. 'Of course! I told you. I have a favour to ask you.'

'So you have. What is it?'

He shook his head. 'Later. You're still quite starchy. I'll wait until you've had your second glass of wine.'

Elsa picked up her wine and sipped it, thinking it was already her second glass really. 'Why don't you drink, Laurence, or is that an embarrassing question?'

'I just decided not to, years ago. I've never regretted my decision.'

He obviously didn't feel the need to elaborate further. Elsa frowned a little. 'But don't you get bored at parties when everyone's drunk and getting tedious?'

He shrugged. 'If I am, I just drive myself home. Now, what do you want to eat?'

'Pâté and steak and chips,' said Elsa decisively. She usually took hours to make up her mind.

'You must leave room for pudding. The chef trained in Vienna and his tortes are amazing.'

'My mother went to Vienna once with some friends. She learnt to make apple strudel. So come on, tell me, what's this favour?'

Laurence gave her a considering look as if weighing up waiting until the food had been eaten before asking it, or going straight for it. 'OK. I want you to be my partner at a very swish ball.'

'Do you?' Elsa was stunned. She'd expected him to ask her to make a dress, or alter something, or even take up his jeans. 'Why?'

'Because you're very good company and I'd like to take you. And' – his smile was definitely rueful – 'it's being run by someone who is always producing women for me. I'd really like to bring my own this time.'

'That dress wasn't mine, you know,' said Elsa quickly, in case he thought she looked like that on a regular basis, with her hair and make-up done and a fabulous dress on. 'I've given it back. I haven't got a ball dress of my own.'

He dismissed this concern with a shake of the head. 'That doesn't matter. It's a costume ball.'

'A costume ball?' Elsa was intrigued.

'Yes, only it's not just dressing up. We all have to be in Regency dress.'

'Oh my goodness.' Would that involve quite a tricky corset? She managed not to share this thought with him.

Laurence laughed, seeing the way her mind was going.

'But really, you don't have to make your dress. You can hire one. In fact, I can hire both our costumes.'

He was obviously completely unaware of the enormity of his suggestion. She struggled to find the words that would convey her dismay at this idea. 'Asking a dress-maker to hire a dress from goodness knows where is like asking . . .' She paused, struggling for a metaphor. 'I don't know, asking a top chef to stop by for a hamburger and fries.'

Laurence appeared to consider this. 'I think most chefs would be prepared to do that, if pushed.'

Elsa tutted. 'Well, I'm not prepared to hire a musty old curtain that smells of sweat and is historically incorrect!'

He seemed a little dashed by this. 'Does that mean you won't come with me?'

It suddenly occurred to Elsa how churlish she had sounded. She'd been invited to a lovely occasion and all she'd done was moan. She had no idea what sort of hire place he had in mind and the costumes might be of the very finest, in authentic fabrics and every last detail attended to. Her mother would be appalled. 'Oh, I'm sorry. I didn't mean to be rude. What must you think of me?'

Again Laurence was thoughtful. 'I think you're a very busy woman and the thought of taking time and trouble to make a dress for yourself isn't on the cards just now.'

Elsa bit her lip and nodded. That was it exactly.

'It isn't for another month, if that helps. I knew it was a big ask,' he said quietly. 'Maybe I should take you out to dinner several times to make up for it?'

Elsa was still silent. Part of her wanted to go to the ball, very much; to be Cinderella, not just the fairy godmother with the wand who made the beautiful dress, only with a lot more effort than waving a foil-wrapped stick with a tinsel star sellotaped to the top. She'd had a taste of it at Ashlyn's wedding and rather enjoyed it. But the other part was very comfortable slicing through swathes of tulle with life-threateningly sharp scissors, taking in seams, adding bugle beads, keeping in the background. Who was she – really?

'I do wish you'd say something,' said Laurence. 'I'm beginning to think I asked you to come to an orgy without realising I was speaking in code.'

'I'm sorry.' Elsa sighed and smiled at the same time. 'I've been dreadfully rude. You ask me to a lovely party and I just fret about it taking up too much of my time.' Among other things, she added silently.

'I hadn't taken into consideration your perfectly justifiable feelings about hiring a dress.' He put his head on one side. 'Is there anything I can do to make things better?'

'You could ask someone else, someone who could actually dance, which you know perfectly well I can't do. After all, you must know plenty of other women. And they wouldn't make a big fuss about hiring a dress, either.'

'But I asked you.' The corner of his mouth moved. 'Even knowing your limitations.'

She put her hand on his, trying to make up for her rudeness. 'But that's what I'm saying! You could have someone without limitations.'

'I have a plan for your limitations. I'm going to arrange for you to have waltzing lessons, or at least one. Then you will be able to dance.'

'But why not choose someone who can already?'

He laughed with exasperation. 'You're a very hard woman to ask out!'

Elsa looked aghast. 'No I'm not – I came here, didn't I? I'm just a hard woman – actually, I'm not a hard woman at all. I'm soft as soap . . .' Then, realising that she'd got mixed up and that soap was usually hard, she went on, 'Or something very soft – but I don't want you to have to go to all that trouble and expense when someone else would do.'

He looked at her in exasperation. 'No, they wouldn't *do*.' He spoke slowly as if to a small child intent on mis-understanding. 'I do know lots of women I *could* ask, but you are the one whom I *have* asked. It'll be fun; we'll have fun.'

'Oh.' He did seem genuinely to want her to go.

He smiled to ease her moment of anxiety. 'It would be worth all the trouble and expense just to see my friend's face when I walk in with a beautiful woman – or as her boyfriend might put it, a bit of top totty. Please say you'll come.'

Elsa wasn't sure what to do. She did want to go, she realised. It was a very flattering invitation, and she liked Laurence, but did she have time to make something? As long as Carrie didn't suddenly make a decision she could. 'OK. I could probably make something for it if I can do it now, but the moment someone I'm doing a wedding dress for makes a decision, I'll have to drop everything. I've got a couple that need final fittings and finishing off as it is.' She paused. 'I work evenings too.' She regarded him under her new fringe, trying to look firm. 'And I will have a waltzing lesson. Only one though. I won't have time for more.'

Now he put his hand on hers. 'Thank you, Elsa. I'm really pleased.'

Elsa felt a slight tingle. He had nice hands and she rather liked the feel of it. Fortunately for her peace of mind, at that moment the waiter came to take their order. Elsa used the time she wasn't placing her order to get her head round the fact that a very nice man had asked her to a costume ball and that she was going to have waltzing lessons, just like an ingénue in a Georgette Heyer novel. The nice man also seemed quite keen on the idea. There was a lot to take in.

When the waiter had taken their orders and their menus Laurence said, 'So you'll definitely come?'

'Yes, I will. And thank you very much for asking me.' After a pause she said, 'But you'll owe me, big time.'

He laughed and then became serious. 'Anything you ever ask me, I'll be happy to do for you.'

She smiled. He was reasonable looking, apparently comfortably off, and single. So what was wrong with him? There must be something, or he wouldn't be asking her out.

'What do you do for a living?' she asked. If he said 'undertaker' she'd know.

'Something in the City,' he said, smiling. 'If you're not careful, I'll tell you all about it.'

'No thanks, you're all right.' She smiled. He was all right.

Chapter Thirteen

Bron lay in bed for a few moments to see if Roger was stirring. Sunday morning was his favourite time for sex – he had usually had a bit too much to drink for it on Saturday night and was too obsessed with getting ready for work on weekdays. Although it really did nothing for her now, Bron knew that avoiding sex wouldn't help her relationship. She counted to ten and slipped out of bed and into the bathroom feeling relieved and guilty – but more relief than guilt. Maybe they did need a weekend away together somewhere, although in her heart of hearts she knew it would take more than that to fix it.

When she came back into the bedroom he was awake. He peered sleepily at her. 'If there's nothing else going on here this morning, you might as well bring me breakfast in bed,' he grumbled.

Bron pulled on some clothes as quickly as possible to stop him getting too interested. 'What do you want?'

'You know what I want, but you're obviously not going to give it to me.'

Bron forced a smile. 'I meant for breakfast, silly. I've got lots to do today before we go to your parents'.'

'I'll have eggs and bacon, toast and coffee. Oh, and half a tomato.'

'Not toast in bed, Roger, please!'

'Oh, don't be so anal.' Then he moved down in the bed, turned over, and apparently went back to sleep instantly.

Downstairs, she put the kettle on and then opened the cupboard and found her secret stash of chocolate. She sighed. Roger wasn't all bad by any means, but he wasn't particularly alert when it came to their relationship. Was he really happy to carry on as they were? Wouldn't he like something more like it was when they first got together?

She got a packet of bacon out of the fridge. When she'd made Roger's breakfast and taken it up, she'd come down, make a cup of tea and dip chocolate in it, while she read yesterday's paper. It would be a few golden moments of self-indulgence before the hurly-burly of Sunday properly began.

When she took up his tray he seemed to be fast asleep. Should she wake him? Just leave the tray and risk it getting cold, or take it downstairs again? She could eat the toast herself. But before she could make a decision, he groaned, farted loudly and said, 'Did I tell you there's a cricket club do on at the pub this evening? You won't have to do any cooking at all today, with Mum making lunch.'

'I have just made your breakfast,' she pointed out, but without rancour; she couldn't be bothered to argue with him this morning.

'Doesn't count. You never do during the week.' He sat up and smiled. 'This looks nice. Could you bring me up the motoring section of the paper? I know you're only interested in the girly bits.'

Bron considered telling him that he hadn't mentioned the cricket do but decided she didn't want to risk an argument. If their life together couldn't be exciting, let it be peaceful.

That evening, Bron was aware that Roger wanted her to look good so she took trouble with her make-up. Her hair was freshly washed and blow-dried and her nails were a reasonable length for once. She took out her favourite dress. It was last year's but still looked pretty and fresh with its shortish, flirty skirt, spaghetti straps and delicate floral pattern. It was one of those dresses that had never really been in fashion and so was never really out of it. She pulled out a pale orchid-coloured pashmina to wrap up in if she felt cold, but the evening was verging on the sultry and she probably wouldn't need it. She tied it round the handle of her bag so she wouldn't lose it, and then went to present herself to Roger who had his feet on the coffee table, reading the sports pages of a Sunday paper he'd cadged from his parents.

'How do I look?' she said. She hated herself for needing to check, but if she didn't, Roger would tell her she looked wrong anyway.

He glanced at her. 'OK.'

'Is it the skirt? Too short?'

He shook his head. 'No, it's fine. Quite classy.' A compliment! She couldn't believe it! 'So don't open your mouth and ruin it,' he added.

'What do you mean by that exactly?' she demanded.

He sighed. 'Nothing! Don't get all worked up, it was only a joke. I just meant don't go boring everyone with tales of the salon. Having to cut out a tangled roller is just not that funny. A lot of the wives who'll be there have got really high-powered jobs.'

That was her put in her place. And as he had roared with laughter when she'd told him about this incident when they first met, she felt hurt and nostalgic for happier times. Was this relationship really salvageable? And if not, what were her alternatives? She knew the answer really, but didn't want to acknowledge it. Secretly, she had compiled a list of clients – either people she'd already worked for away from the salon, or people who'd go with her if she left. But knowing Roger would be unhappy about this only made her feel more guilty.

'Well, darling, hairdressing isn't exactly rocket science, is it?' he went on, possibly sensing he'd hurt her feelings and trying to make her feel better.

'Actually, rocket science isn't rocket science,' she said,

feeling tired before they'd even set off. 'It's quite simple.'

Bron had heard this somewhere, but didn't really know if it was simple or not. She clattered out of the room on her high heels that weren't all that easy to walk in before he could answer. She took refuge in the kitchen and sipped a glass of water.

Oh, how she didn't want to go to this do! She'd hardly know anyone, and the ones she did know she didn't particularly like: they were all city traders or lawyers or the like. And Roger had been right about the wives – they all had careers they could talk about with pride. She knew perfectly well that what she did was just as challenging and difficult as what many of them did, but she also knew that society – *that* society anyway – assumed that hair-dressing was a job for thickos. At times she considered getting a T-shirt that said 'I'm a hairdresser, please speak slowly' but thought people probably wouldn't understand it was meant ironically. A T-shirt with 'I have twelve GCSEs, three A levels and had a good offer for a place at university, and I chose to be a hairdresser' probably wouldn't help her case either.

When they arrived at the pub they had to fight their way across the crowded room. It was a country pub, one that Roger knew well from going with his cricket crowd, but Bron had only been to it a couple of times. The cricket club took over one of the rooms so it felt more like a club than a pub, really.

'What are you drinking?' Roger asked. 'You're driving.'

As she always drove when they went out with his friends this was no great surprise. 'Orange juice and soda, please.'

While she waited behind Roger as he fought his way to the bar, feeling, as always, like a child waiting for its mother to pay it some attention, she looked around. She recognised a few faces and then her gaze landed on one she knew well. It was Sasha, the owner of the salon where she worked, and her *bête noire*. What was she doing here, of all places?

She looked away quickly, hoping Sasha wouldn't see her. It was already going to be a difficult enough evening – the last thing she needed added to it was her boss.

Roger handed her a glass. 'Come on, I can see the others over there.'

Deeply depressed, Bron followed Roger to the area where Sasha was, ensconced among Roger's friends as if she was already part of the gang.

'Hi guys,' said Roger. 'Cheers!' He raised his pint glass, not bothering to introduce Bron, who wondered why on earth he'd brought her.

She smiled into space and sipped her drink.

'Hi, Bron!' said Sasha. 'Bet you didn't expect to see me!'

Bron forced a smile. 'No. I don't expect you thought you'd see me, either.' It was interesting that Sasha seemed quite at home among all these high-flyers, but perhaps owning a salon raised your status somewhat.

'Oh, I knew you were coming.' Sasha looked at Bron in a knowing way that made Bron feel as if everyone was in on a secret except her. 'Roger said he'd bring you.'

Bron looked at Roger, who was looking perfectly comfortable. Sasha and Roger knew each other slightly, she knew that. But she didn't know that Roger had spoken properly to Sasha, ever.

'Don't look so stricken,' said Sasha. 'I phoned him about putting an ad in the cricket programmes.'

'That's right,' said Roger. 'Local advertising is very important to us. If we could get a sponsor for the kit . . .'

'Well, that's good,' said Bron, quietly but more firmly than usual. 'If your cricketing chums come to the salon, I won't have to cut their hair for free.'

'Bron?' said Sasha teasingly. 'You're not moonlighting, are you?'

'I cut Roger's mother's hair and any of the WAGs who do teas for me when I'm on the rota.' Sasha didn't know about Bron's recent spate of weddings; Bron really hoped Roger wouldn't say anything.

'Why don't you tell her to book an appointment at the salon?' said Sasha, still smiling to imply she was joking, but there was the usual edge to her voice whenever she spoke to Bron. 'We haven't got so many customers that you can afford to give out freebies!'

Bron smiled back. She knew perfectly well that Sasha meant every word and, for once, she had the perfect answer. 'If Roger's mother came to the salon, she couldn't guarantee to get me. She might have to make do with one of the other stylists.' Bron made an I'm-a-ditzy-girl expression, but she meant what she'd said just as much as Sasha had.

'Oh, Mum wouldn't mind who she had to do her hair,' said Roger, missing all the undertones. 'It doesn't matter to women of that age what they look like.'

Even Sasha seemed a bit horrified at this, although she had made that really ageing suggestion for Bron's client.

'Well, you know what I mean,' he went on. 'A bit of a snip here and there, it can't matter who does it.'

'So who cuts your hair, Roger?' asked Sasha.

'Bron,' he said, getting slightly pink.

'I can tell. Come and see me next time you want it cut. I could do things with hair like that.' Sasha gave him a look that excluded everyone else present.

'Oh, please do,' said Bron. 'There's a really tricky bit where he's going a bit thin. You might be able to do something clever to disguise it.'

Roger stared at her, his mouth slightly open.

'Sorry,' went on Bron, her inner bitch still off the leash, 'didn't you know you were going a bit bald? It's perfectly normal, you know, as you get older.' Then, aware that she might have gone a bit too far in asserting herself, she said,

'I feel a bit hot. I'm just going into the garden for some air.'

No one in the group objected to her leaving, she realised as they made way for her. The back doors of the pub opened on to large gardens that led to a small stream. Bron abandoned her empty glass and walked out into the fresh air. Then, her heels piercing the grass with every step, she headed to where she could see willows weeping picturesquely into the water. She pulled her pashmina around her shoulders to help keep off the midges. Once she could stare into the water she would feel calmer.

She'd have to go back in eventually, she realised, but she really didn't want to. They weren't her sort of people, they were Roger's, and they made her feel like the child on the edge of the group in the playground. She was not exactly ostracised, but she wasn't included, either. And when did Roger get so friendly with Sasha? It wasn't that she felt jealous, but she was confused.

She wrapped her arms around her and rocked a little, trying to sort herself out in her mind.

The glow of a cigarette drew her attention to the group of trees nearby. She'd just taken in that she wasn't alone when the smoker spoke.

'Sorry, did I startle you?' said a man's voice.

'Er – no – not at all,' said Bron, taken aback.

'I'm trying to give it up,' he said as he emerged. 'But it does have its advantages.'

He was tall and needed a haircut, thought Bron immediately and then realised he was familiar. But as she couldn't remember where or when she'd seen him, she didn't comment.

He seemed to be wearing working clothes. A shirt, pale with washing, was half tucked in to a pair of faded jeans that had rents below the knee. Not for fashion's sake, Bron guessed, but through wear.

'Hang on – we've met before!'

Bron gave him a questioning look. 'Maybe . . .'

'Yes! Just before Ashlyn's wedding. You were leaving when I came to put Major back in the house.'

'That's right.' Bron nodded slowly, remembering clearly now – she'd had to rush back for Roger, always Roger.

'I hope you don't feel accosted.' He frowned slightly. 'Perhaps if I introduced myself – my name is James.'

'I'm Bron. And no, it's all right. I don't feel accosted.' Bron wasn't quite sure how she felt. He seemed nice enough and friendly, and not at all threatening, not that Roger would come to her rescue if she needed him. She shivered.

He tipped his head on one side a fraction. 'Are you OK?'

Bron pulled her shawl about her more tightly, as if to protect herself from his questions. 'Fine.' She realised that she'd sounded strained and hoped he wouldn't notice.

'It's all right, I'm not trying to pick you up. I just thought you seemed a bit . . . well, never mind.' He smiled again and she noticed he had a very nice smile. His face was brown and there was a fair bit of stubble going on round his jaw, but it was a kind face. 'Actually, you look great, but not happy.'

'I said, I'm fine,' she repeated, with more conviction this time.

'So what are you doing on your own out here? You're not having a cheeky fag, so what is it?'

Bron sighed. 'I just fancied some fresh air, that's all.'

James chuckled. 'I'm afraid these days the air can be fresher inside the building than it is in the garden. Although I swear I'm giving up.' This last comment was almost to himself.

'It's quite hot in there,' said Bron.

'But your friends will be wondering what's happened to you. In fact, even as we speak your girlfriends are deciding which one of them should come out and check on you.'

Bron sighed. 'No they're not. I'm not here with girl-friends, my partner's inside. He'll probably be wondering where I am.' She closed her eyes for a few seconds, wishing he wasn't – not so much so she could feel free to chat with this James person, but because they no longer made each other happy. Anyway, he probably hadn't even noticed she'd gone. He obviously preferred to spend time with people like Sasha rather than her.

'On the other hand,' persisted James, 'if you're out here it's probably because you've had a row.'

'No! Well, not really.'

'Do you know, somehow, that seems sadder. All couples row from time to time, but for you to want to come out here on your own when you haven't rowed makes it more likely there's something else that's wrong. You seem so sad about it.'

Bron turned away from him a little. He was far too perceptive for comfort. She might not be happy with Roger – in fact she definitely wasn't – but she didn't want to discuss his shortcomings with a stranger.

'Do I sound like a counsellor? Sorry! I just know that couples have ups and downs.'

James dropped his cigarette end and then stubbed it out with his boot. It was a tiny little roll-up, hardly a cigarette at all. The boot, however, was heavy and stained with soil. He picked up the remains and put it in a little tin. Bron wondered if he was in a relationship and if so whether he was speaking from experience.

'It's perfectly natural,' she said, meaning to be consoling if he was sad.

'Oh yes. As long as the good times outweigh the bad.'

Bron realised then that the good times hadn't done this for a while. There were bad times and there were OK times. That was all. She hoped things were better for him.

'I'm sorry to have intruded,' he said.

'Oh you haven't – not really. It's nice to have someone to chat to.' She regretted these words the moment they were out. Now he would know exactly how barren her relationship with Roger had become and she really hadn't intended to broadcast this fact.

'So you didn't go to the wedding?'

'No. Mrs Lennox-Featherstone did ask me – which was really kind of her – but I had to get back.'

'That's a shame, it was a very good do.' He smiled. 'Great food!'

'So I heard. Elsa, the dressmaker, who ended up as one of the bridesmaids, told me all about it.'

He frowned. 'That's a bit odd, isn't it? Choosing your dressmaker to be your bridesmaid? Although if you really got on . . .'

Bron chuckled as she tried to explain. 'It was a last-minute thing. The real bridesmaid dropped out and Elsa was made to stand in for her. She wasn't keen, I can tell you.'

James laughed. 'Well, she looked the part. Very pretty, I thought.'

'Thank you! I mean, I think she looked pretty, but I'd done her hair for her so I can take some of the credit.'

'So you're a hairdresser?'

Bron tried really hard not to get tense. 'Yes.'

'Cool.'

Bron shot him a glance. Was he mocking her? It didn't really seem so but perhaps he was just hiding his feelings about it. 'I like it,' she said defiantly. And then her phone started to sing from her handbag.

'Oh, excuse me. I'd better see who this is. Sarah!' she said a moment later. 'No, this is a perfect time to call.'

Chapter Fourteen

'Carrie's in town.' This was the message that Sarah had passed on to Bron and Elsa via a few frantic phone calls. They were all going up on the train to London to meet her, quite early, in part so Elsa could go to a fabric shop. Bron was coming along for moral support and Sarah was going to try and persuade Carrie to use her. Not only would it make the whole adventure more fun, and put good work Bron's way, it would mean whoever did Carrie's hair would not be swooping in at the last minute, not yet a member of what was becoming known between them as the Wedding Team.

Sarah had put off calling Hugo to confirm that Carrie wanted to see his work and what time they were all due to meet at the hotel. If only she could be normal with him. It was all very well her wanting to keep their relationship professional – but could she be? Maybe she'd be lucky and get his answering machine.

But Hugo had answered right away – sounding as if he'd just got out of bed and Sarah panicked briefly in case she'd woken him up. But then she reminded herself that not only did he have come-to-bed eyes, but he had a been-in-bed voice too, unfortunately for her peace of mind.

'Sarah,' he drawled. 'What can I do for you?'

When Sarah said 'What can I do for you?' she sounded brisk and businesslike. When Hugo said it he sounded as if he was offering sophisticated sexual techniques, possibly involving chocolate.

'Sorry to ring on a Sunday night, Hugo,' she said, 'but I just want to make arrangements for our meeting with Carrie tomorrow. Have you any thoughts? We're meeting her at four.'

'I can't make four, I'm afraid, but I could do six?'

'I'm not sure that would fit in. I mean, I'd have to ring Mandy and see—'

'Don't worry. Mandy and I are old friends. I'll ring her.'

Well, this was one less thing for her to do, at least. 'Great. So, did you manage to find a venue?' Sarah strained to make this sound like a casual request. She really didn't want him to know how hard she'd been working to sort this problem for herself and failing miserably.

'Ah – little hitch there, I'm afraid.'

A squeak of anguish escaped her but she managed not to reproach him for raising her hopes – just. 'Oh, fine. I'll find one myself. You don't need to worry about it,' she said, with more confidence than she felt.

'Oh, I've found a venue and you'll love it. Not absolutely what anyone's expecting but really amazing. There's just a little matter of whether or not it's licensed for weddings.'

'That's very tantalising.' She tried to sound cheery, as if this news weren't tearing her in all directions: first hope, then despair. Ending up relatively cool was difficult. 'Where is it? If it's in the far north, I can't have it. My sister's getting married on the same day. I'll have to box and cox.'

'What?'

'I'll have to run between weddings. I can't let my sister down and Carrie is my most prestigious client to date.' Sarah paused, aware that if she went on talking about it, the impossibility of the situation might make her cry.

'Ah.'

Back under control, she said, 'So where might this perfect-yet-flawed church be?'

'If it comes off it's in Herefordshire. I don't want to tell you more in case it doesn't.'

Herefordshire was at least in the same quarter of England, which was hopeful. 'Nothing more you can tell me? I'd quite like something to tell her. Or you haven't got pictures of it by any chance, have you?

'Sorry, not of this venue, I'm afraid. I'm going to be showing her a range of my work but I'm avoiding churches and things because the place I have in mind is really a bit different and until I'm sure—'

Sarah interrupted him. 'You do know she wants traditional? Just like Ashlyn?'

'People don't always know what they want until they see it. Trust me, Sarah.'

She sighed. She knew this was true but suspected Carrie might be different. She was a top Hollywood A-lister; compromise wouldn't be part of her life. 'You don't have to find the venue for me, Hugo.'

'I did offer.'

'I know, but it's my job. It's up to me to do it.'

'Don't sound so downhearted, Sarah,' said Hugo. 'It will all work out. Things always do.'

Sarah hadn't realised her feelings were so apparent. Why didn't Hugo understand the urgency of the matter? Why was he so wretchedly laid-back all the time? 'Not weddings, Hugo. There are TV programmes based almost entirely on videos of wedding disasters; that's why people employ me, so they don't have to sell their horror stories to claw back some of the cost of their fiasco.'

Hugo was silent for a few moments. 'Why don't I come over and take you out for a late drink? You sound as if you need cheering up.'

Just for a second she allowed herself to consider it. The idea of drinking brandy, albeit only as friends now, with Hugo took her right back to Ashlyn's wedding. It had been lovely – too lovely. 'Thank you so much but I've got to be up at dawn and I've loads still to organise.'

After they had disconnected, she allowed herself two minutes' reminiscence about Ashlyn's wedding and then carried on with her phone calls. She must be very careful where Hugo was concerned. She'd made it clear there could be nothing between them, so perhaps she was being unfair to think he'd even dare risk asking her again, even if a part, a very tiny part, of her half wished he would. She really couldn't afford to be distracted. She had to focus on the job in hand. Her reputation depended on it.

Bron arrived on the platform just as the train pulled in. She had several carrier bags with her and gave the impression of a schoolgirl going on an outing.

'So sorry,' she gasped to Sarah. 'I thought I had loads of time but then I couldn't find a parking space, and then one machine was out of order and I had to run all the way to the other one, and then back to the car . . .' In spite of her difficulties, she seemed very excited. 'It's so brilliant of you to swing it for me to come!'

'It's all right!' said Sarah, returning Bron's spontaneous hug. 'I've got our tickets. Quick, Elsa, bag that table.'

They organised themselves and eventually collapsed into their seats, all of them relaxing now they were actually on the train.

Bron got out one of her carrier bags. 'I know it's silly but I brought little bottles of champagne to drink. To get us in the mood!'

'Oh, Bron, what fun!' said Elsa, glancing at Sarah, wondering how she'd react to this.

'And things to eat.' A small pink cool bag came out of the carrier. 'And this!'

'This' was a copy of *Celeb* magazine. On the cover was Carrie Condy, news of her approaching wedding advertised all over the front.

'Give me that!' said Sarah. 'Mandy said something

about them being interested. It would be amazing publicity for us all if they covered it.'

'Of course they'll cover it!' Bron was passing out straws to go in the champagne bottles. Then she opened the cool bag. There were little smoked-salmon canapés and quails' eggs.

'I've only just had breakfast,' said Elsa, nevertheless taking a roll of salmon filled with cream cheese.

'So you managed to get away OK?' Elsa asked Bron as she eased the cork out of her little bottle.

'Mm, yes, at last! Work wasn't hard, Mondays are quite slow and I'm owed loads of holiday. Roger was a bit harder to get round.'

Having taken Sarah's call in the pub garden the previous night, she had immediately made preparations. While actually at the pub she had asked Sasha for the day off. She had shrugged and said, 'Suit yourself.' Once she was home she had peeled some potatoes for Roger's supper the next night. The last thing she had wanted to do was to stand in her spindly heels at the sink, in her pretty dress. But Roger had told her early on in their relationship that he was a 'potato man'. Rice and pasta were a poor substitute, in his opinion. However, he wasn't much good at peeling them. If she didn't want a row, she must make things as easy as possible for him.

Having peeled them she cut them into chips, the squared-off, chunky way he liked them. When he got home from work he could cook these in the deep-fat fryer that had been their present from his parents. Bron hardly ever used it. Then she'd rummaged and found a couple of steaks she'd had in the freezer for a while and took them both out. He wouldn't need two but she could turn the other into a stir-fry the next day. She didn't actually go as far as cutting a tomato in half for him, but she considered it.

When she'd got his dinner ready as far as she possibly

could, she went upstairs, showered and then put on the sexy and extremely uncomfortable underwear he had bought her last Christmas, because he liked to see her in it. When he came up to bed she was sitting up, perfumed, lightly made-up and adorned by black and red nylon, prepared to ask if it was all right if she went to London to see a client. Although Carrie Condy was only a potential client as yet, she didn't tell him that. When he heard the name he was impressed. He didn't want to show this, obviously, but Bron could tell. Later she wondered if she'd really needed the underwear to get round him. As she shuffled off to her side of the bed, now back in her own comfy cotton PJs, as near to the edge as she could get, she looked back over the day. The party had been grim. When she got back in from outside she'd been feeling more positive about herself, but the others had managed to wear away this spurt of confidence. No one had actually been rude, but she was firmly kept in her place as Roger's totty, without an identity of her own.

Those few minutes in the garden had been the only relief from it. After she'd spoken to Sarah, she and James had chatted for a bit longer. She remembered now that he'd said he was Ashlyn's parents' gardener – such a pleasant change from the commodity brokers, car salesmen and IT consultants she had been talked at by for the rest of the evening.

Bron, determined to let none of the previous day's irritations affect her day out in London, had got to the supermarket early and bought her picnic. She'd seen the magazine at the checkout and fallen on it.

Sarah, sitting next to Elsa and dressed in a business suit, was poring over it. 'It says here she's getting married in a "secret location". Well, they've got that bit right! Secret even from the wedding planner.'

Elsa said, 'Are you OK, Bron? You're still looking a bit stressed, in spite of bringing the party with you.'

'Oh no, I'm fine now I'm here.' She smiled brightly. She reached across to her friend. 'That's a nice scarf you're wearing.'

Elsa looked down at it. 'Is it all right? I thought I should make some effort to brighten myself up.'

'You definitely should,' agreed Bron. 'Now let's get this champagne down. It's not awfully cold, I'm afraid.'

'It is awfully early, though,' said Sarah doubtfully.

'Have a cup of coffee afterwards,' said Bron. 'We're not meeting Ca— I mean our friend till when?'

Sarah lowered her voice. 'Four, and well done for not saying the name. Although it's in *Celeb*, no one is supposed to know about it.'

Elsa laughed. 'It is ironic, isn't it? Still, cheers! Here's to a great day out.'

They all clinked bottles and settled back in their seats.

'So what's everyone doing before we get to meet the client?' asked Bron after a few minutes of companionable champagne-drinking silence.

'I'm going to a fabric shop,' said Elsa. 'I'm hoping to get loads of samples for her. I've got quite a lot already but more is definitely more.' She belched politely. 'It's very fizzy, that champagne.'

'It's supposed to be. The straws make it more intoxicating. Stop looking so worried, Sarah! What are you doing?'

'I've got various bits and pieces that I want to find out for my sister, such as how quickly you can get a passport – why she hasn't got one I don't know. Anyway, what are you going to do, Bron? Go with Elsa?'

'You're very welcome. It's a lovely shop.'

'To be honest, to go shopping, in Oxford Street, without Roger, or anyone, would be total bliss. Brilliant not to have to rush to catch a train afterwards, too.'

'Mm,' agreed Elsa. 'But Sarah? Who's paying for the hotel room? Not you, I hope?'

'Carrie is, at least for us two. If she takes Bron on, then her room will be paid for too, obviously. If she doesn't,' Sarah went on quickly, 'it'll be absorbed by everything else. We don't need to worry about it.'

Bron sighed. 'I can't tell you how much I hope she takes me on, but the chances are minute. She's bound to have her own stylist and hairdresser.'

There was a silence. No one wanted to agree with her, but they all knew she was right. 'I need some bits and pieces for work too,' said Bron. 'I don't like buying my stuff through Sasha if I can help it.'

'Why don't we go and do what we need to do and then meet up for a late lunch?' suggested Sarah. 'Then we can go and meet Carrie afterwards?'

'Wonderful,' agreed Bron. 'We have all got each other's numbers, haven't we, in case I get lost and need to be talked my way to the restaurant?'

Having confirmed they had, they sat in silence for a while. Elsa was thinking about her evening with Laurence. He'd been the perfect gentleman, taking her home, kissing her on the cheek. That was lovely, of course, but Elsa realised she wouldn't have minded if he'd been a tad less gentlemanly. A kiss on the lips would have been perfectly acceptable.

Chapter Fifteen

All three women were a little bit giggly – from nerves and the one glass of wine Sarah allowed them for lunch. They walked into the foyer of the hotel, which was constructed from shiny marble and glass. Glamour pinged from the walls as sunlight does from frost. Classical music, potted palms and beautiful young men in tail coats and fitted waistcoats added to the atmosphere of calm yet animated luxury.

Elsa and Bron exchanged glances while Sarah went to reception to announce their presence. Bron felt she was there under false pretences, although she had brought some photographs of styles she'd done, and some magazines for ideas. Elsa felt her normal black V-neck and trousers, the scarf notwithstanding, weren't nearly smart enough. As Sarah waited for the girl at the desk, so lovely she could moonlight as a model, to phone up, she offered a little prayer that Hugo's venue was a real possibility. Then another that he wouldn't announce it in front of Carrie and Mandy when he joined them later. If the news was bad she wanted it in private. She'd just have to trust him.

Miss Condy had, apparently, taken over an entire floor. Bron's confidence dipped lower. You don't hire that many bedrooms and not put a hairdresser in one of them, not if you're a Hollywood A-lister.

No one spoke in the mirror-lined lift. Apart from anything else, they didn't want the beautiful young man accompanying them to know how nervous they were.

They all wanted to pretend they visited superstars all the time. No one was fooled.

Mandy Joseph let them in, obviously expecting them and not, as Elsa secretly feared, turning them away from the door when she saw them. She ushered them through a massive sitting room to an almost-as-massive bedroom. Carrie herself, looking tiny in real life and wearing sweat pants and a strappy top, was sitting on the bed painting her toenails. She leapt up when the girls came into the bedroom.

'Oh hi! I'm making such a mess here! Now you've come we can have champagne. Mandy and I don't let ourselves have it unless someone else is here. We'll need two bottles. Are they in the fridge?' Her expression as she looked at her PA made it clear that while she was lovely and had very good manners, she was used to having her needs supplied more or less instantly.

As Mandy, equally accustomed to supplying those needs, moved away to fetch the champagne, Sarah smiled and held out her hand. 'I'm Sarah Stratford, your wedding planner. This is Elsa Ashcombe, who'll make your dress if you want her to. And this is Bron, who is my favourite hairstylist. She's mainly here—'

Bron interrupted. She didn't want Sarah to have to tell a whole lot of lies on her behalf. 'I could also paint your toenails if you wanted me to.' She smiled a girl-to-girl smile. 'It's really hard to do your own, isn't it?'

She so wanted to be part of the team and to make herself useful, if possible.

Carrie smiled back at her, accepting the offer. 'That would be fantastic – I'm making such a mess – but later! Now let's have a drink.'

'Mandy?' asked Sarah as they went through to the sitting room where the champagne was being opened. 'Did Hugo call you? About coming this evening with his portfolio?'

145

'Oh, Hugo!' said Carrie, rolling her eyes in ecstasy. 'The perfect romantic Englishman. He's so . . . ooh, sexy. That voice!' She wriggled deliciously and Sarah felt depressed. How could any man resist if Carrie decided she fancied them? Not Hugo, she was fairly sure of that.

Carrie was smaller, prettier and nicer than anyone had expected her to be. She was not a tyrant-princess. She just wanted her dream wedding and had people around her to make sure that what she wanted was what she got.

'So, who's in all the other bedrooms on this floor?' asked Bron, relaxed by a couple of gulps of champagne.

'Security, mostly.' Mandy's cool expression was kind but very professional. 'And we're expecting some of Carrie's family to visit. It makes it easier if everyone is on the same level.'

Bron felt a little better. Mandy hadn't mentioned stylists, or hairdressers, or even, rather surprisingly, a personal trainer.

Sarah's experience told her that while Carrie couldn't be sweeter, it didn't mean she wouldn't be demanding. And Mandy Joseph would ensure her every whim was catered for.

Sarah topped up everyone's glass.

'Cheers!' said Carrie, raising her glass high. 'I know we're going to have a brilliant time and you guys are going to get me the wedding of my dreams!'

'And here's the cake I want,' said Carrie, seemingly hours and several glasses of champagne later. 'Look, I took a picture of it on my phone.'

Everyone crowded round the phone except Mandy, who was gathering glasses and tidying the room. The picture was of what appeared to be a spherical tree, like a lollipop of cake on a stem. Half way down the stem was a smaller sphere which disappeared off the end of the picture.

'I saw it in the window of this dreamy cake shop in

Vienna,' said Carrie. 'And it's just what I want! So original! I don't want those tacky statuettes of the bride and groom on my cake. I want this!'

Silence settled over the room as they contemplated the tiny image.

'I'm not sure that's a real cake,' said Sarah, reluctant to rain on this lucrative bride's parade. 'I think it's just a fake.'

'It had real icing on it,' said Carrie. 'You could see the little flowers.'

'I think it might be a ball of oasis, you know, that foam stuff that florists use – iced, to look as if it was made of cake,' went on Sarah.

'I don't think a real cake would stay up there unless it was glued on,' said Elsa. She had retaken all Carrie's measurements, just to make sure, and they had spent some time going through her sketches, so she felt she knew Carrie pretty well by now. 'It would need some sort of armature.'

'I really want that cake,' said Carrie definitely.

A tense few seconds ticked by. 'If it's physically impossible to make that cake, it might not be possible to have it,' said Mandy firmly.

No one moved or spoke. Sarah found herself staring at the pattern on the carpet, not daring to look at her client, whom she felt she'd let down. Elsa put herself in her happy place, which was among fabric swatches, hoping Carrie wouldn't cry. Carrie sighed deeply.

'Hang on,' said Bron suddenly. 'I've worked out how to make it.'

Everyone looked at her. 'How?' said Sarah.

'Well, we'd need to get a pole we could fix a series of discs on to, to make the spherical shape. We'd make the cake in large round tins – or square ones – it wouldn't matter. Then we'd just cut them to shape. Or we could use one of those spherical tins people use for Christmas puddings, if we could get one large enough.'

'But how would you get it round the pole?' asked Elsa.

'You'd fit it from the sides, in two halves,' said Bron. 'Then ice it so it's completely spherical.'

'Well, that's amazing!' said Sarah. 'Thank you so much, Bron. I'll get you to do some sketches I can give to whoever I get to make Carrie's cake.'

'I want Bron to do it,' said Carrie.

'What? But Bron doesn't do cake. She's a hairdresser and make-up artist.' Sarah felt a bit thrown by this suggestion.

'She worked out how to make the cake – I think she should do it,' said Carrie.

Sarah looked at Bron, trying to work out if she desperately wanted to be rescued or could rescue herself.

'I do do cakes, actually,' Bron said. 'I've done some quite elaborate ones.'

'What sort of cakes?' asked Sarah.

'Well,' Bron began. 'It started when I was at college. Someone's little brother was having a birthday and wanted a train cake – there was a series on television and he was desperate to have it exactly the same. They couldn't get one made so I said I'd do it.'

'Wow!' said Carrie.

'Then I did one for my aunt and uncle's ruby wedding anniversary. That was fun. It was covered in red roses and I put gold leaf on the tips of the petals. It looked amazing.'

'It would!' said Sarah. 'Why have you never told me this before?'

Bron shrugged. 'Well, it never came up. Besides, I've never charged anyone for a cake. They've always been presents.'

'Well, I'd pay you,' said Carrie.

'I'd love to have a go at it, said Bron quietly. 'I'll have to borrow a kitchen to do it in, one that's been passed by Health and Safety. But I'd see it as an amazing challenge.'

'But have you ever made cakes like that – in a

professional way? It looks very complicated . . .' said Sarah, wondering frantically if Carrie would know or care if Bron didn't make it, as long as she got the cake she wanted.

Bron laughed. 'Not quite like that, obviously, but if Carrie wants me to do it, I'd be more than happy to have a go.'

'I really want you to do it,' said Carrie firmly. 'You worked out how to do it and I'd really like to think that I know the person who made my cake.' She drew breath. 'In fact – we could have a parade of trees all up the room – just like my cake – with my cake at the end!'

'Excellent idea,' said Mandy.

'Yes,' agreed Sarah. 'Maybe we could hire the trees.'

'What sort of trees would they be?' asked Mandy.

'Bay, or box, probably,' said Sarah.

'But wouldn't it be nice to have fruit on?' suggested Mandy.

'We could wire in little oranges if you wanted,' agreed Sarah. 'It could look very elegant.'

'Elegant would be good,' said Carrie. 'People always seem to think that if you're over a double-D cup you want tacky.'

'Or,' said Bron, 'we could have fake versions of the cake. Like the one that Carrie saw in the shop.'

'Oh yes,' said Carrie. 'That's what I want. Really classy!'

The reason Carrie had wanted a wedding just like Ashlyn's dawned on Sarah. 'So you won't be wanting personalised confetti then?'

'Nu-huh.' Carrie shook her head. 'I want to be thought of as a serious actress. Nothing too show-biz or common.'

'That's brilliant, Carrie,' said Sarah with relief. 'That's the kind of wedding I like doing best.'

It crossed her mind that economies could be made if

149

Carrie and her sister shared some of what a wedding needed. She'd make Lily pay her share, of course, but prices came down for things like napkins if you were ordering a thousand.

'You could have a little bead or something in each whorl of icing,' said Bron, her mind still on cake.

'Swarovski crystals!' said Carrie. 'Or would that be tacky?'

'I have a contact with them,' said Elsa. 'I could get you a good deal, I should think. It would be good publicity for them, after all. And we could put some on the dress to tie in with the cake? And maybe embroider some little trees? It would be very subtle, only visible if you looked really closely, but on the hem or the veil – it should be possible.'

Carrie sighed dreamily. 'That would be heaven! As long as it's in good taste,' she added.

'There's a difference between a bit of bling and bad taste,' said Sarah. 'This is your wedding day, you must have what you want. I won't let you do anything over the top, I promise you.'

'The reason we went with an English wedding planner was to avoid anything Carrie's future mother-in-law could say was vulgar,' said Mandy.

'My sister's having just the same problem with her future mother-in-law!' said Sarah, and then wished she hadn't. Discretion was supposed to be her middle name, after all.

'So it's not just because I'm American?' asked Carrie. 'People assume I'm going to be what they call in Manhattan a Bridezilla.'

'Oh no. Anyone can be difficult at any time,' assured Sarah. 'That's what I spend a lot of my time doing, making sure everyone is happy.'

'She's very good at it,' said Bron loyally.

'More champagne, I think,' said Carrie. 'Mandy, could you ring room service for me?'

'Don't forget you have to go out for dinner,' said Mandy. 'And Hugo should be here in a minute.'

'Just one more drink each,' said Carrie. 'Then, if Hugo's coming, I'd better put my face on.'

'I could do it for you if you like, and finish your pedicure,' said Bron.

Carrie frowned. 'I haven't got those things you put between your toes. Shall we ask room service for some, when they bring the champagne?'

Bron shook her head. 'I can do it with loo paper. Don't worry. Here, you sit down. I'll sort you out.'

'Mandy?' Carrie asked, her foot on Bron's lap. 'Did we book someone to do my hair for tonight?'

'You didn't say you needed anyone, Carrie, but I'm sure—'

'I'd like Bron to do it. I've seen what she did with Ashlyn's hair and it would be good to see what she can do with mine.'

Sarah glanced at her watch. 'But Hugo will be here in ten minutes. Will you be ready?'

Carrie waved a leisurely hand. 'Whatever. You get used to being seen in your curlers by gorgeous men.'

'I brought my brushes with me. I'll do your make-up when I've done your toes.'

While Bron was doing what she did so well, Elsa went off into a corner. She wanted to staple samples to drawings and Carrie had asked if she could name the fabrics so she knew if she was asking for organza (sheer but stiff), chiffon (fine, sheer and floaty), or georgette (drapier, a bit thicker and less sheer than chiffon).

Sarah cleared a table for Hugo. He would need somewhere to show his albums and folders. Fortunately the sitting room was amply provided with tables, especially when all the bottles and glasses were cleared away. She glanced at her watch again. It was unlike him to be late. She knew he knew Mandy and had met Carrie before but as she was organising this wedding she felt responsible for everything to do with it, including everyone's time-keeping.

Mandy's mobile phone rang. Going by what she said, it must be Hugo, and he was going to be late. 'Not a problem,' said Mandy and disconnected.

Sarah felt anxious, then reminded herself firmly that he was the first contact. She really wasn't responsible for him.

By the time Hugo turned up, Carrie was looking every inch the star. Everyone had got involved in what she should wear. Eventually an outfit in the softest shell-pink suede was decided on. Bron had tonged her hair into an amazing style that seemed to defy gravity, and her make-up was so subtle it was barely apparent.

'Oh, honey!' said Mandy. 'You look to die for!'

'Where are we going again?' asked Carrie. 'I can't remember?'

'It's a dinner for the backers of Come Back Again,' said Mandy. 'You look just great!'

Carrie inspected herself critically in the mirror. No one else could find fault with her but she was the last arbiter and she had to be satisfied too. To everyone's relief, she was.

There was a knock at the door and Mandy ushered Hugo in.

'Carrie! Sweetie!' They hugged and Sarah turned away as he picked her up and swung her round. 'You are the most gorgeous thing not sold in a cellophane box at Harrods!' he said, putting her down.

Then he strolled across to Mandy and kissed her cheek. 'Mandy, how is the sexiest PA in Hollywood?'

'In London, Hugo,' said Mandy, friendly, but not buying the flattery. 'I presume you know these guys?'

Elsa and Bron smiled in a friendly way. Sarah just nodded.

He raised an eyebrow. 'OK, shall we get on with it?'

Sarah had never doubted his skill, but when she saw what else he had produced, apart from the wedding photos, she was truly amazed. Carrie and Mandy were extremely impressed.

'Hugo, honey! We have got to have you. Don't you think, Mandy?' said Carrie. 'Sarah?'

Sarah did her best to smile. 'He is very good.' She wanted to go on to say, 'But are you sure you don't want Mario Testino or someone?' but couldn't. Her feelings towards Hugo were so confusing. If Carrie had implied Hugo wasn't up to the job she'd have defended him like a tigress.

Hugo packed up his things. 'So,' he said to Bron and Elsa who were helping clear up yet more glasses. 'What are you girls doing now?'

'We're going out to dinner,' said Bron.

'We're giving them a lift,' said Carrie. 'I wanted them to come to dinner with us, but Mandy thought it wasn't a good idea.'

'Why don't you come with us?' Bron asked Hugo.

Sarah busied herself so she couldn't see his reaction to this invitation. She wasn't ready to engage with him yet. She still felt too confused. Then she chided herself for being silly. Where was the harm in having a friendly dinner with him? Elsa and Bron would be there. She looked up.

'Hugo . . .' she started, just as he said, 'Actually, I have plans.'

Shortly after that, he left.

Chapter Sixteen

A little while after Hugo had gone, all five of them piled into the car arranged to take Carrie to her dinner date. She was going to drop Sarah, Bron and Elsa at their hotel on her way, to save them getting a taxi. They were all best friends by now and Bron, having made Carrie look as if she wasn't wearing any make-up and was just naturally beautiful, which was the perfect look for the film that she was negotiating, had been booked to do hair and make-up for her wedding.

'I just feel us girls are part of a crew now,' said Carrie as the chauffeur held open the car door. 'It'll take the stress out of the whole wedding thing.'

While the others chatted gently, Sarah looked out of the window, as always loving being driven through London in the evening. Summer or winter, it always held a feeling of excitement and promise. She was happy with the way things had gone. Carrie was delighted with everything that had been arranged so far and while she was still intent on getting married in a pretty church on a summer Saturday, she was more aware of the difficulties of achieving this dream.

They swept along Park Lane. Hyde Park seemed to be in a celebratory mood. Some trees were decorated with fairy lights and Sarah had a sudden urge to stop the car so she could get out and walk. She didn't, of course; she was being sensible. After they'd all freshened up for dinner, she would escort her team to a wonderful restaurant for a meal. But just briefly she'd wanted to take off her shoes and walk through the grass and smile at the people and pretend she didn't have any responsibilities.

The car slowed at some lights as they passed a boutique hotel when they were somewhere in Belgravia and Sarah saw a taxi draw up outside it. Hugo, now wearing a dinner jacket, his hair artistically ruffled, came down the steps and opened the door of the taxi and ushered in a very beautiful young woman. Her heart clenched for a moment. A second later she'd convinced herself it was nothing. He was entitled to go out to dinner with whomever he liked.

She turned back to the others. 'Did you say that *Celeb* magazine was interested in covering the wedding, Mandy?' she asked.

Mandy nodded. 'It's not definite yet, but they're interested.' She lowered her voice. 'They contribute to the cost quite a bit if they have exclusive pictures.'

'Well, that's brilliant! Would you need Hugo as well?' Sarah was suddenly hopeful. Maybe she wouldn't have to work with him after all.

'Oh yes,' said Carrie. 'Even if they sent one, we'd need him for the more intimate shots you wouldn't want in a magazine.'

'Oh. I hadn't thought of that.' She sat back down in her seat. 'And do you have a preference for a videographer? You will want the wedding videoed, won't you?'

'Absolutely,' said Carrie. 'I may ask people I know in the business to do it for me, but if you have anyone you can recommend . . .'

'I'll give you all the details.' Sarah pulled out her notebook and jotted it down.

'This is the hotel you asked for, ladies,' said the chauffeur a little while later.

As they landed on the pavement, having scrambled out of the limo and kissed Mandy and Carrie fondly goodbye, Elsa said, 'I'm never sure I like being called "ladies".'

'Well, trust me, there's no acceptable way of referring to a group of women,' said Sarah crisply, still a little unsettled by her glimpse of Hugo. 'I've tried them all: girls, women, ladies; they all sound bad.'

In the foyer of the hotel, Sarah looked at her watch. 'Shall we meet back down here at half past, then?'

'OK,' said Bron. 'But if you want me to do your hair, let me know. I'm going to have a look at Elsa's.'

'Does that mean you think it needs doing?' Sarah patted her head anxiously, ignoring Elsa's squeak of surprise.

'Yes,' said Bron. 'You wash it, I'll blow-dry it for you.'

'But you've just done Carrie's,' Sarah objected, 'and if you're doing Elsa's as well . . .'

'Doing Carrie's was what my dad would have called "speculating in order to accumulate".' She grinned. 'It's brilliant that she wants me to do it for the wedding. It is unusual for her not to have her own stylist.'

Sarah shrugged. 'Maybe it's because she hasn't got that many close friends and wants people she knows around her.'

Bron shook her head. 'She must just not get on well personally with her stylist. But it's great news for me! And, I get to make her cake! Thank you so much for bringing me along, Sarah.' And she hugged her friend.

Later, with everyone's hair newly styled and Sarah's a good couple of inches shorter, they found an Italian restaurant within tottering distance – Bron's heels weren't up to much forward motion. As three women on their own, they were welcomed with much flattering attention and given a table next to the garden. They could look out through the French doors to trees hung with fairy lights and what turned out up close to be plastic lemons.

Considering how lovely it was, Sarah felt touched with melancholy. She couldn't help wondering if Hugo was sharing a similarly luscious London garden with the beautiful girl she'd seen him with. Or they might be in some smart club, dancing the night away before kissing each other to death in the back of a taxi. She stifled a sigh and took the menu she was being handed.

'This is fun,' she said, determined to shake off her strange mood. She'd had a really successful day with Carrie, and her hair looked great. What Hugo did in his spare time was no business of hers, even if she did think, rather wistfully, that it could have been her this evening, being whisked off to dinner. She gave herself a mental shake – she must enjoy herself, for the others' sake if nothing else. 'This is almost like a hen night.'

'Well, I wouldn't know,' said Elsa. 'I've never been on a hen night but I get the impression they can be very raucous. I have seen some pictures.' She made a face. 'We won't be getting drunk, will we?'

'A bit, maybe,' said Bron. 'It's not often none of us is driving.'

'True,' said Sarah. 'Let's order.'

This took a fair bit of doing as they kept forgetting about the food and talking about bits and pieces that had happened during the day. When at last the waiter had taken back the menus and promised to bring the wine right away, Elsa said, 'Hen night or not, it's going to be fun.'

'I must say, it's the sort of hen night I'd have if I was ever going to get married, which I'm not of course,' said Sarah, more out of habit than anything else.

'Aren't you?' said Elsa.

Sarah shook her head. 'Definitely not. I've seen them go wrong too often. My sister was married for about six months before it collapsed.'

'And now she's getting married again?' said Bron.

Sarah nodded, a pained expression on her face. 'You should have seen the dresses she wanted to wear. Little wasp-waisted things, boned to the hilt.'

'But they're lovely!' said Elsa. 'I make those sort of dresses.'

'Not for people who are pregnant, you don't,' said Sarah.

'Oh no,' Elsa agreed. 'Maybe I don't.' She paused. 'I wonder what I'd put your sister in, if I had a choice.'

'Have you had lots of pregnant brides to deal with?' asked Bron.

'A couple. It's not usually a big deal, except for the photos.'

Sarah sighed. 'I wish you'd talk to Lily. She's insistent that her mother-in-law will go mad if anyone suspects she's not a virgin bride. Mad, really.'

'So what is she having?' asked Elsa.

'Not sure yet. But at least this time she's in a proper relationship, with a decent man. They've been going out for over a year.'

'I'm not sure that's long enough,' said Bron, picking up a breadstick and crunching the end of it.

'No? How long have you and Roger been together, then?' Sarah caught a sad note in Bron's voice but wasn't sure if she wanted to talk about it.

'A couple of years.'

'So,' said Elsa. 'What kind of dress would you have, Bron?'

'Oh, I don't know. Haven't thought about it.'

Sarah, who had moved on from wedding dresses said, 'I wonder if I could branch out and arrange hen nights? The trouble is, I'm not sure I'd want to deal with the tacky extras – the cowboy hats, the French maid outfits.'

'You could arrange classy hen nights: spa holidays, maybe even learning something, like cooking or – I don't know – pottery,' suggested Elsa.

'What, make your own dinner service?' said Sarah.

'Useful when it came to the first row,' said Bron brightly. 'Oh, here comes the first course. I'm glad we decided to share one. It's huge!'

'Shall we order some more wine now?' suggested Bron. This done, Sarah asked, 'So, Bron, if you haven't thought about a wedding dress, have you thought about your hen night?'

'And can you please invite us?' said Elsa. 'All my friends from school are either abroad or living with someone, determined not to get married on moral grounds.' She frowned. 'I only kept up with those two.'

'Ah,' said Sarah. 'Norma No-Mates.'

'That's me,' said Elsa, cheerfully. 'Still, I can say "Always the bridesmaid, never the bride" now, because I've been one. A bridesmaid, I mean.'

'You're young. You've got plenty of time. You might get married at any minute!' said Sarah.

Elsa shook her head. 'Not in the foreseeable, anyway. No, it's Bron's hen night we should be thinking about. She's got a man, after all, which is key, let's face it.'

'I'm never going to marry Roger,' said Bron.

The words were like a brake on the general chatter and there was a small silence before Elsa spoke.

'Aren't you?' she said. 'Of course, there's no reason why you should. I probably just got carried away by Carrie's wedding.' She stopped, abashed. 'Have I made an awful pun?'

'We'll forgive you,' said Sarah.

'So do you feel like Sarah, morally opposed to marriage?' said Elsa. Something about Bron indicated she had things on her mind she might want to share, but needed a little persuasion to do it.

Bron shook her head. 'Nope. Not generally, just for me and Roger.'

The tinkling of mandolins and Italian tenors, the sound of other diners scraping their knives and forks and murmuring to each other seemed to make the silence that suddenly fell more intense.

'Why not?' whispered Elsa.

'Because . . .'

In the pause, while Bron was trying to express the thoughts that had thrummed away in her subconscious for months now, their main courses arrived. If the waiters wondered how the lighthearted group of young women who'd come in could have changed into the tight-lipped people who dismissed them with only the politest of smiles, they didn't comment, but the atmosphere changed completely.

Bron ignored her chicken alla Milanese and picked up her glass. 'We just don't get on any more. I could never be the wife he wanted, however hard I tried. I'm not sure if we should even be together.'

'What do you mean?' Sarah put her hand on Bron's.

Bron sighed. 'I always thought if I tried my best, conformed to how he wanted me to be I could make it work, but I just can't. He despises my job, despises me and always has to be the one in charge.'

'Oh, Bron, I'm so sorry,' said Elsa, putting her hand on Bron's other hand.

Sarah said, 'We – I – I mean, we knew he didn't like you doing weddings, and going out at night, but I didn't realise things were that bad.'

'Well, they are.' Now she'd admitted it, both to herself and out loud, Bron felt tears starting at the back of her throat. She drank some more wine and tried to push down the growing feeling of despair that threatened to engulf her.

'Well then, you must leave him,' said Sarah firmly.

'I know,' said Bron, 'but I can't until I've got somewhere to go to.'

'Your parents?' suggested Elsa.

'They live in Spain,' said Bron. 'I could go and stay with them, of course. They'd love to have me, but I couldn't work there, or at least, not till I'd learnt some Spanish.'

'My flat is so tiny, there isn't room for me in there what

with all the office stuff,' said Sarah. 'But if you needed a place to go . . .'

'That's awfully sweet of you,' said Bron. 'But it's not that urgent. He may be a bit of a bully, but he doesn't hit me or anything.' For some reason her voice cracked and she suddenly started to cry.

Elsa, sitting next to her, instantly put her arm round her. 'Oh, honey. Don't cry, it'll be all right.'

The hubbub of the restaurant buzzed around them, oblivious to Bron's distress.

'I know.' Bron sniffed loudly, trying her hardest not to sob, 'but it's just dawned on me how awful it will be leaving him.'

'Why?' asked Sarah. 'Are you in love with him? In spite of everything?'

'No. If I'm honest I don't think I've loved him for ages now. We've just fallen into a habit.'

'Then won't you be glad to get away?' asked Sarah gently.

'I will be, but I hate rows and he'll shout.'

'Well, shout back!' said Sarah, firmer now.

'I could do that, if I had the engine running in my car so I could leap into it and drive off when it got too awful,' said Bron, trying to lighten up a bit, 'but there's no point in shouting if I've nowhere to go. And the thing is' – she gave a huge final sniff and wiped her nose on her paper napkin – 'now I've made my decision, I feel I must do it at once. Or soon as.'

'We've got to think,' said Sarah. 'Surely between us we know someone with a big enough floor.'

'My floor's huge but it would be dreadfully uncomfortable, although you're very welcome to it,' said Elsa doubtfully. 'And I do have a sofabed.'

Bron shook her head and dried her eyes. 'I really don't think I want to camp on someone's sofa, although it's terribly kind of you to offer. When I tell him I'm leaving, I want to be able to tell him I've got somewhere else to go,

161

or he'll persuade me leaving him is a really stupid idea. Which it would be, if I didn't have anywhere else.'

'Oh, I don't know,' muttered Sarah. 'I'd rather sleep on a park bench than live with a man I didn't love.'

Elsa turned her attention away from Bron for a moment. 'You've obviously been badly hurt in the past, Sarah.'

'That's another story.' Sarah waved a hand dismissively. 'Right now, we've got to focus on Bron. Don't we know anyone who'd like a nice lodger for a while?'

'Roger's mother would,' said Bron, 'but I don't think that's an option. What?'

Elsa was wagging her finger in the air, biting her lip, as if she were trying to remember something. Then she said, 'I've got it, I've got the answer!'

'What answer?' asked Bron.

'To where you should live,' said Elsa. 'When I was giving back the bridesmaid's dress . . .'

'Yes?' said Sarah encouragingly.

'. . . Ashlyn's mother told me she's got a cottage. She was complaining that her tenant had let her down or she couldn't get insurance or something. She's going to do something with it later – can't remember what – but doesn't that sound ideal? It would at least tide you over until you could find a place of your own.'

'So it's near Mrs Lennox-Featherstone's house?' asked Sarah.

'Yes! Bron, you wouldn't even have to move away from the area. You could stay at the salon,' said Elsa.

'That sounds brilliant,' said Bron quietly, but with a bit of optimism in her eyes now. 'I just hope it's not too good to be true.'

'I don't see why it should be,' said Elsa, at last sticking her fork into her plate of pasta. 'She's nice. A bit mad, but she says what she thinks.'

'Yes she is,' said Sarah. 'Some brides' mothers can be nightmares, but although she was very fussy and wanted everything just so, she didn't keep changing her mind or anything. She was good to work with.'

'Ring her when we get back,' said Elsa. 'I've got her number. I'm sure she'd be thrilled to have a tenant.'

After that, they had a wonderful evening. The restaurant was kind to them and they were all much happier now. Bron phoned Roger, who seemed surprisingly relaxed about her being away, which made her less anxious. Sarah, the problem of where Bron should live solved, pushed thoughts of Hugo and his gazelle-like friend out of her mind. Elsa, pleased to think she'd found the solution for Bron, revealed her sharp sense of humour to good effect, and the waiters, obviously relieved that the group had started laughing again, plied them with liqueurs on the house.

'What's this?' asked Sarah when the glasses arrived.

'Strega, signorina,' said the waiter.

'What's it like?'

'Fuel oil,' said Elsa. 'I had it with my parents once.'

'That doesn't sound very nice,' said Sarah, looking at her glass anxiously.

'It is, sort of,' explained Elsa. 'Not sure why.'

'OK,' said Sarah. She took a sip and coughed. 'Mm. I see what you mean.'

'And desserts?' broke in the waiter, happy now his offerings had been accepted.

'We might as well,' said Bron. 'After all, we none of us have wedding dresses to get into.'

'I have got a ball gown to make though,' said Elsa, after the waiter had taken both the menus and their orders.

'Ooh, tell us!' said the others.

When it was time to go home, Bron took her shoes off and walked barefoot back to the hotel, supported by the others who had more sensible shoes.

'That was the best evening out I've had in a long time,' said Sarah. 'Who needs men?'

The other two didn't reply.

Chapter Seventeen

The prospect of living on her own when she'd never done it before was daunting, but now she'd made the decision Bron was determined not to slip back into the inertia that had kept her with Roger for so long.

She telephoned Mrs Lennox-Featherstone during her lunch hour the next day, not wanting to lose a moment longer. Much to Bron's relief, she was very quick on the uptake.

'Bron? The hairdresser? Lovely to hear from you. What can I do for you?'

'Well, Elsa, the dressmaker?'

'Charming girl, lives in black. Yes?'

'She said you had a cottage you might like to rent.'

'Absolutely, I have! Can't get it insured as an empty property and I wasn't planning on doing anything to it until the autumn. It's far too soon after the wedding for me to get my head round all that. So if you wanted it for a while I'd be only too delighted.' She had paused. 'It might be rather wonderful having a top-rate hairdresser so close.'

Bron had laughed and assured Vanessa that she could summon her at any time, day or night, to do her hair. The rent was really low and she felt it was the least she could do.

'But I can't actually show it to you until the weekend. You're not in too much of a hurry, are you?'

In fact, Bron had been hoping to see – possibly begin to move into it – a lot sooner than that. 'Well . . .' she began.

'I'm doing a course every night this week, including Saturday, now that I think of it. But if you wanted to pick the key up after eight on Saturday, that would be fine.'

'So I had to be satisfied that that,' she had told Elsa on the phone when she'd finished thanking Mrs Lennox-Featherstone and convincing her she'd be the perfect tenant.

'But you'll be able to pack and stuff, won't you? If you want to leave anything round here, just let me know.'

'That's kind of you, Elsa. I'll try and fit it all in my car but if I need somewhere to put stuff, I'll be on to you. I don't want to tell Roger until I'm certain . . . It might be uninhabitable.'

'Well, I think you're being really brave about all this,' said Elsa. 'And you know Sarah and I are here for you if you need us.'

Bron felt touched yet again by how supportive they were both being. 'Thank you. I don't feel very brave, just hideously guilty. He hates change. Even though I don't think he really loves me, he won't want me to leave.'

She spent the rest of the week planning her escape. She put a lot of clothes into bags, telling Roger she was having a clear-out. There was an awful lot of stuff that she'd paid for and was intending to take – things that he wouldn't need personally – but couldn't until she'd at least told him she was going. He may not have been the most noticing man on the planet, but even he would think something was up if she started unscrewing mirrors and shelving units from the walls.

On Saturday morning she felt distinctly nervous and slightly less confident in her decision. Roger had been very nice all week, and she almost wanted to change her mind. But she wouldn't let herself. She had Elsa and Sarah to give her moral support and she knew that even if she and Roger didn't hate each other, they didn't really make each other happy.

'I'm going to see a friend,' she said, perched on the bed while he ate the breakfast she'd brought him. 'It means I'll miss cricket but I'll be back in time to cook you a lovely supper. I thought I'd get a couple of steaks and make real chips.'

'Great,' said Roger, tucking into eggs and bacon. 'I need a big meal after all that running around.'

Bron smiled, patted his foot under the duvet and left.

She hadn't really lied, she realised, just not told all the truth. For while Roger was at cricket, she was going to be packing her stuff. Only after the dinner, the bottle of wine and the ice cream and hot chocolate sauce, would she tell him she wouldn't be having Sunday lunch with his parents but would be leaving home instead.

She felt bad about his mother. She'd have to go and visit her later, when Pat'd got over the shock.

Having done her shopping, buying supplies for her own first days in her new home as well as Roger's farewell meal, she drove home. She'd allowed plenty of time for him to leave for cricket but, strangely, his car was in the drive when she got back.

Had cricket been cancelled for some reason? She couldn't think why. It was a lovely day, perfect for it: sunny, but not too hot.

Planning to tell him she'd wanted to put the steaks in the fridge before meeting her friend, she put her key in the lock and instantly knew something was wrong. There was perfume in the air that wasn't hers, but was familiar. Then she heard laughter coming from upstairs. She knew instinctively what she'd find, but her feet carried her upstairs anyway.

She found Roger and Sasha in bed together. Sasha was sitting on top of Roger. She was wearing the ghastly underwear that did so much for his libido and so little for Bron's.

She felt sick. She thought she might indeed vomit, but actually, she almost felt more sorry for Roger and Sasha as they looked at her in horror and then Sasha let out a small scream and fell off Roger.

'Oh God, Bron! I thought you were out all day!' he said, fighting to get out from under Sasha's controlling thighs.

Sweat broke out over Bron's face as the reality of the scene threatened to overwhelm her. Even though she no longer wanted to be with Roger she felt horribly betrayed. It was their bedroom he was having sex in, on her sheets, with her boss. She took a deep breath and went to the wardrobe, took out a large carrier bag and then started unloading the top of her dressing table into it.

'Well, I came back,' she said, slightly calmer now. After all, she kept repeating to herself, she'd been leaving him anyway.

Roger just lay there, blinking at her.

'Oh, Bron,' said Sasha, sitting up now, the sheet barely covering her ample bosom, 'this is only a bit of fun. No need to take it too seriously. It doesn't need to change anything.'

Bron stopped putting nail varnish into its box. 'You're wearing my underwear – you must have changed out of yours! But don't worry,' she went on quickly. 'The last thing I want is for you to give it back to me.'

'You're not going to say anything to anyone, are you?' asked Sasha.

Typical of her boss to worry about her reputation. Looking, albeit rather reluctantly, at her now Bron realised Sasha suddenly seemed older and less glossy and groomed than she usually did. She was several years older than both of them and an unexpected spark of compassion rose in Bron. 'At the salon? Probably not. I don't want

Roger any more anyway. You can have him as your young stud if you like.'

'Hang on!' Roger sat up, suddenly full of righteous indignation. 'What do you mean you don't want me any more! I was going to marry you, Bron!'

Bron started to laugh. It was all so ridiculous. And so clear. Roger had, he thought, moulded her into the perfect wife, but a perfect wife wasn't enough. He wanted a mistress as well – one who just happened to be her boss.

'I'm sorry not to be more flattered, but you never asked and I wasn't going to marry you back,' said Bron. 'I was going to tell you I was leaving anyway – tonight.'

'What do you mean? Where would you go?'

'I have a place arranged, thank you for your concern.'

He tried to speak for a few moments and then managed, 'But my parents think you're perfect for me!' Roger was still in denial. He might well have thought about upgrading from a mere hairdresser to the salon-owner but it had never occurred to him that the hairdresser might leave him. He was outraged.

'I'm very fond of your mother, Roger, but you're going to turn into your father very soon, and he's a fascist.' It was bliss finally letting it all out.

'How dare you talk about my father like that!' Roger jumped out of bed, naked, his whole body jiggling with indignation. It was hard not to see the funny side. She stifled a giggle.

'Sorry to hurt your feelings, but you must admit he makes Genghis Khan seem like a bleeding-heart liberal. I don't know how poor Pat has put up with him all these years. And you're just the same!'

'I don't know how you can say that!' He was now struggling into a pair of boxer shorts. 'I give to charity, don't I?'

'So does the Mafia, Roger! And I should warn you,' she said to Sasha, 'that he won't bother with foreplay after the first six months. As for looking for your G spot, without Sat Nav, he hasn't a chance.' She frowned. 'Maybe that was a bit unfair. Sat Nav can lose far easier-to-find places than that.'

'Now you're being disgusting.' Roger was now wearing trousers and it gave him a bit of confidence.

Feeling her own confidence growing by the minute, Bron stood up straight and confronted Roger. 'You're a fine one to talk! You dress your girlfriend up in my underwear and say I'm being disgusting!' she said.

'Bron!' A T-shirt gave Roger the upper hand, or so he thought. 'You're blowing this up out of all proportion.'

'At the risk of being thought disgusting again, I think you've been the one doing that!'

'Really, I had no idea you had such a filthy mind!'

She shrugged, for the first time a little rueful. 'I didn't intend to give you the character-assassination speech, but you did rather ask for it.' She moved to the dressing table, opened a drawer and took out a large plastic bag she had ready. And to think she'd been feeling guilty about leaving him. She swept everything on the table into it.

Sasha was getting back into her clothes and Roger put on his socks and shoes. 'You're over-reacting,' he said. 'Typical bloody woman!'

Bron sighed briefly, her anger abating a little. Originally, she had only been going to take what she really needed. She wasn't going to take everything she'd paid for, just because she could. But now she was intent on stripping the bedroom of anything she'd bought personally. There was a huge dress carrier ready in the wardrobe and she slid the dressing-table mirror and one of the bedside lights into this while Roger was still staring at her.

'You can't take the furniture!' he roared.

'I can if I paid for it. I won't take the mattress though. It's been sullied.' She had to stifle another giggle. 'Sullied' was such a lovely word and she hadn't realised she'd known it until it popped out. Adrenalin was keeping her going, she realised, aware that later the shock of all this would hit her. But at this moment, she was on a high.

She was aware of Sasha and Roger whispering to each other, probably wondering if she'd gone off her head. She'd never felt so *on* her head. The bathroom was the next place to get the treatment, although she left the shaving mirror as it had been a present from her to Roger and she couldn't see properly in it anyway. She then went downstairs to the kitchen.

Her carrier bags were full so she found a bin-liner and started filling it with gadgets: the blender, the toaster and the steamer. Roger came in while she had the knife block, full of knives, in her hand.

'You can't take that!' Roger's trousers were half tucked into his socks. 'It was a present from my parents!'

'Yes,' replied Bron, half admiring him for being so confrontational when she was so well armed. 'To me!'

'Shall I put the kettle on?' suggested Sasha from behind him, now fully dressed and anxious to soothe the situation if she could.

'If you're desperate for a cup, that's a good idea,' said Bron. 'I'll be taking it in a minute.'

'You cannot just strip my house like this!' Roger was pulsating with indignation. 'It's robbery!' He wasn't even trying to win her back.

'OK, I'll leave the kettle,' Bron conceded, 'although it's mine by right.' She knew there was a kettle in the cottage. Mrs Lennox-Featherstone had sent her an inventory of what was there.

She surveyed the kitchen and considered taking the saucepans, but then left them. They'd been her parents', left behind when they moved to Spain, and they weren't very good ones. Her cookery books she decided were just too heavy; as it was she could only just drag the sack into the hall before going back for another.

'What do you need that for?' demanded Roger, seeing her detach the bin-bag from the roll. 'You've taken everything that isn't nailed down!'

'There's the standard lamp in the sitting room!' Bron had to bite her lip to stop herself laughing. She had no intention of taking the standard lamp, although that too had come from her parents.

'This is bloody ridiculous!'

'OK then, Roger, I'll do a deal with you. Help me get this lot into my car and I won't take anything else if you really need it.'

'I've put a couple of sugars in your tea, Rog,' said Sasha. 'For the shock. This must be so upsetting for you.'

Bron shook her head in disbelief but didn't say anything. Roger hated being called Rog even more than he hated sugar in tea.

When she drove away twenty minutes later, Bron gave a little toot of triumph on the horn. At that moment she felt she could conquer the world.

Chapter Eighteen

Bron's calm gave up on her when she was halfway to pick up the keys from Mrs Lennox-Featherstone. She pulled into a lay-by and did some deep-breathing exercises, but they didn't stop the shaking that was convulsing her body. She burrowed in her bag and found some Rescue Remedy and after a few moments she calmed down.

'Is it the Rescue Remedy, or is it the time you take to take it that calms you?' she wondered out loud, partly to test her voice for tremors. She blew her nose, then she checked her make-up, removed the accumulation of it that had landed under her eyes, and drove on. Vanessa had said she could pick the key up anytime, but if she wanted a guided tour first, she'd have to wait until after eight. Bron had fully intended to wait until someone could show her over the cottage, but then she hadn't intended to find Roger in bed with her boss. Shit happens: plans have to change.

The door of the big house was opened by the house-keeper – she presumed. Elsa had mentioned there was one.

'Oh, hi!' Bron said breezily. 'I'm a bit earlier than expected, but could I have the key to the cottage?'

The housekeeper said, 'Come in. Mrs Vanessa is out, but she left a message about the key.'

Bron followed her anxiously into the hallway. A 'message about the key' did not sound like the actual key, which was what she needed. Supposing she couldn't move into the cottage directly, what could she do? She didn't want to land on Elsa's or Sarah's floor, although she could as a last resort. She didn't really want to talk about what had happened, not yet. It was too raw. She wanted to establish herself in her new home first. Although not having to meet Mrs Lennox-Featherstone just then was a bit of a relief.

The housekeeper came back with a bulging plastic bag. 'Here you are. You'll need the duvet and the sheets and things. Mrs Vanessa always lets the house with bedding.' She smiled.

Bron smiled back with relief. Her new landlady hadn't mentioned bedding on the inventory but in her haste to get away, she'd forgotten all about it anyway. She had a feeling there were a lot of things she'd forgotten.

'You have to get the key from James, next door,' the housekeeper went on. 'The man came to read the meter. He let him in.' She frowned a little. 'You want tea or something? You not looking well.'

Bron forced a smile. 'Oh, I'm fine! I'll just take these and find my new home. Please tell Mrs – er, Mrs Vanessa how grateful I am to have somewhere to live.'

As she drove away, with bedding but without a key, she thought this must have sounded rather odd.

There were the two cottages, side by side. She could tell which one was hers because there was a fairly muddy old Volvo outside the other. James, who had the key, must be in, which was a huge relief. She didn't really want to sit in her car for hours waiting for him. It would have looked so pathetic.

She got out and went up the short path to the front door and knocked. She could hear music playing and tried to identify it as a distraction while she waited. What on earth was she going to say? 'Hi, I'm Bron, your new neighbour. Can I have the key?'

She didn't have a chance to say anything much. As James opened the door, a large dog streamed out into the garden, circled her and went back into the cottage. By the time James had finished telling it off and then congratulating it for returning a lot of the preliminary stuff was redundant. Then she realised she recognised him and cursed herself for not making the connection before. He was the gardener, and the man she had met on the riverbank.

'It's you,' he said. 'How nice.' And he smiled.

She looked into his friendly face and all her fortitude threatened to desert her. She'd been so strong and brave during and after the ghastly scene with Roger, and now she felt like bursting into tears. She'd probably have felt stronger if he'd been hostile and a stranger.

She couldn't speak. She just stood there, smiling weakly.

'Come in,' he said. 'You look as if you could do with a cup of tea or something.'

She must look awful, she thought as he stepped aside, pinning the dog against the door so that she could pass him into the cottage. He was the second person within about ten minutes who had said that.

She found herself in a sitting room. It was tiny, with windows on two walls. There was a sofa pushed under one window and a table under the other. There was a fireplace on the other wall and in one corner a staircase was half concealed behind an open door. Through another door she could see a kitchen built on to the back.

The dog circled her again, banging into her body from time to time.

'Sit!' said James. 'This is Brodie. She's a rescue dog and I haven't had her long. She's still a bit over-excited when visitors come. It's Bron, isn't it?'

Bron nodded. She was still feeling shocked. She knew it was delayed reaction but she couldn't shake herself out of it.

'Come and sit down. I'll get the kettle on. Unless you think you need something stronger?' He frowned at her. 'I think I've got some brandy somewhere. I needed it for a recipe.'

Bron perched on the edge of a sofa that you'd disappear into if you weren't careful. She couldn't make the decision for herself. Brandy might indeed be a good idea.

Brodie – possibly sensing Bron's need for comfort – came and sat on her feet, raising her head so Bron could rub her chest. Bron obligingly did this, finding it soothing to rub something soft and furry. It was a way of communicating that didn't involve actually speaking.

Bron allowed herself to inch further on to the sofa until she could lean back. The dog instantly jumped up beside her and put her head on Bron's lap. She didn't know if she should make Brodie get down. She thought she probably ought to but the warm weight of the dog's head was comforting, so she carried on stroking her.

'Oh, Brodie!' said James reproachfully as he came in with a tray. 'Get down! Bron doesn't want your hairs all over her.'

Bron shook her head, trying to convey that she liked the dog and didn't mind at all about hairs. He seemed to understand.

'I'm training her not to jump up on people who don't appreciate it – or rather to wait until she's invited. I'll presume you invited her.'

She tried to return his smile.

He put the tray down on the table and then handed her a glass with an inch of brown fluid in it. 'Here, take this, then I'll find something for you to put your tea on. Do you take sugar?' he asked, as an afterthought.

Bron shook her head again.

'Oh good. I haven't got any.' He produced a small three-legged stool from under the table and put it near Bron. 'There.' He set the mug of tea down. 'Have you got everything you need?'

Bron nodded, trusting the power of speech would come back eventually. She sipped the brandy. It warmed her instantly and she began to feel calmer.

'Are you feeling any better now?' James stood looking down at her kindly.

She nodded, but realised she should give some explanation as to why she needed brandy at four o'clock in the afternoon. 'You must be wondering why—'

'I know you're going to be my new neighbour, and everyone knows that moving is one of the major stresses of life.' He smiled. 'So you don't need to say anything about why you're a bit upset.'

'That's very tactful of you, but it's probably only fair to tell you that I've just left my boyfriend.'

'Good choice,' said James. 'You didn't seem that happy with him when we met the other evening. I mean, I shouldn't presume but . . .'

'No, well, it was soon after then that I decided to leave him. I heard about the cottage – next door – being available, and arranged to move in.' This all sounded very sane and controlled. She probably didn't need to say anything else.

'Was he very upset? Your boyfriend, when you left. I'm not really curious, but you were in a bit of a state when you arrived . . . you don't need to tell me if you don't want to,' he added hurriedly.

The brandy reached Bron's sense of humour and tickled it into action. Feeling much more herself again, she started to giggle. 'Well, he was a bit upset, but mostly because I was taking the furniture with me.'

'Were you?' James seemed surprised.

'Only the small stuff. I had paid for it.'

'Oh, that's all right then.'

'And I was in rather a bad mood.'

'Really?'

Bron nodded and sighed. 'I'd discovered him in bed

with my boss!' She frowned. 'Oh God. I've got to go to work on Monday. How horribly embarrassing!'

'I should coco,' said James, chuckling softly.

Bron chewed at her lip. 'I'm not sure if I *can* go to work, actually.'

'If you like your job then maybe—'

'I don't like it that much and I've seen her in my peep-hole bra, which I have to tell you was not something I chose myself.'

'If you say so . . .'

'I do! It was a present from Roger, one of those gifts that are supposed to be for the woman but actually are more for the man.'

James held up his hands in surrender. 'You probably won't believe me, but I promise I've never bought anything like that for anybody.'

'It's all right, I do believe you.' Bron was rather embarrassed now, she'd said a little more than she'd meant to. 'I still can't think what to do about work.'

'It might be awkward if you stayed. Was your boss a friend as well as a love-rival?'

This made Bron giggle a little. 'Not really. She never liked me, always made me wash hair and sweep up if she possibly could.' She looked up at him. 'I'm a very talented hairdresser.'

He sensed her defiance and the corner of his mouth moved. 'I know.' He hesitated and then said, 'And I know it's an awfully clichéd expression, but why don't you phone a friend?'

'I will later. I feel too exhausted to talk too much now.' Bron finished her brandy. 'Men, eh? Who'd have 'em?'

'He was only one example. We're not all like that.'

She sighed deeply. 'I know, but it'll take me a while to trust again, that's for sure.'

There was a moment's silence. 'Have your tea.' He

moved the little stool closer to her. 'Would you like a biscuit?'

'No thank you, I really should get settled in next door.'

'Well, wait till you've finished your tea. I'll come over with you and make sure everything's working. Vanessa told me a new tenant was moving in – a young woman – and said I might need to turn on the electricity at the mains and things.' He paused. 'It'll be nice to have a neighbour again.'

Bron struggled to her feet. 'We'd better go then.'

James, having found the key, carried the bedding while Bron retrieved her case and some of the things she'd liberated from the house.

The little cottage smelt a bit funny to Bron as she entered.

'Alan, the man who lived here before, was an artist. He might have smoked the odd spliff,' said James.

Bron smiled. 'That explains it.' She didn't ask if James had shared the odd spliff with the artist, but he answered her question anyway.

'I don't like my head being messed with,' he said. 'Tobacco is bad enough. I'm definitely giving up.' He grinned. 'Don't worry, you haven't moved next door to a crack den or anything.'

'I'm sure I haven't.'

'Listen, why don't I make supper for us a bit later – when you've had time to move your stuff in.'

'Well, I did bring food . . .' Then she froze. The bag of groceries – just enough to tide her over for the first weekend – was still sitting in Roger's fridge.

'You left it behind?'

She nodded.

'I'll knock on the door when it's ready. It'll be something simple – eggs, I keep my own hens. Anyway, would seven be too early for you?'

'Not at all. I should be sorted out by then. I'm really grateful for all your help.'

When she was alone, Bron got out her phone and found Elsa's number.

'I've done it,' she said when Elsa answered. 'I've left him.'

'Well done! What's the cottage like? Have you had time to settle in yet?'

'Er no.'

'Well, all in good time.' Then, sensing there was something Bron hadn't told her, Elsa asked, 'Is everything all right? Do you need me to come round?'

'No, no, I'm fine . . . err . . .'

'Yes?'

'I found Roger in bed with Sasha, my boss from the salon.'

Elsa dropped her phone.

Chapter Nineteen

After a quiet Sunday spent with her parents, eating lunch, going for a walk and watching an old film while she finished off putting some scarlet silk binding on a corset, Elsa woke up the following morning full of energy and ideas.

Without bothering to get dressed she went straight to her workshop. She had done all she could for Carrie until Carrie made a few decisions. There were two designs for bridesmaids' dresses, one long, one ballerina length. Ashlyn had had this, and so Elsa had assumed Carrie would want the same options. As to quantity and size of bridesmaids, Carrie was, as ever, hard to pin down.

So today she would get on with her own ball gown. The moment she heard from Carrie about the designs she had sent her, she would drop everything to get on with her dress, but just for now, she could concentrate on herself.

She got out her swatch books, going through them to make sure there wasn't anything more suitable – or more lovely – for her overskirt than the material she had already picked out.

She got out her book of costumes and found the picture of the one she wanted to make. It was very pretty and although her enthusiasm for creating it was total, the thought of wearing it was more daunting. Ashlyn's wedding had been a one-off; she much preferred to be anonymous, to wear clothes that didn't draw attention to her. And if this was the reason, as her mother insisted, that she didn't have a boyfriend, then so be it.

The phone rang; the voice on the end of it was commanding. 'Elsa? Is that you? Vanessa Lennox-Featherstone.'

'Oh, hello.' Elsa glanced at the clock. It was only ten to eight in the morning! Who else but Mrs Lennox-Featherstone would ring so early?

'So sorry to ring you at sparrow's fart,' said her caller, making the word 'fart' sound positively patrician. 'Tried yesterday but couldn't get you. Thing is, I've got an appointment for you. To have your colours done. Today. That OK?'

Damn! She'd so hoped that colours thing had been forgotten about. Still, she supposed she'd have to go now. And today, when she was going to do something for herself. She cleared her throat, coughed and ummed and erred a bit, but eventually had to concede that today was fine.

'Fab! But I'm going to come with you so I know what you've been told and I can check up on you.'

'Oh!' Elsa didn't quite know how she felt about this. It was very kind of Ashlyn's mother to give her a present but she didn't really think she wanted it. Sadly, she couldn't refuse – she just wasn't brave enough.

Mrs Lennox-Featherstone told Elsa she'd pick her up on the way to the studio. 'She's a marvellous woman – she'll tell you exactly what to wear and how to wear it. Tips on make-up, too. You'll have to throw away half your wardrobe, of course, but it's worth it! See you at half ten then. Byee!'

If this woman, whom Elsa already hated, and Mrs Lennox-Featherstone thought they could bully her into throwing away her black V-necked tops they were in for a surprise. She may be too shy and cowardly to defy them when they were actually present, but they wouldn't know – or indeed care – if she did nothing about changing. And why should she? She looked just fine in black.

Defiantly she went into the kitchen. A cup of Women's Tea would sort her out. When describing this to friends she said it was what you drank if you needed a strong whisky, but couldn't have one – possibly because it was still before eight in the morning. Once fortified, she went to shower and dress.

The doorbell rang promptly at ten-thirty and Elsa found Bron on the doorstep. She looked different – giggly and a bit wild-eyed.

'Bron! What happened? Did you decide not to go back to work after all?'

'I went in, just to see. And although I thought I could go on working for her, I found I couldn't. She did beg me to stay – terrified I'd tell the world, probably. I should have taken pictures with my mobile, I could have blackmailed her for millions!'

Elsa laughed. 'Well, you look great on it, I must say. What a shame your landlady is such a bully!'

'She's not really, once you get used to her. I met her as I was going back to the cottage and she said I should come along. I didn't have anything else to do and I thought you might appreciate some support.'

'Yes I do, of course I do. Let's go.'

Vanessa Lennox-Featherstone stood outside her sports car wearing a geranium-red suit that exactly matched her car. She may have been a woman of a certain age but she was no slouch in the style department. Elsa, clutching her bag defensively across her chest, admitted this with trepidation.

As she walked to the car Vanessa said, 'Morning, darling. Do hope this isn't terribly inconvenient but Hilary is incredibly booked up and we got a cancellation. Has Bron told you what's happened to her? Nightmare! Thank you so much for telling her about my little house. She's going to be the perfect tenant.'

'I hope so,' said Bron.

'Of course you are! A hairdresser on my very own land – how much better could you be? I usually go up to London to have mine done but now I can pop along to see you.'

They all clambered into the car. Elsa, the smallest, folded herself into the back, Bron got into the front with Vanessa.

'OK,' said Vanessa a few moments later. 'Everyone in? Seatbelts? Off we go then.'

The back of the car dipped slightly as Vanessa roared off.

'We're going to have huge fun getting Elsa out of the ubiquitous black. Such a waste of your beauty, darling.'

'I wouldn't say—'

'Of course you wouldn't. But I would.' She stopped at the crossroads. 'Ashlyn's having a brilliant time on her honeymoon, by the way. She's lucky to be able to have a nice long one. They're visiting her in-laws for an extended time now, of course.' Vanessa looked both ways and shot across. 'I went on an outward-bound course in Scotland for mine. Bloody freezing, I can tell you!'

The studio where Elsa's torture was to take place was in a pleasant housing estate on the outskirts of town. It didn't look too daunting on the outside, but Elsa was not reassured. Awful things could go on behind a neat front garden with a picket fence and an up-and-over garage on the side. She'd seen movies – she knew.

The woman who opened the door was not daunting, however. She was very attractive and well groomed, there was no getting away from it, but she also had a warm and friendly smile. She didn't look like a style Nazi; she wasn't wearing strange binding garments which would indicate rigid ideas of right and wrong. But Elsa refused to allow herself to be reassured; she was going to resist what was about to happen, no matter what. She spent all her life making clothes to her clients' exact requirements. To be a client (courtesy of Vanessa) and be told what to wear went against the grain.

Bron and Vanessa obviously warmed to Hilary straight away, but it was easy for them – Vanessa already knew her and they weren't going to be given a forcible makeover. A vision of herself being strapped into a dentist's chair while make-up was applied flashed into her brain.

'Do come in,' said the woman. 'I'm Hilary. Hi, Vanessa, lovely to see you again.'

'Darling!' Vanessa kissed Hilary warmly. 'This is Elsa, who needs the makeover, and this is Bron, a *wonderful* hairdresser – did the hair for Ashlyn's wedding and turned little Elsa into Audrey Hepburn. Don't you just love that fringe?'

'Absolutely! You've got lovely big eyes, Elsa – or is that just because you're terrified?'

Elsa laughed, partly because Hilary was spot on in her diagnosis and partly because it seemed polite. Elsa was nothing if not polite.

'Well, come in, everyone. Through here. Anyone got anything they want to take off? No? It's a lovely day, isn't it?'

Hilary ushered them into a large room full of sunlight. There was a row of mirrors down one end and a huge rack full of clothes. There was also, to Elsa's eyes, enough jewellery to supply a medium-sized market stall. Further along was a counter and shelving where different kinds of hats were displayed. It would be good to have some idea of what suited you before you took yourself off to a hat shop, thought Elsa to take her mind off what was to come. They were very expensive items on the whole.

'So, is Elsa going to be a season?' asked Bron. 'I'd say she was an Autumn, myself.'

Hilary shook her head. 'We don't do it like that any

more – too restrictive – and another golden rule, never second-guess! But I can see exactly why you said that.'

Hilary was one of those people able to make people feel at their ease, even when contradicting everything they'd just said. They must send them on courses to learn the technique, thought Elsa, still a little resentful.

'Now.' She swept Elsa further into the room, making a quick dash for the exit impossible. Then, like a magician with a flock of doves, she produced a flurry of white gowns from a cupboard. 'Anyone who's going to comment on Elsa's colours must wear one of these in case the colour they're wearing confuses the issue.'

'Oh, absolutely!' said Vanessa, grabbing a gown. 'This is such fun! I almost want to have my colours done all over again!'

A moment later Elsa felt she was surrounded by dental patients. She felt exactly like one herself as she sat in the chair. She only just stopped herself asking for a strong anaesthetic.

'Now dear, have you got any make-up on? Good, saves me having to take it off,' said Hilary.

'I can't wait to see you in some colour, darling,' said Vanessa. 'Black is quite wrong for you, don't you agree, Hilary?'

'Possibly, but first we've got to discuss what the right colours do for you.' Hilary paused, making sure everyone was paying attention. 'When you look at an attractive, well-put-together woman, you don't think, Wow, look at that jacket—'

'Don't you?' asked Bron. 'I quite often think that.' She glanced at Vanessa. Embarrassingly, Vanessa noticed.

'Oh God, don't tell me I've got this wrong!' She tugged at what she was wearing under her gown. 'I *love* this jacket! I was absolutely sure it was fine for me.'

Hilary started to laugh. 'It *is* fine, Vanessa. Really. It's perfect for you.' She turned to Bron and Elsa. 'Vanessa is a wonderful client. She really took it seriously. She's the only woman I know who actually threw out everything in her wardrobe that wasn't on the colour swatch.'

'Wow,' said Bron, out loud this time, but very quietly.

'I didn't throw it away, I gave it to a charity shop,' said Vanessa.

'And she keeps her swatches in her bag when she's buying anything new,' Hilary said triumphantly.

'Well, there's no point in paying for the specialist help and not following the advice, is there? Now, can we get on with Elsa?' Despite her outgoing personality, Vanessa obviously didn't really like being held up as a shining example.

'OK.' Hilary got everyone's attention again. 'What I was trying to say was that we should see the woman before the individual items of clothing, so we say, "she's attractive – oh, what a nice jacket," not, "what a fabulous jacket," without noticing the woman wearing it.'

'I think I follow you,' said Elsa, 'but I'd prefer not to be noticed at all. Are there colours I could wear so I'd just fade into the background?'

'Certainly not!' said Vanessa. 'And if there are, you're not allowed to wear them. Why should an attractive girl like you want to disappear?'

'Well . . .' Elsa began, knowing she didn't really have an answer.

Seeing her discomfort, Hilary moved on. 'Vanessa can wear that very strong colour because it's geranium, not pillar-box red.' She made a face. 'I expect you think I'm mad making those small distinctions.'

'No,' said Elsa, her attention finally caught. 'I know exactly what you mean. I deal with that sort of difference all the time.' She sat up in her chair, suddenly a great deal more engaged in the whole process.

'I know what you mean too,' said Bron. 'When you're getting the right hair colour, just a shade one way or the other can be fatal! It can be twenty years on or off!' She paused. 'Sasha is rubbish at it.'

Hilary glanced at her. 'OK, Elsa, now wait there while we try a few things.'

'When we've got your colours sorted,' said Vanessa, 'we're going to talk about style. It's a crying shame that someone who makes such lovely garments wears tatty black trousers all the time.'

'But these are my best trousers!' protested Elsa.

'Why don't you go and pick out some nice jewellery,' said Hilary to Vanessa, who obediently took herself off to the other side of the room.

'Gold and silver. Everyone can wear either, you know.' Hilary turned to Elsa. 'But you have to understand what they do for you. Then, if you're good, you can try on the hats. And there are some wigs in the second drawer down.'

'Can I stay if I promise not to say anything?' asked Bron softly.

Elsa nodded. 'As long as you tell me what on earth happened at the salon when you went in this morning.'

'But not now,' said Hilary firmly. 'We're here to work.' She picked up a swatch of fabric and laid it on Elsa's shoulder. 'What do you think?'

Elsa looked at it. 'I like that.' She did.

'Good, so do I,' said Hilary. 'What about this?'

Colour after colour was laid on Elsa's shoulder. Then the colours were layered, one on top of each other. Some combinations looked terrible, others brought Elsa's face to life. She was paying attention – and to her horror and surprise she was having fun. She realised that she didn't need to fight it any more. Perhaps there was more to this colours lark than she'd thought.

'Do put some make-up on her,' said Vanessa, who arrived at Elsa's side garlanded with necklaces, belts and chains. 'I'm just dying to see those eyes look even bigger. She's a potential mankiller, you know,' she said to Bron.

'Laurence, the best man at the wedding, is mad for her.'

Elsa laughed. 'No he's not! He just wants someone to go to a ball with him.'

'Same thing, darling, trust me, I know.' Vanessa held an earring up to her ear. 'Too much of a chandelier? I love big earrings.'

'But I've only ever seen you in close-fitting ones,' said Elsa, forgetting to be shy.

Vanessa shrugged. 'I know. I do have to restrain myself a bit. But these are heaven!'

'Go away and play, Vanessa,' said Hilary, 'I haven't finished with Elsa yet. So, Elsa, what sort of make-up do you usually wear?'

'Um, not much. The usual. Bit of mascara, lip-gloss. I have got some eye-shadow somewhere.'

'Colour?'

'Brown.'

Hilary shook her head. 'Do you want to look as if you've been in a fight or haven't slept for three days? No, don't answer, you're not allowed to say yes.' She looked enquiringly at Elsa. 'But at least you didn't say you match your eye-shadow to what you're wearing.'

'If brown makes her look rough, what would black do?' said Bron, teasingly.

Hilary ignored this. 'Can I do your make-up?'

'Do say yes,' said Bron. 'This is so interesting.'

Elsa sighed. 'Might as well, I suppose.' She remembered how Bron had made her look at the wedding; she wouldn't let Hilary do anything too outlandish.

Twenty minutes later the white gown was whisked away and Elsa was revealed. 'Oh my God, I never knew I could look like that! It's amazing!' She suddenly felt that with her new haircut, beautifully made-up and dressed in one of her creations she might just possibly be ready to go to the ball.

'I've made a note of everything I used—' Hilary began.

'We'll have one of everything,' said Vanessa, currently wearing a long platinum wig and a Stetson-style hat. 'I don't trust Elsa to buy it for herself. I may have to take her shopping one day soon.'

'Or I could,' said Bron. 'Please don't be offended but I probably know shops more suited to Elsa's budget.' Nobly, Bron was leaping in to prevent Elsa being dragged off to Harrods where either she would only be able to buy a pair of knickers, or Vanessa would insist on paying. She knew Elsa would absolutely hate that.

'Much better idea,' said Vanessa. 'I always come away with the wrong size when I go to Primark.'

If Vanessa was pleased with the effect this revelation had on her audience, she didn't allow it to show.

Chapter Twenty

Sarah had picked up the phone without thinking. It was eleven o'clock on Monday morning and she'd been on the go since seven-thirty. One minute after nine she'd hit the phones. With luck, this was someone coming back with some positive news.

Hugo's drawl startled her so much she nearly dropped the phone. Coincidentally, she'd caught sight of his name as she went through her address book for possible kitchens for Bron to make Carrie's cake in and hadn't been able to stop thinking about him.

'I want you to come out with me for a day,' he said, unaware that Sarah had broken into a light sweat of panic. 'To look at a venue,' he added.

Sarah cleared her throat. 'For Carrie?'

'Uh huh. The one I mentioned before. It could be perfect.'

Back under control now, Sarah was brisk. 'Has it got the clipped yews, the manicured grass, the ancient grave-stones – preferably with lichen – and the lych-gate?' Sarah knew the answer would be no, or even if it were yes, the venue wouldn't be available on the day.

He laughed. 'No. It's a private house, with a chapel. It doesn't tick all those boxes but it's really original and I think Carrie will love it. Even if she doesn't, I still think you should have a look.'

Sarah was about to refuse – her sense of self-preservation on full alert – but a private chapel might be the very thing. It wouldn't be the same as a traditional country church, but it could be just as appealing.

'You must see it, Sarah,' said Hugo, suddenly a great deal less drawly. 'Even if it's not right for Carrie you need to meet the people. They're not at all sure about the whole wedding thing but if they met you, you could reassure them and probably use them in the future. It would be a really exclusive location for your top clients.'

Sarah felt she couldn't miss this opportunity and accepted, albeit a little reluctantly. 'When were you thinking of going?'

'In about half an hour. Come on, you need to get out of the office sometimes.'

Sarah was desperately torn. The thought of driving out into the country with Hugo was tempting if unsettling. She suddenly longed to get out. Her ear was scarlet from being pressed to the phone and she was tired of being polite to people. If she went with Hugo she could be rude if she felt like it – he wouldn't mind, he was used to it. She would just have to hope he wasn't too nice to her. That would be much more difficult.

On the other hand she had so much to do. She'd actually wondered earlier if she needed an assistant, if only to keep control of the paper that so covered her desk she had no space for her coffee mug.

'No one's indispensable,' Hugo went on. 'It's vanity to suppose otherwise.' While Sarah was working this out he went on, 'Pick you up at half eleven, then. It'll just give us time to get there for lunch.'

Sarah gave in. 'OK.' She put the phone down and realised she probably should have sounded more enthusiastic. She was enthusiastic, sort of, but guilt was having its effect – she should really have continued to work. But supposing this was the perfect venue? She couldn't not check it out – that would be completely unprofessional.

She stood in front of her wardrobe, scanning it as if for something more than just a clean pair of trousers and a top that didn't need ironing. The trouble was, most of her clothes were smart little suits or tracksuit bottoms so worn they would hardly stay up. There was very little casual-but-respectable in between. A suit didn't morph into casual wear once it was a bit tatty, it just remained a tatty suit.

Like every other woman she knew, she did have the ubiquitous black trousers – if only she could find something to put with them she'd be fine. The jacket from one of her more frivolous jacket-and-skirt combinations – in tan rather than black or navy – would go OK with the trousers. Now it just needed a little top for underneath. She rummaged in her underwear drawer and found a black vest. If she added some exciting jewellery it would look OK. She didn't want to look as if she'd made much effort, after all, even if it was a semi-official trip. She would prefer it if Hugo just thought she'd been wearing that when he rang.

There was a snakes' nest of beads in a drawer and she disentangled a few. Unable to decide she put on a selection, mixing coral with some fake jet and a couple of strings of seed pearls.

Now make-up. As this went on more or less auto-matically she had time to examine her soul on the subject of Hugo Marsters. Despite being absolutely sure she should avoid getting too close to him, and that he could only ever be a friend at most, why did she feel fluttery when she spoke to him? And why did counteracting this make her abrasive and churlish instead of just calm? Why couldn't she behave like everyone else?

In an effort to stop looking like a wedding planner on a recce she tousled her hair a bit and wore a redder lipstick than usual. Then she wiped it off and replaced it with lip-gloss. She was still changing her mind and her make-up in rapid succession when she heard a car hoot. Typical Hugo – expecting her to rush out the moment he summoned her.

But she absolved him of any rudeness when she met him

on the doorstep. He had planned to ring the doorbell.

'Hello, you,' he said, kissing her cheek in a practised manner. 'You look a bit flushed. Are you OK?'

The flush was the result of her scrubbing off the bronzer which had made her look like she'd spent a misspent youth in a tanning salon but she wasn't going to tell Hugo this. 'I'm fine!'

'Just checking. Now hop in.'

He opened the car door for her in a way that counteracted his casual demand. He really was a bit of an enigma, she decided as she did up her seatbelt.

'Right, we're off to the country,' he said, and started the car.

'I hope it's not too far out for Carrie,' said Sarah.

'I thought anywhere in the country was fine as long as it was typically English.'

'In theory, yes, but as my darling sister is getting married the same day, I have to find somewhere reasonably near to where she's arranged to be.'

'Which is?'

She told him. 'And she's getting married early, so if I can persuade Carrie to have a later time, to segue into cocktails, possibly, I'll be able to manage both events.'

'Sounds as if it'll be a bit tight to me. And cocktails isn't exactly typically English, is it?'

'Royalty has done it,' said Sarah, meaning to sound firm but with desperation edging into her voice.

'Well, you should see this venue anyway. It could be fabulous but, to be honest, it's in need of a bit of titivation. If you booked it for Carrie, you can have input into that.'

'How come?'

'It belongs to some old friends of mine. As I said, it's where I had in mind but needed to check they'd actually moved in. It's a wonderful old building that's going to cost them millions to restore. They need it to earn them money

ASAP. If you could tell them how it could be more user-friendly, they'd be grateful, and you could have a really fabulous venue you can use at any time, more or less.'

'Hm. I suppose you're right. It's just . . .'

'It's not that far away.' He drove in silence for a bit. 'No chance your sister would change her day – or even her venue?'

'She's not getting married in a venue – it's her parents-in-law's church.'

'Oh.'

'And she can't change the date because she's booked it already.'

There was a moment's silence. 'Double oh.'

Sarah found herself laughing.

'Now, lunch,' Hugo went on smoothly. 'Would you like to have it in a pub first, or shall I ring Fen and ask her to give us bread and cheese?'

'Definitely a pub. You can't just ring people up and demand lunch, even if it's bread and cheese. They might not have enough of either!'

'Good point. We don't want to be squabbling over a stale crust and a heel of mousetrap.'

'We don't want to be taking the food from their mouths!' Sarah could imagine the horror of being told that two – well, one really – completely strange people were turning up for lunch with no time to shop or prepare, but smiled at his rejoinder anyway.

'I don't think it would cause a major panic, they're very laid-back. Besides, I warned them we might turn up for lunch, but I do know a nice little gastropub that's very near them.'

'You would,' said Sarah, almost indignant. He would have a sort of internal map with nice little eateries, boutique hotels and places for tea dotted all over it. She'd heard the odd rumour and it was a symptom of his raffish lifestyle. Restaurants with rooms would be his speciality.

But then she chided herself: why must she always challenge him? He was being perfectly nice to her.

'Be grateful,' said Hugo. 'Everyone needs to be fed and watered, although in your case I think you need a large Pimm's or a champagne cocktail – something to make you relax.'

'I'm perfectly relaxed!'

'Liar,' he said smoothly.

Sarah exhaled. He was right: she was extremely tense. She did a few deep-breathing exercises, hoping he wouldn't notice. She glanced down at her chest to see if what she was doing was obvious and realised she was showing a lot more cleavage than usual and hitched up her top, hoping her beads had covered the worst of it.

She saw Hugo glance down and knew her action had been spotted. She looked out of the window, determined not to say anything until Hugo did. She was his guest, it was up to him to make her feel comfortable. Then the voice of her mother, long dead, came to her. As his guest, it was up to her to enjoy herself.

'It's a lovely day,' she squeaked.

Hugo laughed and Sarah wished he hadn't. It was a very sexy laugh, and she didn't need any added complications. It was proving harder to resist his charms each time she saw him, and that seemed to be much more than usual these days. 'Shall I put the radio on?' he suggested. 'It would save us having to make conversation.'

'What a good idea,' she said, trying not to sound too relieved.

The pub was in a charming place that couldn't decide if it was a large village or a small town. Either way it was idyllic, with lots of buildings with either black beams against whitewashed walls, or silver-brown beams against ancient brick. Sarah's optimism awakened. If Hugo's friends had 'the big house' near here, it was likely to be wonderful, however dilapidated.

Hugo parked his car round the back of the pub. 'Inside or out?' he asked Sarah as he locked the doors.

Sarah looked at the pub, low, beamed, surrounded by climbing roses, and made a snap decision. 'Inside, please.'

Inside it would be dark; if she blushed he might not notice. Outside it would be a dreamy summer day; she might not be able to concentrate on being a businesslike wedding planner. Besides, she'd forgotten her sunglasses and she'd have to spend a lot of time with her eyes screwed up or shut – neither conducive to efficiency.

She followed Hugo into a building that seemed pitch dark after the brightness of the day. The flagged floor was uneven and ancient, beams threatened Hugo's head, and there seemed to be dozens of little rooms. She stood behind him at the bar.

'Hi, Hugo, mate!' said the barman, who was young and Australian. 'Got your table. It's through in the snug.'

As Sarah followed him again she realised he must have booked the table before she'd decided what she wanted to do. Had he successfully second-guessed her? Or was he just thoughtfully making sure he could accommodate her decision? There was definitely a lot more to Hugo than she'd ever suspected.

'So, Pimm's or champagne cocktail? They do both very well.'

'Don't I get the chance of half a lager or cider? Or even a glass of wine?'

'Nope. Make up your mind.'

Sarah, who had heard herself described as bossy, found being bossed strangely relaxing. No wonder people didn't mind when she told them what to do – it saved so much energy not having to make decisions. 'Champagne cocktail then.'

While he was getting drinks Sarah checked out the other customers. They were predominately middle-class,

County, and wealthy. By the bar, however, there was a phalanx of locals, in shirtsleeves, worn corduroys or denim jeans and the occasional flat cap. Perhaps they were paid by the management to make the place look like a proper pub. Then she sighed in self-reproach. Why was she making snippy mental comments about the place? She knew it was because Hugo was well known here and she had made a lot of snippy comments to herself about him over the couple of years she'd known him. A moment of reflection made her wonder if it was because she had been secretly drawn to him even before the kiss and it was in self-defence, but she dismissed the idea rapidly. She really couldn't afford to go there.

He came back with a tray with two glasses on it and two menus tucked under his arm. One of the glasses was a traditional conical champagne glass, of the kind popular before flutes became the fashion. The other was a pint glass filled with a cloudy grey liquid.

'What's that?' asked Sarah, pointing to it, hoping she sounded brightly curious, not suspicious.

'Ginger beer. It's very fiery – perfect if you need a drink but don't want to drink alcohol.'

'Why do you need a drink?' Sarah was genuinely curious now.

'Because you're a very daunting woman to be with unless you're very tired, and possibly a little drunk.'

Sarah put down the glass she had been about to sip from. 'What? Me?'

'Oh yes,' Hugo confirmed. 'On occasion, frankly terrifying.'

Sarah giggled. 'I don't believe you.'

Hugo raised his glass in a toast to her. 'Well, not completely terrifying. Anyway, here's to Somerby being the perfect venue, and here's to you: the best wedding planner in the world . . .' He stared into her eyes and Sarah's stomach lurched.

Feeling totally addled by a mixture of lust and terror, she raised her glass. 'To me,' she murmured and took a sip. Sarah was confused. She wasn't sure if she could resist Hugo for much longer and was starting to wonder whether it really would be such a bad idea to get involved with him. Aside from the fact that she was obviously attracted to him, he was easygoing, fun to be around, he seemed to respect her and despite the odd rumour she didn't really believe he was anything like her ex. But she'd made it perfectly clear she didn't want to go out with him. Part of her still felt this was the right decision, but the other half hoped he might ask her again. This time she might even say yes. Not that she'd ever dream of actually hinting as much to him. No, if it happened, it happened.

'It's delicious,' she said as she set her glass down.

'They do make them well here, as I said. Now, what about food?' He handed Sarah a menu. 'I can recommend the scallops. And considering we're so far inland, the fish is surprisingly good.'

As Sarah looked down the list she wished she was in an era when she could just hand the menu to her escort and ask him to order for her. 'The scallops do look nice,' she said. 'I'll have them.'

'So will I. And shall we share a salad?'

When they'd dealt with the food order and Hugo had sat back down again Sarah said, 'So, tell me about your friends' house.'

'You'll see it for yourself soon. Another cocktail?'

Sarah shook her head and found that it went on swinging internally, even after she'd stopped moving. 'Well, actually, a very large glass of water would be good.' A strong cocktail on an empty stomach hadn't been a very good idea, but being with Hugo somehow made her feel more decadent.

They chatted easily over lunch and Hugo even managed

to persuade her to have syrup sponge and custard, with cream.

As they drove up to the house, Sarah admired the long drive (albeit in need of repair) that passed through parkland currently being grazed by small black cows. It was a proper country estate. She sat up a little straighter.

'They're Dexters,' said Hugo, 'but don't ask me any more questions because I don't know the answers. They're smaller than ordinary cattle but that sums up my knowledge of them.'

'I wasn't going to grill you on animal husbandry,' said Sarah, wonderfully relaxed after their lunch. Lily and Hugo were right, she did need to relax more often.

The house was enormous and beautiful and, as Hugo had said, dilapidated. Sarah instantly understood a couple falling in love with it. 'It looks like a project for one of those television programmes when the really impossible looking gets completed in twice the time allowed but with far less money than you'd think.'

Hugo laughed. 'They did get in touch with the television channel but it wasn't enough of a project for them.' He parked the car and, before he'd pulled on the handbrake, the front door opened and a young woman came out.

'Hugo! Hi!' She was wearing jodhpurs, ancient muddy trainers and a polo shirt with a rip in the sleeve, all of which just seemed to enhance her model figure. Sarah wondered if she'd be quite so insouciant if she hadn't been so blatantly aristocratic. She flung her arms round Hugo's neck and kissed him. Then she smiled at Sarah – she might be posh but she was also friendly.

'This is Sarah. Sarah, Fenella, although she prefers Fen. Fen, Sarah had a champagne cocktail for lunch so she's not quite the brisk professional she is usually. Though even with the edge taken off, she's quite something!'

'Thank you for sharing that with people I've never met

before!' Sarah gave him a look. Although she knew he was teasing, these were potential clients of sorts.

'Oh, don't worry about him,' said Fenella, taking Sarah by the shoulder and leading her into the house. 'He always says outrageous things. It's his way of getting attention. Now come in. Oops, mind the dogs.'

A raggle-taggle selection of dogs came towards them in a wave. There were a couple of bigger ones, which Sarah thought were pointers, and a collection of small ones, who looked unnervingly like copies of the big ones that had accidentally got into the washing machine and been shrunk. They sniffed around Sarah and Hugo but didn't say much.

'Come on,' said Fenella, having herded the pack round the corner of the house to some unseen destination.

They entered an echoing, empty hall big enough for a small ballet troupe to practise in.

'Come through to the kitchen where it's a bit more cosy and I'll make some coffee. Rupert's somewhere about. The trouble is, the house is so bloody enormous we keep losing each other.'

Fenella led Sarah and Hugo through various other rooms and corridors to the back of the house and into a huge, sunny kitchen.

'This is the only room we've got enough furniture for,' said Fenella, 'and even then it's only because we put everything we've got into it.'

'That's not necessarily a bad thing,' said Hugo. 'If you want to rent the house out for photographic shoots, the emptier the better. Although you'll need a few bits and pieces as props and things.'

'I think we've got plenty of those. Ah, here's Rupes.'

A tall man appeared from a door in the corner that Sarah hadn't even noticed. His clothes were as scruffy as his wife's and his welcome just as warm. 'Hi there! I'm Rupert. Welcome to the House of Usher.'

'It's not at all like the House of Usher,' complained Fenella, measuring coffee beans into a grinder.

'It is about to fall down though,' said Rupert, gloomily. 'Or nearly. We've got someone coming to look at one of the valley gutters. I'm dreading him telling me the whole lot needs to be redone. That'll be a few hundred grand, I reckon.'

'It's only over that little wing, right at the end, one of the outbuildings,' said Fenella. 'I don't know why you're making such a big deal out of it. We don't have to renovate that bit yet.' They'd obviously had this conversation before.

'Well, in my opinion you can definitely make money out of it,' said Hugo, 'even in the state it's in. You've got some lovely rooms and as I remember the floors are in quite good nick.'

'Most are, yes, but the dining-room floor is rotten as a pear.'

'Not necessarily a bad thing,' said Hugo. 'You could just put down some plywood sheets and paint them white. White floors are good for photographs.'

'When we've had coffee I'll give you a tour,' said Fenella.

'That would be wonderful.' Sarah began to relax. Rupert and Fenella were nice and their house was lovely. It would be good to bring business their way if she possibly could.

Fenella produced a tin of biscuits but Sarah refused one.

'Not on a diet or anything boring, are you?' asked Fenella.

'Oh no, but Hugo made me eat syrup sponge and custard after an already huge lunch.'

'With cream,' added Hugo.

Everyone laughed and the others began to chat about various friends and acquaintances while Sarah itched for the tour she'd been promised.

'So what are your plans for the house?' asked Sarah, as

soon as there was a break in the chat about what old So-and-so was up to now.

'Mainly to keep it from falling down,' said Rupert. 'Any suggestions that will help us do that will be gratefully received.'

'It would be a perfect venue for weddings,' said Sarah. 'Is it licensed?'

Fenella and Rupert looked at each other. 'We've applied. We haven't had an answer yet. We're quite hopeful.'

'It would be a really beautiful setting. You could charge a huge amount of money per wedding.'

Now her hosts were looking at Sarah. 'How much, do you think?'

'Obviously it would depend on what you could offer, how many rooms could be used. If the wedding party could all stay over and party on until the night, it could be several thousand.'

'What, per wedding?' Fenella seemed doubtful.

Sarah nodded. 'You may not be quite ready to offer the total package just at the moment, but it would be something to aim for.'

'And if you also offered it for magazine shoots, with accommodation, that's another nice little earner,' said Hugo.

'Have you got the most enormous mortgage?' asked Sarah. 'Sorry! That was terribly rude. It's nothing to do with me.'

Rupert dismissed her apology. 'We were frightfully lucky. I inherited it, but there wasn't a bean to go with it, so keeping it standing—'

'Getting it standing, more like,' put in Fenella.

'Is a major headache. It's too far from London for me to be able to commute, and if I had to stay in London that would cost even more money.'

'And I don't want to be here on my own,' went on Fenella, 'especially in the state it's in.'

'I completely understand,' said Sarah. 'It's too big a house to be alone in.'

'We're renting out the land,' said Rupert, 'but that doesn't earn all that much.'

'I do some bits and pieces locally,' said Fenella. 'But I can't earn anything like enough.'

'Don't worry,' said Hugo. 'Between us, Sarah and I will make the house earn its own living. Won't we?'

'We'll certainly do our best,' agreed Sarah.

'Well, that's really kind,' said Rupert.

There was a contented pause. Sarah felt warm and happy at the thought of helping this nice couple and their wonderful house. Hugo smiled across at her as he cradled his coffee mug. They really did make a good team.

'Oh, Hugo,' said Rupert suddenly. 'I meant to ask earlier – what's this I hear about you and Electra getting engaged?'

Chapter Twenty-One

Sarah felt the breath leave her body and her strength drain out of her. It was as well she was sitting down, she thought as she concentrated on looking normal. She hadn't realised, until that moment, quite how much her feelings for Hugo had changed that day. From feeling edgy and unsure about him she had come to see that not only was she more than passingly attracted to him, but she liked and trusted him. It was an emotion she hadn't felt in years. And now this.

'Er – well,' said Hugo, clearly rather thrown.

Sarah was aware that he was looking at her but kept her eyes on a small puddle of coffee that had been left by someone's teaspoon. When she thought of what happened after Ashlyn's wedding, even if it was only kissing, it made her feel sick. If he was engaged he must have been in a committed relationship when he not only kissed her but asked her out. Was he hedging his bets? She couldn't believe how she'd let herself be taken in. At least she could congratulate herself on not agreeing to go out with him and certainly not actively encouraging him to ask again.

'I heard she was mad to marry you,' said Rupert teasingly.

'I think Sarah would say she would indeed be mad to marry me,' Hugo agreed amicably.

It took Sarah every ounce of determination to meet his eyes. She had to compose herself. She'd had a shock, that was all. She'd allowed herself to hope, but the others need never know what was going on inside her at that moment. 'Oh yes. I'd definitely say that.'

For a moment they looked directly at each other. Sarah thought she might have seen a hint of apology in Hugo's expression – an attempt at an explanation – but it didn't make her feel one iota better. What sort of woman did he think she was? Another conquest?

'Sarah's very cynical for a wedding planner,' went on Hugo. Maybe she'd imagined that look. He didn't sound at all contrite.

Feeling she was being mocked was the jolt she needed. She wouldn't let this affect her. She was strong, capable and above all a consummate professional. And it was his life – what did she really care? she told herself firmly. 'Not too cynical – just cynical enough.'

Fenella laughed, apparently unaware of the shock Sarah had received in the past two minutes. 'You're so sensible. My parents complain that people don't stick at marriage these days and give up at the first sign of trouble. But why should you stick together for ever if you're not happy? Luckily Rupes and I are two of a kind. We fit.' She smiled fondly at her husband.

'You're very lucky,' said Sarah, 'but on the whole I think it's better not to get married in the first place. But please don't tell anyone. It would be very bad for business.' Everyone laughed. 'Could I have my tour now?'

Chairs scraped on the stone-flagged floor as everyone got up and Sarah wondered if Electra (what a name!) was the girl she'd seen Hugo with in London. Despite all her lectures to herself, how had she let her guard down enough to think he might genuinely like her? How could she have been such a fool? Still, they had to work together and her professionalism would get her through.

'So,' said Fenella. 'Shall I do the tour guide bit? Or shall you?' she said to her husband.

'Let's all go,' said Hugo. 'I want to see it too and Fen

might not be able to answer all my technical questions.'

'You are unbearably sexist, Hugo,' complained Fenella good-naturedly.

Hugo gave his friend a lazy smile that would have made any girl's stomach clench, Sarah acknowledged – but not hers, not now. She was never going to be so silly as to even think about him again. Thank goodness she hadn't let her guard down too much before! She felt she'd had a narrow escape. If you can kiss a girl like he'd kissed her when you're engaged to someone else, you are a low-down, dirty, rotten scoundrel and not to be trusted. However charming you were.

'Do you mind hanging on while I get my camera?' he asked. 'Some pictures could be really useful.'

'For the "before", do you mean?' asked Rupert.

He smiled. 'I thought Sarah could use them. She has a top celebrity client who might be interested in using Somerby as a venue.'

Hugo went and Fenella said to Sarah, 'So who's your client? Or can't you say?'

'I can't say, I'm afraid, but I'd love it if she chose to come here. Is the house very dilapidated? Oh, sorry, was that rude?'

'Rude but understandable. Come on,' said Fenella, 'I'll show you. In fact it's not too bad structurally, as far as you can tell. The roof is mostly sound and it's not too dreadfully damp. There's woodworm but no dry rot that we've discovered. We did have a jolly thorough survey before we moved in.' She made a face. 'My parents insisted. They wanted us to sell it and buy somewhere sensible. We're getting a roof expert in tomorrow for the bit that Rupert's worried about. That did fail the test. Rupert, can you and Hugo find us when he comes back?'

The two women left the huge kitchen and went through the green baize door to the hallway. Sarah stopped and noticed that the ceiling was dark with centuries of grime but the floor was parquet and in good order. Sarah couldn't decide just then if she thought it would benefit from several coats of paint, or was more picturesque as it was.

The drawing room was beautiful, made so by its semi-circular ceiling-to-floor windows through which summer sunshine now streamed. It too had a parquet floor that needed, according to Sarah's unskilled eye, nothing more than a good polish. The walls had the tattered remains of wallpaper that was more like a mural than paper, although a repeating pattern could be detected. Birds of paradise flitted between trailing vines and classical columns. Distant vistas included pyramids and rolling hills.

'What fantastic wallpaper,' said Sarah.

'Isn't it? We're hoping to get a paper restorer to tell us about it. If we were millionaires we'd get it reproduced and put it back,' said Fenella.

'Even as it is, it's heavenly,' said Sarah. 'In fact I'm not sure that it would be as good if there weren't great bits missing. It might be too much.'

'We had exactly the same thought, but there's probably a middle way.' Fenella paused. 'Do you really think you might persuade your client to come here? I mean, let's face it, although we've started work, it's still in relatively bad decorative order, as an estate agent would say. I'd call it shabby.'

Sarah was outraged by this description. 'No, not shabby! Shabby-chic if you must, decaying grandeur, fading aristocracy, any of those things – but not just shabby!'

Fenella laughed. 'OK. But will you be able to sell it to her?'

'I'm not sure, to be honest. She was so set on the traditional English country church thing and I'd need to see the rest of it. And of course what it really depends on is if you can get your licence in time.'

'Oh, here are the boys,' said Fenella as voices could be heard echoing through the empty house. 'Have you met Electra, Sarah?'

'No.'

'You'd like her. She's fun.'

Sarah managed some sort of smile as if the prospect of meeting Electra was, while not at the top of the list of most-wanted events, at least not at the bottom. In fact, it languished a few places behind Godzilla in a temper. 'It's a beautiful house,' Sarah said to Rupert as the men joined them. 'I can't wait to see the rest of it.'

'The library's through here,' said Fen. 'This is the one without a decent floor.' She opened double doors into a room as enormous as the drawing room.

'Just put something down to cover it and paint it white,' said Hugo, raising his camera.

At least while he was taking a fusillade of shots from every conceivable angle, she didn't have to talk to Hugo, and nor could Rupert and Fenella. It helped. She didn't want the subject of Electra coming up just now. By the time they left, Sarah was convinced she'd feel absolutely fine about Hugo having a fiancée – why she'd allowed him to inhabit the emotional part of her brain even for a nanosecond was beyond her. But she'd have all that soppy stuff well under control any minute now.

'Let's have a look at what's through here,' she said firmly and walked as if she was thinking only of her client, the venue and the floor.

'The pièce de résistance is this,' said Rupert, ushering them through the door of a panelled study.

'Ah, the chapel,' said Hugo. 'Amazing!'

'It's actually quite a recent addition to the house,' said Fenella. 'One of Rupe's ancestors made a fortune doing something dubious like slave-trading – exploiting some-one, anyway – and absolved his sins by building this. It's not to my taste, actually.'

A high, vaulted ceiling, a marble floor and three stained-glass windows at the end made it look, to Sarah's eyes, more like a small church than somewhere for a mere family to worship. In fact, she'd arranged weddings in churches that felt far smaller.

'It's an almost perfect example of the High Church revival,' said Rupert. 'Not exactly a copy of much earlier churches but it reflects the best medieval precedents and shows a return to sacramental tradition.'

'You sound very knowledgeable,' said Hugo. 'Been boning up on it all, have you?'

'Of course.' Rupert laughed a little defiantly. 'I'm almost an expert now.'

'Don't encourage him, Hugo,' said Fenella. 'He'll bang on for hours if you let him.'

'What I need to know,' said Sarah, on tenterhooks for the answer, 'is could you actually use it for weddings? Getting a licence for the house is one thing, but if you could have the ceremonies here, it would be even more wonderful.'

Fenella and Rupert exchanged glances. 'That's what we're hoping for,' said Fenella. 'Like you, we thought using the house for weddings would be nice, but if people could actually get married in the chapel, well, that would be brilliant.'

'The aunts, who I inherited from, were always thinking up money-making schemes and I know they talked abut weddings, but I'm not sure if they got as far as getting it licensed.'

'We haven't followed up seeing about getting the chapel licensed because we thought the house was in far too bad order for us to use it,' explained Fenella. 'We didn't know what we wanted to do anyway. It's only quite recently that we decided the house needs to earn money and not just us.'

'Would it still be consecrated?' asked Hugo. 'Presumably if it is, you could still have weddings here.'

Fenella shook her head. 'Don't know that either. Sorry to seem so stupid. We haven't been moved in all that long.'

'I know,' said Hugo. 'I was at your house moving party when you left the old place.'

Sarah felt that at any moment she might be exposed to distressing details of what Hugo got up to at that party, whom he met, or went home with, and how much fun Electra was. She wanted to get back on track. 'So do you have to go through the house to get into it? I'm just wondering—'

'No!' Rupert interrupted her gleefully. 'The beauty part' – he strode across the aisle to the other side – 'is that it has access to the outside world. It was so the local people could use it too. At the time there was something happening that meant the local church was out of action, and so the ancestor who was building this had the side door put in.'

'This could be so perfect,' said Sarah, almost trembling with excitement and anxiety. Please, she muttered, don't show me this fabulous venue and then let it be unusable. 'I'd be so grateful if you could find out if it's licensed, or still consecrated or whatever. I'm sure I could talk my client into coming here, if it would be legal. It would be just the place.'

'Let's have a look at it from the side door. It's no good trying to persuade her to walk through a ploughed field,' said Hugo.

'We could mow the grass,' said Rupert.

They all went out of the side door. A long path came up a gentle slope from a small wooded area by the road, through parkland to the door of the chapel.

'If she really wants all the extras,' said Hugo, 'I've got a mate who does film sets. He'd turn this into a graveyard as traditional as you liked.'

'I'd try to convince Carrie not to have a fake churchyard,' said Sarah. Too late, she realised she shouldn't have used Carrie's name.

'Oh my God!' said Fenella. 'You're not talking about Carrie Condy, are you? I am a *major* fan of hers.'

'She is a surprisingly good actress for one with her assets,' went on Rupert.

'Mm,' said Hugo, obviously thinking about them too.

Sarah felt herself blush. It was totally unlike her to be so unprofessional – it was bloody Hugo's fault! 'Well, yes, it is her, but please – I beg of you – don't tell anyone! I should never have let her name out like that. I should be sacked!'

'But it's your company,' said Hugo.

'I should think of something else to do for a living!'

'Well, don't beat yourself up about it,' said Fenella, sensing Sarah really was distressed. 'We won't tell anyone. We certainly wouldn't want to jeopardise her coming here. It would be so wonderful!'

'It'll mean a lot of hard work, poppet,' said Rupert to his wife. He turned to Sarah. 'Would she want the whole house? Including bedrooms?'

Sarah nodded, priding herself on being back in full control of her emotions again. 'It would be a hell of a lot of work. She might want to use the bedrooms to get dressed in and stuff, even if she stays in a hotel. But financially, it would be well worthwhile for you to do them up.' She paused. 'I'd get a good deposit for you, so you could do the work.'

'We've got some capital we could use but not really enough. Would the deposit cover all the extra help we'd need to get in?' asked Fenella.

'I'd make sure it would,' said Sarah, determined at that moment to bring her celebrity wedding here whatever it took. It would put Somerby on the venue map as nothing else could.

'So how do you get paid, if that's not a rude question?' asked Rupert.

'I like to negotiate a flat fee if I can,' said Sarah. 'That's what I'm doing with Carrie. Not all wedding planners do it like that, but I prefer it. It gives me an incentive to get good deals so that my clients have saved money by having me. Or at least,' she went on, thinking back to some of the weddings she'd organised, 'not spent hugely more.'

'So we wouldn't have to pay you?' asked Fenella, obviously doubtful.

'No! I'm not saying some of the big hotels don't give me good rates, things like that, but I don't take backhanders. I want to be neutral, so I look for the perfect venue for each client.'

'Very virtuous,' muttered Hugo.

Sarah shot him a black look, but realised she was more angry with herself than him.

'It could all be so perfect!' said Fenella, suddenly all dreamy.

'Yes,' agreed Sarah and then she remembered – her bloody sister's wedding. She turned to Hugo. 'How long would it take to get from Steeple Colby—'

Hugo might have been a complete bastard, but he was quick on the uptake. 'Oh, your sister's wedding?'

She nodded.

'Not sure. An hour, possibly?'

Sarah closed her eyes while she worked things out. How soon could she reasonably leave her sister's wedding, overlooking the fact that she shouldn't leave it at all? What was the minimum time she could spend with Carrie before the event, given that Elsa and Bron would be with her, getting dressed and stuff. When she opened her eyes again she hadn't found an answer to her question. Fen and Rupert were looking concerned. 'Sorry – nothing for you two to worry about. It's just that my sister has chosen to get married the very same day as Carrie Condy.'

'And she can't change—'

Sarah interrupted Fenella's question. 'It's at her fiancé's parents' church, the date is booked and she's pregnant.

They wouldn't be able to get another Saturday for weeks, by which time the baby would be showing.'

'Ah,' said Fenella, obviously understanding the dilemma. 'Do his parents know she's pregnant?'

'I think so, but none of the other relations must know. They'd really prefer for her to be a virgin bride although she's been married before.' Sarah knew she shouldn't be sharing all this intimate information with virtual strangers but it helped to talk about it and Fenella seemed understanding and discreet.

'Well, if you do have Carrie's wedding here, I'll help you as much as I can,' said Fenella. 'After all, a lot of what you do is checking on caterers, things like that, isn't it?'

'Mm,' said Sarah.

'Well, I'm used to doing things like that. And if it's here, I'll want everything to go as smoothly as possible.'

Fenella was very reassuring. It was probably a good thing Sarah had washed a little family linen in public.

'That could be marvellous – I usually arrive at a venue at dawn and leave twenty-four hours later . . .' She made a deprecating gesture. 'Well, sometimes it feels like that. I do have to make sure everything is tidy.'

'It sounds exhausting!' said Fenella sympathetically.

'It is quite full on, but most of the hard work is done beforehand and if you trust your suppliers and it all goes well, it's very satisfying.'

'Well, don't you worry about this end,' said Fenella. 'If Carrie Condy has her wedding here, she won't regret it. I promise.'

Looking at Fenella, Sarah felt confident that she was organised, determined and brave. She hoped she wouldn't need her to be brave to help with Carrie's wedding, but the other two characteristics were essential. 'I'm going to work really hard on getting her to decide on Somerby,' she said. 'And if not Carrie, the very next wedding that might be remotely suitable.'

If effort of will alone could have made Sarah sprout wings and fly home and thus avoid travelling with Hugo, it would have happened. But even more mundane solutions like hiring a car or finding a taxi were too difficult. After all, she didn't want to announce to Fenella, Rupert and Hugo himself that she was so upset with him for not having told her he was engaged that they couldn't share a car. It sounded childish, even to herself.

So when the time came, and she'd hugged both Rupert and Fenella, she got in and accepted her fate.

The moment he'd closed the door of the car, Hugo said, 'Sarah, I want to explain about Electra—'

She flung her hands up in a warding-off gesture, suddenly feeling like her sister Lily. She would have preferred him to wait until she was somewhere that would allow her to leap out of the car on the pretext of calling in on old friends. 'No, no, please don't! Why should you? It's nothing to do with me.'

'The thing is, I feel I should explain—'

'No!' She stopped feeling like Lily and became her own, fierce self again. 'Please don't. It's quite unnecessary.' She laughed, trying to prove that she hadn't been remotely fazed by the announcement. 'Just don't ask me to arrange a wedding on the eighteenth of August! I don't think I could fit in another one on that day.'

Hugo sighed. 'I promise I won't do that.'

'Super.' Sarah was pleased with her apparent insouciance. Maybe if she acted it long enough and hard enough she'd gradually begin to feel it.

'So, keeping my personal life off limits, what did you think of the venue?'

'Fabulous! Really, really good. I just hope it's licensed for weddings.'

'You could get Carrie to get married in a register office a couple of days before and then have a blessing at Somerby. It could look nearly like a proper wedding.'

214

'I had thought of that and it's my back-up solution, but selling the idea to Carrie will be really difficult. It's just not traditional.'

'But it's been done by a lot of celebs lately.'

'I know, but I want to pursue the normal route first. If it's possible, it would be much the best.' She paused, knowing that she should now take time to thank Hugo for taking her to such a beautiful house. She bit her lip. 'Thank you so much for taking me to Somerby. It's really lovely.' There, it was done.

Hugo sighed again. He seemed a lot less cheery than he had been on the outward journey – depressed, almost. 'That's OK, Sarah. I am only too happy to help you. And Fen and Rupert, of course.'

'How did you meet them?' With relief, Sarah steered their conversation off the rocks and into calm water. She could listen to Hugo go on about what Rupert got up to at school until they finally got home.

Chapter Twenty-Two

Bron was just locking the car, having put postcards about her mobile hairdressing service in all the local post offices in the area, and anywhere else who would put one up, when her phone rang. As she burrowed about for it she wondered if leaving the salon had been rash – she could spend more on fuel than she earned driving all over the country to do her work. But how could she have borne to go on working there? She'd be forever picturing her boss in a red nylon thong – not a pretty sight.

She found the phone at last. It was Roger's mother.

'Hello, Pat!' Bron tried to sound upbeat because she could tell that Pat was anything but.

'Bron, I don't know what to say. Are you still speaking to me?'

'Of course! Why shouldn't I be?'

'Because of what that wretched boy has done. And I hear you've had to give up your job, too!'

'Well—'

'Have you found another one?'

'Not yet. I've been quite busy and—'

'Well, that Sasha will have to give you severance pay, all that sort of thing.'

'You don't need to be so upset, Pat. You and I can still be friends. Not sure about Sasha,' she added, under her breath.

Pat was still riddled with guilt-by-association. 'But how, when my son has behaved so appallingly?'

Bron exhaled, quietly she hoped. 'Shall I come round?'

It was Pat's turn to exhale. 'Would you? I hate to ask, in the circumstances, but I've got an important do on tomorrow and I really need my hair doing. Not' – she went on hurriedly – 'that that's the only reason I want to see you. I hope you don't think that.'

Bron laughed. 'I'd love to come and see you and do your hair. We're friends. We must try and keep Roger out of it.'

'Hmph! Sometimes I wish I could keep that boy out of my house! What a way to carry on!'

Bron was glad to be getting out of the house and if Pat paid for her hairdo, and she'd probably insist on it, it would give her a little petty cash to live on. Could she get enough weddings and clients to go properly freelance? she wondered. Or would she have to go further away and find another salon to work in? Carrie's wedding would certainly help.

It was both strange and familiar to park her car in Roger's parents' drive. His father would be at work and had he been home, Bron would have been far more reluctant to visit. She and Pat had always got on well, but Roger's father was another matter. Vince and Bron had never seen eye to eye.

Pat's arms opened to Bron at the same time as she opened the door. 'Lovie! How could he do that? He's such a silly boy!'

Bron returned the hug sincerely. 'We weren't right for each other really. We wouldn't have made each other happy ultimately, or why did he sleep with Sasha?'

'Strumpet!' said Pat and Bron giggled.

'That's a good word!'

'A very satisfying one. I've been practising. Now come on in. I've bought your favourite biscuits; we can get it all off our chests. How long has he been having an affair with your boss?'

This simple question gave her a bit of a shock. 'I've no idea!' The word 'affair' implied it had been going on for some time. Had it, or had it been the first time? Something told her it hadn't. All the lies and deception that must have gone on made her humiliated in retrospect. She shuddered. 'Has she moved in, do you know?'

'I think so.' Pat put her hand on Bron's arm. 'He's bringing her to lunch on Sunday. I insisted. She said she didn't want to come – I heard her in the background – but if you do the dirty on someone, you have to face up to your wrongdoing.'

Bron realised suddenly that Pat was far more upset about this than she was. 'Oh, Pat, let's have coffee and those biscuits. I'm fine about it now. I've got a lovely little cottage to rent – for not too much money – everything's lovely!'

Pat led the way to the kitchen where she clicked the kettle on. 'It's just like you to be brave about it, but he's behaved very badly.'

Pat's expression made Bron think she was about to send him round to her house to say sorry, as if he'd broken a window playing cricket or something.

'Really, don't worry about it. It's fine.' Had Pat not been Roger's mother, Bron would have gone on to say it was a merciful relief not having to live with Roger any more. He was controlling, bad-tempered and not great in bed.

'It's OK, really it is. Now what's this event you're going to? Are you happy with the colour? Or is it just a cut and blow-dry? I could come round early tomorrow if you like.'

'Could you? That would be wonderful! It's this lunch thing with the Golf Club wives.'

Relieved to have got off the subject of Roger, Bron sat down at the kitchen table while Pat made coffee. 'What are "The Golf Club Wives"? It sounds like the title of a sex-and-shopping blockbuster!'

'Not quite as much fun as that, sadly, but pretty daunting. Vince wanted me to get involved with them in case any of the husbands are people he wants to get in with. We none of us play golf but we put on little social events between ourselves.'

There but for the grace of God go I, thought Bron as she nibbled oat and honey biscuits and sipped coffee. She could just imagine it – competitive fundraising with Women Who Lunched.

'The thing is,' went on Pat, 'Mrs Bedlington, the chairperson—'

'You have a chairperson? Golly!' muttered Bron.

'—is quite a dominating woman and I would like to look my best for the occasion.'

'I'll come upstairs and help you choose an outfit if you like. My friend Elsa – you know? The one who made the dresses for that big wedding, who had to be a stand-in bridesmaid? – well, Ashlyn's mother – Ashlyn was the bride, if you remember – well, Ashlyn's mother—'

'I think I'm still following you,' said Pat, 'though it's not easy.'

Bron laughed and went on, 'Well, she made Elsa get her colours done. It was a present for being a last-minute bridesmaid. She made me go too. It was huge fun! There were three of us trying on jewellery. It was just what I needed . . .' Her voice tailed away. Pat already felt quite guilty enough without Bron rubbing it in. She changed the subject a bit. 'Getting people to give up wearing black is always a bit of a problem, apparently.'

Pat seemed totally confused. 'What do you mean, she got her colours done?'

'Oh! Don't you know? It's a firm – well, a franchise, I suppose – called Colour Me Beautiful. They tell you what sort of colours you can wear.'

Pat humphed. 'It sounds a bit like Mrs Bedlington to me.'

'No! It's not bossy, it's liberating! They take all your make-up off, or most of it, and then they hold all sorts of different colours against your skin and you can see which ones work and which don't.' Bron thought for a few seconds. 'Actually, it's not unlike choosing the right colours for people's hair. Some colours make people look like death and others make them glow.' She peered at Pat's hair for a moment. 'I think we could put a semi-permanent on yours, just for a bit of a lift. We haven't got time for foils and all that.'

'Not unless you come at dawn and I'm not sure I fancy having my hair done with Vince snoring in the bedroom.'

Bron laughed. 'Let's go up and sort out what you're wearing and then I'll tell you about my new project. I'm going to make an official wedding cake!'

'Bron, that's marvellous. You always were a grand baker. Are you getting it iced professionally?'

'No!' Bron squeaked her indignation. 'I'm icing it. It's going to be tricky because it's a tree. You know, one of those ones like lollipops that posh restaurants have outside their doors.'

'My goodness, Bron.'

'Trouble is, I don't know where I can make it. It has to be in a properly approved kitchen and also one big enough.'

Pat went quiet for a moment and then suddenly looked very pleased with herself. 'I think I can help you there. The woman I have in mind is away at the moment, but I'll get back to you as soon as I can. She's lovely, I know she'll let you use her kitchen if she can. It's been through all the checks apparently, you know, health and safety.'

'Oh, Pat!' Bron put her arms round her and gave her a hug. 'You're amazing.'

Pat hugged her back. 'Roger doesn't know what he's lost by cheating on you.'

They released each other and Bron gathered up their coffee mugs and put them by the dishwasher. 'I think he did know. He thought he wanted a little woman to be at his beck and call, but in fact what he really wanted was someone more exciting. It's a perfectly valid choice.'

Really, thought Bron, she had been just as bad for him as he had been for her. They had both dragged each other down.

Having helped Pat decide on what to wear for her important lunch with an association she was certain Sarah would condemn as too sexist and retro for words, Bron decided to cook a special meal for James. It was, she realised, a knee-jerk reaction. The way to Roger's heart had been through his stomach and although she didn't want to reach James's heart, he had been kind to her and she wanted to do something nice for him in return.

But what should she cook him? The trouble with cooking for someone you hardly knew was that you had to second-guess their tastes. He'd cooked her an omelette when she'd moved in: he might well be vegetarian. One solution would be to go home tonight and ask him, and then invite him for a meal, but that would make the whole thing seem a bit formal. She would much prefer to just leave a note on his front door saying, 'Don't bother to cook, just come round to mine at about seven.' That way it would be nice and casual. All she wanted to do was to save him the bother of cooking, and perhaps eating something nicer than he might make for himself. Everyone liked to be cooked for once in a while, especially when they lived alone as he appeared to do. She hadn't noticed him staying away at all or a potential girlfriend visiting him. But then she didn't really know that much about him, just that he seemed a kind man who liked to keep pretty much to himself.

Having wandered up and down the high street and stared into the butcher's window for a while, Bron decided she'd just have to ring and ask him.

'James? It's Bron, your new neighbour.'

He chuckled. 'Vague as I can be, I haven't forgotten who you are yet.'

'Oh good. I was just ringing because I wanted to cook you a meal – to say thank you. Tonight OK?'

'That would be excellent.'

'Not sure about that, but I'll do my best.' Bron suddenly found herself a bit more anxious about this than she thought she would have been. 'So, are you vegetarian? We had eggs . . .'

'No.'

'Or vegan?'

He chuckled. 'I think that's pretty much a given. I couldn't be a vegan if I ate meat, now could I?'

'No,' said Bron, feeling silly. 'Any particular hates?'

'Anything except eggs would be great.'

Bron felt herself blush and was pleased he couldn't see her. 'I'd forgotten about the hens. About seven, then?'

Chapter Twenty-Three

⁂

Having decided that she definitely mustn't cook chicken – he wouldn't want to eat his pets' relations – she couldn't think of anything else that wouldn't take hours and hours.

She wandered aimlessly up and down the High Street, searching for inspiration, wishing she hadn't decided to leave her cookery books behind. She'd ask Pat to collect them for her. She didn't want to go back there if she didn't have to. At least there'd be no doubt about them all belonging to her.

Then, somehow, before she knew how it had happened, she found herself outside the salon, staring in the window. She suddenly thought that there was a computer there, she could look up a recipe on the Internet – a tried and tested one that she knew would work.

She was trying to look through the window without being seen when one of her clients spotted her and waved. Before Bron could indicate that she didn't want to be seen, Sasha, obviously more on the ball than she was, spotted her, and shot out of the door, grasping her wrist like the Ancient Mariner, only in fishnet tights.

'Have you decided to come back?' Sasha was wary, testing the water in case Bron planned to rush into the salon and declare Sasha a total slapper, or some such. 'Your job's here if you want it.' Maybe she'd finally realised what a good hairdresser she'd lost.

She didn't add 'provided you don't make trouble' but she didn't need to. Sasha had always been well able to make her requirements known without having to express them out loud.

Bron looked down at her arm, which had the effect of making Sasha loosen her grip. 'Er, no, it's all right. I mean, I don't want my job back.'

Just being next to Sasha on the pavement was horrid enough. Bron would rather do anything than go back into the salon with its bitchiness, long, boring hours and all the little arguments about tips.

'So why are you here?' Sasha's smile was definitely false but a little more relaxed. Bron smiled back, equally falsely.

'I left some things here and I also wondered if I could borrow the computer? I need to look something up on the Internet.' She might as well use it now she was here.

Sasha considered. Would Bron make trouble if she refused? She obviously couldn't decide. 'OK then. If you're not too long.'

'Thanks.' Bron smiled and walked past Sasha into the shop.

A couple of her ladies were sitting under driers. Spotting Bron they called out to her, 'Hello dear! How nice to see you.'

'I was told you'd left when I rang yesterday. Now here you are,' said one.

'Come for your cards, have you? Now, Sasha, don't you make any trouble for her, she's a lovely girl. Always did my hair just as I like it.'

The other one had been looking at Bron thoughtfully. 'Not in the family way, are you? You wouldn't want to be working with all these chemicals if you are.'

Bron, who was wearing a loose summer top over her jeans, decided not to be offended. Sasha gave Bron a they-think-you're-fat look, which Bron ignored.

'Not that you're showing yet!' said the woman, anxious lest she'd put her foot in it.

Bron laughed and revealed her normal flat stomach under her top.

'Well, if you will go round in a nightie that doesn't show off your nice figure, what can you expect?' said the woman, still embarrassed.

Bron laughed again. 'No, I'm not expecting, but I have left. Sasha is very kindly allowing me to use the Internet. I've left my boyfriend too.' It was Bron's turn to look meaningfully at Sasha.

Sasha said, 'If you want to use the computer, go on through. You know where it is. And don't be too long. I'll need to order some stuff soon.'

Bron smiled at her ex-clients. 'You can always contact me privately if you want to.' She rummaged in her bag for the business cards she had for weddings. 'Here's my mobile number.'

Sasha's hatred was almost audible. It's because she's in the wrong, thought Bron. She can't forgive me.

Bron found a recipe quite quickly as she knew which books she had, and could look up most of them. She had just printed out one for pork tenderloin that was easy, didn't take hours and didn't involve chicken. She would need to go back into the main part of the town though. She was just waiting for the printer to wake up and start performing when Sasha came in.

'You're not doing anything you shouldn't, are you? Such as stealing my client records?'

Bron knew perfectly well that Sasha didn't have her client records on the computer because she had never got round to putting them there.

'I'm just printing out a recipe,' said Bron calmly.

'It was wrong of you to give my clients your card,' Sasha went on crossly.

'It was wrong of you to give my boyfriend—'

'Oh, all right!' Sasha snapped, before Bron could go on. 'I'm sorry about that!'

Bron shrugged. Sasha sounded about as sorry as she used to be when slipping in an extra appointment meant that Bron missed her lunch break yet again. In other words: not very. Tactfully, the printer creaked into action and produced Bron's recipe.

'Now, if you've finished with the computer, please go. I'll see you get your cookery books soon.' It did seem as if Sasha was genuinely trying to be pleasant, but she just couldn't do it.

'Thank you, that would be kind,' said Bron graciously and moved swiftly out of the door. When she'd said a long goodbye to her ex-clients, she set off once more for the shops.

It was only when she'd planned her menu, washed her hands and tied a large tea towel round her waist that Bron realised the kitchen in the little cottage was not geared to haute cuisine, or even ordinary family cooking. She'd managed fine up to now, when she mostly lived on boiled eggs, the odd chicken breast or bit of fish, but for anything more than that, its size was prohibitive. She'd been so busy recently, she just hadn't taken it in.

For a start, the only surface big enough to work pastry on was the floor. She'd been planning to make apple pie. She'd never met a man who didn't like it.

She chewed her lip and wondered how she could get round this problem. Supposing she sterilised the floor and covered it with foil? No, she'd need a mile of foil, which she didn't have, and it would all crinkle up. Still prepared to roll pastry on her knees, she considered putting a towel down and using that as a surface. It would give the pastry an interesting texture and she was on the way to fetching a towel when she realised she'd have to roll the pastry out with a wine bottle.

So it would have to be apple crumble and not pie. Roger would have complained horribly but James would probably be perfectly happy.

As she rubbed butter, flour and sugar between her fingers, she realised that problem-solving was one of her favourite things. It was why she'd been so keen to make Carrie's cake. She just hoped that Pat's friend's kitchen was suitable and she would be allowed to use it. Anyway, Sarah would have some ideas.

She lit a fire, not because it was really cold but it had started to rain, making the cottage seem a bit dark. Having a fire and lighting some candles she'd brought with her cheered it up a lot.

Once her living area was more *gemütlich* she put a couple of plates in front of the fire to warm, aware she was probably the last woman on earth under thirty who cared about hot plates, then went back to her cooking. She hoped James wouldn't be late. She didn't want her pork fillets to dry up.

He wasn't late. He arrived with a bunch of flowers that obviously came from a garden and were a wonderfully eclectic mix.

'Oh, they're wonderful!' said Bron. 'What are they all?'

'Well, they're mostly just common things. Those salmony-pink roses are Albertine, the double-double purple ones are really called aquilegia, but are always known as grannies' bonnets. The stripy grass is called gardeners' garters. I'm sure you recognise the moon daisies.'

Bron laughed. 'I'll put them in water and then give you a glass of wine.'

'I've brought wine too. Shall I deal with it?'

As Bron produced the two tumblers she had washed and polished for the occasion, he pulled the cork from the bottle. He was a very calming presence, she decided. And not bad-looking; she wondered once again if he were single. She handed him the glasses before retrieving her potato dish from the oven and carrying it to the table. The table wobbled.

'A bit of fag-packet should sort that out,' he said knowingly, and then added, 'Pity I smoke roll-ups.'

Bron tore the top off a box of cornflakes. 'Here, try this. How's the giving-up going?'

'I've cut down a lot. It's only about five a day now, but I would like to quit completely.'

Bron bent down to wedge the cardboard under the offending table leg. Suddenly she felt terribly shy. She was getting to know James and they were neighbours, but she was aware that they were sharing a very small space and he was a relative stranger. The cottage seemed to have shrunk to half its already tiny size. She stood up awkwardly.

James, perhaps sensing her sudden discomfort, said, 'I've got some dry logs next door. Shall I go and get them?'

When she had lit the tea lights on the table that went with the ones dotted round the place she suddenly realised that it could have all looked too romantic. She wasn't coming on to him, she was just thanking him for helping her settle into her new home. He might be quite attractive in a rustic way but she couldn't even think about another relationship until she'd had quite a bit of freedom first. When he came back with the logs she handed him a full glass.

'Come and sit down. You must be starving. Cheers!' she went on cheerfully, clinking her glass against his. 'Dig in! Oh – I didn't meant that as a ghastly pun, you being a gardener and all.'

'It's all right, I'm not remotely sensitive about it. I used to be in IT until I couldn't stand it any more and decided to retrain.'

Bron took a sustaining draught of wine. 'Perhaps I should retrain. You've no idea how embarrassing it is telling groups of people you don't know what you do for a living.'

'What, that you're a hairdresser?'

'Mm. It's very satisfying and I really enjoy it, but people just assume you're stupid.'

'Are you sure? Why should they think that?'

Bron shrugged. 'Traditionally it's what girls who aren't likely to pass many exams get pushed into doing. But I did it because I wanted to. I passed plenty of exams.'

'As I didn't know that hairdressers were supposed to be stupid you don't need to show me your certificates to convince me you're not.'

Bron giggled and took another sip of wine, feeling much more relaxed. James was very easy to talk to, now her initial awkwardness had worn off – and he listened as if he was genuinely interested, unlike Roger. 'I am branching out a bit, actually.'

'Yes?'

'I'm supposed to be making a wedding cake, but I'm not quite sure how to do it.' Bron smiled. 'Anyway, what about you?' she asked. 'Did you have to study, too? Although isn't gardening sort of instinctive?'

'Instinct helps but it's not enough. Especially if you want to work in one of the great gardens.'

'Which you do?'

He nodded. 'The garden here is lovely and I was terribly lucky to meet Vanessa. Working for her has been brilliant, but I don't want to do it for ever. I want to go into garden design more and to do that you really have to know about plants.'

Bron smiled a little quizzically. 'Traditionally, the boys who weren't expected to pass exams were taught gardening.'

James laughed now. 'Here's to people who aren't expected to pass exams but do.'

As their tumblers collided, Bron said, 'Much more toasting and we'll both be tipsy,' then blushed, hoping she hadn't implied anything. 'Do start. I don't want all this getting cold.'

They ate in silence for a while and then James said, 'So, how are you finding it, living alone?'

Bron considered for a moment. 'It's fine, really. Much better than I thought it would be. I've never lived on my own before and I've always assumed I'd hate it, but I really like the freedom.' She paused and took another sip of wine. As James didn't comment she went on. 'I've got friends and my work, I don't need anything else.'

'Not even a man to do the heavy stuff?'

Bron laughed, aware he was teasing her. 'I've got a very strong back, thank you, so I can do my own lifting. I might need your help if I come across a spider though,' she added, not wanting to appear too strident. Besides, it was true.

It was James's turn to laugh. 'I'll have a glass and a bit of card ready.' He was silent for a moment. 'And I know what you mean about living alone. It's peaceful even if it is a bit lonely at times.'

'I'm certainly going to do it for a while. It means I can have the radio on in the middle of the night if I can't sleep.' She raised her glass again. 'To the single life!'

When they clinked again, she went to get the crumble.

It was shortly before twelve when James, who had suddenly looked at his watch, got up. 'I had no idea it was so late—'

They had been chatting about this and that, books, films, music and the time had whistled by.

'Nor had I.' Bron was a bit surprised; the conversation had flowed easily.

'I've got an early start. But thank you so much for dinner. It was wonderful. One of the drawbacks to the single life is food. Somehow it never seems worth putting too much effort into cooking.'

'Well, I'm glad you enjoyed it. It was just a thank you for being such a good neighbour. In fact' – emboldened by the wine Bron said what she'd been thinking for a while – 'I could cut your hair for you if you wanted.'

The corner of his mouth lifted in a rueful smile. 'I'll bring the hedge trimmers.'

Bron twinkled back at him. 'It's all right. I've got my own.'

As he walked down the path she decided he was really quite cute when he smiled.

Chapter Twenty-Four

❧

Sarah held the piece of card in her hand, flapping it backwards and forwards as she read the words for the hundredth time. She wouldn't even have dreamt of going if she hadn't been in London already but she'd come up to check out the band Mandy wanted to play at the reception and, having done that, she now had this invitation forcing her to pay it some attention.

It had arrived in the post a couple of days earlier, the announcement of an exhibition that included Hugo's photographs. She had been about to recycle it but catching his name made her pin it on her noticeboard instead.

And goodness knows why she'd stuffed it in her bag as she walked out of the door that morning. But as she had, she reasoned, she might as well go. She got out her London street map and worked out a route.

It was in a part of London Sarah didn't know at all. It looked 'up and coming', in that there were a few stylish shops in among the grille-fronted off-licences and video-games stores. The odd brightly painted front door shone out from among the homes for squatters. It would be the place to buy property for those with strong nerves who didn't fear street crime. Sarah didn't qualify for either criteria and was glad she wasn't here after dark. She hailed a taxi from the tube more so she didn't get lost, she told herself, than because she was nervous.

The driver pulled up in front of a huge old warehouse that looked big enough to store elephants. 'Here we are, love. They tell me this is one of the hottest new galleries in town.'

'Oh, right, thank you!'

Once inside the building, Sarah felt pleased to be there. Going to exhibitions was the sort of thing she loved to do but hardly ever let herself make time for. She walked up the stairs trying to convince herself that it was just the exhibition generally she'd come to see and the fact that Hugo's work would be here was just by the by. She chuckled at herself, not even slightly fooled.

The space she arrived at made Elsa's large workroom look like a single bedroom. Here the vast area was divided up by white-painted partitions. The room was full of activity. People were hanging work, realigning bits of partition and, somewhere out of sight, someone was banging ten bells out of a piece of metal. Sarah was confused. She pulled the invitation out of her pocket from where it had been in and out several times already and realised she'd got the date wrong. The exhibition was for next week.

Mentally kicking herself extremely hard, she was about to turn and leave when a girl came up to her. 'Can I help?'

She was tall and thin and encased in tight denim. Her hair was very blonde and blossomed out of her head in wild curls. Sarah thought she was familiar but couldn't immediately place her.

Sarah made a gesture. 'I'm sorry, I got the date wrong. I'll just go.'

'Do you live in London?'

Sarah realised the girl could probably tell that she didn't just by looking at her and then wondered if this was paranoia. 'No . . .'

'Then come and have a look now or you'll miss it.' The girl smiled. 'I know what you country bumpkins are like! Is there an artist you're particularly interested in?'

'Well, I know Hugo Marsters a bit.'

233

'Oh, Hugo! He's great, isn't he? Bloody good photographer, by the way. I'm Electra Handforth-Williams.'

'Sarah Stratford.' So that was why she was familiar. She'd seen her with Hugo that time, when she was last in London. She found it almost impossible to smile. Her hand, she knew, taken by Electra and shaken, would be damp and cold. Why did she ever let herself think Hugo might be interested in her? Electra was enchanting, in the way that Bambi was enchanting. She couldn't possibly even think of competing with such youth and vitality, not to mention beauty.

'Well, come on in. We're still setting up, as you can see, but Hugo's work is hung. I took responsibility for it personally. We're expecting it to attract a lot of attention. One or two pieces have been sold already but he'd promised them for the exhibition and I jolly well told him they had to be there!' She sparkled at Sarah. 'Jolly nice to have a few red spots straightaway!'

Sarah nodded, trying to reflect some of Electra's good humour, and followed her.

'He's *so* good, isn't he? Well, I'll leave you to it. Come and find me if you want to be talked through any of the other artists.'

Electra was right – he was *so* good! Sarah had seen his portfolio at Carrie's hotel and been impressed but these were amazing. Huge black and white photographs filled two of the enormous partitions. One wall was of celebrities, beautiful people, but looking really interesting. She spotted Carrie, her hair flying across her face, laughing, freckled and completely without make-up. Sarah had never seen her look so beautiful. Several famous actors; men and women, young and old; sporting heroes in unusual, casual poses that she recognised but couldn't immediately place; politicians, past and present: all were represented. She gazed and admired and felt ashamed of how she'd just assumed Hugo made his living by doing weddings, never suspecting that he was also a great artist.

Then she was brought up short. She came to a section where no one seemed to be famous and felt sick and faint for the second time that day.

She could hardly breathe as she looked at herself. She was crouching down, looking up into the face of Ashlyn's little bridesmaid. She was smiling and taking a strand of hair out of the little girl's eyes. The little girl was doing the same for Sarah, and now she saw it, she remembered the feel of the tiny, damp hand on her face.

Sarah swallowed. She wasn't used to seeing herself look beautiful and she had to admit in this picture she did. Yet she also looked exactly like herself, so it wasn't just a clever angle or something. Was that how Hugo saw her? As beautiful? Or was it just the artist's eye? But why hadn't he shown her this before? She was acutely aware of Electra, somewhere in the gallery.

Then she came to some photographs of the girl – Sarah felt she couldn't really be more than a year out of her teens – herself. Here Electra was half naked, her flawless back and toned arms making her look like an idealised piece of marble. They were very intimate. There were lots of her, taken in a meadow behind which presided a huge stately home Sarah felt she should have recognised. She was sure it must be where Electra had been brought up.

Electra came up again and handed Sarah a cup of coffee. 'Here, thought you might like this. I thought I recognised you. You're the woman in the photograph.'

As she took the cup it occurred to Sarah that it might have been coincidence that made Electra appear at just the moment she was looking at her photos, but maybe not.

'Oh golly, look at me!' Electra peered at her image. 'You don't think I look remotely fat, do you?'

As it was possible Kate Moss would look fat next to her, Sarah could only say, 'No.'

'I do work out a lot. Look at those abs!'

Sarah's attention was more caught by the tiny, perfect spheres that were Electra's breasts, actually.

'Who, I ask you, would swap that fabulous figure for squealing kids!' Electra laughed. 'I know, I know, everyone wants babies these days, like they were some fashion accessory, but I'd rather have a really fit bod.'

'Well, you don't have to think about having babies for years and years,' said Sarah, feeling like someone's grandmother.

'I know, but I've already decided. Kiddywinks: fine in a photo but otherwise, *not* for me.'

Sarah was about to ask if she'd discussed it with Hugo, who, as far as she could tell, was good with kiddywinks, and might want some of his own. But as it was really none of her business, and she wasn't sure she wanted to hear the answer anyway, she shut it again. 'You may feel differently in a few years,' she said instead.

Electra made a face. 'That's what *everyone* says, but I won't change my mind. I love my career too much. And I love travelling. Might even move to New York. They've got a fabulous art scene over there. Now, if you've finished with Hugo, come and see this work. I think it's *amazing!*'

Ingesting the cup of very strong black coffee – something she rarely, if ever, did – helped Sarah get through. She managed to nod and smile at Electra's intense enthusiasm for the work in the gallery, all the while wondering what Hugo saw in her. But then she told herself off. Electra was beautiful, enthusiastic and obviously bright, and she most probably had hidden depths.

She was relieved when her phone rang. She found a quiet corner, and managed to be quite calm when Mandy said, 'Sarah, honey? You'll be very glad to know that Carrie's made up her mind about the bridesmaids. She wants four and she wants them to have dresses very like her own.'

'And have we decided on which design she likes best?' Sarah had her fingers crossed for Elsa who was getting frantic.

'Not yet, but I will try and encourage her to soon. She thinks the sight of her and four little attendants will be very pretty.'

'Well, that's something, thank you for telling me. I'll get on to Elsa straight away.'

Sarah disconnected. She felt it was time she left but she probably ought to say goodbye to Electra first, it would seem a bit rude just to disappear. She walked over to her. 'Electra, it's been great, it really has. Lovely meeting you and really wonderful having a personal tour of the show, but I've got to go.' She shook Electra's hand and walked away, glad to be out in the fresh air.

She rang Elsa in the taxi that she'd asked to take her to Paddington, rather than wrestle with the tube again. She was feeling jumpy and tired at the same time. That had been something of an ordeal. What with the strong coffee, her photograph and meeting Electra, of all people, she really needed a lie-down.

Elsa took the news calmly. 'That's OK. Even if she wants them to be just like hers, they won't want boned bodices, it would be child abuse. I've already got in touch with my woman. She's coming round for a chat sometime. She's brilliant at beading.'

'Oh good,' said Sarah, sighing. 'I'm really glad that it's all OK.'

'Are you OK, Sarah? You sound a little tense.'

'Fine. Just being in London, busy day, all these people, traffic and noise, you know,' said Sarah, glad that Elsa couldn't see her and realise just how strange she felt.

Chapter Twenty-Five

'OK,' said Sarah quickly, knowing she had a short window of Lily's attention to get the wording of the invitations right. 'Mr and Mrs Gerald Stratford . . .'

'That sounds weird!'

'It's how it's always done. We want traditional, don't we?'

'But she's not my mother!'

'No,' said Sarah, 'but she's Dad's wife and they're contributing a fair bit, you mustn't be ungrateful. She was really thrilled about the baby.'

'Mm, yes, she was. Which is more than Dirk's mother will be.' Lily sighed. 'Maybe she's not such a bad old thing.'

Sarah typed the next few lines on her computer. 'Come and choose a font. There are a few that are very traditional.'

Lily came and leant on Sarah's shoulder. 'Oh, I want that one.'

'No,' Sarah snapped. 'Your in-laws would never wear it. You can have an Edwardian script or, if you must, Blackadder ITC, but that's a bit quirky for the older generation.'

'OK, you do it.' Lily moved to stand in front of Sarah's full-length mirror and looked at her stomach. 'Honestly, it doesn't really show I'm pregnant.'

Sarah didn't look up from what she was doing. 'Not now it doesn't, but it will by August. Trust me. Or even if it doesn't, you can't take the chance. You have to choose a sensible style.'

Sarah was keeping hold of her patience with difficulty. When Lily had turned up at ten that morning she'd decided to set the whole day aside to get her sorted out. Lily had sworn they'd do everything that Sarah said they must, but it was now two o'clock and all they'd done was go out for lunch. Lily refused to focus.

'It's so boring having to be sensible all the time!' Lily wailed.

Sarah exhaled. Her patience was about to desert her, especially with so much still to do for Carrie's wedding – the one she was actually being paid to organise. 'I know, sweetie, and you can have a lovely, gorgeous, fairy-tale dress, as long as it's within budget, but it can't be tight-fitting. Now let's get the invitations finished at least.'

'OK.' Lily flopped down on the sofa and crossed her legs. She was still enviably slim and Sarah was beginning to wonder if perhaps she should indulge her in the Spanish-style dress with full, flamenco-style train and ruffles that her heart was currently set on – provided the Wedding Fairy produced the five grand required to pay for it.

'You've got the card?'

Sarah nodded. 'These invites should have been out weeks ago.'

'It's OK, Dirk's mother has rung up everyone and said the invitations are on their way. Are you sure we don't need reply sections?'

'Absolutely. Sometimes tradition works out cheaper. You don't need favours on the tables either. Although do have a photographer, just for a few formal shots, or you're risking not having any photos at all. Unless you know Dirk's Uncle Joby is really good?'

Lily shook her head. 'I think he may be a bit of a lush, actually.'

'OK, well, I'll make sure that he doesn't get near any alcohol before he's done a few pictures outside the church.

The others aren't so important. Dirk's mother will need a lovely one of you both to put in a silver frame on top of her grand piano.'

Lily's jaw dropped. 'How did you know she's got photos in silver frames on her grand piano? How did you even know she's got a grand piano? That's amazing.'

Sarah laughed. 'I was just guessing, but it's nice to be right.'

'Oh, you're always right. It's what makes you so boring.' Then Lily realised what she'd said. 'Oh, Sarah, I didn't mean it like that! You're not boring at all. It's just the fact that you're always right that's boring. Not you.'

'It's all right. I'm not at all offended. I like being right.' She paused for a second as she hunted for the card she'd bought for the invitations. As was happening annoyingly often these days, Hugo popped into her mind. Did he think she was boring? Probably, if he was with someone like Electra. But it hadn't stopped him kissing her. She had been right not to take it any further. Although even if she now knew it had been a terrible mistake to let herself go that night, she had really enjoyed it at the time.

She put a few sheets of card into her printer. The thing was to keep herself very very busy, at all times, and banish all thoughts of him into the box marked 'toxic', for ever. 'If this doesn't work, I'll get them photocopied down the road. It won't cost much.'

'So do you think a wedding list is a good idea?' Lily had opened a magazine and was leafing through it. 'If so, what about Harrods?'

'Not Harrods, or you'll only get really small things like eggcups and napkin rings.' Sarah considered. 'You could make your own list in a loose-leaf binder, then you can put really imaginative things on it, like . . .'

'A daisy punch?'

Sarah was completely nonplussed. 'What's a daisy punch?'

'Like a hole punch only it makes daisy shapes. There are lots of lovely crafty things I'd put on if I made my own list.'

'You could even put on things you need for the baby.' Sarah was encouraged – Lily seemed to be making a sensible decision at last.

Lily shook her head. 'No. Dirk's mother would never wear it. I'll just have a normal list and if people give us money, use it for other stuff.'

Sarah nodded in agreement. 'It would take far too much organising. Have a list at a department store that has several branches so it's easy for people to get to.'

'I want really nice presents,' said Lily.

'You'll get them! Don't worry, and don't be so mercenary!'

'Dirk's mother said it was a good idea to have a big wedding because you get lots of presents and they set you up for your married life.'

Sarah muttered to herself that if you were mostly paying for your own wedding it probably wasn't cost-effective.

'There, that seems to work,' she said out loud, as her printer spat out a perfect invitation. 'Now I'll get it to do two hundred and then we'll have to fold them.'

'Couldn't I draw some butterflies on them instead?'

'Lily! I know you drew butterflies or kittens on every bit of schoolwork you ever produced, but—'

'I'm good at butterflies and kittens. And it's *my* wedding. This is something I can do for it. The amount of bossing around I've had to put up with, you'd never believe I was the bride. Honestly, I think what I want is the last thing anyone thinks about. I'm not even allowed to have the dress I want.'

Sarah sighed. 'OK, butterflies on just a few, the ones you're sending to your own friends. But don't let Dirk's friends get any with them on. I'll just set the printer up.' She was halfway through doing this when the phone rang.

Sarah's hand fell on it as if it were saving her life. 'Elsa! Hi! What's up!'

'Golly, Sarah, you're very pleased to hear me! What are you up to?'

'Lily and I are printing the invitations for her wedding, or at least we will be in a minute. And yes I know they should have been done weeks ago.'

'Did you? I don't have a clue about any of that stuff.'

'We're also deciding about dresses.' Sarah glanced at her sister who seemed to be buried in a bridal magazine so fat a pregnant woman should probably be advised against lifting it. She lowered her voice. 'Hey, I don't suppose you could come round, could you? Lily's a bit fed up with being so restricted on style—'

'Because she's pregnant?'

'Mm. You might be a bit more imaginative about what she can have than I am.' The thought of another adult to help her with her sister's dottier ideas was wonderful.

'Well, I know you said Mandy would let you know the moment she knew, but I was just ringing on the off-chance to ask if Carrie had said which of my designs she likes yet, because I'm going quietly mad here. I've got all the fabric samples, the drawings all done in detail, bridesmaids' dresses, everything, but I can't start until I hear from her. I know the dress'll take ages because they always do if you're short of time. Sod's law.'

'Tell you what, if you come, talk to Lily and fold invites, I'll ring Mandy and see I can hurry things along a bit. Deal?'

'Deal. See you in about ten minutes. Shall I bring wine?'

Sarah considered. 'White wine, warm. Then we can't drink it until it's cooled down which will mean we'll get the work done first.'

Elsa laughed and they disconnected.

Lily looked up from the magazine. 'You are so Machie— M— Who was that Russian person?'

'Machiavelli. And he was Italian. Why?'

Lily pouted. 'What you said about the wine. Actually, I'm not going to drink at all any more, although I had cut right down.'

'Good! What brought this flash of sanity down on you?'

'Something I read in the paper.'

'Well, I'm really impressed.' Sarah patted her sister's arm. 'You're taking responsibility. Good for you.' Sarah felt ashamed of herself, assuming that Lily was just ignoring her pregnancy when really, she was beginning to take it all very seriously.

'Actually,' said Lily after revelling in her sister's approval for a few seconds, 'it makes me sick.'

Elsa soon appeared with wine, crisps and chocolate biscuits. Both sisters were delighted to see her. Lily took the biscuits and ripped into them. 'The government hasn't told us we can't eat chocolate yet,' she said, tucking in. 'Although, it's only a matter of time.'

Elsa proved to an accurate and willing invitation-folder. To reward her, Sarah withdrew to her office and made the call. Mandy was as ever rather vague. 'Oh, honey, Carrie hasn't had the designs that long and she'll want to make changes. I don't really like to ask her about stuff like this when she's so busy. But I promise I'll try my best. We do appreciate you're all being so wonderful about it.'

'I wouldn't nag,' said Sarah, who felt she hadn't nagged, really, but Mandy was always so charming, 'but Elsa really needs to start work. You know she's got to make the entire dress out of muslin first to check that it fits properly.'

'Oh yes, the toile? That sounds so French! I think we had forgotten. We'll have a think, but in the meantime, give Elsa our love.'

Sarah put the phone down wondering if Mandy and Carrie were joined at the hip or if Mandy was using the

Royal 'we'. If so, did this mean her client was in fact royalty? In which case she could put 'By Appointment' on her business cards. On this happy but fantastical thought she went back to Lily and Elsa.

They were sitting together on the sofa, the magazine spread over both of them. Sarah, seeing them happily ensconced, decided she needed a glass of wine. She came back to the room a minute or two later with two glasses of wine and an elderflower pressé for Lily.

'How's it going?' she asked, handing out glasses.

'Well, Elsa's much better at this than you are!' said Lily indignantly. 'There are loads of other styles I can have apart from the marquees that you think I should wear.'

Sarah bit her lip. 'Thank goodness you reminded me! I must get on to the marquee people as soon as possible. Do you have any idea what size the garden is?'

'Well, if you know how many guests there are going to be, you'll know what size you'll need, surely?' suggested Elsa.

Sarah shook her head. 'We don't want to order one too big and have to take the neighbours' gardens over too. I'd better ring Dirk's mother and ask her.'

'Don't do that. Then they'll know I'm not organising everything!' Lily was so horrified at this suggestion she had to have another chocolate finger to help her recover.

'Oh, Lily! Did you tell them you were doing everything? Didn't you mention at any stage that your sister was a wedding planner?' Sarah's impatience got the better of her for a moment.

'I would have done,' said Lily, 'but I knew you had a top celebrity client having a wedding on the same day. I thought you might not be able to fit me in.'

'Lily, really!' said Sarah. 'You didn't know anything about Carrie when you chose your date. Why didn't you say anything?'

Lily shrugged. 'What your sister does for a living doesn't necessarily crop up when you've just announced your engagement to your future in-laws.'

'She's got you there,' said Elsa. 'But why don't you ask Dirk for the dimensions of the garden? He must have a rough idea.'

'Good plan,' said Sarah, relieved to have another practical person on hand. 'Now, how are you two getting on with wedding dresses?'

'Well, we've found several styles that would do well,' said Elsa. 'There's one with an overskirt that could look very pretty. The ball gown I've made is rather like it. I can show it to Lily and see if she likes it.'

'I could try it on,' said Lily excitedly, sending the crisps flying as she leapt up.

'Well, you could,' said Elsa, 'but . . .' She paused. 'As I seem to have a bit of time on my hands – until Carrie makes up her mind – I could make you a mock-up in muslin.'

'Tell me, Elsa,' said Sarah, 'I've never known. How do you pronounce the word for that? Is it "twarl"' or "toil"?'

Elsa looked abashed. 'I always wait for the client to say it first then I just say what they do.'

'Cop out!' said both sisters together, united at last.

Chapter Twenty-Six

Elsa felt surprisingly shaky considering she wasn't about to do anything life-threatening. It would have been better if Laurence hadn't been there, she decided, then she wouldn't have to worry so much about making a fool of herself. As instructed, she'd found a pair of shoes with medium heels that stayed on quite well and was wearing a skirt. She could have worn her favourite black trousers but she felt she should get used to moving with a bit more fabric around her.

'He's a very well respected teacher. You'll be fine,' said Laurence as they mounted the stone steps to the door. 'There's nothing to be nervous about.'

'I realise I'm not likely to die,' Elsa said, 'you very rarely die when you go to the dentist, either. It doesn't stop you being nervous.'

'If it's any consolation to you,' said Laurence. 'I have never died while at the dentist.'

She shot him a look while he pressed the bell. 'Well, nor have I but I'm still terrified!'

Laurence had rung her the evening after Elsa had helped Sarah and Lily with the invitations, offering to give her a dancing lesson. If wretched Carrie had made a single decision about what she or her bridesmaids should wear, she would have had a genuine reason for refusing, but she had no such excuse. If she hadn't had rather more wine than she'd intended and been feeling a bit giggly she might still have said no, but the combination of time on her hands and a fun evening with Sarah and Lily had her saying yes. And it would be nice to see him again. She found herself looking forward to that part at least. It was a pity that he was too busy for them to go out for a drink afterwards, she thought wistfully.

'What are you frightened of, exactly?'

She made a face. 'Making a fool of myself.'

He laughed. 'Surely it's better to get your embarrassment over in private, rather than on the dance floor with hundreds of others?'

She was about to remind him that she was doing him a favour when the door was opened. Elsa did her best to smile. She didn't want anyone else to know she was terrified. What if there were other people there to watch her? She'd die of embarrassment.

When the door was opened by a man worryingly reminiscent of one of the professionals on *Strictly Come Dancing* her embarrassment meter, already on high, shot up to the top. Had the teacher been like lovely, kindly Len, the expert of experts, she'd have been fine. This young lion was bound to despise her feeble efforts.

'Hi!' said the leather-clad stud in question. 'Come on in.'

At second glance Elsa realised that he didn't look anything like any of those television stars, it had just been her nerves that made her think so. But he was very good-looking and moved like a panther. They seemed to be the only ones there. At least no one else but Laurence would see how bad she was – and he already knew.

'No need to look so worried!' the panther said to her, smiling in a stomach-clenching way. 'I don't bite! I'm Terry,' he added.

'I'm Laurence Gentle and this is Elsa Ashcombe.'

'Well, come in both.'

Terry led the way and when he was more or less out of earshot Laurence said, 'He's much younger than I thought he'd be. I hope he'll be all right.'

Elsa didn't have a chance to reply but she did wonder if

Laurence had ever watched *Strictly Come Dancing*. Didn't he know the dancers were young? A little fillip of satisfaction warmed her – he wasn't totally happy about this now, either.

'Have you got some other shoes, love?' Terry asked Elsa.

Elsa held up the bag with her best shoes in it. 'I'm going to be wearing these,' she said.

'Fine. Come on in to the studio, or do you need to use the facilities?'

It occurred to Elsa that he may have said this because she looked as if she was going to be sick. She really hoped he was wrong and followed the men into the studio.

It was a large, mirrored room with windows both ends. Elsa felt even more intimidated and crept to the corner to put on her shoes. Her medium-heeled courts that she had had for years suddenly felt loose and sloppy. She probably should have sewn some elastic on them or something.

'Elsa really just wants to learn to waltz,' Laurence was saying. Although it was true, her nerves made her irritated with him for speaking for her. She told herself to calm down. Laurence was only trying to help.

'Right, you guys,' said Terry. 'Take hold of each other. You know the hold? You do, Laurence, obviously. Elsa . . .' He moved Elsa's hands.

'OK, we'll start without music, just to check we know the basic steps then we'll really start to dance.'

Elsa felt suddenly awkward. She'd been quite happy in his arms at the wedding, when she had hardly met him; now it felt strangely intimate. They made a few unsatisfactory starts, Terry watching them carefully, his head on one side, patiently giving instructions. Elsa caught a glimpse of herself in the mirror. She looked as stiff as her dressmaker's dummy. Laurence could dance so it was obviously all her fault. Or was it? They were both getting a little frustrated with each other.

'You know some people are born to dance?' said Elsa, pulling away from Laurence. 'Well, I think I'm born not to dance.'

'You do seem to be taking a while to pick it up,' he replied, and Elsa thought she detected a slight note of impatience in his usually mild-mannered voice. Well, she had said she couldn't dance. 'It's quite simple really. Forward side together, back side together.'

Terry looked at Laurence and then at Elsa. 'You know what? I think you're the problem, Laurence. You're making Elsa nervous. Why don't you go off and come back at half past and see how we're getting on?'

'Oh,' said Laurence, rather nonplussed. 'You don't think I'm helping?'

'No. You keep giving Elsa advice that isn't the same as mine. You go away and we'll get on fine.'

Laurence gave her an odd look and, as he left, Elsa noticed a rather dejected air about his slumped shoulders.

With Laurence sent to the shops for a paper Terry took Elsa in his arms, having started the music. 'Right now, don't look down, don't think, just move with the music. Back on our right foot – excellent!'

After a faltering start, something fell into place in Elsa's brain. She stopped thinking about her feet, she just listened to the music, felt the pressure of Terry's arm on her back as he gently guided her, and moved about the floor with him, apparently glued to his chest. It was brilliant. She could see the two of them – what a contrast to her and Laurence – moving as one. She didn't look awkward and stiff any more.

'That was amazing!' she said a little breathlessly, a few minutes later. 'I could really feel myself doing it.'

'You see, you had the steps in your head and in your feet. You just needed to forget about both for it to all happen.' Terry smiled down at her, obviously pleased with her progress, and to have enabled it.

'Can we do it again?' she asked eagerly.

Round and round the floor they sailed – to the right and to the left and Elsa managed both. She didn't hear the door open and it was only when the music stopped that she noticed Laurence looking at her, and at Terry with his arms around her.

'Well done,' he said quietly.

'Isn't it great? I finally got it! It's like *My Fair Lady* or something!'

'What?' Laurence frowned.

'Sorry,' said Elsa. 'I'm a bit addicted to old musicals.'

'Quite right too,' said Terry and then glanced at his watch. 'I'm afraid my next pupil will be here in a minute, but I want you two guys to practise together before the ball.'

'Thank you so much, Terry,' said Elsa, her eyes shining with enthusiasm. 'That was wonderful! I never dreamt I could dance like that.'

'Yes, thank you very much,' said Laurence. He still seemed rather subdued. 'Now, how much do I owe you?'

'Oh, you must let me pay,' said Elsa, hunting for her chequebook. 'I had the lesson.'

'But I arranged it for you, so you could come to a ball, with *me*.' Laurence's cheque arrived on the table before hers did. 'Forty pounds? Thank you very much.'

'Laurence, you must let me pay. You can waltz perfectly well already. I needed the lesson.' Elsa would never have described herself as an ardent feminist before, but suddenly her whole worth as a woman seemed to depend on her paying for her own waltzing lesson.

But Laurence was adamant. 'No! I arranged it all because I want you to be able to dance. It's my shout. I won't have any argument.'

Once they were outside the studio, Elsa thanked him again. 'You really should have let me pay.'

'Nonsense, it was worth it. You can dance now,

although I wish . . . anyway, Terry, he was good, wasn't he? You seemed to be getting on very well when I got back . . .' Laurence looked at his feet.

Elsa bit her lip. Surely he didn't mind that it was Terry who had unlocked the key that enabled her to dance? He was the teacher, that was his job, and he had to hold her tightly. It was part of the dance. Laurence couldn't possibly be jealous of Terry, could he? She smiled to herself – she was fairly sure that Terry was gay.

Chapter Twenty-Seven

Bron found the address, tucked away between a pub and a primary school, without difficulty. Pat's directions had been perfect. Four women who needed their hair doing in a kitchen that may well be suitable for making Carrie's wedding cake, all arranged by Pat as promised. Bron was excited as she parked the car.

The house was delightful, she thought, as she started unloading her kit from the boot. She left one load on the doorstep and then went to get the rest of it. Someone had opened the door before she had a chance to ring.

'You must be Bron,' said a pleasant-faced middle-aged woman with a bad perm. 'I'm Veronica. Let me give you a hand.' Veronica picked up Bron's tool kit. 'Do you mind doing it in the kitchen? There's plenty of space there.'

'Not at all,' said Bron, thinking how much easier it would be for her to ask about borrowing it if she didn't have to ask to see it specially.

'And you've got at least five clients. Pat said you wouldn't mind.'

'Not at all,' she said again. 'I'll get a production line going. It would speed things up if people washed their own hair, though.' She was aware that people loved the therapeutic effect of having their hair washed by professional, massaging fingers, but without a back-wash, it sometimes involved a lot of water down the back of people's necks and it would mean the others had to wait longer.

'Through here,' said Veronica, leading Bron to the most

delightful room. It was large, sunny and overlooked an overflowing cottage garden. There was a long stainless steel counter along one wall with a four-oven range cooker and a double sink. Bron could see various other appliances and another washbasin but couldn't really look properly just now.

Four women were sitting at a table drinking coffee and eating biscuits although it was only nine o'clock. They all looked up when Bron came in. Pat, who was already there, got up and kissed her and introduced her to the other women.

'We're turning Veronica's kitchen into a hairdressing salon,' she said. 'She's being very nice about it, and providing tea and biccies.'

'I was just saying to her, I can get through you all a bit quicker if those of you just having a cut and a blow-dry could wash your own hair?' Bron smiled. 'I can do whoever's going first, of course. Veronica? That should be you, I think.'

A little while later, Veronica and Bron re-entered the kitchen. The four women at the table were talking all at once, and very excitedly.

'We've been chatting!' said Pat. 'About Bron setting up her own business.'

'Yes?' said Veronica.

'Mm. We were just saying: good for her; going out, getting work, being her own boss,' Pat went on.

'And then we wondered if we could do it,' said another. 'How do you find it, love?'

Bron considered. 'Well, it's very early days, but it's nice to work for yourself. If I got enough work not to have to worry about money, it'd be brilliant.'

The women exchanged glances. 'Well,' said the one Bron remembered may have been called Barbara, 'we don't have to worry about that. I mean, we already do a lot of catering for nothing,' she explained. 'Our children have all moved out and we've time on our hands. We'd do catering. It's what we're good at.'

'Well,' said Veronica. 'You have been busy. Drawn up a business plan yet?'

'No,' said Barbara, 'you can do that. You're on cakes. You've had the practice.'

Bron steered Veronica to a chair and changed her wet towel for a dry one and draped a gown round her. She could see that everyone was so enthused by their idea they might forget why they were there.

'So I'm involved in this, am I?' said Veronica, while Bron gently pulled a brush through her hair.

'Definitely,' said Pat. 'Why should young people do all the entrepreneuring? This would give us something to do outside the home, and I think parties would be fun.'

'We wouldn't be guests,' said one of the women. 'We'd just be standing around holding trays.'

'That would be the Aitch-Trot,' said another, sounding knowledgeable.

Everyone looked at her enquiringly.

'I read it in the paper last Christmas. It means "handing things round on trays". It was Hugh Fearnley-Whittingstall who said it.'

There was a collective swoon at the name. 'I love his programmes.'

'And I like a man who knows what to do with a joint of beef,' said Veronica.

'So do I,' said Pat, 'and I haven't got one.'

Bron thought there was a hint of belligerence about her ex-boyfriend's mother today and suddenly panicked in case her split with Roger had precipitated something between Pat and her awful husband. Pat seemed so much feistier away from him. Bron was pleased to see this side of Pat coming out more. She would have to encourage it further.

'But you wouldn't want to break a new one in now, surely,' Bron said. 'After the years you've put in on Vince.'

'Hmph.' Pat sounded dismissive. 'Didn't do me much good though, did it? But don't worry, I'm not planning on leaving him or anything drastic. But I am going to get this little business of ours going. You've been an inspiration to me, Bron.'

'And us,' said another. 'Look at you, snipping away in Veronica's kitchen. You can take your skills anywhere, and so can we.'

Bron smiled at the woman, who currently had a very nice bob that needed a bit of a trim. If she became a regular client, Bron might suggest a few highlights, so that the balance of blonde to grey was better.

'So what sort of events would we be doing?' asked Veronica, with her head on her chest, while Bron divided her hair into sections.

'Everything: weddings, funerals, children's parties.'

'Oh, not children's parties. I'm not organising games. I'm rubbish at all that stuff,' said the woman with the bob.

'We wouldn't have to be there during the party. We'd just do the sandwiches—'

'And make Peter Rabbit biscuits. I've still got my cutter. I used to pride myself on getting the blue just right.'

'I used to love doing the food,' said one woman. 'It was the parties I hated. Same with adult ones, too.'

'So this is perfect for us!' said Pat. 'We get to do the bits we like best.'

'I can't do fancy cakes,' said Veronica, upright now, staring into the propped-up mirror. 'Well, I can do the cake bit but I can't do the icing.'

'I can,' said Bron, feeling relaxed enough to put her penny's worth in. 'I've made some very fine trains in my time. If you need one, or anything complicated, you can ask me. And while we're on the subject . . .' She moved quickly on before her nerve could go. 'Veronica, Pat tells me this kitchen has been passed by Health and Safety.'

'That's right.' Veronica obviously had her mind on her

hair as she went on, 'I think maybe just a little off all round. I'm not in the mood for any major changes.'

'Fine. I'll just kiss your hair with the scissors, you'll never know you've had it cut. Would it be possible for me to make a cake in here? It's a posh wedding cake.' She nearly added 'for a celebrity' because she knew they'd love the gossip, but managed to stop herself in time. 'I'd make sure I paid for every penny of gas and electricity, and of course, not use it if it's inconvenient for you.'

'I don't know,' said Veronica. 'My husband might not like it.'

'Husbands, ha!' said someone.

'She's great at cleaning kitchens,' said Pat. 'I'm going to have to clear up mine myself on Sundays now.' She sighed. 'It's so sad. She used to leave it gleaming.'

'No, well, Sasha didn't ever sweep up at the salon, either,' said Bron, wondering how she could persuade Veronica to let her use her kitchen. 'There, do you think that's enough? Shall I dry it now?'

'That looks fine. Yes, please do, dear. Maybe next time I'll let you take a bit more off.'

As Bron got through her clients, their enthusiasm for their new project grew. Veronica, looking very elegant now, sat at the table with a big pad of paper, writing down ideas.

'What we want are a few events where we know people, so it doesn't matter if we make a few mistakes,' said Veronica. 'Just to begin with.'

'What shall we call ourselves?' said Pat. 'We need to get some cards printed.'

'What about the Catering Ladies?' suggested the woman whose locks were in Bron's tender care at the time.

'It's straightforward,' said Veronica, 'but is it a bit boring?'

'No, I think it sounds fun,' put in Bron. 'It sounds as if you're a team of strong women, determined to make things happen.'

'Well, we are!' they chorused.

'Shall I put on the kettle so we can celebrate?' suggested Veronica.

'You can get cards done very easily,' said Pat. 'Let's decide what to put on them.'

'But no professional dos until we've had a bit of time to practise,' said Veronica. 'We'll do things for nothing except the cost of the ingredients until we've got a few under our belt.'

Bron thought for a moment as she ran the dryer over her last client's hair. 'Um, I might have a wedding you could do on those terms,' she said. 'A friend of mine's sister is getting married and they've got hardly any money. I'm sure they'd be thrilled if you could do the food for just the food, if you know what I mean.' She was aware Sarah had been worrying what to do about the catering for Lily's reception and as far as she knew she hadn't found anyone yet.

'What sort of food would they want?' asked Veronica.

'No idea. Would you like me to ring my friend?'

'When you've finished me,' said Bron's last client. 'If my hair dries naturally it goes all spiky.'

'Spiky is cool,' said Bron, 'but I won't let you be spiky if you don't want to be.'

When all the hair was done and everyone satisfied it was lunchtime. Veronica, a natural caterer, produced some sandwiches, little quiches and salads she'd made in advance. Bron accepted a quiche and got out her phone.

Sarah took a while to pick up which gave Bron time to finish her mouthful and realise that the pastry was delicious. 'Sarah? Where are you? You sound very faint.'

'I'm carrying rather a lot of wedding dresses,' said Sarah. 'From a charity shop. For my sister to try on. Hang on, let me just put these in the car . . .' There was a clunk and the sound of rustling and then Sarah was back on the phone. 'Right, I'm all yours.'

'It's about Lily I'm ringing,' said Bron. 'What sort of food does she want at her reception? I've got a wonderful team of women here who'll do the food for you.'

'Oh, who are they? I'm bound to have heard of them.'

'Um – well, you won't have, because they're a brand-new business.'

'Brand-new? Oh, Bron, I don't like to use people I don't know. Lily's future mother-in-law is being very definite about how she wants everything.'

'I can guarantee they're fantastic cooks. I've just eaten the most delicious quiche. Melt-in-the-mouth pastry.' Everyone in the room was looking at her and she crossed her fingers, sensing they saw this as an omen. If they got this job their business would be on a roll. 'Even better, they'll do it for the cost of the food, no labour, because they're new.'

'Really?' Sarah suddenly became a great deal more enthusiastic. 'That would save a fair bit. Who did you say they were?'

'The Catering Ladies. They've just formed. It would be a good idea to book them now before someone else snaps up the opportunity.'

'Oh well, if you tell me they're really good. I should imagine Dirk's mother will want a buffet.'

'Not an Aitch-Trot?'

'Sorry? I didn't quite catch that.'

'Never mind.'

'Why don't you come over to Elsa's at about seven? She's going to help sort Lily out with a dress. You can bring me sample menus and things, if you've got them.'

'Fine!'

Bron disconnected and looked at her rapt audience. 'Can you produce me some sample menus for a buffet before five tonight? If so, you've got a job.'

'Fantastic! Of course we can,' said Veronica.

'So can I borrow your kitchen for the cake?'

'You've got us our first commission; of course you can.'

Chapter Twenty-Eight

Lily looked at herself in Elsa's long mirror. 'I don't know. It's a bit – dreck. Looks like net curtains.'

'It could certainly do with a wash,' said Elsa briskly. 'Try the next one.'

Sarah and Lily had gone round to Elsa's for her professional advice. Sarah had had a trawl of the local charity shops to see if anything was suitable. Lily had been forced to come round to the idea of a 'pre-loved' dress, but not willingly, despite being reassured that Sarah would make sure it was dry-cleaned thoroughly before Lily's big day.

Now, Sarah handed over the next offering. This had big hoops, lots of beading and was grubby round the hem. 'Here you are, but don't let the label drop off. I can take back the ones we don't use but I must remember which charity shop they came from.'

'I can't believe they let you do a sale or return,' said Elsa, hooking up Lily.

Sarah shrugged. 'It took a bit of sweet-talking but that's my job.' Then she sighed. Sometimes she found her job very difficult. Lily was proving to be even more demanding than her A-list client.

'Oh!' Lily squeaked. 'That's too tight.'

No one spoke for a few seconds. 'I think that could be described as a pregnant pause,' said Sarah.

Elsa and Lily glared at her.

'I could let it out if you love it,' said Elsa. 'I might have to sew an extra bit of material into the bodice. I'll check the seam allowance.'

'Don't bother. I hate it.' Lily plucked at it and sniffed, fighting tears. 'I can't believe I can't fit into that dress just because I've got a tadpole swimming about inside me. What size is it?'

Sarah and Elsa exchanged glances. 'About eight to ten, I should say,' said Elsa, tactfully. 'They don't often have the size in them,' she added.

'Take it off,' said Sarah. 'You've still got a couple more to try. If only I could have got to one of those charity shops that specialise in wedding dresses, I might have found better ones.' She took the dress from Elsa and put it into its bag. 'That's still an option if none of these are any good, but we are getting short of time.'

The last dress was much better and billowed generously round Lily's still slender form. 'Oh, I like this!' said Lily. 'This must be a size twelve.'

'Don't get so obsessed with sizes,' said Elsa. 'I'm going to pin this so it fits you and you can see what you think.'

'I don't suppose you've got any wine, Elsa,' said Lily. 'I can't help feeling this would be a lot less stressful if we had a little glass of white.'

'No alcohol until Bron gets here,' said Sarah firmly. 'She's bringing a takeaway round at seven. Anyway, I thought you were off it.'

'Sometimes I am, sometimes I'm not. Don't be a spoilsport,' said Lily. Sarah was just about to protest when Lily went on, 'What's that dress up there, under the muslin?'

'Ng,' said Elsa, her mouth full of pins. She took them out. 'That's the ball gown I was telling you about. For the ball I'm going to with Laurence.'

'Oh, can we see it?' asked Sarah, needing a break from shop-soiled wedding dresses, even if they were 'pre-loved'.

'Oh, let's,' agreed Lily, probably bored with them too.

Elsa went across and removed the muslin cover from

her dress. She was pleased with it. It had little puff sleeves and a bodice in pale blue. The dress split just under the bust revealing a primrose-coloured underskirt. The edges of the gown were trimmed with tiny embroidered flowers, with the odd seed pearl picking up the colours. It had been a real labour of love.

'That's fantastic! I can't believe you made that,' said Sarah.

'Thank you for your confidence, O Great Provider of Two Important Clients,' said Elsa dryly.

'Oh, you know what I mean. It's just it's so exquisite. How did you find the time to do all that embroidery?' Sarah was peering at it closely.

'I cheated. That's some very fancy ribbon. I sewed on the pearls. It's effective, isn't it?'

'Extremely! You really should take this up pro-fessionally,' said Sarah, giving Elsa's arm a playful push.

'That's what I want!' declared Lily. 'That's my dress!'

'Actually, it's my dress,' murmured Elsa.

'I mean, that is exactly the sort of dress I want!' Lily was pointing at the gown as if she were trying to put a spell on it, possibly to make it fit her perfectly.

Both the other women looked at the ball gown and then back at Lily.

'Something like that could work well,' said Elsa. 'The bump would be quite unobtrusive.'

'There won't be a bump!' declared Lily.

'There probably will be,' said Sarah, for what felt like the millionth time. 'But it will hardly show. That's a lovely idea, Lily, well done!'

'Do you want to have a white wedding, everything traditional?' asked Elsa.

'My mother-in-law does,' said Lily. 'What we want doesn't seem to be important.'

'The dress is always the bride's choice,' said Sarah, 'especially if there isn't a mother to be pacified. No, Lily,

I'm not saying it's a good thing we haven't got Mum any more, but it is one less person to consult on things.'

'Right,' said Elsa, 'put the first one back on.'

'But we hated that. It was all grubby.'

'And a bit tight,' added Sarah, ignoring Lily's frown.

'Never mind about that. I've got an idea.' Elsa was on a roll. 'Come on, Lily.'

'Couldn't I try on your dress?' Lily asked as she struggled into the dress. 'It's so much nicer.'

'You can, but later. I want to see what I can do with this one.' She stepped back, her head on one side. 'Dye it, that's the first thing. I think a soft apricot.'

'Yes,' said Sarah, warming to the idea. 'I like that. What about you, Lily.'

'Apricot's cool. After all, I shouldn't really wear white. I'm not a virgin.'

As the proof of this was already showing, the other two didn't comment.

'And then we need an underskirt. If you liked pale yellow, I've got some material left over from my dress,' Elsa said. 'In fact, let me go and see what other scraps I've got. This is going to be good!'

Elsa's enthusiasm was catching. She brought back a bag of bits and Sarah and Lily rummaged through them.

'Actually,' Elsa went on, 'although it's dirty, this is quite good material. I'll take out the sleeves and give you little puff ones, like I've got – you've got good arms so that's a perfect look for you.'

Lily looked at an arm, trying to admire it underneath the bulky satin.

'Are you sure you'll have time to do this, Elsa?' asked Sarah.

'Of course. It shouldn't take too long. Now, Lily, take it off,' ordered Elsa, 'and let's have a good look.'

With the dress back in her hand she examined it a bit more closely. 'Yes, I can put in an extra panel with the material from the sleeves.' There was a terrifying rip as Elsa demolished a seam. 'Don't worry, I know what I'm doing.' Seeing Sarah and Lily looking a little anxious as she picked up her shears, she said, 'Why don't you try on my dress, Lily? Sarah, you help her. I won't be a minute here, then I'll make you a sketch.'

Elsa was perched on her chair unpicking a seam a little more carefully than the one she'd dealt with before and Lily had finally taken off the ball gown. Not that Elsa was proprietorial about her clothes but she was glad to see it safely hanging up again, unscathed.

'It's so gorgeous!' she kept saying, 'and my bump hardly shows at all!'

As this was the first time she'd acknowledged she had a bump, or at least one bigger than a tadpole, Sarah felt this was progress.

'Bron will be here with the takeaway soon,' she said. 'Cover Elsa's dress up again in case something bad happens to it.'

'Is Bron nice?' asked Lily. 'She does hair and make-up, doesn't she? Could she do mine?'

'No, she couldn't,' Sarah wailed, and then regretted it. 'Sorry, Lily, she could probably advise you, but she's booked for Carrie. Carrie wanted her specially.'

'Oh, so although I'm your sister, I don't get the best people?' Sarah couldn't work out if she was teasing or not.

'Lily, who does your hair normally? That's the best person for you,' said Elsa.

Lily shrugged, picking up a scrap of the ribbon that had decorated Elsa's dress. 'I haven't been for ages. There's no one I trust. Can I have this on my dress?'

'Sorry, I haven't got any more. And it costs a fortune,' Elsa replied. 'I'll find you something just as lovely though.'

'Bron might be able to recommend someone for your hair,' said Sarah, hoping against hope that Bron would know a hairdresser so far away from her own area. She had a nightmare-flash of there being no one but her to put her sister's silky locks into a bun on top of her head. Donating a kidney would be very much easier.

Bron arrived with a Chinese takeaway and a couple of bottles of Pinot Grigio on the dot of seven. 'I wasn't sure if I should bring wine. Are we working or not?' she asked.

'Wine is always a good idea,' said Lily. She shot Sarah a look. 'Well, for people who aren't pregnant, anyway.'

Sarah smiled. 'Bron, this is my sister, Lily. Lily, this is Bron,' she said.

'You do hair and make-up?' said Lily, cutting to the chase without preliminaries. 'Sarah says you can't do mine for my wedding.'

Bron took in the situation after a couple of seconds. 'I'm sorry, but I really can't. What sort of style did you have in mind?'

'You should have it in a bun on top of your head, with ringlets over your ears,' said Elsa, confirming Sarah's worst fears.

'Like you'll wear for your ball?' said Bron. 'Up-dos are quite time consuming. Don't, whatever you do, have your hair cut before now and then.'

'Oh, I won't,' said Lily.

'And are you having a veil, or not?' asked Bron.

Elsa, Lily and Sarah all looked questioningly at each other. 'You don't have to if you don't want to,' said Sarah.

'You could have a really pretty tiara instead,' suggested Elsa. 'I've got a couple you could try now.'

'Not having a veil would save money, wouldn't it?' said Lily.

'Definitely,' said Sarah.

'Then I won't have one.' She looked at her sister quizzically. 'You see, I can be economical sometimes.'

While Sarah hunted in Elsa's little kitchen for plates and

cutlery and Elsa performed magic with scissors, pins and an old wedding dress, Bron and Lily talked about hair. They were a good team and once again they had proved themselves stalwarts, especially when this was a wedding they weren't supposed to be involved in.

'You'll need to have a couple of practice runs before the big day,' said Bron. 'Especially if you don't have a regular hairdresser. One dummy run is enough if you do get to know someone.'

'I can't afford to keep going to the hairdresser,' said Lily, worried. 'That's partly why I haven't been for so long.'

'OK, so what you need to do is find a hairdresser who has students. They advertise for models in the window. They do your hair very reasonably, and if the student was good and you got to know each other, she'd probably do your hair for your wedding day.'

'Would you trust someone with so little experience?' asked Elsa, looking up from her seam-ripping.

'If she and Lily have built up a good relationship, there's no reason why not,' said Bron. 'I did all my friends' hair when we were going to a big do. They were very pleased.'

'But you're a very good hairdresser,' said Sarah, putting down a roll of kitchen towel as she perched on the sofa.

'Yes,' Bron agreed modestly, 'but possibly not the only one.'

Sarah and Bron discussed the Catering Ladies and Lily chatted to Elsa as they tucked into the takeaways.

'So, Elsa,' Sarah asked a little later, while they were all still shovelling up egg-fried rice and prawn crackers. 'How did your ballroom dancing lesson go?'

'Oh! It was wonderful. I was a complete klutz at first – couldn't do it at all. I kept stepping all over Laurence's feet, but then Terry sent him out and I danced with him! It was a miracle. Suddenly, I could do it. He sort of clamped me to his body so I couldn't go wrong.' She stopped, aware that the others were looking at her oddly.

'So, was he gorgeous?' asked Lily. 'The teacher, I mean?'

'Mm. Quite. An amazing dancer. I think Laurence was a bit jealous of him, actually.'

'Oh, so he's keen then?' said Bron.

Elsa shook her head. 'I don't know if it was that, more that he was annoyed that he couldn't teach me to dance.'

'Men can be quite controlling,' said Lily. Everyone looked at her. 'Even Dirk is, a bit. My first husband was a real bully!'

'Oh, love,' said Sarah. 'I hate to think of you with that horrible man.'

'Roger was a bit of a bully,' said Bron. 'Or maybe it was me who allowed him to be.'

'Men are very unreliable,' confirmed Sarah, the resident expert.

'No,' said Lily firmly. 'Not all of them. Dirk, for instance, can be a bit bossy, but he'd cut off his arm for me; and when he is bossy, it's because he's looking out for me.'

'Dirk is very nice,' agreed Sarah.

'And he's not the only nice man,' said Elsa. 'Laurence is quite nice too. And I think he's reliable.'

'I'm probably just a cynical old wedding planner,' said Sarah laughing, wanting to change the subject. 'I'm dying of thirst. Anyone else need a drink of water?'

'So,' Elsa said when she'd returned, 'have you decided about your cake yet, Lily?'

'It would be good if you could make it, Bron,' said Sarah. 'If you used the same ingredients as Carrie's cake there'd be the economy of scale.'

The other women looked at her.

'I mean,' Sarah ploughed on, 'if you were buying ingredients in bulk, like dried fruit, it would be much cheaper. You'd have to keep exact records of how much of everything you used for each cake, of course. I wouldn't want to diddle Carrie.'

'Although she could easily afford to pay for my cake ingredients,' said Lily.

Seeing Sarah take a combative breath, Bron said, 'But Carrie's cake has to be sponge. It would be really difficult to support the weight on a pole, otherwise.'

'Does Carrie know this?' asked Sarah.

'No, but honestly, would she really mind? I suppose you should check, but it was more the shape she wanted,' said Bron. 'Still, a sponge cake isn't very traditional.'

'And we wouldn't be able to send sponge cake to all the far-flung aunties and uncles, would we?' said Lily.

'It would have to be fruit to do that,' agreed Bron. 'I suppose I could just about fit it in, but I will be pushed for time.'

'I know!' said Sarah, her brainwave sending the prawn crackers flying. 'We'll ask Aunt Dot! She's a wonderful baker and would love to do it!'

'Aunt Dot?' asked Lily, frowning.

'Yes – not sure if she's a real aunt, but she makes brilliant cakes. I'll get the ingredients for her. Bron, do these catering-lady friends of yours have a Cash and Carry connection, do you think?'

'I should think so. Veronica makes cakes for WI markets,' said Bron.

'Brilliant.' Sarah raised her glass, her worried look leaving her for the first time in a while. 'We've got the dress, the caterers, the cake and the hairdresser all sorted for you, Lily. Let's have a toast!'

'Hey,' said Lily when she'd taken the smallest sip. 'I've had a brilliant idea! You must all come to my hen party! Elsa and Bron, I feel like you're my new best friends.'

'Surely you don't want a hen party when you're pregnant,' said Sarah without thinking. 'You won't be able to get drunk.'

'Sarah,' said Lily, very dignified all of a sudden, 'a hen party is an opportunity to get together with one's female friends before you get married. You don't have to get drunk to have a good time.'

'No, Lily,' said Sarah, suitably chastised but liking the role reversal.

She felt a pang of guilt. She knew she had to go to Lily's hen night, but she really didn't want to. It wasn't anything to do with Lily, more her friends. They were bound to want to do things that just made Sarah feel jaded. Still, she'd go, and probably have a brilliant time. And everyone was always saying she needed to lighten up.

Chapter Twenty-Nine

❧

'And you're sure you gave the driver the right address?' Sarah was sitting in the car next to Hugo as they drove to Somerby. It was high summer now and the surrounding countryside was lush, in part owing to the sudden spell of rain they'd been having. Sarah prayed it would clear very soon.

'He's got the postcode, he's got Sat Nav, and I gave him some basic directions. He'll be fine.'

'Sat Nav does mad things sometimes.'

'I know.'

'And neither Mandy or Carrie will be able to help if he goes wrong.'

'Probably not, but he won't go wrong. He'll be very experienced, professional. It'll be fine, Sarah, now relax.'

Sarah exhaled loudly and looked out of the window. 'I'd feel happier if I could have sent a driver I know. If only they had given us a bit more notice.'

'Carrie didn't know she was going to be in the country until just recently. She couldn't have known earlier.'

'And poor Fen, having to rustle up lunch for us all. Although I suppose she has had just enough time to get in caterers, if she felt she needed to.'

'Mm.' Hugo obviously wasn't listening. He'd heard all this several times before and knew a response wasn't really called for.

'And what's the house going to look like in all this rain!'

Hugo glanced at her, giving her an opportunity to see

his charming crooked smile. 'Wet! Now stop fretting. It's going to be fine.'

She did feel less anxious about Carrie and Mandy's last-minute visit to Somerby, to which she had been summoned, but the pang she got from Hugo's crinkled eyes and sexy mouth was not helpful. How could she react like that to him when she had so much on her mind and when she'd told herself that he was off limits? Two damn weddings on the same day should be enough to stop her having unsuitable feelings for an unsuitable man, surely? How can there possibly be space in her mind for anything except the job in hand? Her guard was weakening, she could tell. He was so attractive and so skilled at calming her fears, she found it hard not to keeping wondering, 'What if?'

And she couldn't stop thinking about his exhibition. The quality of his work, the fact that some had been sold before the show even opened, was amazing. He was so talented. And yet here he was, helping her with a wedding, albeit a celebrity wedding. Then she thought about Electra and felt down again. It wasn't only that she existed, and that he was engaged to her, but the fact that she seemed so wrong for him. He loved children: she had seen him with them, and she had seen him photograph them. And he'd just been telling her about his nephew and niece as they hit the motorway. His face lit up when he mentioned them. What was he doing with a woman who cared more about her abs than being a mother? If she thought they'd be happy together, it would be easier – possibly.

'If only it would stop raining!' she moaned, using the rain as an excuse for her sudden despondency.

'I think the sky is lightening over there,' he said, then switched the windscreen wipers up to full.

The house was still beautiful, thought Sarah as they came within sight of it. On a small hill, surrounded by parkland

and trees, it looked like a painting, animated by raindrops falling on the leaves of the trees. There were two big black cars parked in front of the house, announcing clearly that Carrie and her entourage had arrived. Sarah had hoped she and Hugo would be first but at least the others had found the place.

Hugo stopped the car at the bottom of the drive. 'Let's just have a moment to ourselves to enjoy the stillness before we go in, shall we?' He smiled reassuringly at her and once again her stomach did a flip. Why did he always have to be so nice to her?

Sarah wound down the window. The smell of summer wafted into the car. She couldn't identify any particular scent but the mixture was wonderful. Somewhere a bird sang, a solitary sound among the gentle pit-pat of water on leaves. If she hadn't been in her smart working clothes, and had a mac or something, she would have got out and smelt the air at closer quarters, but she couldn't.

Neither of them spoke for a few minutes until Hugo said, 'Shall we go on?'

'Not just yet.' Sarah wanted to stay in the car, listening to the gentle hiss of the rain and the bird before she had to go back to being the high-powered wedding planner she was every other minute of her life. But she couldn't do that either. She took a deep breath and said, 'We'd better get going now.'

Hugo turned the key in the ignition and they drove up to the house.

Fenella must have been listening for the car. She rushed out the moment they reached the front door and pulled open the car door before the engine had stopped. 'Thank God you're here, it's not going well. They must have whistled down here! We weren't ready really, and I got up at five.'

Fenella was looking elegant in a harassed way in silk

trousers, matching top and a floaty jacket. The top was half tucked into the trousers as if she had been interrupted while dressing.

'It'll be fine,' said Sarah, surprised at how calm she sounded. 'Don't worry. We just need to paint the picture for her.'

'They're muttering about the condition everything is in. It's not the traditional setting Carrie wanted, and I don't know what else!'

'Don't worry, Fen,' said Hugo, giving her a friendly hug. 'Uncle Hugo's here. He'll make everything work out.'

This did make Fenella give a little chuckle as she exchanged glances with Sarah. There was no doubt, he *was* a calming presence.

Carrie, Mandy and a couple of men Sarah didn't know were standing around in the dining room. Sarah could see that the floor had been covered with hardboard and painted white and looked amazing, but the room felt cold and Carrie, in a strappy top, was rubbing her arms. Mandy was similarly attired and they did not look happy. A wet summer day in England must have felt arctic to them. Sarah knew she'd have to find something for them to put on or they'd never agree to anything.

'Oh, hi! Sarah! You're here. At last,' said Carrie, coming forward and kissing Sarah. Sarah felt her reproach – not only for suggesting this unsuitable venue but for being late. 'And Hugo!' He got a warmer reception, possibly because his arms were warm and she was cold.

'So sorry you were kept waiting,' he said when he'd released her. 'We hit very bad traffic in Hereford.'

While Hugo was chatting to Carrie and Mandy and soothing ruffled feathers, Sarah touched Fenella's sleeve. 'You haven't got a couple of pashminas or cardigans or something for them to borrow? They won't come here if they're cold.'

Fenella hesitated only a moment. 'Pashminas. I've got

loads of them. People always give them to me as presents. I'll be right back.'

As good as her word, she came back while Hugo was still making Carrie and Mandy giggle in a shameless way.

'Here, ladies, take one of these each,' she said gracefully, as if it was perfectly normal to dole out shawls in English country houses.

Carrie and Mandy were charmed and grateful. Fenella had colour coded them too.

'Sorry,' said Hugo to the two dark-suited men, 'I'm Hugo Marsters, photographer to the stars.' He laughed to show he was being ironic. The men he was addressing didn't laugh back.

'We're Carrie's lawyers,' said one and went on to introduce himself and his colleague. 'We're here to see Carrie doesn't get ripped off.'

One of them had a smile as practised as Hugo's but it did nothing for Sarah. She just laughed lightheartedly, pretending that everything was wonderful and all was going just as she'd planned it. 'I thought that was my job!' Then she put her hand on a cashmere-jacketed arm. 'Fen, are we in time for lunch?' She could do charming too.

'We're having it in the kitchen,' said Fenella. Her fake cheerfulness was less skilled than Sarah's. 'I thought it would be more cosy in there. The Aga's going full bore.'

As the party filed through the house, Sarah could see a lot of work had gone on since she'd last seen it. But instead of the oohs and ahs of appreciation she was expecting, Sarah heard murmurs of disapproval. Anxiety clenched at her stomach and she hoped Fenella had provided wine. If Carrie turned down Somerby, which reeked of upperclass elegance, where on earth else could she provide that she would like and with only a month to go? If Carrie had a couple of glasses of something she might feel more positive.

The huge kitchen was a picture of country-house

glamour, she thought. Fenella and Rupert had obviously made a real effort to make it look picturesque but practical and in her opinion, they'd brought it off superbly.

A huge variety of pots, pans and kitchenalia, antique and modern together, were displayed on the wall above the Aga and the range cooker. Copper-bottomed bowls, little pans, cheese-graters, nutmeg-graters, a wire egg basket shaped like a hen, balloon whisks, ladles, conical sieves hung next to spatulas, colanders, spoons and a string of garlic.

The enormous built-in dresser displayed a large collection of china jelly moulds, huge old serving platters, a set of pewter side plates and a random collection of breakfast saucers. Some of it was bright Majolica wear, some were faded English classic designs. None of it matched but all of it was quality. The hooks were hung with jugs and mugs and on the top was a basket full of flowers. In Sarah's opinion, it was a magazine editor's dream. She just hoped Carrie and her party appreciated it.

The long table was laid for lunch and Rupert, wearing a striped apron and a broad smile, took a huge roasting tin out of the oven.

'Welcome to Somerby!' he declared. 'I thought as it was such a filthy day we'd have a proper bit of roast beef. Home-reared. With roast potatoes and Yorkshire pudding.'

'Er, Carrie doesn't eat red meat,' said Mandy.

'Nonsense!' said Rupert. 'You're not going to turn down organic beef reared on English grass. Full of nutrients you can't get any other way.'

Sarah held her breath. Rupert's bluntness might not be welcome and most Hollywood stars not only didn't eat meat, but also avoided anything likely to add even a millimetre to their already stick-like figures. This was the sort of thing she should have anticipated, she chided herself.

'Well,' said Carrie, thankfully as charmed by Rupert as she was by Hugo, 'I guess it wouldn't hurt just once.'

'Come and sit down,' said Fenella, who had also been holding her breath. 'Hugo, you go that end, Carrie, you go on one side, Mandy the other. You two . . .'

With easy manners Fenella seated everyone, looking as if she was making the placement up as she went along, but Sarah could tell she'd thought about it carefully. She herself was placed between the two lawyers but she didn't feel like sitting down.

'Can I do anything?' She spoke brightly as if totally confident that everything was under control.

'Could you just take this water?' said Fenella, giving the same impression. 'And Hugo, can you pour wine for everyone?'

'I don't drink—' Carrie began but Hugo's charm caused her to accept half a glass of wine from what appeared to be a very grand bottle. It even had dust on it.

Sarah was about to be impressed until she remembered that when there was building work going on, dust was inevitable.

'So tell me, Carrie,' said Hugo, smiling into her eyes, 'what made you want a traditional English wedding?'

She smiled and shrugged. 'Well, you know Rick, my fiancé, is English, originally. But I guess I just fell in love with those great Jane Austen movies and when I saw Ashlyn's pictures . . .'

'Then it's my fault?' Hugo raised an eyebrow.

Carrie laughed, pushing him gently. 'Not your fault at all – just your skill that showed me what could be done.'

'I promise you, Somerby can provide not only tradition but originality,' said Rupert with assurance. 'And that's a rare combination.'

Sarah smiled to herself. A rare combination indeed – virtually an oxymoron.

The meal was superb. Rupert was either a sensational

cook or the beef was so good no one could ruin it, but it was tender and tasty. The roast potatoes were numerous and crunchy and the vegetables were piled high in platters, covered with butter. Gravy came in two-pint jugs, one up each end of the table.

To begin with, the two lawyers ate almost in silence, obviously relishing the food. Twice Rupert got up to carve more, and Sarah noticed that he'd cooked two huge joints of beef. Even Mandy and Carrie ate well. Hugo made sure that glasses were topped up, either with wine or with water, and everyone began to relax.

'The thing about this place is its history, Carrie,' said Sarah, feeling obliged to get the conversation back to the matter in hand while Rupert retrieved massive apple pies from the oven.

'Some of the rooms are a little bleak,' said Mandy. 'Carrie, you commented on that the moment you saw them, didn't you?'

'Oh, Rupert!' said Hugo. 'Haven't you got your family portraits up yet, or are they still being cleaned?'

There was just the tiniest pause before Rupert answered and it could have been because he was finding space for a very hot dish. 'Oh yes, they are.'

'Rupert has the most superb collection of family portraits going right back to the eighteenth century. Or did you get some of the earlier ones too?' Hugo went on expansively.

'No,' said Fenella quickly, 'his brother got all those.'

Hugo leant towards Carrie and whispered, 'His brother is a duke, you know.'

Sarah heard Carrie and Mandy gasp and wished that Hugo had chosen a less noble title for Rupert's brother to be. It would be so easy to check dukes – there weren't many of them. Still, if it did the trick, did she really care?

'Family fortunes have declined a bit latterly,' said Rupert. 'Now, Carrie, if you'd kindly pass me those carrots, I'll have somewhere to put this down.'

'You'd think the brother of a duke would have servants,' muttered one of the lawyers to Sarah.

'Not these days,' said Sarah, 'very passé.'

Hoping he would know what passé meant, she sighed and took another sip of wine. It was very good, she decided, even if the dust was recent, and she really hoped Fenella and Rupert hadn't spent too much money on the lunch.

'Cream from the farm next door,' said Rupert, putting a jug on the table that was almost as large as the gravy jugs had been. 'We feel strongly about food being as local and as seasonal as possible,' he added.

'Does that mean it doesn't have calories in it?' asked Carrie, smiling prettily.

'Only good calories,' said Fenella. 'Obviously we don't eat like this all the time or we'd be fat as pigs, but if you are going to have a traditional roast lunch, it's better if you know the provenance of everything.'

'This pastry is fantastic. Melt-in-the-mouth,' said Hugo. 'Have another little slice, Carrie. Rupes, you really can cook.'

'So can I,' muttered Fenella, 'but he's more flamboyant about it.'

When everyone was only just able to move, Fenella said, 'Well, I think we should have the proper tour now. Carrie and Mandy have only really seen the dining room, but I'd like them to see all the rooms, plus a couple of bedrooms that are finished now. More will be finished on the day, of course.'

Again Sarah could see how much work had been done since her last visit and, sometimes, what work hadn't. A lovely antique basin and ewer were placed strategically under a drip. Fortunately nothing splashed into it until after Carrie and Mandy had passed into the next room.

The drawing room was a masterpiece. Someone, maybe

even Fenella or Rupert, had extended the wallpaper by turning it into a mural. Now the pillars and exotic birds were the foreground for an Egyptian scene, with pyramids and sand dunes in the background. It was a masterpiece of simple painting and *trompe l'œil*.

'Tradition and exotica,' declared Hugo. 'I like that. You really feel that behind the wall you can see this view. Did you copy the idea from Hazlehurst? Family seat,' he muttered sotto voce to Mandy, who was near him.

'Sort of. We had to scale it down quite a lot,' said Rupert, after exchanging desperate looks with his wife. 'These rooms may seem spacious, but to me they are on the small side.'

'That's what you get from a venue like this that you never could from anywhere else,' said Hugo. 'The personal touch. I mean, you could rent a castle if you wanted, with a lake, a pagoda, anything. But at Somerby you'd get intimacy, style, a secret place that the tourists don't know about. One word sums it up perfectly – class.'

At that moment Sarah realised that only Hugo could have said those things. She certainly couldn't, or at least, not in anything like the same grandiose way. Rupert and Fenella were far too modest, but Hugo had no shame – thank goodness.

'Another bonus, in my opinion,' said Hugo, 'is that yours would be the first wedding ever to be here. Others will follow, but you'll be the first.' He crinkled his eyes at Carrie in a way that no normal woman could resist. 'I think you are a trendsetter, aren't you?'

Carrie shrugged, raised her shoulders and agreed in her body language that yes, maybe she was. 'It would be quite cool to be the first to discover this place,' she said to Mandy.

Mandy shivered in agreement.

'We do want something for you that is totally unique,' Sarah broke in. 'Nowhere else I've researched has anything like the charm of Somerby.' She paused. 'It's good from the security angle, too. The way the roads are, it'll be very easy to keep the paparazzi under control.'

'That's a good point,' said one of the lawyers. 'That does have to be taken into consideration.'

'We'll have that checked out later,' said the other.

There was a moment's silence while this all settled, and then Fenella said, 'Let's carry on with the tour,' and she led the party to the room that opened off the chapel.

The chapel should do it, thought Sarah, aware that Fenella was probably pinning her hopes on this too.

There was a long silence when Rupert opened the door and Carrie, Mandy and her two lawyers regarded what was in effect a miniature church.

'Holy cow!' said one of the lawyers under his breath.

'This was for just one family?' asked Mandy eventually.

'Originally, yes, but the villagers used it when their own church was being repaired,' said Rupert. 'It's why it has this other entrance here.' He opened the door.

By some miracle the sun came out from behind a cloud, shining on the wet path that led through the park down to the road. It glimmered like white marble.

'Your carriage could take you all the way up to the chapel door,' said Fenella, 'if you liked.'

'Or you could walk up, with your retainers – brides-maids – behind you,' offered Sarah.

'Then after the service and the outside photographs, you slip into the house while your guests go round the long way,' said Hugo. 'Giving you a few moments to freshen up before your greet them.'

Carrie bit her lip and nodded, still non-committal. No one spoke. No one from the Somerby side wanted to say anything that would scupper their chances and no one from Carrie's team appeared to have anything to say, obviously waiting for her approval before they dared speak.

At last Sarah couldn't bear it any longer. 'I'm just thinking how wonderful your cake will look silhouetted against that fabulous window, with the parkland beyond.'

There was a pause as long as the Forth Bridge before Carrie eventually spoke. 'Oh yes,' she said softly. 'That would be truly fabulous.'

And Sarah silently sent a prayer of thanks up to God.

Chapter Thirty

'I can't believe we pulled that off,' said Fenella to Sarah as they watched the two black cars go down the drive. It had stopped raining and they were all standing in front of the house having said goodbye to their visitors.

'It was touch and go,' said Rupert.

'I think it was your stately background that clinched it,' said Sarah, laughing. 'You'll have to produce some family portraits now. You can probably pick them up from auctions quite cheaply.'

'No need,' said Rupert. 'There are dozens in the attic at home.'

Sarah glanced at Hugo who was laughing.

'I'm going to let the dogs out,' said Fenella, unaware of Sarah's discomfort. 'The poor darlings have been cooped up all day. You excelled yourself with the roast, Rupes.'

'Yes, the lunch really was fantastic,' agreed Sarah, on safe ground again. 'The apple pie was truly heavenly.'

'Fen made it.' Rupert watched his wife go into the house. 'She doesn't do such a good roast as me and refused to take her share of the credit.'

'Well, it was all stunning,' said Sarah.

'We'd better make a list of what still needs doing before the big day,' said Rupert. 'I can't believe we've done it. How much will we be able to charge, do you think?'

Sarah told him. 'Wow,' he said. 'Fan-bloody-tastic.'

And they grinned at each other, Rupert shaking Hugo's hand and hugging Sarah.

With mugs of tea now in their hands, they toured the house again. Everyone made notes and Hugo took photos from every angle. 'Remember, you'll want a before and after album,' he said. 'And maybe some shots for a brochure.'

It was only when they were alone for a few moments that Sarah turned to him. 'Hugo, I can't thank you enough. If it hadn't been for you, she never would have gone for it.' She wanted to make some gesture, to mark her gratitude and was about to kiss his cheek but, suddenly feeling a little awkward, she stood back on her heels again. She would have liked to say something about his exhibition too. She opened her mouth to tell him how impressed she'd been, then caught his glance. He looked quizzical and wryly amused, and yet slightly wistful.

'Hugo . . .' she said.

'Sarah,' he said back, but before either of them could go on, Rupert came back and the moment was gone. She couldn't tell if he'd sensed her desire to say something or not.

'Are you sure you won't stay for supper? Cold beef and apple pie?' asked Fenella as they stood in the hall.

'No, really, I should get back. It's six o'clock already and I've got loads to do,' said Sarah.

'You could stay the night,' Fenella went on, 'test out the spare beds. As you saw, we have several.'

'Honestly, Fen, we'd better make tracks. Sarah's not the only one who has to work in the morning.' Hugo put his hand on Fenella's shoulder and kissed her cheek.

'Not a wedding, surely?' Fenella asked him, kissing him back.

'Nope, thank God,' said Hugo and turned his farewells to Rupert.

Sarah was hugged firmly by both of them and it was only when she was in Hugo's car and they were halfway down the drive that she realised she'd never asked them if the chapel was now licensed for weddings. She said so to Hugo.

'Do you want to go back and ask now?' he said, braking slightly.

'No, they'll just be relaxing with a glass of wine. I can always ring them tomorrow. There are bound to be lots of things I need to ask them.' She yawned. 'Wretched Carrie, she still hasn't decided what wedding dress to have. Elsa begged me to try and get her to commit.'

'I don't think she means to be unreasonable, she just doesn't realise that things take time to make or organise, or whatever.'

'I know,' Sarah agreed. 'I also forgot to confirm that her wedding cake will have to be sponge and not fruit. Bron says a pole wouldn't take the weight of a traditional cake. But at least she decided on Somerby. And I know it's the right choice. Fen and Rupert will do a fantastic job.' She chuckled reminiscently. 'You were outrageous, saying that Rupert was the son of a duke.'

'Oh, but he is,' said Hugo, glancing at her. 'Not a very grand one, but a duke's a duke.'

'Oh my goodness!' said Sarah. 'And he seems such a nice guy.'

'The two are not mutually exclusive, you know.'

Sarah stretched back in her seat, feeling relaxed, if a little weary. They'd done a good day's work between them. 'I know.'

'Why don't you close your eyes and have a doze?' said Hugo.

'You must be tired too.'

'I'll chew gum. That'll keep me awake. And put on some music.'

Some African jazz music filled the car with the limpid notes of a saxophone and Sarah let her eyes close. Count your blessings, she told herself. Carrie's wedding is on its way. Rupert or Fenella would have told her if there was a problem with the licence. It was going to be really beautiful. Somerby was idyllic – beautiful even in the rain, though of course it would be much better if it didn't rain. She was fine with Hugo. Yes, he was gorgeous, but they could be just friends now, and so what if he was engaged to someone else. Far better to have him as a friend. And she wasn't remotely jealous. She wasn't that sort of woman. She'd enjoyed those kisses but they seemed almost a lifetime ago now. And to show how cool she was about it all, she'd offer to take him out for something to eat when they got home. She owed him.

'Your phone is ringing,' said Hugo.

Sarah snapped awake, found her bag and then scrabbled for her phone. It was Lily.

'Sarah! Can you come over? I'm not feeling very well.'

'What sort of "not very well"? Is it the baby?' Sarah was wide awake now.

'It might be. I've got a pain. Oh, Sarah, I'm so frightened!'

'Hush, it's going to be all right,' she soothed. 'But where's Dirk?'

'Spending the night with his best friend. I've rung him but he said to ring you. He's miles away.'

'Sweetie, I'm miles away.'

'He's in Liverpool.'

'Oh,' said Sarah.

'Where do you want to be?' asked Hugo.

'Just a minute, Lily.' She turned to Hugo and told him Lily's address. 'How long to get there?'

'About an hour. Less if we're lucky with traffic.'

'Lily? I'm about an hour away. I'll get to you as quickly as possible, but really you should ring the doctor. Or Dad.'

'No. I want you.' Lily sounded tearful.

'I'll be there soon. Don't worry, Lily, please. Why don't you have a bath while you're waiting? It might ease the pain and if you do have to go into hospital or anything you'll be nice and clean.'

Lily accepted this was good advice and they disconnected.

'I can't believe I said that,' said Sarah, 'about her being nice and clean. I'm barking!'

'Well, it did the trick. Lily will be occupied until we can get there. It'll distract her.'

'That was what I thought, but how do you know it would? You've never met Lily.'

'I've met plenty of girls like her. They revert to childhood if they're frightened.'

'Lily is a bit like that. Better than she was though, and being pregnant must be quite nerve-racking sometimes. I really hope there's nothing wrong. I know she got pregnant by accident but she'd be devastated if she lost the baby. But Hugo . . .'

'What?'

'You don't have to take me to Lily's. Home is much nearer. You've been such a star already, you don't have to do anything else. Take me there then I can pick up my car. You don't want to be involved in Lily's dramas.'

'Don't be silly, it would take you much longer to get there that way. We don't want Lily to be alone a moment longer than necessary. Besides, I want to help.'

Sarah spent the rest of the journey trying to work out if Hugo had insisted on driving her for her benefit or for Lily's.

Lily was enveloped in white towelling from slippers to her head. 'Oh, Sarah! You should have told me you had someone with you!' she said, smoothing her hair and going all girly the moment she spied Hugo. It was a reflex action with some women when confronted by an attractive man, Sarah realised.

'I thought you must have guessed,' said Sarah, examining her sister for signs of imminent miscarriage. 'Can we come in?'

'Of course.' Lily smiled at Hugo. 'Who's this?'

'This is Hugo. Hugo, Lily. Are you all right?'

'Let me get you something to drink or a snack? I could make a sandwich or something.' Lily was looking at Hugo, over the embarrassment of being seen *en déshabille*.

Sarah looked at him too. He may well be hungry. It was hours since lunch and although Fenella had offered cake with their mugs of tea she was fairly sure that he hadn't had any.

'Don't worry about me, how are you?' said Hugo. 'Sarah's been really worried about you.'

Lily glanced at her sister a little guiltily. 'Oh, I think that may have been a false alarm. The bath helped.'

'So you're not in pain any more? There hasn't been any – you know – other signs anything might be wrong?'

'Shall I put the kettle on while you two have a chat?' Hugo, the epitome of tact, left the room.

'You won't know where anything is!' Lily complained after him.

'I'll find what I need,' Hugo called back.

'He can't make tea in a house he's never been in!' said Lily, and then, 'He's gorgeous!'

'That doesn't make him incapable! Now sit down, do, and tell me how you are. We've made a mercy dash to get to your bedside and you're worried about Hugo finding the tea bags!'

Lily subsided on to the sofa and Sarah sat next to her. 'Oh well, I had a bath, like you said, and the pain sort of – went away.'

'What, completely?'

'Mm. But tell me about Hugo! He's even better looking in real life and not a bit like Bruce, really. I thought you told me he was just a colleague?'

'He is.'

'Are you trying to tell me there's nothing in it? When he drove you to my bedside, so to speak? Sarah, are you telling piggies?'

Half of Sarah wanted to laugh at Lily's malapropism

and half of her wanted to strangle her sister for teasing her. She had to nip this in the bud immediately before Lily said something hideously embarrassing. 'We were together – working. We were looking at the venue where Carrie is going to have her wedding.'

As Sarah hoped it would, this diverted Lily's attention from Sarah's supposed love life. 'Go on then, what's it like?'

'I will tell you, Lils, but first I want to know why you're so fine now when you were practically in tears on the phone.'

'I told you, I had a pain.'

'And it went, just like that?'

Lily bit her lip and inspected her fingernails, which had transfers of cartoon kittens on them. 'Mm.'

Sarah studied her sister. 'Is there something you're not telling me?'

Lily nodded.

'What?'

'Well, I got into the bath . . .'

'Hurry up. Hugo will be back any minute!'

'OK, I'm telling you! Be patient.'

Sarah fixed her with a glare she hoped might get Lily to tell her what had happened.

'I farted,' said Lily, beginning to giggle. 'I got into the bath and lay back and then – it just happened. Bubbles and everything. Afterwards I felt loads better.'

'So you didn't think to ring me?'

Lily shook her head. 'I was quite lonely. It's lovely to have you here. And Hugo's dreamy.'

Dreamy Hugo came back into the room. 'I've made some tea and I found a whole lot of left-over balti. Shall I heat it up?'

Sarah started to laugh. She looked at Lily who had her face in a pillow. 'That's a good idea, but not for Lily. Indian food seems to give her wind.'

They spent the rest of the evening eating and watching *Sex and the City* DVDs. It was cosy and surprisingly enjoyable.

While Hugo was making more tea, Lily said, 'It's good that you've got a man who's so in touch with his feminine side.'

When Hugo came back in he asked why Sarah was laughing so hard, but she wouldn't tell him.

Chapter Thirty-One

❦

Bron had a dilemma; while she had a perfectly good plan for making Carrie's cake on paper, she didn't really know it would work until she'd made some experiments. It was too early to make the actual cake, but she needed some dummy runs, to make sure it would all work. For this, she needed tools. Roger had a shed full of them, but she wasn't going back there. The obvious solution was James – he was a gardener, they always had tools, didn't they?

Her problem was getting up the courage to talk to him. After his initial friendliness and welcoming attitude their friendship hadn't really progressed. He'd wave at her when he saw her and they'd shared the odd cup of tea over the garden fence as it were, but that was all. She hadn't even seen him for a day or so. For the first time in a very long while, Bron had found herself thinking about a man other than Roger. A man with a very cute smile. And although it wasn't that she wanted to fall into another relationship, five minutes after Roger, part of her was miffed that he hadn't even asked her to go for a drink.

The trouble was, she was developing a bit of crush on him – probably because he was so different from Roger – but she had no idea how he might feel about her. She knew he was single. They got on well, but it was not the sort of question you could ask outright. Bron blushed at the very thought. It really was a little soon after Roger and a crush didn't necessarily mean anything, did it?

He probably wasn't avoiding her. It could just be that they were never home at the same time. He went off to work with Brodie early in the morning, and in the evenings Bron was often out doing hair. Word was getting around that she was available for after-hours hairdressing and she was really busy. She was enjoying it too, she reflected. Had she known how much freelance work she could get, she would have left the salon ages ago, if she hadn't been so under Roger's controlling thumb.

But this evening she had arranged to be free. She would be ready to shoot out of her house the moment he arrived home, be it on his bicycle or in the car. She really did need his help. She would lure him into her house with cold lager or hot tea, depending on the weather, and ask about tools. He was bound to have some, or at least access to them. She heard his car pull up and almost fell over herself getting down the stairs and out of the front door.

'James!' she called.

He turned suddenly. 'Bron! Are you all right?'

Bron realised her call must have sounded a bit panic-stricken. Why had her usual social skills deserted her? She didn't want him to think she was desperate or had designs on him – well, not really. 'I'm fine, but I did want to ask you a favour. Would you like to come in and have a drink or something? Tea? Lager? Elderflower pressé?'

'Cool. I'll just go in and shower. After all that rain the garden has gone mad and I'm stinking.'

James arrived on her doorstep smelling of shower gel. His hair, which she still longed to trim, was damp.

'Lager?' she asked. 'It's after six and you've had a long day.'

'Yes please.' He grinned and took the can. 'I don't need a glass.'

'Shall we go and sit outside? Now the weather's cleared up it's nice to make the most of the garden.' Bron picked up a bowl of crisps she had ready and brought her elder-flower drink with her.

An old bench near a rickety table had been set at the end of the garden, designed to catch the last of the sunshine. Bron set down the crisps and her drink.

'I'm just going inside to get something.' She came back with a large lined pad on which she had made her plans. 'It's this cake. I think I mentioned it to you. Now I've got to actually make the wretched thing.'

'Wretched?'

'Well, not really. I'm just not convinced I can make it work. I need a really strong pole stuck into a base that won't fall over, whatever happens.'

'It's a topiary tree, isn't it? So a flower pot filled with concrete with the pole stuck in it would work.'

'Where would I get a steel pole? Or would wood be strong enough?'

James considered. 'I think steel would be best really. Pity, because wooden mop stick is easy to get hold of. But it should be possible to get a steel pole too. Would a length of scaffold be too thick?'

Bron considered. 'Maybe not, as long as the cake on top was big enough so it looked in proportion. And scaffold would be hollow, easier to stick things into it.'

'Show me the design again.' James took the pad and examined her drawings in silence for a while. 'So you need metal discs to support the cake. Where will you get those?'

'Well, if I was using a broomstick, I could buy loose bottom quiche tins. You can get them in most sizes. But I'm not sure they'd come in a big enough size to look right with a length of scaffold.' She wrinkled her nose. 'It's not easy being an artist in cake. Hair is much easier.'

He laughed. 'Don't worry. There must be a solution; we just have to find it. How many discs do you think you'll need?'

'I think about six should do it. I suppose if we used metal I could make a fruit cake, which could be useful.'

'I haven't heard cake being described as useful before, but I suppose there's a first time for everything.'

Bron inclined her head. 'A fruit cake on a camping trip is very useful indeed, but in this instance it means I could start baking now. Fruit would be much more expensive, of course, but I don't suppose Carrie would care.' She frowned again. 'At least I don't have to make Lily's cake as well.'

'Lily? Who's Lily?'

'Oh, Sarah's mad younger sister. She's great fun but a bit scatty and she wants to have a very traditional wedding costing half nothing. My friend Elsa is adapting a wedding dress from a charity shop for her; I've found some caterers who'll do the food for cost and the church flowers are being done by the previous wedding. Her aunt is making the cake. Sarah's having to be really ingenious to get it all sorted.'

'No wonder,' he said, with one eyebrow raised.

Bron laughed. 'Sarah would probably like it if Carrie had a fruit cake then we could bulk-buy ingredients. Maybe we could still do that. I could give the fruit and stuff to Sarah so that their Auntie Dot or whoever it is can make it. What do you think?'

He allowed these details to go straight over his head without consideration. 'I have no idea.'

Bron sighed, aware she was asking his opinion just because he was a man. It was a bad habit she'd picked up from being with Roger and she must break it!

'So,' James went on, 'tell me how you get the cake – whichever kind you decide on – on to the discs and the pole?'

'I'll cut each section of cake in half and fit it round the pole, on top of discs. Then, when I've got a rough sphere I'll ice it so it's completely spherical.'

'You'll need lots of cake. And icing.'

'Definitely, and I thought, as it's for Carrie, a little crystal in the centre of each flower. Look.' She drew his attention to the drawing of the four-petal flowers that were going to cover the sphere. 'Very bling, don't you think?'

'Won't they crack people's teeth?' said James.

Bron laughed. 'No! Only the inside of the cake will be served.'

'In which case – very bling indeed.'

'So, being a gardener,' she said, 'could you find me a nice concrete pot? I'd paint it to make it look old if I had time, but I really don't think I have.'

'What's going to happen to it afterwards?'

Bron shrugged. 'I don't know. I'm going to do a series of polystyrene ones as well.'

'Why on earth would you make polystyrene cakes? This woman's not on some weird diet, is she?'

'No!' Bron laughed. 'It's because we want two rows of them, leading up to the larger, real cake. Apparently the venue has got the ideal place for it, and it'll look really fab. I couldn't possibly make nine cakes and they wouldn't all get eaten.'

'I see.'

'Although there will be lots of extra cake. This one's for show, really.'

'So how many people are coming to the wedding?'

'I'm not sure. I don't think even Sarah knows. Carrie keeps changing her mind. I'm making the big cake for fifty, and enough cake for another hundred. It's all very last minute for such a big wedding.' She realised she shouldn't have mentioned Carrie's name as it was still supposed to be confidential, but then she realised that James didn't read *Celeb*, so probably wouldn't have recognised the name even if she'd said it in full. 'You don't know any blacksmiths, do you?'

'No, but I know a half-decent welder. He'd fix the discs to the pole for you.'

Bron had to stop herself clapping her hands like an over-excited schoolgirl. 'Brilliant! Who's that?'

'Me. I was at art college before I did IT, before I became a gardener. Believe it or not, we did welding.'

Bron marvelled again at how different James was to Roger. Roger might have wanted to be in charge all the time but he wasn't the most practical or helpful of men.

'Oh, that would be marvellous! Can you find the bits?'

'You mean the pole and the discs? I could get some made out of sheet metal if you give me the dimensions.'

'That's fantastic!'

'I can even distress the concrete pot for you.'

'Oh, James, you're such a star. I've been really worried about the technical side of it. Now I know we can really make this work.'

He smiled slightly. 'I haven't been part of a "we" for ages.'

A breath of sadness touched the atmosphere, and suddenly Bron felt the urge to give him a comforting hug. She knew it would be the wrong thing to do and so said, 'It's not always all it's cracked up to be.'

Then she realised she'd sounded cynical, not comforting, and she wished she had hugged him. He was so lovely! 'What are you cooking for supper?' she said quickly, to change the mood as much as anything.

He blinked. The mood-changing thing had obviously worked. 'Nothing much. An omelette probably. As usual.'

'Why don't we walk to the pub? I've got nothing much in either,' she said, crossing her fingers that he'd say yes.

'So you haven't got a date tonight, then?'

For a moment Bron didn't know what he was talking about. 'No, why?'

'Nothing. It's just you're usually out in the evenings.'

She laughed. He'd noticed – was that a good sign or not? It probably said more about the summer television schedules than it did about his interest in her.

'Oh, I'm not going on dates. I'm doing people's hair! My older clients – who gather in flocks at each other's houses, quite often – take up my days. But I've got a few working women, or women who have children and want their hair doing when they've got someone to look after the children, who I do in the evenings.'

'I see. I thought you had a hectic social life.'

Still shocked at his mistake, she said, 'Not at all. I've only just left Roger. I'm conserving my energy.'

Later, when they walked to and from the pub, she was still wondering how he felt about her. They'd had a lovely evening, chatted easily, she'd even laughed at his jokes, but she still had no idea if he saw her as anything more than the girl next door he was giving a helping hand to. He was not only a very attractive man under his scruffy clothes and too-long hair (which he hadn't taken her up on her offer to cut yet) but, despite being quite easygoing, he was also completely inscrutable. And she'd never found it easy to understand men. Perhaps it had been this that had stopped her realising what Roger was really like until too late. She sighed. At least she'd get to see a bit more of James now he'd agreed to help her with the cake.

Having ascertained how, with James's help, she was going to make the structure, Bron knew it was time to begin the trial run. Veronica, the owner of the officially-approved-of-kitchen had a Cash and Carry card and Bron arranged to meet her so she could buy some ingredients. Although in theory she was confident her cake would work, she wanted to give herself lots of time to practise. They met up in the car park of the huge warehouse.

'Hello, dear!' said Veronica, waving as she locked her car. 'This is such fun!'

'But you must come here often! You're always making cakes!'

'But not for celebrities – that's quite different. Oh, and your friend Sarah asked me to make the cake for her sister as we're doing the catering anyway. Apparently the family friend who was going to do it can't, for some reason. I hope you don't mind.'

'Not at all. Why should I?'

'I didn't want you to think I was muscling in on your new career as a cake-maker.'

Bron shook her head. 'I promise you, I have more than enough on my plate as it is.'

'So the freelancing's going well?'

'Yes, I'm really busy. And I like it much more than I thought I would. I was worried I'd miss working with other people, but going to people's homes is much more fun. I sometimes do whole families. The book work is a bit of a nightmare though, I must say.'

'Is it?'

'Well . . . not really, I suppose, but Roger always dealt with the finances so it's a bit of a learning curve for me doing it.' She'd always rather resented him taking charge all the time but now she realised that could be quite a useful quality sometimes.

'I'm quite used to book-keeping after making cakes for the WI stall for so long.' Veronica paused. 'Sarah said with things like flour and butter and margarine, which will go into both cakes, we should buy ingredients together. Then I'll work out how much of them went into Lily's cake.'

Bron shook her head. 'And I thought my books were complicated!'

'I should think it will work out about equal. Your cake is much bigger, but mine will be full of expensive fruit and brandy and stuff.'

'Whatever you think, Veronica. I'm sure you and Sarah can work it out between you. I just want my cake not to drop to the floor in a heap of crumbs!'

Veronica chuckled. 'We can use my business credit card. Now, have you made a list of what you need?'

'I think so. This isn't for the final cake, though, only a practice one. I want to make sure I can get the icing to stay on OK. It would be so awful if it dropped off.'

Veronica found a cart that to Bron seemed more suited to shifting planefuls of luggage than packets of flour and sugar.

'I can't believe we need anything that big,' she said as she followed her friend through the doors into the building. Once through she stopped. 'This place is huge! Like an aircraft hanger.'

Plastic-wrapped blocks of food were stacked from floor to ceiling, only accessible by fork-lift truck. They created tower blocks of tins, packets, bottles – anything that contained food. To Bron it seemed like a combination of the largest DIY store she had ever seen and a cut-price supermarket, where the products were left in their cartons and not displayed.

But it didn't only stock the everyday items on Bron's list. Her cake was destined to look fabulous but the ingredients were simple enough. When she saw what was available in this monster store, a sort of buying rush swept over her and she wanted everything, in mammoth quantities.

'Oh look! Liquorice pipes by the box! I must get some for my dad for when I next go over.' She put a box on the trolley. 'And it's all so cheap!'

'You need to remember that the prices are shown without the VAT,' said Veronica, gently touching Bron's arm. 'I can claim it back but you have to pay it upfront.'

Bron refused to be cast down. 'I'll keep the things that are for me separate. I can't have Carrie paying for Dad's liquorice pipes. Oh, and look at that! Boxes and boxes of Dairy Milk – imagine never running out!'

Veronica chuckled. 'You don't want to risk your lovely figure eating too much chocolate. They'll tempt you terribly if you buy them.'

'Mm. I suppose so.' She put back the lifetime's supply of chocolate she had heaved on to the trolley. 'I'd better get out my list.'

'And try to stick to it, or you'll end up spending a fortune and not have the things you need. Believe me, I know!'

Bron was very pleased with her haul. She hadn't deviated from her list too badly and when she had, she'd been able to justify it. When they got back to Veronica's large and officially hygienic kitchen, she had some huge baking tins, enough foil to line a large room, almost as much silicone paper, baking sheets, cooling racks, sackfuls of silver balls and other decorative bits she thought might be useful as well as kilos and kilos of butter, flour and sugar. Several trays of eggs topped the stack of ingredients on the floor. She could collect the crystals from Elsa once she knew what she was doing.

'Shopping in such huge quantities is exhausting!' she said, helping Veronica in with a huge pack of flour. 'Everything is so enormous.'

'And you walk so far because the place is so huge,' said Veronica. 'It's a mile between the cornflakes and the porridge oats. I reckon I don't need to do any other exercise if it's a Cash and Carry day. My upper body strength is very impressive these days.'

Bron looked at her arms, which were trembling slightly with exertion. 'Mm – I think I need to work on mine.'

Veronica filled the kettle and while she waited for it to boil said, 'So, dear, are we going to be able to share a kitchen? Ideally, we wouldn't coincide, but you need a dummy run and each layer will take time and I've got my usual baking to do.'

Bron hurried to reassure her. 'I'll be very tidy, I promise you. I'm a very organised cook.'

Veronica laughed. 'Well, Pat really misses you; that Sasha never lifts a finger, apparently.'

Bron tried to look insouciant. She failed.

Chapter Thirty-Two

Bron was putting up Elsa's hair on the night of her ball with Laurence. As it was short, this took a long time. Elsa was as nervous as any bride under her gentle fingers but was trying to make bright conversation.

'It's only three weeks to go to the wedding – how many cakes have you made now?'

'Several. James won't eat them any more.'

Elsa looked at her in surprise. 'What do you mean? I thought men always liked cake.'

'My first couple of efforts he accepted gratefully but the last time he said, "I'm sorry, I just can't eat any more." I said, "It's not cake, it's trifle." He said, "But it's made of cake, isn't it?"'

Elsa giggled. 'So what did you do with it?'

'I was very brave and took it up to the big house and gave it to Vanessa. She was thrilled. She was having people for dinner the next day. I was really flattered. I hope they didn't get drunk. It had loads of sherry in it. I'd bought some at the Cash and Carry. So,' Bron went on, 'are you honestly telling me you haven't seen Laurence since your ballroom dancing lesson?'

'Mm. Now I'm really anxious about seeing him again. He was a bit . . . I don't know . . . off after the lesson. And I thought I'd done quite well. I went whizzing round with the teacher.' She smiled. 'I've been practising.'

'Oh, show me!' said Bron, delighted. 'Only not until I've finished your hair and done your make-up.'

'We were supposed to practise together but he's been

299

away. He has to travel on business quite a bit, apparently. Anyway, I'm nervous now because we didn't work together last time.'

'Nonsense,' said Bron. 'You'll be fine.'

'There,' said Bron, half an hour later, 'let's look at you.'

Elsa moved to the full-length mirror fixed to the wall in her workroom. She had looked at many a bride in it, but hadn't often studied herself so carefully. Bron came and stood behind her, hair lacquer in her hand in case a couple of hairs dared escape. They both felt satisfied with their work.

Her dress had turned out brilliantly, Elsa thought, possibly because she'd had quite a lot of time to spend on it as Carrie still hadn't decided what she wanted. The little puff sleeves, high waist and low cut neckline really did make her look like an illustration from the cover of a Georgette Heyer novel, she thought. The overskirt opened over a soft petticoat of palest primrose. She didn't say so to Bron, but before she'd started, she'd checked the colours with the swatches from when she'd had her colours done.

Her hair, gummed into place, padded out with false pieces and adorned with delicate fake flowers and a million Kirby grips, looked historically correct. She wore elbow-length gloves and had a light shawl draped across her elbows.

'Oh, Elsa!' cried Bron, kissing her. 'You look fantastic! Honestly. Look at you. So lovely. I must take a picture. Stay there.' Bron ran to get her phone and took several shots while Elsa regarded herself critically, looking more at the details and cut of the gown than her face.

But when Bron showed her the pictures Elsa said, 'Golly, I do look quite pretty. Maybe I should always wear my hair like this.' She laughed. 'If I don't go near any magnets and the grips don't all fly out, it could be a whole new look for me.'

'Silly,' said Bron. 'Your ordinary, everyday hair makes

you look pretty, but this is special because it makes you look like a painting.'

Elsa had to admit she did look the part. She wondered what Laurence would think; she hoped he'd be suitably impressed.

She stretched out a foot, getting into the whole business now. 'It's good these slippers are so fashionable. These were really cheap.'

'So if you leave one behind at the ball you won't mind,' said Bron.

They both giggled.

'I don't think Prince Charming's been invited.'

'Isn't Laurence your Prince Charming?' asked Bron.

Elsa shook her head. 'I don't know. I mean, I really like him, and we seem to get on well, but maybe he just wanted someone to take to the ball, or he'd have been in touch more, don't you think? He's only phoned me once to confirm when he's picking me up.'

Bron shrugged. 'Maybe something will happen tonight.'

Elsa felt herself go pink at the prospect. She had been thinking about Laurence quite a bit recently and she'd often found herself imagining what it would be like to go out with him – properly. 'Maybe.' She looked at Bron. 'I've gone all nervous and girly!'

'That's good. Sometimes getting ready for a party is the best bit. Now let's have a final look.' She turned Elsa's head this way and that, checking it all over.

'So how about you and James?' asked Elsa, not wanting Bron to feel left out of her happy anticipation.

'Well, he's being brilliant helping me with the cake. He's made a stand for it and has really taken trouble with it, but I don't really know how he feels about me as a woman.' She sighed.

'Well, how do you feel about him?'

Bron shook her head. 'He is lovely and very attractive but I don't know if I've just got some sort of crush on him because he's been so helpful, and anyway, after Roger, anyone would seem attractive.'

'Lovely, attractive and helpful – he sounds perfect!' said Elsa.

'Yes, but I've only just come out of a relationship, I probably shouldn't even be thinking about another so soon. And I think he's had his fingers burnt too. Anyway, I think he just sees me as the girl next door.'

Elsa regarded her friend thoughtfully. 'Would that be OK by you?'

Bron shrugged and sighed. 'I expect so. I really should try life on my own for a bit longer before I hitch up with another man. You're so cool, Elsa, living on your own, running your own business.'

'You're running your own business and living on your own!'

'I am now, but I should have done it before, really. It's so liberating. I was scared at first but it's so much better than living with someone you don't love. Sarah was right,' said Bron, absently gluing down a couple of stray hairs with a squirt from her aerosol can. 'Right, that's you. Now get up and show me your best waltz! Is this the Viennese one or the ordinary? I've watched *Strictly*, I know my stuff!'

Elsa put on a CD she'd recently bought. 'I learnt both. I really didn't want to be caught out – and neither of them is at all easy to do on your own!'

'Wow!' said Bron a few minutes later, having watched Elsa move and dip and sway. 'If he doesn't sweep you into a passionate embrace after that, he must be gay.'

'Oh, I don't think so! I may not have a lot of experience but I think I would have picked that up at least.'

'Well, you'll probably find out for definite tonight. Ooh! I'm so excited for you,' said Bron, kissing Elsa's cheek. 'You look so lovely! Wait till I show Sarah. Now, I must go. Good luck.' And she swept up her bag, blew Elsa a kiss and hurried out of the door.

Laurence *was* suitably impressed by her appearance. In fact, he was speechless for several long seconds before he said anything. 'You look – amazing,' he said eventually, going pink. 'Absolutely amazing. I knew you'd look great, but I never imagined you'd get every detail so perfect.'

Elsa laughed, thrilled with the effect she'd had on him. 'I notice you're not in period dress, however.'

'No. I thought I might not reach the required Colin Firth standard and we're allowed to get away with white tie and tails.'

'I think that's cheating,' said Elsa. 'You could have hired an outfit – you were going to hire outfits for both of us!'

'I know, but I remembered what you said about wearing curtains that smelt of sweat and opted for my own recently cleaned tails.'

Elsa laughed, suddenly feeling more happy than nervous. It was a glorious evening, she felt beautiful and Laurence seemed delighted to see her.

He was still looking at her. 'You know it's just possible that you might steal the thunder of the birthday girl, but don't worry, if she looks like wanting to tear your eyes out, I guarantee to get you away safely.'

Elsa laughed again. 'To be honest, I wasn't expecting to have quite so much time to spend on my dress. I'm still awaiting Carrie's orders. I turned down another bride, thinking I'd be too busy to do it. But that's quite handy because I'm doing Sarah's sister's dress now. Not from scratch, it's an alteration – or rather a complete makeover-job.'

'Fascinating,' said Laurence, taking her arm. 'You must tell me all about it sometime. But now it's time for Cinderella to go to the ball. Are you bringing any sort of coat, apart from your pashmina?'

'It's not a pashmina, it's a shawl!' insisted Elsa. 'Pashminas weren't invented then – or at least they didn't call them that.'

'Well then, grab your reticule and let's hit the road. You'll be glad to hear I've put the hood up on the car.'

Elsa laughed. 'That's a relief. My hair will probably fall down anyway, but it would be nice to get to our destination first.'

Then, as she arranged herself in his Morgan, she said, 'I'm so glad your friend isn't seriously into Marie Antoinette and that lot, you'd never fit hoops and those wigs they wore into this car.'

The ball was at a country house hotel that was the perfect Regency period. 'Your friend – Natasha did you say? – must have chosen it specially. It's perfect!' said Elsa as they drove up and then round the back to park the car.

'Actually, I think this hotel is owned by friends of hers and she fitted the ball round the venue. Now, can you walk in those shoes, or shall I carry you?'

Elsa put her head on one side. 'Supposing I said you had to carry me?'

'I'd throw you over my shoulder in proper fireman style and off we'd go!' said Laurence.

'OK, I'll share with you the fact that these shoes are very comfortable and stay on well. Although the heels aren't quite high enough for proper dancing.'

'You don't need high heels for dancing, do you?' Laurence gave her a startled look.

Elsa tossed her head, enjoying the feeling of the fake ringlets against her cheek. 'You're the expert.'

'Actually, I'm not sure about that any more. Terry was much better.' He frowned and took her elbow and handed her a glass of champagne he took from an offered tray. 'Take this and come on.'

Now they were actually here and about to face a room full of strangers, she felt her nervousness return, especially when she saw a group of people armed with clipboards who seemed to be inspecting everyone as they arrived.

'I so don't want to do this!' Elsa muttered to Laurence

from between gritted teeth. 'I would never have come if I knew I was going to be on parade!'

'I'm sorry,' he muttered back, his arm round her waist, which although it felt rather nice didn't help her ruffled state. 'I wouldn't have done either. I never would have put you through this if I'd had an inkling there was any sort of costume competition. I agree it's totally barbaric.'

Mollified a little by this rather extreme language, she allowed herself to be inspected. As she and Laurence stood smiling gamely she muttered from behind her smile, '"Judge not, that ye be not judged." We're not cattle – we shouldn't have to be scored on our points!'

'But you're not on your pointes,' he teased, obviously trying to make her feel better, 'you're wearing ordinary shoes and you told me quite definitely that they're comfortable.'

She nudged him hard in the ribs. 'How do you know about pointe shoes?'

'I have a sister who did ballet.'

'I bet she could have waltzed without the lessons.'

'Probably, but that's not enough reason to take my sister to a ball.'

Elsa didn't have time to work out if this was a compliment or not before the woman whom Elsa assumed was Natasha spoke.

'Thank you, Elsa,' said their hostess, holding her score card so it couldn't be seen. Elsa relaxed her pose. 'I must say Laurence, you have picked the most lovely partner.'

Elsa could see the speculation in her eyes. She hoped Natasha wouldn't get her in the Ladies on her own and ask her about her relationship with Laurence – she wouldn't be able to help her. She didn't really think she could say they were 'just good friends' because she didn't know him very well and anyway, she hoped he saw her as a little more than that. It was all too new to be examined by someone else.

At last the party was allowed to start again and Laurence said, 'Come on, you need another drink,' and she followed him to the bar.

'I could murder a large fizzy water,' she agreed.

They waltzed together afterwards, and it went better this time. Their first attempt had been a bit of a disaster and Elsa almost wished she could stand on his feet again like they had at Ashlyn's wedding. But now supper was over and they'd done some country dances since: that had helped Elsa relax a bit. She found it was hard to remain tense and worried about your feet when you're being whirled up and down and passed from hand to hand.

'You're getting good at this,' Laurence murmured as they did a perfect left-hand reverse.

'I tried to practise on my own at home, after the lesson.' She looked up at him and he seemed lost in thought, then he glanced down at her, smiling. He really did have lovely gentle eyes. 'I know, I'm sorry, I should have come and practised with you. I've been dreadfully busy lately.'

'It's OK, I didn't expect you to.'

They gazed at each other for a while and Elsa suddenly felt a little awkward. She was just wondering what to say next when the music stopped and Natasha's consort, who, unlike all the other men, was in Regency dress, went to a microphone.

'Ladies and gentlemen, we're about to announce the winner of the costume competition.'

Elsa felt tense. She'd always dreaded hearing her name or her number, or indeed anything, called out. And while she didn't think she was in any danger now, she still felt anxious. Then Laurence took her hand and squeezed it, looking down at her encouragingly.

'In reverse order . . .' A name was announced and Elsa relaxed; the woman who came forward for her bottle of champagne was immaculate. Elsa was fairly sure that her dress was an exact copy of a period costume from a painting.

There was no way she was likely to be called for now.

The second prize went to another stunning creation, far grander than Elsa's gown – this one was suitable for a duchess. Elsa by contrast was very ingénue, her dress suitable for a girl in her first season. She was no longer in her teens but she felt sufficiently inexperienced in the ways of the world for this to be appropriate. Apart from anything else, she hadn't wanted to make anything too complicated in case she'd had to drop it to start on Carrie's creation.

'And the winner,' called the man, who actually looked very smart in his tight pants, tail coat and exotically tied neckcloth, 'who wins a weekend for two here in this lovely hotel, is . . .'

Elsa looked round for someone to step forward and then realised it was her name she had heard. Laurence was looking down at her, smiling. He mouthed, 'Ready?' and when she gave a little nod he took her hand and led her to the front. Everyone clapped like mad. In theory it was the worst moment of her life, being the object of everyone's gaze, in the forefront rather than the background. But from somewhere came a sense of theatre: spontaneously, she performed a deep curtsey and accepted a bottle of champagne and an envelope as if she'd been born to receive such accolades.

'Thank you so much,' she said, stuttering a little. 'I can't believe I won!'

'Your dress wasn't the grandest,' said Natasha, kissing her cheek, 'but it was the prettiest and you look so lovely in it. Where did you get it made? I can tell it's not hired.'

'Oh, I made it myself,' Elsa said making a dismissive movement with her fingers.

'But it's amazing!' said Natasha. 'Did you hear that? She made her dress herself!'

Now the prize-giving was over, other women gathered round Elsa and Natasha. They inspected Elsa's dress more closely.

'It's lovely. And you do it professionally?'

Elsa nodded. 'Mm. I make wedding dresses mostly.'

'You haven't got a business card in your reticule have you?' said Natasha.

Elsa was writing her website address down for what felt like the tenth time when a woman said, 'You don't take on work-experience students, do you? My daughter's doing A level Art but all she ever does is sew. She loves it and wants to go to fashion college.'

Elsa considered. 'Although I do occasionally have help, I've never had anyone for work experience. But I have got a big commission coming up. It might be very useful if your daughter can really use a needle.' She thought of all the crystals that would have to be sewn on by hand. She could try her out at least.

'It's in a fortnight. If you say you'd have her, my Mummy Points will sky rocket,' said the woman. 'The only work experience that is even near what she wants is working in a clothes shop.'

'Well, my work will be quite menial but it'll be with lovely fabrics. Tell her to get in touch.'

Elsa was quite happy chatting to these women eager for her services about what she knew best but then Laurence touched her elbow.

'Come on, we've got to do a victory waltz. On our own. This is when we really find out if your dancing lesson paid off!'

Chapter Thirty-Three

Something happened. Perhaps because Elsa was feeling good about herself after her work had been validated by all those eager people, or because they'd already had a trial run, or for some other, inexplicable reason, but something happened. A switch went on and she and Laurence truly connected.

She didn't notice the applause, she only heard the music and felt Laurence's arm lightly on her back, intimating to her which way to go. She floated, rising and falling on the music of the Viennese waltz. In her head she was in the Vienna Opera House for the night of the Opera Ball. Round and round they went and she felt she was in heaven.

The feeling wasn't only about the dancing, she knew that. She felt a charge between them; now they felt like a man and a woman, not just two random people who happened to be at the same party.

She was aware of other couples joining them on the dance floor and when the music finally ended she and Laurence were at the edge. He was smiling faintly; the corners of his eyes creased slightly. Apart from the fact that he was pleased with her, she couldn't quite interpret his expression. She felt a flutter of excitement in her chest as he looked deeply into her eyes. Then he released the hand he had been holding and took her chin. She closed her eyes and waited for his kiss.

His lips had barely brushed hers when he suddenly pulled away. Someone was tugging at his sleeve. It was Natasha.

'Laurence, I'm really sorry to interrupt' – she shot an apologetic glance at Elsa – 'but you're the only person guaranteed to be sober.'

Disappointment and reality arrived simultaneously. She'd been dancing like an angel, with Laurence, and he had been going to kiss her, properly. The circumstances might never be right again and kind, gentlemanly, sober Laurence was going to have to rescue another damsel in distress.

'It's Jamie,' explained Natasha. 'He managed to really gouge his hand opening a bottle of wine. Maggie is beside herself. She can't drive, they've got a babysitter who has to be got home, and she thinks Jamie should go to hospital. I do too, actually.'

Elsa thought she saw Laurence close his eyes for a moment, expressing irritation, or possibly frustration. But then he was his usual helpful self. He glanced at her, almost as if he were asking her permission. She smiled back.

'Come on, let's have a look,' he said.

The kitchen could have been a scene from *Holby City* before the ambulance crew arrived.

There was a man sitting at the table holding a blood-stained tea towel round his hand. A woman, presumably his wife, was leaning over him, alternately upbraiding him for being so stupid and asking him how he felt. Other people stood around offering opinions – some said the wound, which Elsa couldn't actually see, should be stuck up with sticking plaster, that was all that was necessary. Others said he should go to A and E. One person was all for calling an ambulance.

When Laurence entered the room everyone went quiet. 'What happened?' he asked, and everyone started to talk again.

'Bloody fool was trying to open a bottle with a knife. It slipped and it went straight into his wrist.' This was his wife. 'He's going to bleed to death if someone doesn't do something! And he's drunk,' she added.

'I'm fine! I said I'd drive!' said the man concerned, obviously not only in pain but somewhat inebriated.

'No you're not. Even if you hadn't cut your hand half off you couldn't drive,' said someone else.

'Let's have a look.' Laurence knelt by the man and unwrapped the tea towel. He didn't say anything, just wrapped it up again very quickly. 'Maggie's right,' he said. 'A and E for you.'

'I don't drive,' wailed Maggie. 'And I must get home – we've got a new babysitter, I can't leave her there all night!'

'Don't worry, someone will get you home,' said Natasha, who had joined the group. 'But I think Laurence should take Jamie to hospital. He's sober and he's done a first-aid course. Haven't you, sweetie?'

Laurence raised an eyebrow. 'A couple of years ago, and it doesn't qualify me to do major stitching.'

'You should still drive him in. You could take his car.'

'How am I going to get home?' demanded Maggie. 'I don't mean to sound unsympathetic but I'm frankly livid! He gets drunk when he promised he wouldn't and then bloody injures himself. A taxi will cost a fortune!'

'Someone will take you home, don't worry, Maggie,' said Natasha soothingly. 'There must be someone who lives your way.'

'But I don't want to wait for someone to decide they want to go home. I want to go now! I need to be at home with my babies! Besides,' she added a bit more calmly, 'I don't want to drag anyone away from the party. It's too early to leave.'

'Your car will be safe here, Laurence. I know how precious your Morgan is to you,' said Natasha, still concerned with Laurence and Jamie.

'That doesn't help me,' said Maggie. 'If I could drive, I'd take it.'

Natasha shook her head. 'Laurence is very picky about who he lets drive his car, Maggs.'

'Listen, everyone!' Jamie, still clutching his tea towel, claimed the room's attention. 'I'm bleeding to death here, and all you lot can talk about is Laurence's bloody car!' His blood-letting hadn't done much to sober him up.

'There's another problem,' said Laurence. 'Someone's got to see that Elsa gets home safely.'

For the third time that evening Elsa realised everyone was looking at her. She must have been getting used to it because she felt quite calm. 'I can get myself home. I'll take a taxi or' – she smiled and added jokingly – 'I could drive Laurence's car – except that it's not insured, of course.'

No one laughed. There was a long pause as people waited for Laurence to say, 'Hell will freeze over first,' or something similar. But when he did speak he said, 'Actually, it is insured. How much have you had to drink?'

Elsa was only insulted for a second or two before she replied. 'Half a glass of champagne when we arrived. No alcohol since. And I've eaten a huge plate of bœuf bourguignon.'

'You're not telling me you're going to let some girl drive the Morgan!' exclaimed one of the other men, aghast.

Laurence gave him a look which indicated he'd rather some girl drove it than him, and the man looked away. 'It's insured for anyone over the age of twenty-five with my permission. How old are you, Elsa?'

She smiled sarcastically. 'Over twenty-five, thanks for asking.'

'Seriously, Lau, you wouldn't let a girl you hardly know drive your car!' Natasha was stunned. She shot Elsa an apologetic glance. 'I mean, I know you two haven't known . . .' She tailed off. 'We could get someone else to do it, if it's insured. Not everyone here is drunk, for goodness' sake!'

'I'd rather have Elsa.' Laurence looked intently at her, and she felt herself blush.

'Are you sure?' she asked.

For a moment it felt as if there was no one else in the room. He nodded. 'I trust you.' He fumbled in his pocket and produced the keys.

When Laurence and Jamie had gone off to A and E in Jamie's car, Maggie and Elsa walked over the gravel to the Morgan. Elsa didn't think she should mention to anyone that she hadn't driven for quite a long time. She didn't want to add to Laurence's anxiety and she was too touched and thrilled by what Laurence had said to want to spoil it. Besides, she felt supremely calm. Her only worry was being able to find her way home after she'd taken Maggie and the babysitter back. But if she got lost, she'd do what she'd always done, ever since she first passed her test – she'd ring her father and get directions. He was guaranteed to know the way to anywhere from anywhere. The fact that it was quite late by now didn't bother her. That's what dads were for.

Maggie was unaware of Elsa's inexperience. She talked all the way to her house, either not noticing, or not commenting on any difficulties Elsa might have with driving a completely strange car in the dark. Once Elsa had found the lights and they'd both got their seatbelts on, she chattered away about how irresponsible her husband could be, how she really must learn to drive, and what a fabulous party it had been.

Elsa didn't speak. She just concentrated on getting them both to Maggie's house safely. She wasn't looking forward to driving back home alone, but she had her mobile close to her. Luckily the babysitter's boyfriend came and collected her.

It was only after she'd parked Laurence's precious Morgan safely outside her house that she started to shake. After she'd made sure for the hundredth time she'd locked it she went in, laughing at how she'd been so calm and now her palms were sweating and she was shaking as if from shock.

'This is so silly!' she told herself, trying to be firm. 'Nothing bad has happened – you don't have to panic now! What sort of a woman are you?'

She knew what sort of a woman she was, really. She was shy and previously lacking in self-confidence. But recently things had changed. She felt more confident about her work as a dressmaker, had survived performing in public and had been quietly efficient in an emergency. Sadly, her body seemed to think she was still a wimp. She decided she needed hot chocolate. She put the champagne in the fridge and took her shoes off.

She was on her third digestive biscuit when her mobile went. It was Laurence.

'Everything all right?' he asked casually.

Elsa was not fooled. 'Fine. Did you get Jamie sorted OK?'

'Oh yes. There wasn't much of a queue for once. We got him stitched up and I've just driven him home.' He paused. 'Elsa, would you mind very much if I came and got the car now? Maggie will have their car picked up from yours in the morning.'

She smiled. 'That's fine. I haven't gone to bed yet.' Her heart fluttered once more. He was coming to collect his precious car of course but she would have to invite him in; he'd been a hero tonight, her hero, and she remembered their almost-kiss.

'Are you still wearing your lovely dress?' He broke into her thoughts.

'No. I changed into my dressing gown. But I'm quite decent.' She tried to sound casual.

He laughed. 'I love the thought of you driving through the night in my car, looking like a Georgette Heyer heroine!'

She flew into her bedroom. Decent she might have been but her hair was currently a disintegrating bird's nest of hair lacquer and pins – not a good look. She'd taken off the false bun but had just left the rest, planning to take it out in the morning when she could wash out the spray. But she didn't want Laurence drinking hot chocolate across her kitchen table looking at her in such a state. If he was going to see her dishevelled she wanted it to be for the right reasons!

She'd got the worst of the lacquer out by giving her hair a good brush when she heard him arrive. She went downstairs and let him in.

He was deeply apologetic. 'I'm so sorry to be so neurotic. I love my car!'

Elsa laughed indulgently. 'I think I picked that up. Do you want to come in and have some hot chocolate? I've just had some. It's very soothing.'

'Sounds terrific.' He paused. 'But would you think I was frightfully anal if I looked over the car first?'

'Yes. But I understand. We're all allowed to be anal sometimes. I'll put the milk on. Close the bottom door behind you when you come up and I'll leave the flat door open.'

While Laurence was being anal about his car, Elsa went back to the bathroom to carry on brushing. She felt ridiculously excited. She'd had a wonderful evening. She liked Laurence tremendously. Would he make a move again? she wondered, and really hoped so. She gave her teeth a quick brush but didn't allow herself to put on lipstick. That would look a bit desperate with her dressing gown.

'You look different,' he said, a little while later, looking at her over the top of his mug. 'I don't mean because you're not dressed up any more. There's something else.'

Elsa looked down. She was fairly sure it was the leftover make-up that still smudged her eyes and the way that all those products that Bron had put on it gave her hair a bit more body than usual.

'Maybe it's the satisfaction of having driven your car safely back,' she said, looking back up at him and smiling.

'There isn't a mark on it – or at least, not one that wasn't there before.'

'It was incredibly trusting of you to let me drive it. Now I can tell you that I hadn't driven for ages. I was dreadfully nervous.'

Retrospective horror passed over his face. 'But you felt OK once you were on the way?'

'Yes, actually. I had Maggie for support and there was no traffic to speak of. I actually quite enjoyed my journey back here. It was only when I got home that I went into shock.'

He shook his head slightly. 'I would never have put you through that if I'd known.'

She bit her lip, suppressing a smile and regarded him with her head on one side. 'That's the second time you've said that to me this evening.' He looked a bit blank. 'The costume competition? That involved having to do a Viennese waltz on our own?'

He smiled. 'You were superb, and you certainly deserved to win the competition. Who will you take for your weekend away, or shouldn't I ask?'

'You certainly shouldn't ask. Have another biscuit.' She reached for the tin and passed it to him, fervently hoping he wouldn't see her blushing.

He looked around her workroom, admiring all her handiwork as he gave her a detailed account of an A and E department on a Saturday night. She was about to suggest making some more hot chocolate when she saw him yawn. 'Have you far to go tonight?' She almost whispered the words.

The charge she'd felt when he nearly kissed her before couldn't have been only one way, could it? It seemed so strong. And much as she knew he adored his car, he hadn't really needed to come in for a hot chocolate. But she didn't want to make a fool of herself by being too forward. She suddenly felt rather shy.

'Mm. Quite far.' He blinked at her but she couldn't quite read his expression.

She took a breath. 'Unless you've got to be somewhere very early in the morning or something . . .' She paused.

'I haven't got anything in particular to do tomorrow morning, actually,' Laurence said.

She decided to take a leap of faith. 'You could spend the night here,' she said before losing her nerve. 'The sofa in the workroom converts to a double bed.' Oh, why had she said 'double' when just bed would have done? She felt herself blush again.

'I don't want to put you out.'

Why was he being so polite? She wasn't his maiden aunt. She laughed nervously. 'Of course you wouldn't put me out!' she said. 'I wouldn't have offered if it would. I'll go and get some bedding. You can work out the mechanism. There's a lever somewhere.'

While she found the spare double duvet and some sheets she wondered if there was anything she should do. Why was it all so difficult? She was definitely out of practice. Perhaps she should just lure him into her bedroom and forget the sofabed. But that just wasn't her style and, anyway, she remembered her bed was strewn with clothes – hardly romantic. If he wanted to sleep, alone, he could and she wouldn't lose face. It wasn't that she necessarily wanted to have mad passionate sex with him (although part of her did) but she did want him to kiss her.

The sofabed looked embarrassingly double when Elsa got back with her pile of bedding. They arranged it together, placing pillows, trying to anchor the bottom sheet.

'There,' she said. 'I hope that'll be comfortable.'

'A plank would be comfortable after the night I've had.'

'You should have said. I've got a nice plank I could have rigged up for you,' she teased, feeling bolder.

He gave a tired laugh and then looked across at her in the soft light of a table lamp. 'Come here, you.' He put his arms round her and hugged her for a long time. Then, after what seemed a lifetime of waiting and wondering for Elsa, he found her mouth.

Any doubts Elsa may have had about her feelings for Laurence were dissipated within seconds of his lips touching hers. She wanted him desperately and knew he felt exactly the same. The kiss went on and on; they stopped only to breathe, and then their mouths found each other's again and continued.

At last they sank on to the bed. Elsa's dressing gown fell open and Laurence found his way to her skin and her breasts.

In her turn she undid his shirt buttons and relieved him of his dress shirt. His chest was wonderful to her and as her hands explored it tentatively she thought how aesthetically pleasing a toned male body was.

'Elsa,' he said later, huskily. 'We have to decide whether to stop or go on.'

She knew what she wanted to do: a lightning bolt of insight told her clearly she did not want to stop and that she must say so. Laurence wouldn't push it if she showed a moment's reluctance.

'In which case I'll have to go out to the car.'

'Why?' For a panic-stricken moment she wondered if he'd suddenly remembered he hadn't locked it or something, in which case his mind hadn't been as connected with hers as she'd thought.

'Condoms,' he said bluntly. 'Part of a best man's kit – or at least, sometimes. They're still in the glove box. Back in a minute.'

Elsa used the time to make the bed more comfortable but Laurence must have travelled at the speed of light. He was back before she'd had time to miss him.

Chapter Thirty-Four

Elsa woke and knew something was very, very different about her. A second later she realised what it was. The cause of this vast change was lying asleep beside her. He was, she decided, entirely fabulous. She moved a little closer to him, intending to gently wake him up but then she remembered.

'Damn!' she whispered. 'Bloody packet of three!'

She sighed deeply and got out of bed as carefully as she could so as not to wake him. If there were no more condoms there could be no more sex and she really didn't know if she could snuggle up to him without wanting it. She didn't want to put pressure on him, either.

It was difficult not to feel smug, she mused, as the water washed away what felt like several cans of hair lacquer and, reluctantly, their night together. Her body looked superficially the same but felt so different. When she turned off the shower she examined her face for traces of their passion and was certain she could see them. 'Post-orgasmic glow' her friends at college used to call it. She'd better not make plans to see her parents this Sunday – her mother would definitely notice.

Laurence was in the little kitchen area before her, washing up the cocoa mugs and boiling the kettle.

'Morning!' she said breezily, drying her hair with her fingers, suddenly feeling underdressed in an outsized T-shirt and a smile. 'Shall I make the tea?'

'First things first,' he said and took her into his arms. 'Oh,' he said a moment later. 'No knickers. How delightful.'

A little while later she sighed, and pulled away. 'I'd better put them on.'

He gave her a last, lingering kiss before he released her. 'Yes, I suppose you had.'

Reluctant to leave him, she said, 'I've got a nice big towel if you'd like a shower?'

'Big enough for two?'

She giggled. 'The shower's not big enough for two. You have to watch your elbows even if it's just one of you in there. I'll make breakfast.'

With a lingering pat on her bottom, he moved past her into the bathroom.

'I'm so sorry. I've completely run out of bread,' said Elsa when Laurence re-emerged in his rather crumpled dress shirt, the sleeves rolled up. He didn't look quite as debonair as last night but he looked just right to her. 'I usually have a loaf in the freezer I just peel bits off when I need some, but that crust was the last bit.'

'Well, it's just not good enough!'

Elsa laughed, as much with surprise as anything else. Laurence was always so polite. A night of passion had obviously had its effect on him, too. 'I know, let's go out for breakfast!'

'Do you know somewhere?'

She nodded. 'A lovely pub that does fantastic bacon rolls. It's a little way away but their coffee is really good too! We could buy the Sunday papers.' She paused. 'Or do you want to get home?' she asked, trying not to sound too anxious. She didn't want him to go – not for a few hours at least. She wanted to know all about him, his favourite music, food, what he read – everything.

'No, bacon rolls and Sunday papers sound good.'

Boldly, for her anyway, she teased him: 'You don't want me to drive your car so you can take Jamie's back to his house, then?'

The way he looked at her, with creased eyes and one side of his mouth lifted in a smile, made her stomach clench. 'Jamie can organise his own car. I've done more than enough for him already.'

She nodded. 'Right. I'll go and get some clothes on.'

'Not too many.'

She turned back to look at him, her head on one side in query.

'I mean, it's a lovely day and it's going to be hot.'

She laughed. 'OK, but as it is a lovely day, can we have the top off the car?'

'Of course. I'll meet you down there.'

Oh, the joy, thought Elsa as she hauled a skirt out of her wardrobe. It was rather pretty fabric. She'd made it with a remnant left over from something else. Sadly, there hadn't been much material and it was rather short so she'd never actually worn it before. Suddenly being too short seemed just right. She decided against rubbing on some fake tan. Streaky, while a good look for bacon, didn't work so well on legs.

She should have known that sports cars and short skirts were a bad combination. She'd been in his car often enough, but it was something of a shock to realise showing her knickers was almost inevitable. Still, nothing to be done about it. He'd seen them before, after all. She clambered in and shut the door.

'Right, well, it's in Bronnley, just a couple of miles away. Left at the crossroads.' Having delivered her directions, Elsa spent most of the journey tugging subtly at her skirt. She hadn't managed to tuck it under her when she got in and now it was rumpled up, exposing more than just thigh. She didn't want Laurence to think she was leading him to something he couldn't have. Then she thought of the loo in the pub. They were almost bound to have a condom machine. She blushed with guilty pleasure. Chaste for years, she'd suddenly become a sex fiend! It was lovely.

They were sitting in a sunny bay window, trying to do the crossword, sipping coffee and waiting for their rolls when Laurence's phone rang. Elsa ignored it. She wanted to solve just one clue to prove she wasn't illiterate and was working on an anagram.

'It's for you,' he said, and handed it to her.

There was something very panic-inducing about receiving a call on someone else's phone; it could only be an emergency.

'Elsa?' It was Sarah and she did sound pretty worried. 'Thank goodness! I've been trying to track you down for ages! Your phone is off, or out of battery or something. I tried you several times and then I was forced to ring Bron. She told me you were at your ball last night and when I still couldn't reach you, I got Laurence's number from Vanessa.'

Her phone, Elsa realised, was still in her historically correct reticule where it must have quietly died. 'So what's so urgent?'

'Carrie! She's on her way to yours.'

'On a Sunday?'

'Sorry, she's off again tomorrow. She's going to decide which dress. I think Mandy must have made her. We're meeting up at yours at about eleven. Is that OK?'

No, it wasn't OK. Her studio flat was probably full of traces of what had gone on in it the night before. Laurence looked at her quizzingly. She shrugged.

'Elsa?' Sarah squawked.

'Oh God. Yes, it's fine. We'll be there as soon as we can.' She disconnected and looked up at Laurence.

'No time for breakfast?' he said, with that lethal eye-brow/smile combination.

'Yup,' she agreed, but as she spoke the barman announced from the bar that their breakfast had arrived. 'Carrie and everyone are on their way to mine. It means she's at last made up her mind about which design she wants, but . . .'

'You don't want everyone to know what we got up to last night?'

'I would rather not. I don't want to seem prissy but it would be a bit embarrassing.'

'We'll take the rolls with us and eat on the way,' said Laurence.

She was at the bar, paying and wrapping baps in napkins before Laurence had a chance to tell her he didn't allow people to eat in his car. She didn't absolutely know this was a golden rule of his, but if it was, she hoped that hunger would soften his attitude.

'Tell me when you want a bite of roll,' she said, halfway through hers. 'I didn't realise how hungry I was until I started eating.'

'Well, supper last night was a long time ago. And a lot has happened since.'

'Mm,' she agreed with her mouth full. 'And apart from having to have a tidy-up to make sure there's nothing incriminating lying around, I'm really pleased to be able to start on that dress at last. She's a lovely girl but she's a nightmare client. She keeps changing her mind about things. Well, once I've started on the dress, she can't change her mind again! I'll have to tell her.' She paused. 'You couldn't go just a bit faster, could you?'

Laurence glanced at her, and suddenly, she wished she hadn't said that as the tail of the car went down and they roared forward.

Sarah, Bron, Hugo and a man Elsa didn't know, but thought she recognised from somewhere, were all waiting outside her door as they drove up.

As she clambered out on to the pavement, Elsa heard Bron say, 'Not wearing the black trousers this morning then?'

Elsa made a face and found her keys. 'I'm so sorry to keep you waiting. We'd just gone out for breakfast. We ate it on the way here.'

'It's fine,' said Sarah. 'You're back before Carrie is, which is all that matters. Do charge your phone though.'

As she led the way up the stairs to her flat and workshop Elsa said, 'Sorry, I knew my battery was a bit low when I went out last night, but then forgot to charge it when I got home.'

'Probably distracted by other things,' muttered Bron.

When the whole group landed in her workroom the sofabed, still in bed form, seemed to scream for attention. Elsa shot Laurence a look and scooped up the duvet. Laurence started turning it back into a sofa. He was biting his lip, trying to keep his amusement to himself.

Sarah, the soul of tact, caused a diversion. 'Does everyone know each other? Elsa, you don't know James, do you?'

Elsa smiled at him, clutching pillows. 'Weren't you at Ashlyn's wedding? You do seem vaguely familiar.'

'Yes I was. I remember you. You were the bridesmaid.'

'And I was the best man,' said Laurence.

Bron caught Elsa's eye, raised her eyebrows and nodded her head in Laurence's direction. Elsa knew her blush would tell Bron everything she wanted to know.

'Hugo?' said Sarah, possibly to take the heat off Elsa. 'Do you and Laurence know each other? Hugo's a photographer. Carrie wants some candid shots of her choosing dresses and things.'

'Of course we know each other,' said Hugo casually. 'Hi, Laurence. How's it going?'

'It's been a bit hectic,' he said. 'I took Elsa to a ball last night and ended up taking some bloke to A and E with a badly injured hand.'

'Elsa!' said Bron. 'You didn't get blood on your lovely dress?'

'Oh no. Elsa didn't come with us to hospital. She drove the wife home in my Morgan.'

There was a tiny pause. 'Good God!' said Hugo. 'I can't

believe you let her . . . no offence,' he went on to Elsa. 'But his Morgan . . .!'

'She drove it perfectly,' said Laurence proudly.

'But you couldn't wait until morning to check, could you?' said Hugo laughing.

'No,' said Elsa firmly. 'Right, I'm just going to get rid of this lot then make some tea. Laurence and I have had bacon butties and I'm desperate for a cup.'

'I'd love some,' said Bron. 'I'll just go and fetch the fake-cake from the car.'

'I'll go,' said James.

'I'll help you make tea then,' said Bron. 'Well?' she whispered as she found some more mugs and the tea bags whilst Elsa put the kettle on. Elsa's dreamy look said it all. She suffered a twinge of what felt decidedly like jealousy. Not that she begrudged Elsa her happiness.

'Oh, Bron, he's so lovely! We didn't stop . . .'

'Too much information! I should be so lucky.'

'Things still not progressing with you and James?' asked Elsa sympathetically.

Bron sighed. 'I know men are supposed to think about sex twenty-four/seven, but I think James thinks about bedding plants twenty-four/seven!'

Elsa giggled. 'That is quite funny.'

Bron shook her head, trying not to laugh. 'No it's not, it's pathetic. Have you got any sugar? Come on then, let's take these through.'

James appeared holding what looked like a huge spherical lollipop on a stick and a plastic box. 'I brought the cake as well, was that right?'

'Yes, fine. I want Carrie to sample it.'

James grinned. 'And you just happened to have some handy when the word went out that she was arriving?'

Bron shrugged.

'Cake!' said Hugo, bearing down on the box that Bron

326

was opening. 'I love cake!' And he took a large slice, closely followed by Laurence. The others took more modest slices. It really did look delicious.

'This is to die for, Bron,' said Hugo, about to help himself to another slice.

'Don't eat it all!' said Sarah. 'Leave some for Carrie and Mandy—'

'There's loads,' said James. 'Don't worry.'

'It is really lovely,' said Sarah. 'You're good at this, Bron. And how pretty is that fake one? How did you make it?'

'That was easy,' said Bron. 'It's just a ball with icing on it. The real cake will go on this.'

'This' was the pole with the metal discs that now was stuck into a stone pot. 'I don't know if Carrie will want to see all this really, but I brought it for you as much as anyone.'

'If you can make the real cake look half as good as that one, it'll be dreamy,' said Sarah. 'You are talented.'

Hugo, disconcertingly as far as Elsa was concerned, had begun wandering about taking photographs. 'Sorry,' he said, catching her anxious look. 'I'm doing some candid before shots for the wedding.'

'It's true,' said Sarah. 'Mandy was most insistent that Hugo be here.' She sighed. She still hadn't quite got used to working with him. Her emotions were all over the place and she didn't like it. It was so much harder to be her usual professional self when he was around and yet she couldn't help secretly being pleased to see him. It was all very disconcerting.

'It's useful to have someone around who's willing to eat cake,' said Bron. 'James has given it up.'

'Not for ever, just for a few days,' he said.

'I must get my samples out,' said Elsa, going to a huge cupboard in the corner. 'I've got four designs here and enough bits of fabric for her to see how they'd look over one another.'

'Oh wow,' said Bron, looking at Elsa's drawing. 'They really are fairy tale.'

'This is the one I like best,' said Laurence.

'That's Lily's dress,' said Elsa. 'I've finished it. It's under that sheet over there.'

'Mm. It's simpler than all these,' Laurence went on.

'I don't think Carrie wants simple,' said Bron.

'Well, we're just about to find out,' said Hugo, looking out of the window. 'She's here!'

Chapter Thirty-Five

❧

Sarah watched as Elsa talked Carrie and Mandy through her designs. She was very impressed. Since Elsa had been forced into a bridesmaid's dress less than two months earlier she'd transformed into a much more confident young woman. She'd always been brilliant at her job but there was a sparkle to her now that hadn't been there before. Due, in no small measure, to Laurence, she felt.

Bron had been brilliant too. Carrie and Mandy had eaten quite a lot of cake for people so interested in keeping thin, and Carrie had adored the fake-cakes and would have ordered them to go all the way up the drive had she not been talked out of it by Mandy and Sarah and a panic-stricken Bron.

The impressive device for holding the proper cake had been admired and the designs for the final creation proved to be just what Carrie had wanted.

James and Laurence had slipped away to the pub at the earliest opportunity. Hugo was the only man in the room now, taking photographs, making jokes, flirting gently. Sarah forced him out of her mind and went over to join Carrie and Elsa by Elsa's flip chart.

'This is the one, Sarah,' said Carrie, tapping the drawing. 'Only with many more crystals. I want to glitter like a fairy!'

Sarah took one look at the drawing and saw it was already fairly well spangled. 'Where else do you want crystals, Carrie? I can't see where you'd fit them on.'

'Down the seams of the bodice,' said Elsa. 'They'll come down into a point and then flare out as the dress becomes full. Imagine a sort of Elizabeth the First busk, coming down into a point.'

'She was known as the Fairy Queen, wasn't she?' said Bron.

'Sort of,' agreed Hugo, capturing Mandy and Carrie together, fingering a fragment of crystal-nylon that shone like gossamer.

'Are you having wings?' asked Bron. 'To complete the fairy look?'

Sarah intercepted a look of horror from Elsa.

'No,' said Carrie, luckily. 'I think that would be a bit tacky.'

Silently several people sighed with relief.

'Will you be able to finish it in three weeks?' asked Sarah quietly, while Carrie was posing again for Hugo.

'Oh yes,' said Elsa. 'I'll have to crack on, but I've got nothing else going on now. There's a chance I'll have a work-experience girl to help me sew on the crystals.'

'And the bridesmaids' dresses?' Mandy, usually quite happy to be demanding on Carrie's behalf, did now seem abashed that not only had Carrie not previously chosen her wedding dress, but that she'd been equally vague about what her bridesmaids should wear.

'They're going to be much simpler than Carrie's,' said Elsa. 'It should be fine.'

'I've just had a thought,' said Carrie. There was a general holding of breath. 'While wings would be tacky for me, they'd be darling for the little ones. Don't you think?'

Elsa was firm. 'If I simplify their dresses even more, they can have wings. I think wings would be quite sweet and they're perfectly possible, but with the amount of spangles currently on that design, they'd be OTT.'

'Oh that's fine! You decide how many spangles, as long as I can have wings,' said Carrie.

'Way to go, Elsa,' muttered Bron and Sarah.

Now everything had been sorted out and everyone seemed happy, or potentially so, with the dresses and cake, Mandy looked at her watch and said, 'I think we'd better be going, honey. It's been great! You must be so pleased that Carrie has finally made up her mind about the dress, Elsa.'

'I do think that's a lovely choice,' Elsa agreed, not allowing the frustration she had suffered at not knowing what she would have to do until the last minute to show. 'And if you want a stand-up ruff, let me know. It could look very fairy-like.'

After much air-kissing Mandy and Carrie finally left.

'You're looking quite stressed, Sarah,' said Elsa, who was obviously fizzing with enthusiasm.

Sarah shrugged. 'I shall probably have to source a fairy coach pulled by two white horses now, with this fairy theme. Luckily I do think I know of one.' She looked earnestly at her friend. 'You're a star, Elsa. You handled Carrie so well. I know I can trust you absolutely. This dress will make you a fortune, I promise. You'll have to take on proper staff, never mind work-experience girls.'

'Well, thank you for choosing me for Carrie,' said Elsa, hugging Sarah.

'And you, Bron, the cake is delicious, the fake-cakes are going to look stunning . . .'

They would have gone on exchanging compliments for longer but Hugo hooked one arm through Elsa's and the other through Sarah's. He looked firmly at Bron, having to rely on the force of his personality. 'Come on, ladies. Let's join the others in the pub. We've got a lot to celebrate.'

'I really ought to start work straightaway,' said Elsa.

'No. It's a Sunday, you can have a celebratory drink first, and then work. Same for you, Sarah. And Bron. No one is lifting a finger until you've all acknowledged how well you've done. Come on.'

'He's awfully bossy, isn't he?' said Sarah to Bron, still linked to Hugo.

'Mm,' agreed Bron. 'I rather like that!'

Sarah didn't comment but she decided that at that particular moment she rather liked it too.

James and Laurence were surrounded by Sunday papers. They'd obviously been enjoying a quiet time while the others had been involved with Carrie. They both got to their feet and the three girls threaded their way between them and collapsed into the squashy chairs.

'Right,' said Hugo. 'It's a celebration. Do we want champagne?'

'I take it it all went well?' said James.

'It did,' said Elsa. 'But no champagne for me, thank you, Hugo. I don't want to be a party pooper but I really do have to work later and I'm quite tired as it is.' She glanced at Laurence who twinkled back at her. Part of her would have liked to be here on her own with Laurence. She hoped they'd have a moment at least to arrange another date before he had to dash off again.

'I'd love a glass of white wine,' said Bron, who, unlike the others, *didn't* have to work later.

'Sarah,' said Hugo. 'What about you? If you'd like champagne I'm sure I could persuade them to do it by the glass.'

Touched, Sarah smiled back at him for a few seconds. 'No thank you. What I'd really like is a grapefruit juice with soda water.'

'Are you sure? I know you like a bit of fizz.' He smiled at her.

Sarah became aware of her friends watching this discussion and blushed a little. She nodded and turned to James, who was seated next to her. 'That cake-stand thing is brilliant!' And they chatted about how relatively easy it had been to construct, if you knew how.

Hugo came back with the drinks and as he dispatched them, Sarah found herself wondering about Electra again. Although she was extremely attractive, if he'd known her so long surely he must see that she wasn't right for him? Or was it only wishful thinking on her part? Maybe they were perfectly suited. Maybe he wanted something a bit different, exotic, someone who was adventurous and wouldn't be by his side all the time.

'So, Hugo,' asked Laurence, breaking into her thoughts. 'Do you get fed up with all this girly dressy stuff?' He winked at Elsa, who blushed and smiled and looked down.

'Well—' he began.

'He's awfully good,' said Bron. 'I've seen quite a lot of his work in Sarah's albums – he's great!'

'Well, thank you, Bron.' Hugo bowed. 'Besides, it's not all I do.'

'That's true,' said Elsa. 'His portfolio is very impressive.'

Hugo bowed again and laughed.

Sarah had been wondering if she should confess to having visited his exhibition before it was even open. Now would be the perfect time, but would it make her seem stalkerish? She decided to be brave. 'Actually, Hugo, I've been meaning to tell you. You know that exhibition that you're in?'

He laughed. 'Think so. I'm in it, after all.'

'Well, I went to see it. I was in that part of town.' This was a lie, but only a small one. 'So I popped along. It wasn't open yet.' She laughed and took a sip of her drink. 'But I met your friend.' She didn't mention her name because it would look as if she cared enough to remember it. 'Who was it?'

'Electra.'

'That's it! Lovely girl. She showed me round. You're really good, Hugo. You're wasted on weddings . . .' Suddenly she felt rather self-conscious.

Elsa and Bron glanced at each other, confused. Why hadn't Sarah mentioned this?

'So you've seen it?' He leant forward eagerly. His usual laid-back manner seemed to have left him.

'Yes. I said. I thought it was amazing.'

'But the picture of you. I was going to ask permission . . .' He hesitated, seemingly unsure of himself. It wasn't like him at all and Sarah was rather touched. Confident, assured Hugo, anxious for her approval. Then she told herself not to be so silly. They were colleagues; he was being professional, wanting to make sure he hadn't broken any rules.

'Do you ask everyone you photograph for permission – obviously you would famous people, but all the others?' She was curious. That would have involved a lot of work.

'Well, not always. But I wanted to ask you.'

Sarah became fascinated by the fact that condensation had formed on her glass. 'It was a lovely photo.'

'What was it of?' asked James.

'It was just one of Sarah at Ashlyn's wedding,' said Hugo. 'With one of her bridesmaids.' He sounded non-chalant now. Sarah thought she must have misinterpreted his earlier concern.

Laurence, who had been half listening and half looking at the motoring section of the paper, looked up. 'Is that Electra Handforth-Williams, you mentioned?' he said.

'That's right. Do you know her?' Hugo asked.

'I've only met her a few times. She always seems to be on her way to some far-flung country when I do. She's a great traveller, apparently.'

'Yes,' said Sarah, feeling she could risk talking about her now she was general conversation. 'Very adventurous.' Sarah felt Hugo's gaze on her but ignored it.

'I went inter-railing after leaving school,' said Elsa. 'With a friend. I love Europe but I don't think I could settle down anywhere but in England.'

'That's just how I feel,' said Laurence.

Sarah, who had Hugo in her line of sight noticed him nodding and heard him say, 'Me too. I love this country, can't imagine living anywhere else. A house in the country, dogs and children – at least three . . .' She stared at her now-empty glass. What *was* Hugo doing with Electra then?

Chapter Thirty-Six

Sarah, Elsa and Bron were in the back of a white stretch limo. They were on their way to Lily's hen night that was arranged at a location that not only catered for hens, but that was suitably convenient for where everyone lived.

Elsa was thinking about Laurence and wondering when he'd next text. He was away again at the moment on business, and they'd only had a chance to exchange brief 'I'll call you's after the pub that day before he had to leave. He was obviously very busy as his texts, though friendly, had been a bit sporadic and his phone calls practically non-existent. She just hoped he'd still be keen to see her again when he returned, although he seemed rather vague about that too. She couldn't help feeling a little anxious. He was the first person she'd really liked in a very long time

Bron was thinking about James. She thought she'd been giving him subtle hints, but he still seemed to see her only as the girl next door. And despite being newly out of a long-term relationship, albeit one that was dead in the water, she knew she really fancied him. It was a feeling she hadn't felt in years. But she'd just have to trust in fate. He was proving to be a good friend and better that than nothing.

And Sarah was thinking about Hugo, as she seemed to do constantly these days. Telling herself he was unavailable didn't seem to stop her from dreaming about him. It was all so futile.

'So, how's it all going, girls?' she said now. 'Elsa, how

are the fairy wings coming along for the bridesmaids? And the dresses? It must be bedlam.'

Elsa seemed fairly relaxed about it. She was wearing a dress in a wonderful deep red and the glow that had been apparent on the Sunday morning of Carrie's visit was still there, although slightly diluted.

'I think it will be fine. I've got my woman, the work-experience girl and I've even roped in Bron's cooking ladies – fortunately it's too early for them to start making vol-au-vents. We bought the dresses and dyed them – Carrie wanted a lovely shell pink which I think I've just about achieved, haven't I, Bron?'

'It's a lovely colour,' Bron agreed. 'I'm going to try and reproduce it in icing. I've had a commission for a wedding cake made out of cupcakes in tiers. That would be the perfect soft shade I need.'

'You're both so talented! I'm so impressed. How lucky I am to have you both on board. Go on telling me about the dresses.'

'Well, we ran up some really stiff petticoats – like those long tutus they wear for *Les Sylphides*?'

Sarah shook her head. 'I'm so sorry, I know absolutely nothing about ballet.'

'Doesn't matter. They go under the dresses and then over both there's a layer of chiffon that opens down the front. They have little ruffs to go round their necks. They're adorable, they really are.'

'That's all right then.'

'The ladies are all sewing on crystals like mad,' Elsa went on. 'They're AB crystals – that stands for Aurora Borealis if you're remotely interested. They really sparkle.'

Sarah was more interested in speed than crystal types. 'Couldn't you glue them on? It'd be quicker.'

Elsa shook her head. 'Very high risk. If you get one wrong you're left with a horrible gluey mark. I will glue them down the bones though and sprinkle a few on to the skirts. They'll be a bit more random, but I wouldn't ask anyone else to wield the gadget that melts the glue.' She shuddered slightly, obviously thinking of what could happen if it all went wrong. 'Fortunately we managed to buy ballet slippers in exactly the right shade. I don't think we'd have had time to get them dyed to match.' She paused. 'They're having crystals on too.'

'So what about Carrie's dress? That's the really important thing.'

'It's going OK, I think. The toile fitted beautifully and she didn't want too much changed, thank goodness. I think she's finally caught on to the fact that there's a bit of a rush on and it won't get done unless she sticks to the plan. She does want a huge stand-up ruff, like in the pictures of Queen Elizabeth the First. I've got some little tiny stones for that.'

'Phew,' said Sarah. 'You're a star. Now, Bron, what about the cake?'

'Well, we finally managed to work out a really quick way of doing the fake ones.'

'We? Is that the cooking ladies, too?'

Bron shook her head. 'James.'

'That sounded a bit soulful!' said Elsa, who knew all about Bron's frustrations over James. They'd discussed it quite a bit recently, over cups of supportive mid-work tea.

'Well, I've given all the signals I can and he hasn't picked up on them. Just as well I'm so busy I can hardly even think about him.' As Bron said this she knew that it didn't matter how busy she was, she still spent a lot of time thinking about James.

Sensing Bron didn't really want to talk about it, Sarah said, 'So, have you heard from Laurence, Elsa?'

Elsa sighed. 'He's working abroad at the moment and he's really busy too, and so can't ring me all that often. It's lovely when he does, though. And he sends sweet texts.

Mind you, I haven't had one for a while . . .' Her doubts crept in again.

'I've put him on the list as your partner,' said Sarah. 'I can take him off if you want.'

'No, I'd love him to come to the wedding, but I don't think he'll be back in time.'

'Oh well, his place is open,' said Sarah. 'You're very sweet together.'

After Elsa had denied and then accepted that she and Laurence did seem suited, she said, 'He'll probably come back and not like me after all. It's always a mistake to have sex too early on in the relationship. What?'

Bron and Sarah were laughing. 'I don't think that's a mistake you've made often, Elsa,' said Sarah. 'And anyway, I don't think you need to worry about Laurence. He's obviously smitten. Although he'd better be careful, you're looking particularly hot tonight, if I may say so.'

Elsa pulled at her dress. 'Do you like it? I've got really into red since I had my colours done. Whilst we're on the subject of men, what about you and Hugo, Sarah?' she went on deftly, still preferring not to be the centre of attention if she could avoid it. 'What was that about him taking a picture of you and putting it in an exhibition?'

'It was lovely. He made me look – well – beautiful.'

'You are beautiful,' said Elsa promptly.

'Hm,' said Sarah, 'but you're looking at my beautiful soul.'

'No!' Elsa contradicted.

'Well, Hugo wasn't, for sure,' said Bron.

'What do you mean? He takes pictures of everyone – it doesn't mean a thing,' said Sarah.

'Come on, I noticed the way you stare at him when you think no one's looking. You do like him, don't you?' asked Bron.

'Of course I like him! He's Hugo! Everyone likes him!'

'I didn't mean it like that,' said Bron. 'And you know it.'

She smiled. 'Has the cool, calm and collected but cynical wedding planner to the stars finally succumbed . . .'

Sarah blushed. 'Don't be silly. He is attractive, there's no denying it but . . .' She didn't want to tell the girls he was spoken for. It would involve too much painful interrogation. 'Until this wedding – both weddings – are over, I haven't time to think about Hugo.'

'But you do really like him, don't you?' persisted Elsa.

Sarah let out a big sigh. 'You don't give up, either of you! All right. Yes, I do, but it's not to be – it's all too complicated, believe me. Anyway, let's not talk about me. This is Lily's night.'

'But Lily's not here yet,' Elsa pointed out.

'It's still her night,' said Sarah firmly.

'Hm,' said Bron. She didn't want to push Sarah too far, not tonight at least. 'So, what's the plan for this evening?'

'I don't know much at all,' said Sarah. 'Lily said she didn't want me to have anything to do with it. One of her friends has done it all, including hiring this limo. I do hope she's going to pay for it – we don't want to have a frantic whip-round at two in the morning. Actually' – she lowered her voice conspiratorially – 'I'm going to try and slip away a bit early. I'm sure Lily doesn't want her big sister cramping her style.'

'Well, I don't want to be up late,' said Elsa. 'I get up really early these days.'

'Oh,' said Bron. 'I was looking forward to a girls' night out.'

'Well, maybe we should have one then,' said Sarah unexpectedly. 'Maybe we should go on the pull.'

The thought of sensible, well-organised Sarah going on the pull made the others giggle rather more than necessary, Sarah thought as the car pulled up to the kerb in front of the first bar.

'Hiya! So you're Lily's big sister!'

The girl on the pavement confronting her was wearing

white leather shorts, long white boots, a fringed jacket and a cowboy hat. Lily and her two other friends were dressed in the same way. Lily had various extras – L-plates, garters and feather sex toys – draped round her neck. Sarah did her best to smile.

'That's right!' she said.

'Lily says you can be a bit of a spoilsport, but you won't on her hen night, will you?'

'Of course not! Whatever gave you that impression?'

Lily was examining her French manicure. Her shorts were pulled tight over her belly and Sarah thought she looked a bit deranged.

'Well, I'm in charge,' said Lily's chief bridesmaid, who was called Charlene. 'And we're going to have a great time. Aren't we, girls?'

Everyone cheered – Elsa and Bron very quietly. Sarah could tell they wanted to go home too.

'So, where do we start?' said Sarah, faking enthusiasm for Britain. 'I'll get the first round in! Which bar are we going to?'

'Let's have one here first,' said Bron.

'Not so fast,' said Charlene. 'We can't just go drinking whenever we want. We have to play the game. Lots of games, really.'

'Oh, come on, Charles,' said another of Lily's friends. 'You can't expect us to go paying forfeits and stuff without a few glasses of wine or a cocktail or two first! It's unreasonable.'

Sarah bit her tongue to stop herself reminding everyone that Lily was pregnant and shouldn't be drinking at all.

'We're going to a club,' said Charlene. 'It's all arranged. We just have to get past the doormen.' She glanced at Bron, Elsa and Sarah, hinting that they were either inappropriately dressed for a hen night or just too old and unattractive.

It took them a little time to file into the club and the doormen seemed to check out the credentials of the girls for a lot longer than necessary. It took Sarah even longer to make her way to the bar but she persevered – all thought of spending the evening drinking mineral water or non-alcoholic cocktails had vanished. She needed at least one drink to get through this.

She realised when she finally got back to the table with the drinks that Lily's friends were already fairly well tanked up. 'Here we go, girls.' She handed Bron and Elsa their drinks. 'We might as well get drunk. It's the only way we're going to get through this.'

'OK,' said Charlene, unaware of any dissent among her audience. 'Here's what Lily has to do!'

There was a cry of 'Whoa' and everyone took a sip from their glasses.

'First on the list . . .' She looked around at her audience, claiming everyone's attention. 'She has to kiss a stag.'

'Maybe we should ring the RSPCA,' whispered Bron to Sarah.

'A proper snog, mind, not just a kiss on the cheek.' Charlene was insistent. 'She has to collect three items of clothing from three different men; get a massage – it can just be shoulders, we don't want anyone stripping off.'

'You surprise me,' murmured Bron, who was starting to feel giggly. It was all so silly.

'And, finally, she has to get up on that stage and swing round the pole!'

'But she's pregnant!' said Sarah, unable to stop herself. 'She shouldn't be doing things like that!' Then she wished she'd kept her mouth shut.

'Oh, and the drinks?' Charlene ignored Sarah's protest and was again checking to make sure everyone was listening.

'We drink with our right hands for the first half-hour and our left for the second. Anyone gets it wrong, they have to put a couple of quid in the middle. Then we buy the next round.'

'That sounds complicated!' said Elsa, struggling to join in.

'Well, it doesn't matter if you mess up, it just gives us more money to drink with,' said Charlene.

'Right,' said Elsa, hoping she wouldn't have to find a cash machine.

'The male strippers come later,' went on Charlene. 'It's a full Monty, so I hope nobody's prudish.'

'As if!' said Bron, with an Oscar-winning display of enthusiasm. 'Bring on Robbie Coltrane, I say.'

Elsa leant in and whispered behind her hand, 'I think you'll find you mean Robert Carlyle.'

'Mm, maybe I do,' she agreed, laughing in spite of everything.

They had a few more rounds of drinks. Lily ticked off various things on her list while the others had to go through a collection of suitable hen-night games until Charlene suddenly called out, 'Flies!' and with a varying degree of alacrity, everyone except Bron, Elsa and Sarah, who looked on bemused, and Lily, who was allowed to just watch and laugh, threw themselves down on the floor and waved their arms and legs in the air. Sarah, feeling as if she was indeed a dying insect, looked at her watch. Ten past ten. No chance of going home for at least a couple of hours.

'OK!' Charlene, who had obviously missed her vocation as a drum majorette or sergeant major, got to her feet. 'More drinks! Come on, you lot.' She looked pointedly in Sarah's direction. 'Join in.'

'I asked those guys over there to play flies,' said one of Lily's other friends, 'but they wouldn't. They're wearing kilts. I think they're being spoilsports.'

Unusually for her, it took Sarah several moments to pick up the significance of this and she realised her brain just wasn't operating at its usual speed. 'Could I just have water this round?'

'Nope,' said Charlene. 'You had water last time. I want everyone to have a proper drink while the show is on.'

Lily, who had discovered a real talent for picking on men on stag dos who were up for a laugh, said, 'Yes, lighten up, Sares. You're supposed to be having fun. That man was only being friendly, you know.'

Sarah smiled guiltily, remembering the young man she'd sent away with a flea in his ear. 'I know and I *am* having fun. How are you getting on with your list?'

'I've just got to snog a stag.'

'But you've snogged at least three people, haven't you?'

Lily nodded. 'But they lied to me and said they were the stag when they weren't. It's my last dare,' she said comfortingly, as if that made everything all right. Gaily, she went off on her mission.

Charlene came back and handed out the drinks. Sarah took a glass. It was pink and fruity and sweet and for a blissful few sips, Sarah thought it might be non-alcoholic. Too late she felt its kick and realised she'd drunk a very strong cocktail very quickly. How many had she had? she wondered. She'd lost count. She would definitely have water next time.

The crowd were going wild. The five men on the stage were gyrating wildly, their polished muscles gleaming. Sarah, who'd accepted yet another cocktail by mistake and then decided she might as well give up her futile attempt at counting, did appreciate they were good at what they were doing, and all had very good bodies, but she didn't really enjoy it.

She glanced at Elsa and Bron who also had glazed expressions on their faces. Lily, Charlene and the other two, whose names Sarah had never quite grasped, were jumping up and down screaming with glee. Lily had already been invited on stage to join in the show. She'd been very good, Sarah admitted, not at all embarrassed by the things she was asked to do by a man wearing nothing but a feather-thong. If only she felt more in the mood for all this. Being a wedding planner was making her old before her time! Maybe she should stop feeling so responsible. Lily was an adult, after all.

'OK, Sarah?' Elsa shouted into her ear, obviously aware that her friend was not enjoying herself.

'I just need a glass of water. I don't know how many of those cocktails I've had, and they're so sweet.'

'I'll get you one if you like,' said Elsa.

'I'll go!' said Sarah, rising from her seat and then sitting down again. She was suddenly aware that she'd had far too much to drink.

'It's all right,' said Elsa. 'I won't have to pay for it, I don't think. I've run out of money.'

'There's some in my bag if you need it,' said Sarah. 'I got some out before I came.' She burrowed under her feet and found her bag, and in it, her purse. 'Oh. I don't know how I can have spent all that money.'

'I'll get the water. Then it must be time to go home!'

Somehow Charlene roped them into yet another game of truth or dare, and, already rather befuddled, Sarah found herself having to down a few more drinks as a forfeit. She felt a desperate urge to lie down but first she really needed to find the Ladies.

When she came out again it seemed to take her a while to find the door of the building but at last she got out on to the pavement. Elsa and Bron were there, looking concerned.

'Charlene took Lily and the others in the limo. They said if we didn't want to go to another club we didn't have to,' she said.

'That's good,' said Sarah, aware of having to enunciate very carefully, as well as keep herself upright; everything was weaving in and out of focus horribly quickly. 'I really don't want any more to drink. I've had too much already. Let's call a – a – car that takes you places.'

She watched as Bron and Elsa went through their purses, looking for money. 'Take mine,' she said grandly, swaying and steadying herself against a wall. 'I've got plenty of money.'

'No you haven't,' said Elsa. 'Yours has been rifled already. Those cocktails were very expensive.'

Sarah felt very very tired and sat on a convenient step. 'If I have a little rest first we can walk home.'

'I don't think so,' said Elsa firmly as she and Bron exchanged glances. They'd never seen Sarah like this. They all needed to get home, and safely. 'First off, these shoes are killing me and second, it's bloody miles away.'

'Oh,' said Sarah, and closed her eyes.

'We need to phone someone,' said Bron.

'Who? I'm not phoning my dad – only as a last resort, anyway,' said Elsa. 'I don't mind calling him if I'm lost and need to be given directions, but he'll have had a glass or two of wine by now, or be in bed. And Laurence is away.'

'Well, I can't phone James. He gets up really early. It wouldn't be fair.'

Sarah opened her eyes briefly when she heard either Elsa or Bron say, 'Hugo!'

'Oh yes,' she murmured and closed her eyes again.

Sarah seemed to have been asleep for a long time. She'd had some very strange dreams including a car ride and Hugo. He was taking her somewhere. Bron and Elsa were there and they seemed to be talking about her, but she couldn't really understand what they were saying. Then she woke up and it was all real, if still a little hazy.

'Thank goodness I wasn't dreaming that I was walking down the street naked,' she said and Hugo, who seemed to be on his own now, laughed.

'Come on, sweetheart, let's get you to bed.'

'I don't want to go to bed with you, Hugo. Even if I do really like you.'

'Do you?'

Sarah nodded. 'Mm. But I'm not going to sleep with you because you'll break my heart.'

'You don't have to sleep with me, but I wouldn't break your heart at all.'

'Wouldn't you?'

'No, but we won't talk about that now.'

In the morning it all came back to her in terrifying detail. She realised that not only had Hugo taken most of her clothes off and tucked her into bed, but he'd left a big glass of water and bowl handy for her. Realising that he'd seen her when she was very, very drunk was more painful than the hangover.

'Have a bacon sandwich,' he advised when he rang her a little later to see if she was all right. 'And a pint of orange juice.'

'I'm so, so sorry,' she said, too ill to be embarrassed. Was it possible for a head actually to split open?

He laughed. 'You're a very endearing drunk, Sarah. Don't worry about it.'

When he was sure that she had what she needed to work on her hangover and had disconnected, Sarah remembered what she'd said about him breaking her heart. She also remembered him saying that he wouldn't. She hadn't believed him then and she didn't believe him now.

Chapter Thirty-Seven

Bron was in her little garden, working on what she hoped was her last fake-cake, thinking that at least she was very quick at creating flowers in icing so when she came to do the real cake, in a couple of days' time, she should be an expert at it. She needed to be as Carrie's wedding was mere days away now.

'Hi,' said a female voice. 'Am I disturbing you? I've come over to see how you're getting on, and to make a hair appointment, if I may.'

She looked up to see Vanessa.

'My goodness!' Vanessa went on, gesturing towards what Bron was doing. 'Look at that! It's fantastic!'

Bron was pleased. 'It's the last. I'm hoping I won't need to do any more. Do you like them?'

'They're beautiful! Could I commission you to do one for me?'

'Of course. You might be able to have one of these when the wedding's over. I don't know what Carrie will want to do with them.'

'To be honest, I'd rather have one without crystals,' said Vanessa.

'Mm, I know what you mean, but I think as Carrie's dress is covered in them, the crystals are necessary. Can I get you a cup of coffee or anything?' asked Bron.

'Yes, but I'll make it. What would you like?'

'I've only got instant, I'm afraid,' said Bron, suddenly a little daunted by the thought of her landlady making her own coffee.

'That's fine. Too much of the other stuff gives me the jitters.'

Bron laughed and started another flower. Now she was doing the top of the sphere, she had to stand on a box to work. She wondered why, if she wanted her hair doing, Vanessa hadn't just rung up to make an appointment. Did she have another reason for calling or was she just being friendly? When Vanessa came out a few minutes later with two steaming mugs and settled herself on the bench beside Bron, Bron soon realised that she definitely had something else to talk about. Once they'd fixed a time for Bron to do Vanessa's hair the following week and Vanessa had grilled her on Carrie's wedding preparations and said she couldn't wait for the next issue of *Celeb* to come out – she made it her business to keep up with all the gossip – she turned to Bron and said firmly, 'Now tell me, how are you and James getting on?'

Bron swallowed a big gulp of coffee. 'Well, we don't see much of each other, we're both very busy—'

'I wondered,' Vanessa interrupted her. 'I noticed him helping you with your cakes.' She gave Bron a piercing glance. Had her landlady been spying on her? Knowing Vanessa, she wouldn't put it past her.

'I think he's very attractive – not that I go for younger men – but he is good-looking, I've always thought,' Vanessa went on.

'Yes, he is, very good-looking.' Bron was wary.

'But you don't fancy him? No chemistry? I mean, it either works for you or it doesn't.'

Bron couldn't quite believe her landlady's audacity, then she laughed.

'Oh, am I being too blunt? If you don't fancy him—'

'It's not that.' Bron blushed.

'Ah, so you do like him?' Vanessa was obviously determined to find out. 'I was only saying to Donald the other night what a good pair you'd make. He told me not to interfere of course, but . . . Anyway, if you do fancy him, then what's the problem?'

Bron wondered if she should match Vanessa's frankness. Probably Vanessa would only prise it out of her eventually; she was like a terrier with a bone. Vanessa gave her an encouraging smile. Bron looked down at her coffee. Perhaps it would help if she confided in someone like Vanessa, it was sort of like confiding in her mother. 'I don't think he fancies me. I thought I'd given him enough hints. I've invited him to meals, given him cake, got him to come round to Elsa's with these' – she indicated the fake-cakes – 'so he could see how nice my friends are, but nothing.' She sighed. 'If he fancied me, he'd have made a move by now, surely. We do get on well, but I think he just sees me as a friend.'

'Nonsense! Of course he fancies you. Lovely girl like you, right next door. He is a man, after all.'

'But as you said, if there's no chemistry . . .'

Vanessa sipped her coffee and then shook her head. 'I'm sure it's not that.' She thought for a moment and then patted Bron's hand. 'It's possible he thinks it's too soon for you after . . .?' She paused.

'Roger.'

'Right. Well, no man wants to be a rebound. Too much pride. And although I don't know all the details, I got the impression he'd come out of a relationship that ended badly for him when he first came here, a couple of years ago. He probably didn't want you to rebound on him and break his heart all over again.'

'Do you really think so?' Bron said quietly, realising there might be some truth in Vanessa's words. It *was* very soon after Roger and he might well think she was a complete slapper for even thinking about someone else so soon. He was probably trying to let her down gently. How embarrassing.

Vanessa warmed to her theme. 'I do. He's quite

sensitive, you know.' She paused. 'So what are we going to do about it?'

'About what?' Bron was puzzled.

Vanessa made a gesture that indicated Bron had missed something very simple. 'You must be proactive, darling! You must do something to make it happen. Good God! If women waited for men to get things going, the population would have died out millennia ago!'

'Oh. Do you think so?'

'It's a fact. Now, what are we going to do about that silly man not taking advantage of what's under his nose?'

Bron shrugged. 'He's being incredibly helpful. He made all the bases for these.' She indicated her tree. 'And he's made the framework for the real cake.'

'You don't need a helpmate – although a man who's practical is a bonus . . .' Vanessa said, going off on another tangent. 'Mm, let me see . . . I know – you need to get him to the wedding. Why don't you ask him to drive you over? After all, you'll need help with those trees. You wouldn't get more than a couple in your little car.'

'But he'd have to take time off work.' Bron began to feel a glimmer of hope. Maybe Vanessa was right, and he just needed a little more prodding.

'That's easy. I can help you there. He's got loads of holiday owing him. Tell you what, I'll suggest he takes you. He can say no if he really doesn't want to, but I think he just needs a bit of a push. How long are you staying over at the house where the wedding is?'

'A couple of days. I don't really think I can transport the cake iced and it's going to take a while to do.' She took another sip of coffee. 'Although I am very good at these flowers now, it will be a bit different on the actual cake. And then when the cake's done, I have to do Carrie's hair and make-up. There are bridesmaids too, although they're little ones, so I won't need to do too much with them.'

'Two or three days together should do the trick.'

Vanessa was in her own little matchmaking world once more. 'He may feel it's not fair to jump on you when you're living next door in case you didn't appreciate it. It would be awkward if you didn't, after all.'

Bron sighed. 'I don't see what else—'

Vanessa patted her hand again in a mothering way. 'You'll think of something when you're thrown together in difficult circumstances, but you've got to remember that men can be very slow.' She stood up and brushed her skirt down. 'Leave it to me, darling. I love matchmaking!'

James did take Bron to Somerby. She didn't know exactly what Vanessa had said to him, but he'd agreed he could take the time off and that helping Bron was a good thing to do. He'd gone to park the car and Rupert was going to tell him where to put the fake-cakes and the pack of dogs had followed them. Sarah was giving Bron a tour.

'They've done so much to it!' Sarah was saying. 'I keep forgetting you didn't see it before, but it was quite empty and barren-looking, but now, it's amazing!'

As they wandered around, Bron made suitably impressed noises. It was amazing. A real country estate, like in a novel. Imagine anyone actually living here. As Sarah rattled on about this cornice and that, Bron sensed she was quite tense. It was a big job, finally pulling everything together, especially when you had your sister's wedding to attend to too.

'You look tired, Sarah, are you OK?' asked Bron.

'Oh yes, just pre-wedding nerves.' She laughed, in rather a forced way Bron felt. 'All wedding planners get them, worse than the bride.'

'Is everyone here? Hugo?' She was dying to ask if anything had happened between Sarah and Hugo the other night.

'Yes, he's here, already snapping away.'

'I hope he didn't take advantage of you after Lily's hen

night,' Bron teased. 'Elsa and I were a little worried, leaving you alone with him, but he was most insistent.'

Sarah groaned. 'Don't talk to me about that night. The evils of drink.'

'But he looked after you OK?' Bron persisted.

'Yes, of course. He put me to bed, left a big glass of water and a bowl and went home.'

Bron detected a note of disappointment in Sarah's voice. 'Is that all?' she asked.

'Well, it was all rather embarrassing. I told him I liked him.'

'And?'

'It's no good, he can't like me . . .'

'I'm sure he does, Sarah. He was awfully concerned for you. When we rang him, he didn't hesitate, he just got in the car.'

'He's kind and I think he is fond of me but . . .' She hesitated. 'He's engaged to a friend of Fen and Rupert.'

'What?' asked Bron in surprise. 'Are you sure? I thought he was single. He's certainly never mentioned her.'

Sarah nodded. 'I know, but he is, believe me.' She sighed. 'Don't say anything. I don't want him to know I even care.'

Bron frowned, but before she could reply Sarah continued. 'I mean, I don't, not really. Anyway, it's all too complicated and I've got far too much to do to be worrying about such things. Come on, here are your sleeping quarters.'

Sympathy for her friend made Bron drop the subject, but as she followed Sarah to a converted pigsty or whatever it was, she wished there was time to talk about it properly. She sensed Sarah wanted to tell her more. Was Hugo really engaged? If so, would he really have dropped everything like that when he'd heard she needed help? And shown such obvious concern for her? Bron might have been a little drunk herself that night but she could have sworn Hugo looked at Sarah with much more than just fondness.

Perhaps there would be a moment in the next two days when she would tell Bron everything. Bron was a good listener and she'd be there for her friend whenever she needed her.

'They're going to rent these converted buildings out, but you're the first in here,' Sarah said as she opened the door. 'Gorgeous, isn't it?'

'It is! I love the whitewashed walls and the rag rug. It's like a little place in Greece or somewhere.'

'But as it's England, there's a wood-burning stove. Not that you'll need it now. I can't believe this weather! As long as it lasts until Sunday, it can rain all it likes after that.'

'James says we need rain. He was worrying about his greenhouses. Vanessa has promised she'll water everything while he's away but I'm not sure he trusts her.'

'Will he be all right in the caravan? I didn't want to put him in here, with you. I told Fen things weren't at that stage yet.'

Bron made a face. 'He'd better make a move soon or Vanessa will sack him.' She chuckled. 'Or I'd better make a move soon or she'll sack me!'

'Is she that bad? Anyway, you don't work for her, do you?'

'No, it's just that she was very firm about it the other day. And she made him bring me, with all my trees. She's wonderfully bossy sometimes.' She explained to Sarah about Vanessa's little pep talk.

'Mm, I remember her as a bride's mother. Blunt isn't the word for her.' Sarah smiled. 'Right, I'd better get on. Come up to the house when you're ready and I'll show you where you can start putting your cake together.'

Sarah walked back up to the house, mentally ticking off various items on her to-do list. She must find her clipboard and start ticking things off for real. She was glad Bron had arrived safely, with the cake in tow. It seemed a lifetime ago that she had arrived herself, eager to be shown around, to see how much of a transformation had gone on.

The dogs had milled about her ankles as Rupert kissed her.

'So, did you get everything done?' she asked

Fenella laughed. 'You'll have to see for yourself, but I think we've done a pretty good job. There are the occasional grot areas, but I'm sure we can hide them. We've worked pretty much non-stop at it.'

'Oh, well done! Please, show me everything.'

'Does that mean that you don't want coffee first?' asked Rupert, ever the host.

'If you'd be a love and make it, we'll come and get it soon,' said Fenella.

'The path up to the chapel looks amazing!' Sarah was very impressed. 'And it's wonderful being able to offer the whole package. People could have always got married first and then had their own ceremony here, but this is just perfect.'

'The local vicar has been so helpful,' said Fenella. 'And his roof fund is doing quite well too!'

Sarah laughed.

'Carrie and Rick had to visit the vicar at least twice,' Fenella went on.

'Oh, it's Rick now, is it?' said Sarah, teasingly. 'You'll be on first-name terms with all the stars soon.'

'I really hope so!' said Fenella. 'But thank goodness they stayed in a hotel. If she'd seen the state of this place she'd have thought it would never be ready in time. The security's going to be mega.'

'Yes, and you're lucky this time, once Somerby gets on the venue map, which it will after it's starred in *Celeb* magazine, you'll be papped all the time.'

Fenella looked horrified. 'You are joking?'

'Well, only a bit.'

'You mean you're only a bit joking? Or that I'll only be papped a bit?'

'Both! But as I told Carrie that day, the situation does make it easy for it to be kept under control.'

'Oh, Lordy! Well, come and see the drawing room.'

It was beautiful. The blend of gorgeous parrot-strewn wallpaper and mural was complete, with *trompe-l'œil* plants creeping over the cornices on to the ceiling. The walls had perspective, giving the impression that a garden of Eden extended into the hills. Sun and light, both real and fabricated, filled the room with gold.

Real palm trees stood in pots in the corner, adding to the exotic atmosphere. Garlands of flowers linked painted pillars and actual ones so realistically that Sarah almost expected an antelope to come out of the mural and put its nose into a vase of leaves that covered the fireplace.

'Oh, Fenella!' exclaimed Sarah, her eyes wide as she took in all the detail. 'It's paradise! It's perfect!'

'I did the painting myself,' said Fenella proudly. 'It's taken almost all the time since I last saw you. I had to help Rupert with the rest of the decorating, too, so I've had some long days.' She yawned and then laughed.

'I'm so impressed. Now, show me the rest,' said Sarah.

'Ah, well, this is the bit we couldn't get done,' said Fenella, indicating a corridor. 'I thought of hanging a sheet over the entrance, but it might look a bit as if we're still decorating,' she went on. 'We are, of course, but we don't want to advertise the fact.'

Sarah considered. 'Mm, tell you what, why don't we get some pots or jars or something and stick branches – big branches – in them. It'll look as if there's a wood in your house, but a few fairy lights and people won't go down here. It'll fit in with the real/fake theme and if you don't put up physical barriers people wander about all over the place, looking for the loo.'

Fenella's face took on a look of panic. 'I think that's a

great idea, I really do, but I haven't time to do it. I'll just stick a notice up, "Trespassers Will be Prosecuted".'

Sarah laughed. 'But think how much funnier it would be if there was a wood here! Bron's friend James . . .'

'The one who's sleeping in the caravan?'

'Yes. We'll ask him to do it. He's a gardener. Once he's helped Bron with the fake trees he can hack at real ones. Do we know where the cake is going to be yet?'

'Here.' Fenella opened the door into the dining room.

'Oh, wow!' said Sarah, thrilled. 'This is fantastic! You've created the most perfect space for the grand entrance!' She could now easily picture the long double row of fake trees, sparkling in the lights, leading to the wedding cake, bigger than the others, at the end of the row. 'You must have completely redecorated – there's nothing shabby about your chic now!'

'It took us for ever,' said Fenella, tired at the memory of it all. 'We didn't give in and rent a scaffolding tower for two days and I was perched on the top of a ladder, which I really hate, having to go back down again every time my brush needed more paint.'

'Couldn't you have hung the tin off the ladder or something?'

'I could have if I'd had a proper paint kettle, but we just had these massive tins of white paint that I put a bit of colour into. Anyway, Rupert, who was rebuilding the pigsties – where Bron will be staying – came in and said it was bloody ridiculous. He went into town and came back with the tower. He'd only hired it so it had to go back but I wanted to keep it. *So* much better than those horrible ladders. We've still got loads of decorating to do, after all.'

'You've done a fantastic job, Fen, I don't know how you did it in the time.'

'By working all the hours God sends,' said Fenella.

'It's been worth every second, really it has. And now it's done, you've got this amazing venue.'

Fenella nodded. 'It's what kept us going.' She sighed deeply. 'Do you really think we have to bother with the branches in jars thing?'

'Yes,' said Sarah. 'I'll ask James when they arrive. He'll do it. And Elsa will be here soon too. She might have time to help him.'

Elsa arrived shortly after Bron and James and was shown the bedroom Fenella had allocated for Carrie so she had somewhere to use while she was in the house. She could leave her things there, have her make-up touched up and generally use it as a base. It would also be useful for the bridesmaids.

'It's our bedroom, actually,' Fenella said wistfully. 'It's the only one currently with an en suite, so I had to give it up. We're a bit short of bedrooms that don't desperately need sorting out.'

'It's beautiful!' said Elsa. 'And so huge! You could have a ball in here.'

'Yes, it is a good size.'

'It's about the same size as my workroom at home,' said Elsa, feeling the need to impress on Fenella just how massive this bedroom was, 'which is the entire floor of an old factory.'

'Oh, that is quite big, isn't it?'

Elsa nodded. 'I'll go down and get my rail, then I'll start bringing up the dresses. When are the bridesmaids coming?'

'I've got it written down somewhere. They're not coming all at once, fortunately.'

'After they've had their fittings and I've done any alterations I can help you. Sarah said she'd been making unreasonable demands and that I must be useful.'

Fenella laughed. 'Sarah's great, isn't she?'

Elsa nodded. 'But she admits she can be quite demanding. She does have very high standards.'

'Nothing wrong with that. Anyway, will you and Sarah be all right in those little attics?' Fenella went on. 'You have got one each, which is better than having to share, but they are rather tiny. The bathroom works OK if you run the hot tap for ages. Hot water comes through eventually.'

'They looked sweet; we'll be fine there,' said Elsa. 'I loved the curtains – gorgeous fabric.'

'Probably genuine antiques,' said Fenella. 'We found them in an old trunk. Well, this isn't going to get the baby bathed. I must find James and get him to hack down some trees. There's a small wood nearby – I'm sure we won't miss it. We can't have *Celeb* magazine discovering our undecorated passageway!'

Bron was in the kitchen, looking at her real cakes. There were six of them and the top one was already iced. It was a little dome of green-icing flowers with crystal centres. She'd taken so much trouble with it and got it so perfect she hoped she could do the rest of the icing as well. She had several large plastic boxes of icing already made up, enough spare nozzles and icing bags to set up a small shop and was all ready to go, except she was nervous. She'd practised her flowers until she could do them really quickly, but doing something in the safety of Veronica's kitchen, with Veronica on hand for advice, was one thing. Now she had to assemble the layers and actually finish the thing.

Fenella came in. 'How are you getting on? Do you want a hand taking it all upstairs? I'll ask Rupert. I'm still trying to find enough sheets. I know I've got loads, my mother gave me all her old ones, but I can't find them! I've done most of them—' Fenella stopped as she noticed Bron's slightly frazzled look. 'I'll find Rupert. He can help you.'

Bron would have preferred James because he knew what he was doing by now, but he'd been sent into the wood with a pair of loppers, a pruning saw and a ladder. She fully accepted that he was the best man for that particular job, but he was also the best man for transporting her cakes; he was experienced with cakes by now and knew how they should be handled. She wasn't sure she wanted to trust her confectionery to Rupert, who, nice as he was, might drop something vital.

Still, she smiled politely at him when he appeared, wearing paint-spattered jeans and a jumper with the welt hanging off.

'I gather you need some help?' And he picked up several sections of cake that had been stacked together and disappeared out of the room.

While Bron had some idea where she needed to be, she wasn't exactly sure of the way. Rupert was lovely but she was worried that his busyness might mean he didn't treat her cake with the care and attention it required. She picked up the top she had already iced and followed him, as swiftly as she could with such a delicate burden.

She could hear him talking in a loud voice to someone and she knew he wasn't paying attention. She hurried and found the staircase, currently covered with drugget – a trip hazard if ever she saw one – terrified that any moment she would come across Rupert and a pile of cake crumbs.

Now she was nearer she could hear that Rupert was talking to Hugo. The men were laughing and teasing each other. Just too far away to yell, 'Mind my cake!' she sped along the hallway, which was wide enough for two women to take exercise side by side in hooped skirts. Where was Rupert? She knew he wouldn't have let her get lost on purpose, he was far too kind and gentlemanly, but he had a lot to do and had long legs.

Relief flooded over her as she found the right room. Already someone had placed her fake cakes in two rows leading to the long windows, where the real cake would stand.

'You thought I was going to drop the cake, didn't you?' said Rupert. 'Go on, admit it.'

Bron sighed deeply. 'Yes I did.'

'It would have made a wonderful photograph,' said Hugo. 'You wouldn't like to drop it on purpose, would you?'

Bron scowled at him as crossly as she could manage. He laughed.

Elsa was tired of smiling. She loved children and these little girls – daughters of Carrie's far-off cousins – were not naughty. But like anyone else who was five years old, they found it difficult to keep still. They wanted to run around playing fairies, flapping their arms and encouraging each other to louder squeals and more hysterical laughter. They also found the huge bed very tempting.

Their mothers were too busy chatting with each other to do much to rein them in – they were very excited to be involved in a celebrity wedding.

'Now, Isolde,' said Elsa firmly. 'Can you just let me check if this fits? It won't take long.' She should probably be firmer with them, she realised, but it was too late now.

'So what's Carrie's dress like?' asked one of the mothers, having realised that Elsa needed help.

'Fabulous,' said Elsa, her mouth full of pins.

'Can we have a peek?' asked the other mother.

'Not a chance,' said Elsa. She took out the last pin. 'You haven't got long to wait and she'd kill me if I let anyone see it before she has. There, that wasn't too bad, was it? Now, Imogen, your turn.'

It was time for Sarah to go. There was nothing much she could do now. She'd said goodbye to Elsa and Bron. She hadn't seen Hugo since this morning. He was probably off somewhere with his camera. For one brief moment she wondered if Electra would turn up to the wedding but then dismissed the thought. She had the guest and staff list and Electra's name wasn't on it – there wasn't even a plus one against Hugo's name. Bron had iced the last but one section and was now icing the entire thing into a ball. Elsa was hand-sewing the bridesmaids' dresses so that they fitted properly. And James had created a very mysterious wood in front of the blocked-off corridor. All was as well as it could be. Later everyone was going to sit in the kitchen and eat cottage pie and drink red wine. Sarah wished she could be with them.

'The florist will arrive very early tomorrow,' she said to Fenella, who had a clipboard. She felt Fenella would be the perfect custodian of it in her absence. And she did have a copy of her various lists in her handbag. She was running through everything in her mind. 'Let me know if there are any problems. I'll be at the end of my mobile – mostly. Right, the orchestra – I suppose I mean band, don't I? Whatever, they should turn up a couple of hours before they're needed. They like to eat something and then have a bit of a practice.' She frowned suddenly. 'Are they staying here? I can't remember.'

'B. and b. in the village,' said Fenella. 'I can't fit in another soul. We will be able to soon, but not now. Thank God Carrie and her entourage are staying at the hotel.'

'I know. The caterers will be early too. I've used them lots of times; they're very reliable.'

'Right,' said Fenella, writing on her clipboard. 'Horse and carriage?'

'Carrie's coming from the hotel in a car, she'll be put into the horse and carriage – we've found the perfect spot – and will be driven up the road and then up the drive to the chapel entrance. You don't need to worry about the horse and carriage because they'll just go back when they're finished. They've got a huge great lorry they can put it all on. Anything else you're not sure of?'

'The press,' said Fenella, seeming worried. 'Do I have to feed them or anything?'

'Absolutely not. We're only feeding the *Celeb* lot and they've been given strict instructions. I've warned the local pub that they'll be inundated. That'll have to do. Mandy has arranged some extra security. She'll handle all that.' Sarah put her arms round Fenella and hugged her. 'I do wish I could stay with you all. I'll be back as soon as I can.'

'Enjoy Lily's wedding. And don't worry about a thing. We'll manage,' Fenella said, with a little more conviction than she felt.

And Sarah finally got into her car, waved and drove away.

Chapter Thirty-Eight

Sarah was already tired when she arrived at Dirk's parents' house. Although things were going well at Somerby at the moment, she knew from experience that there were many, many slips that could occur between cups and lips where weddings were concerned.

She was let into the house by a stray aunt who smiled at her vaguely and then went back to whatever it was she had been doing.

Sarah found the kitchen and went in. A middle-aged woman with the kind of facial lines that indicated bad temper and discontent was putting cutlet collars on a rack of lamb. 'Who are you?' she demanded, sounding none too friendly.

'I'm Sarah – Lily's sister.' She smiled bravely. Her role was not so clear-cut here. While Lily expected her to organise everything, she was there as Lily's sister, not as a wedding planner. It meant that she had to do everything she usually did, but very discreetly. It made everything a lot harder work.

'Oh, hello.' The woman gave her a cursory glance. 'You're nothing like her, I must say.'

Sarah didn't know if this was a good thing or not in this woman's eyes.

'Is Lily here?' she asked.

The woman shook her head. 'No, she's at the flat, claiming she's tired. She'll know what being tired is all about when she's had the baby! Poor Dirk!'

'I think Dirk is very lucky,' said Sarah firmly, infuriated

by this woman already. 'Lily is a lovely person and she's going to make a brilliant mother. She's also going to make Dirk very happy. He's to be congratulated on his good taste.'

Sensing slightly too late that she'd been rather rude the woman managed a smile. 'Of course.'

'And I'm a wedding planner, and I'm here to help you all I can, Mrs . . .' Sarah's professional memory deserted her. If this woman'd been a client Sarah would have had her name on a file. Because she was Lily's future mother-in-law, she hadn't and so couldn't remember it.

'Boscastle,' said the woman, 'I'm Dirk's mother. Yes, I remember now, you've been organising that film star's wedding. What's her name again?'

'Carrie Condy.'

'Oh yes, that's right. And where is she getting married?'

'At a lovely old house in Herefordshire,' said Sarah. It was unlikely Mrs Boscastle was intending to inform the small number of publications to whom this would be hot news, but she didn't want to be too precise. 'So how is everything going here?'

Mrs Boscastle inclined her head. 'It's a shame it's too late to do anything about the food.'

'There's a problem with the food?' This was a bit heart-sinking. Those ladies should have been perfect! They were fairly near, they were doing it for cost, and they had the sort of friendly personalities that made them ideal for the job.

Mrs Boscastle nodded. 'It's a buffet – hopeless! It'll be all little nibbly things. No one will get enough to eat, Lily's— Some people will get drunk and the people who should be together won't be. A sit-down meal would have been far better. I could have arranged place settings.'

'You still could if you wanted to, Mrs Boscastle, if you think you've got time. You could seat people and then we can ask them to come up and get their food table by table.'

Sarah actually assumed something like this had already been done. It wasn't a last-minute job. To do it properly you had to take your time or you had people's exes sitting next to each other and fistfights threatening to break out before the first waltz – or at least before the last one.

'Well, I thought Lily and Dirk would see to it.' Mrs Boscastle frowned, indicating she knew perfectly well Lily and Dirk couldn't be expected to know the ins and outs of all their relations. 'I'm cooking this for a few chosen friends tonight. There's one thing I can control.'

Sarah became aware that she might be arranging fish and chips for the unchosen many and wondered exactly how many of them there were. 'Would you like me to help you do a table plan?'

Mrs Boscastle regarded her sideways. 'Could you do that?'

Sarah nodded. 'As I said, I'm a wedding planner,' she told her again. 'That sort of thing is part of my job. Although it is usually the family that does it, I do assist.' She remembered Ashlyn's wedding and her anxieties about seating the missing bridesmaid's parents.

'It's a good offer—'

But just after these words had left her mouth Sarah realised that Lily had first call on her time. 'I could give you an hour or so, but what about your dinner guests?'

'Oh, we couldn't do it tonight, we'll have to do it in the morning.'

Sarah was very firm. 'I'm going to be very busy with Lily in the morning.' Just how busy, she had yet to find out. Lily had said she'd arranged a hairdresser, the dress was lovely and they were using family cars to transport everyone. In theory, it should all be fine. Theoretical weddings always went swimmingly. It was the real kind that were unpredictable.

'Perhaps you could come when my guests have gone? About ten? Is that too late for you?'

Considering Sarah already felt she could sleep for weeks without even turning over it was definitely too late for her, but she smiled. 'I'll pop back about ten then. If you have a list of all the people who've been invited it won't take us long.' She fervently hoped she'd said this firmly enough to make Mrs Boscastle dig out the list.

Just as escape was in sight, Sarah remembered something else. 'The marquee came all right?'

'Oh yes. It's taking up the entire garden, but I must confess my herbaceous borders look very much better as part of the floral arrangements. Some friends of mine are coming in to do table displays tomorrow.' She smiled. 'It's very useful having friends with skills.'

'I couldn't agree with you more, Mrs Boscastle.'

Lily was sitting on her bed with her scrapbook – the one she'd started in childhood – spread out in front of her. Her dress was hanging in a bag on the back of the door. There was an open case sharing the bed with the scrapbook.

Lily got off the bed and came to Sarah, flinging her arms round her neck. 'Sares! It's so lovely to see you. I've felt so lonely without you.'

'Shouldn't you save all that stuff for Dirk?' Sarah returned the hug with equal affection. 'What have you done with him?'

'He's staying with Freddie, his best man. He's fine.' Lily sighed. 'I'm not making a horrible mistake, am I, Sares?'

'Of course you're not!' said Sarah, hiding the panic she felt with another hug. 'You've known Dirk for ages, he's lovely, you've lived together happily. It will all be fine.' She didn't mention the fact that Lily was carrying his child – that would sound like emotional blackmail. 'Scary mother-in-law, though!'

This made Lily giggle a little. 'Isn't she terrifying? She must be to scare you.' She sighed. 'I couldn't have managed without you, you know.'

'Oh, you could—'

'I mean, in my life. You've always been there for me; since Mum died, you took over her role. You've been brilliant, Saresy.'

Sarah felt her throat constrict and tears come to her eyes. She held Lily close to her. 'Oh, love! I haven't been brilliant at all, I've been critical and bossy and all those things.'

Lily put her sister away from her gently and smiled. 'That's what I mean – that's what mums do.'

'Silly!' said Sarah. 'So how have you been, really?'

'OK, it's just . . .'

'What?'

'In some ways I feel sort of numb.'

'Numb?'

Lily nodded. 'The other day I was testing my feelings for Dirk, to make sure I wasn't making another dreadful mistake and . . .'

'What?' Sarah held Lily's hands to encourage her to say what she was worried about.

'And I imagined that I heard something awful had happened to Dirk.' Sarah made to speak but Lily stopped her. 'I couldn't feel anything! That's what I mean about being numb.'

Sarah relaxed a little. 'Perfectly normal. Many's the bride who's told me much the same thing. Don't worry about it. It's just the panic of the big day approaching.' She paused. 'I went round to Dirk's mother's. She wants me to pop back and do a seating plan with her. Has she any idea how long a seating plan takes to organise? Why the hell didn't she think of it before?'

'Because we told her we didn't want a seating plan!' Lily got up off the bed, revealing to Sarah that her pregnancy was at last beginning to show a little. 'What is the bloody woman up to now? She's hijacked this wedding from the very beginning.'

'Oh, love!' Sarah put her arm round her sister again. 'It'll be all right. If you really don't want a seating plan I'll tell her that later. It'll save us both hours of stress. I'll talk her round. Don't you worry.' She paused. 'Now, is everything else under control?'

Lily nodded. 'I think so. My bridesmaids are turning up tomorrow. They've all got their dresses. They're having their hair done but they're not allowed up-dos. My hairdresser said she could only do one, and that's mine.' Lily looked at her sister. 'It was so good having that chat with Bron about it all. I'm going to do my own make-up. I've practised, and after all, I know best how I like to look.'

'Oh, I'm so proud of you – you've really grown up in the last few months, Lily!'

'I know.' Lily sighed. 'I don't like the idea but I think maybe it's time I grew up a bit. I'm going to be a married woman and a mother.'

Sarah chuckled. 'Have you got your music all sorted out? For the reception? I know you had to have all the hymns that Dirk's family wanted for the church, but you've picked out your favourites?'

'Oh yes. Dirk did that a while ago. And we tested the sound system in the marquee.'

Sarah sat on the bed. 'Can I look at your scrapbook? I know you did the dress one but this one holds all your hopes and dreams, doesn't it? Does it relate to what you're actually having on your wedding day?'

'Not really, but I was a bit Barbie-obsessed in those days. Loving my dress though!' she added, brightening up. 'Did you pay Elsa for all the work she did? I know I didn't.'

Sarah shook her head. 'We had a bit of a row about it but she wouldn't take any money. She said me getting her Carrie's dress was enough. Poor girl! Carrie didn't decide until the last minute about what dress she wanted, or what she wanted the bridesmaids to wear. They're going to look sweet as anything, but what a rush for Elsa.'

Sarah allowed herself a couple of seconds to think about Ashlyn's little bridesmaid and the photograph Hugo had taken of them both. Then she shoved the vision aside and concentrated on her sister. Now was not the time. She must focus solely on Lily. 'Anything else you need me to sort for you?'

Lily nodded. 'The receiving line. Mona is insisting on having one.'

'Well, they are usual.'

'I really don't want people who know me, my friends and relations, noticing that I'm pregnant.'

'The dress will disguise it quite well, and you're not exactly huge.'

'If Aunt Margaret sees the slightest bulge, she'll say, "Up the duff, are we, ducky? That's nice!"'

Sarah giggled, knowing she shouldn't. 'I'm sorry, but you sounded exactly like her when you said it.'

Lily giggled a little too. 'But you do see I can't risk her saying that in a line-up. Mona will hear and she might say something.'

Sarah considered. 'Tell you what, have two line-ups. You and Dirk, and then, a long way away, the parents, bridesmaids, best man, whoever.'

'She'd never wear it! She's been so difficult about it all. She's such a snob.'

'I'll talk her into it. Make out it's what the posh folk do.'

Lily giggled again. 'My big sister Sarah, fighting my battles.'

'That's what big sisters are for. Now, what are you going to do tonight? Early night? A DVD in bed? Hot bath?'

'I don't know.' Suddenly Lily began to cry. Not scorching, temperamental tears, but large, hot, silent ones, pouring down her cheeks.

'Oh, lovey, what is it?' Sarah cuddled her. 'What's the matter?'

'I don't know! Nothing really. Everything.'

'Have you eaten?'

Lily shook her head.

'That's probably why you're feeling weepy. I'll go out for something,' said Sarah, ever practical. 'Fish and chips?'

'Ooh yes, my favourite! But no vinegar, I've gone off it.'

'We'll watch some *Sex and the City* or something while we eat it, then I'll go round and explain to Dirk's mother you don't want a seating plan and tell her about the line-up arrangement.'

Lily looked up at Sarah. 'You won't be able to change her mind. She'll make you – us – have one.'

'Would it break your heart if she did tell people where to sit?'

'No!' wailed Lily. 'Not that much. But the line-up thing is really worrying me.' She sniffed. 'She'll die if she hears people referring to my bump and I don't want my wedding day ruined by scenes.'

You and every other bride, thought Sarah, but most of you are doomed to disappointment.

Lily was right about Mrs Boscastle being determined to have things her way. Her dinner guests had been swept out of the way and the kitchen table cleared for action.

'Lily did tell me that she and Dirk had decided they just wanted people to sit where they wanted,' Sarah said firmly. 'With whom they wanted.'

'They're young things,' said Mrs Boscastle equally firmly. 'They don't know how important these things are. We'll do it together. I'll get my husband to make labels on his computer tomorrow morning. Then we'll just stick them on to folded cards.'

'That's going to be quite time-consuming,' said Sarah. 'Are you sure there won't be other things he'll want to be doing? Checking the wine is chilled? Manly things like that?' Mr Boscastle had yet to appear. If he was anything like his wife, he might have ideas of his own.

'No. Those WI women, or whoever they are, will arrange the wine. At least I hope they will. They don't seem very well organised and quite inexperienced.'

Sarah bit down hard on her lecture about those women working for nothing, only charging for the food and being very obliging in every way. Mrs Boscastle wasn't supposed to know about all the economies Lily and Dirk had had to make. She did hope it was just Mrs Boscastle being difficult though, and that there wasn't really anything wrong with them.

'They'll be fine. And I'll help you put the place cards out if your husband makes them. Now there's just the receiving line to sort out.'

Mrs Boscastle shook her head. 'Lily and Dirk said they don't want them but I had to over-rule them. They're essential.'

'They are quite out-dated,' said Sarah, mentally crossing her fingers against the lie. 'But what many of my . . . er . . . upmarket clients do nowadays is have two. It makes it move faster.'

'Two? And how can that possibly make it go faster?'

As Sarah had no idea how, she had to busk it. 'Family members do chat to the parents a bit more, which means people are kept waiting. If they go to the bride and groom first, and then move right away to the family, they pick up momentum.' Sarah was very glad that no one, particularly Hugo, could hear all this drivel – he'd be bound to laugh. Although, if he'd been here, she realised, she'd have felt so much better about the whole thing.

'Oh, well, if that's what people are doing these days . . .?' Mrs Boscastle looked at Sarah questioningly.

'I helped at a very smart wedding the other day and they were very pleased with the way everything worked.' This wasn't actually a lie, it was a fact – it just didn't relate to the receiving line.

'Very well then. Now, let's get on with the seating plan.

My husband was as upset as I was at the thought of a free-for-all. You seem moderately efficient. We should have it done in a jiffy.'

Mrs Boscastle was efficient too – almost as efficient as she was snobbish – and they made good progress. But the snobbishness did begin to rankle. Something disparaging was said about almost everyone. Lily's relations' names were all scrutinised as if Mrs Boscastle were trying to detect something about them to indicate class.

Mrs Boscastle had obviously forgotten that Sarah was Lily's sister, and all the relations she was being so snooty about were hers too. Hugo, never far from her mind, came into it again, this time in a really useful way.

Sarah started dropping names in the casual way Hugo had made Rupert do it when they were trying to persuade Carrie to have her wedding at Somerby. Without actually saying so, she managed to imply that these names were relations of hers and Lily. Mrs Boscastle became a lot more friendly after that. Sarah's pièce de résistance was actually true – Aunt Margaret, who was so wonderfully tactless, bound to reveal Lily's secret to the world, really was a Lady. Mrs Boscastle loved it.

Sarah drove back to Lily's very late. She let herself in and saw her sister fast asleep on the sofa, the television flickering to itself. Although she felt a bit guilty about it, Sarah decided not to move the bride-to-be. Having made sure Lily wouldn't get cold in the night, she sloped off to bed. Lily and Dirk would have a lovely double bed to sleep in the next night, after all.

Chapter Thirty-Nine

Everyone was up early at Somerby. Bron tiptoed into the kitchen to make a cup of tea before she carried on with her icing, only to find Fenella and Elsa already there. Fenella was anxious.

'I'm sure it's fine, but Sarah did tell me that the florists would be here by seven at the latest – there's loads to do. The chapel, the drawing room, the dining room, they're all having big displays.'

'What about the bridal flowers?' asked Bron.

'Thank God Carrie's bringing those with her. Can't remember why, but they're being done separately. Mandy said she'd make sure they got done and everything.'

'It's only half past seven now,' said Elsa, checking the big kitchen clock. 'They've probably got lost.'

'Have you much to do on your dresses, Elsa?' asked Bron, pouring water on to a tea bag.

'No, they're mostly done. I just hope Carrie's not too late though. I still need to do a final fitting and there are some crystals I can't sew on until I've finished the main sewing. Can you remember what time she's supposed to get here?'

'I think Sarah said about four,' replied Fenella. 'She can't make it before.'

'Oh God, that doesn't give me much time for her hair and make-up,' said Bron. 'You'll probably need half an hour with her, won't you, Elsa? At least the cake will be finished and I can focus utterly on the bride.'

'Most brides do need more than two hours to get ready,' Elsa agreed, beginning to get edgy herself, although she calmed down a little when Fenella said she was sorry, she'd misread Sarah's instructions and Carrie was due to arrive at around three.

Then the phone rang and all three women jumped. Fenella flew to it and the others listened anxiously from the moment they heard Fenella say, 'Are you sure you're all right?'

It could have been Sarah saying something bad had happened to her.

Fenella's side of the conversation was tantalisingly brief and it was only after a tense few minutes that Bron and Elsa discovered what the disaster was.

'I knew it!' said Fenella, her hands on her temples, her eyes shut. 'That was the florist. She's had an accident. She can't come. She's OK but the van's undrivable and the flowers are all mashed to pieces.'

There was a moment's horrified silence. Then Elsa said, 'Phone Sarah. She'll know of someone else. Don't worry. We can sort this out.'

'Yes,' agreed Bron. 'We're a team. We can fix anything.'

They realised this was more of a disaster for Fenella than for them. Flowers were vital if Somerby was to really shine. If *Celeb* magazine took photos of it looking less than its glorious best, the wonderful publicity of a celebrity wedding would be completely wasted. Not to mention the fact that Carrie would be upset with Sarah.

'OK,' Elsa went on, taking control. 'I'm calling Sarah. Shall I tell her or shall you?' she asked Fenella as she waited for it to connect.

'I will,' said Fenella and took the proffered phone. 'Come·on, Sarah! Answer! Damn, it's gone to voicemail.'

'Leave a message. Let her know how urgent it is!' said Bron.

When Fenella handed Elsa back her phone Bron got up to make more tea.

'OK,' said Elsa, 'worst case scenario, we have no florist,

so we have to do it. What are the most important areas?'

'The chapel,' said Fenella. 'Bron, your fake-cake trees mean we don't need too much in the dining room. At least, we can get away with less there. Have either of you done any flower-arranging?'

They shook their heads. 'But we're both artistic and practical, we can do stuff if we have to,' said Bron. 'We can't let Sarah down. Or Carrie. We'll make it work somehow.'

Fenella's phone started playing 'Für Elise'. 'Sarah? Thank God!' She explained the problem, murmured uh-huh a few times and scribbled down a number.

'She's given me the name of another florist. She did a wedding you guys were at in June? Sukie someone?'

'I don't think we met ever, but the flowers at Ashlyn's wedding were fantastic,' said Elsa, a little disappointed at not having to create floral extravaganzas – she liked a challenge.

'I hope she can do it,' said Bron. 'She's probably at some other wedding or other, even as we speak.'

'We'll find out in a minute,' said Fenella. 'It's ringing. Sukie? You're not in the middle of anything, are you? We've got a major emergency!'

As most of Fenella's conversation seemed to be directions with the occasional floral reference, Bron and Elsa gathered that Sukie was on her way. 'We could have done it,' said Elsa. 'Between us.'

'Not without flowers,' said Bron. 'I don't know if you've noticed but there isn't much growing currently. The garden obviously hasn't reached the top of the to-do list yet.'

'OK,' said Fenella, slamming her phone down on the table. 'She's on her way – sounds terribly nice, by the way – but she says she probably won't be able to buy enough flowers without driving for miles. She'll get what she can but we've got to get as much ivy as possible, to stretch them. We have got plenty. Thank goodness Carrie wanted traditional country arrangements and nothing that needed strelitzias or anything. Bird of Paradise flowers,' she explained to her confused audience.

At this moment James appeared, looking for tea and toast. 'Oh, James, the florist has had an accident,' said Bron.

'Yes.' Fenella turned to him. 'You were so brilliant with the fake trees, do you think you could gather ivy for us? The florist needs it to bulk up the flowers. We haven't got much else.'

'I wouldn't say that,' said James taking in the situation. 'Obviously the garden has been neglected for quite some time, but if you're looking for big, showy things, there are some wonderful acanthus – bear's breeches . . .' Sensing that his audience was still in the dark, he went on, 'They've got huge pinky-mauve flower spikes and they work brilliantly in arrangements.'

'Of course, you'd know this,' muttered Bron, feeling a bit thick for not having realised this sooner.

'And there's a Rosa glauca with fantastic hips. Big swathes of that could look amazing.'

'Listen, James,' said Fenella, 'I'm terribly glad you know all this stuff and that it's there somewhere in that jungle, but if you could just hack some of it down, and a load of ivy, we'd be thrilled. Then Sukie can do what she can with it.'

'If I can just have something to eat first . . .'

'Of course you can!' Bron flew to the bread bin she'd been introduced to earlier, glad to be useful. 'I'll make it!'

'You're a star,' said Fenella. 'Now what else can possibly go wrong?' Her phone rang again and the tension in the room shot up again. 'Sarah? Yes, Sukie's on her way. What a nice woman. And James says there's lots of stuff in the garden I just hadn't noticed.'

They chatted for a bit longer and then Fenella

disconnected. 'Sarah's making place names. Apparently they weren't going to have them but now they are; it's all frightfully last minute. She sounds reasonably calm, but it's not nine o'clock yet. Anything could happen between now and—'

'Don't say that!' said Elsa. 'Supposing Carrie's really late and I don't have enough time to finish her dress?'

'Oh, I'm sure she won't be late for her own wedding, she's a professional!' said Bron, and looked around. Everyone was glaring at her. 'What? Oh, sorry – do you think I was tempting fate?'

The last crystal was applied to the last flower made of icing. The cake was finished at last. Hugo, who seemed to be everywhere with his camera, took a selection of shots, mostly, it seemed to Bron, while she had her tongue out in concentration.

'That's fantastic, Bron,' he said. 'Really good. Are you going to take up a whole new career in cake-making?'

'Probably not, but it's another string to my bow. I might go and help James now.'

'Just one last picture . . . thanks.'

'How's it going?' Bron asked Fenella who was holding the ladder for James.

'Well, the caterers are here, they seem fine.'

'That's good. What about the flowers?'

'Sukie came with a van full of them, but she said she will need the ivy because you need so many. She's got Elsa making little posies for the tables. What with all the stuff James found in the garden I don't think anyone will know there was ever a problem. Luckily I don't think Carrie's instructions were all that precise.'

'What time is she due?' Bron helped release a long single strand of ivy that James had unpeeled from the wall.

'Quarter of an hour ago. Elsa is getting frantic. Sukie put

her to work to encourage her to burn up her surplus energy.'

'I could help Sukie, if she needs me. I can't do anything much until Carrie gets here, then Elsa and I will be fighting over her.'

'Actually, if you could hold the ladder, I can go and see how it's all going. If bloody Rupert had let me keep the scaffolding tower, James would have been fine on his own.'

'I'm fine on my own anyway,' said James from above.

'No you're not. Ladders are dangerous,' said Fenella firmly. 'I'm going to break out the cake I made the other day, to keep us going. I forgot to have lunch.'

'I'm not sure James is all that keen on cake,' said Bron.

'I would rather have a sandwich,' he said, smiling down at them. 'I didn't have lunch either.'

'Goodness me,' said Bron, after Fenella had left, 'you must have stripped the entire building of ivy.'

'Well, finding the ladder took a while and Rupert suddenly discovered a rose bush perfectly placed to rip the wedding dress to shreds. I had to deal with that first.'

'Thank goodness you were here. And you thought you were only coming to help me!'

'That wasn't the only reason,' he said. 'Right, I'm coming down now. Hang on tight and don't let me step on your hand.'

Bron watched him descend the ladder, trying not to notice that his jeans were a bit tighter and newer than usual today. It was a good look for him.

Bron and Elsa were frantically washing their hands. Carrie had arrived, half an hour late, and they both wanted her.

Bron was laughing, slightly hysterically. 'James and I were carrying the ladder back to the barn where it lived. We were just passing my pigsty when we heard the car.

He turned round suddenly and the ladder when through the window! My bed is covered in glass.'

'That's awful!' said Elsa. 'What did you do?'

'Nothing! I just came running up here.'

'Will James sort it out?'

'I don't know. But I haven't got time to worry about it now. The really awful thing is, we were getting on so well, I was going to say something but . . .' It had happened in rather a rush and she'd had to run up here to prepare for Carrie.

'Oh Bron . . . well, never mind, at least you'll have an opportunity to see him later.' Elsa sighed.

'Have you heard from Laurence?' Bron asked.

'No, I haven't heard from him in a while,' Elsa said as she dried her hands. No good thinking about that now. 'Right, I think I'm clean. I'd better go and find Carrie. Rupert told me she's in an awful mood.'

Bron made a face. 'My nerves are already in shreds. There's something about the sound of breaking glass that goes right through you.'

'I heard Fenella ringing Sarah. Carrie is not happy that she's not here. Although she did know about Lily's wedding, she still expected her to be here for her.'

Bron glanced at her watch. 'She must have left by now, don't you think?'

Elsa shrugged. 'They won't have started the speeches yet, surely? Lily was getting married at two – it takes at least an hour for the ceremony, the photos and getting back to the house.'

'She won't make it, will she? Which means we have to cope with a grumpy superstar all on our own!'

Chapter Forty

The moment Sarah had thought would never arrive finally came. Lily, on her father's arm, processed up the aisle to Purcell's 'Trumpet Tune'. She looked truly beautiful in the dress Elsa had made for her and probably only those who knew she was pregnant would notice her tiny bump. As Sarah, wearing a silk chiffon dress with a jacket in a soft yellow that toned in beautifully with Lily's underskirt, was sitting on the bride's side she couldn't hear any hissings or mutterings that might have come from the groom's section of the church. This was a relief.

As unobtrusively as possible, Sarah got the corner of her hanky up to her eyes, thinking that maybe she wasn't the cynical wedding planner she once was, and wondered briefly if Hugo had anything to do with it. Whatever the reason, her eyes took some dabbing.

Dirk, who looked young and handsome, seemed relatively serene, although there had been a bout of tears earlier, Sarah had been told.

Lily had behaved unexpectedly calmly. All the weepiness of the night before seemed to be over. Her hair and skin shone with the bloom of pregnancy and her dress looked lovely, gently opening over down the front like a gown in a medieval painting. Elsa had done wonders.

Earlier there had been a moment that caused Sarah's heart to falter, just slightly, when Lily, inevitably, had asked, 'Does my bump look big in this? Mona's really insistent that I don't look pregnant and I promised her I wouldn't.'

Sarah decided to lie. After all, it didn't actually look big, it just looked visible. 'Not at all. You look really, really lovely. I just wish Mum could have seen you.' Sarah felt her throat tighten and she swallowed.

Lily's eyelashes fluttered briefly. 'It's all right, you've seen me. And Dirk will see me, and Dad. And Mum may be looking down on us from somewhere.'

As the sisters hugged Sarah felt a moment of role reversal: Lily was comforting her and she was the one close to tears.

Lily had accepted the place settings, agreeing with Sarah that at least with her in-put, there shouldn't be too many disasters. She was very relieved not to have the formal line-up her future mother-in-law wanted, but the two-part version as suggested by Sarah. Sarah, torn in two by her sister's wedding and her first celebrity one, felt pleased to have made Lily's day easier. She knew that she'd already done loads – in fact it was through her and her contacts that it had all been done so thriftily. But Sarah also knew that she might have to scoot off early when Lily might still need her support.

There had been a few hitches before they got to this point, of course. The marquee, which had been such a bargain to hire, developed a split. Hardly surprising, considering its age and the very low rental, but it had meant Sarah had to spend quite a lot of time up a ladder with a roll of gaffer tape.

Mrs Boscastle's fine herbaceous border was the backdrop for one side of the marquee, but there had been a very small budget for flowers. Her friends, aided by the Catering Ladies, each of whom Sarah would have awarded an MBE had it been in her gift, put their many skills to good use and had made table arrangements out of what blooms there were, all of which seemed to come from their own gardens. The WI and its ilk, so despised by Mrs Boscastle, had added the final touch to make the marquee fit for a wedding. Sarah crossed her fingers that Sukie had managed to save the floral day at Somerby. She was very good, and it was a major stroke of luck that she was available, but would she have been able to get hold of enough material for something suitably sensational?

Sarah glanced at her watch as her father and Lily were deposited at the front of the church. It was twenty minutes past two.

By the time Lily's second bridesmaid went up to do a reading Sarah knew they were running very late. In theory she should get into her car now and make haste to Somerby, possibly adding the cost of speeding tickets to Carrie's bill. But she couldn't do that, she realised as Lily's friend stumbled over *The Prophet* – it wasn't Carrie's fault her wedding day coincided with Sarah's sister's. It was just a horrible coincidence. Should she have said no to Carrie? No, she couldn't have. A wedding like that could make her name, or – if it all went wrong – break it.

Nor could she run away yet, not until after her father had made his speech. The best man, the groom and any other random orations could go on without her, but she had to hear her dad.

Outside the church, the photographer, booked only for a very few formal shots, was rather surprised to be hustled along quite so briskly, but he knew Sarah, wanted to be used by her again, and did what he was told.

'You don't want all those pictures of the relations,' Sarah muttered to Mrs Boscastle, as they watched the bride and groom smiling up at each other. 'Frightfully common!'

Sarah, who'd booked this photographer when she'd developed cold feet about Uncle Joby's reliability, was very glad she had. He was far more interested in chatting up Charlene than taking photographs.

Nor was there time for the bride and groom to have a glass of champagne and a cuddle in the car on the way to the reception. This was something that Sarah always suggested if it were possible. It was a moment for the newly-weds to be alone to savour the moment before the hurly-burly of the reception.

This time, however, Dirk's friend, who'd been entrusted with getting them to the reception safely, was told the priorities had changed – they now had to be there in record time. Fortunately it was very near by and anyway, Lily wasn't drinking.

The double line-up worked brilliantly. Sarah, hanging round Lily so between them they would remember the names of the more obscure family members, did overhear people asking her when the happy event was due, but if they said similar things to the families, at least Lily didn't know about it.

'Right,' said Sarah to Lily, 'let's get people sitting down with a glass of wine – save the fizz for the toasts.'

She whisked to her father's side and explained her problem. He was already aware that Carrie's wedding was due to happen a couple of counties away.

'But, love, we can't start straight into the speeches until people have something to eat. It's a buffet – it'll take ages.'

'Dad, I know that, and I feel awfully mean.' She paused. 'Maybe I should just abandon Carrie. There's a good team over there. They don't need me.'

'Now, love, don't say that. Your mother would have been so proud of you. And you know Dirk and Lily are on your side. They want you to do Carrie's wedding just as much as they want you at this one. You do what you need to do.' He leant forward conspiratorially. 'And if that bitch' – he indicated Mrs Boscastle – 'pardon my language, with a mouth like she's chewed on a lemon, gets uppity, tell me and I'll sort her.'

Sarah hugged her father, chuckling into his ear. 'That's where I get my bossiness from. It's you.'

'No time for sentiment, girl,' he said. 'Get those glasses filled. I'm getting ready to start!'

She moved deftly through the crowd to Veronica, in charge of the Catering Ladies. 'I want you to make sure everyone has a plate and then just move among the tables with plates of food and bottles of wine, serve people where they are. I desperately need to get to Carrie's wedding!'

As the Catering Ladies were all quite excited at the thought of Carrie's wedding, they were keen to help. 'Leave it to us. We'll get this lot fed and watered before they've had time to work out what their names are.'

Sarah wondered if power was going to her head. Although she organised weddings she usually deferred to her clients. Now she practically was the client she let her organisational skills let rip. Everyone was seated, somewhere, in minutes flat. No one was allowed to complain if they were not on the table allocated – they just saw Sarah and did what she told them.

She was up by the top table, where, in theory, she was sitting, in seconds. 'Lily, darling, do you mind if Dad does his speech now? I really have to leave soon.'

Lily, who most of her life had been awkward and attention-seeking, had been transformed by marriage. 'Saresy, you've been so brilliant, you go when you like. We'll be fine without you, won't we, Dad? Charlene will do her bridesmaid bit, if necessary. Come on, Dad.'

'Dad' nodded obligingly. 'We'd better let them get one drink down them though. My speech won't stand up to total teetotalness.'

Sarah smiled and patted his shoulder, wishing she didn't have to stick to total teetotalness herself. 'OK.' She perched on the edge of her seat and got out her mobile phone, hoping no one was looking and would think her rude. She tried the Somerby number but couldn't get an answer so she pressed in Hugo's number almost instinctively. He'd know what to do. 'Hugo?' she whispered, leaning down as if she was picking up her napkin. 'We've only just sat down but I should be able to set off from here in about fifteen minutes.'

'Ri . . . ght,' said Hugo, in a way that meant it was not right. 'Carrie's not frightfully happy at the moment. No chance you can get here a little sooner?'

Sarah took in all the unexpressed urgency – she understood 'not frightfully happy' meant 'in a major strop' and knew she had to get there instantly, if not before. If Carrie got really upset with Sarah for not being there and refused to pay, it would bankrupt her and ruin her reputation. She'd had an instalment of her fee, but not enough to pay all the suppliers.

'I'll have to leave now then. I was going to stay to hear my dad's speech.'

There was a pause and then Hugo said, 'Listen, you stay where you are. I'll collect you.'

'But, Hugo, there's an hour between us, it won't be any quicker if you come and fetch me – longer in fact.'

'Stay where you are. I'll come and get you. Trust me.'

He disconnected, leaving Sarah to wonder if she could in fact trust him or not. Well, she would just have to. It was bad news that Carrie was so upset. She'd known it was possible, of course. It wasn't that celebrities were any more difficult than anyone else, but they were used to a certain standard. And if Sarah had paid for a service she'd be very annoyed if she didn't really get it, even though everything had been left in good hands. It was always going to be tight but it would have been just about doable if the service hadn't gone on so long. But it had. And now she was in a major bind, torn between letting down her sister and her biggest-ever client. Although, to be fair, her sister was being brilliant about it.

Sarah stayed seated, drumming her fingers on the table for a few seconds before she realised what she was doing and stopped. 'Please get your food faster,' she silently urged the guests. 'Drink up!' She took a sip of her wine, forgetting for a moment that she wasn't going to. Forcing her mind away from her anxieties she remembered how pleased she'd been to find the wine at a supermarket. She'd tasted it in the car park, found out it was all right, and then gone back in and cleared the shelves. It was less than half price once the reduction for quantity had been taken into consideration.

The Catering Ladies were doing a very good job. She saw a wodge of sandwiches being delivered over several hats to some surprised relations who were having a good catch-up. Then she noticed Veronica coming towards the top table with plates in her hands. Smoked salmon and salad – perfect! She'd explained how unhappy Mrs Boscastle had been with the buffet idea and now she might be fooled into thinking she'd got her own way in the matter after all.

Sarah chatted to her father and stepmother, trying to hide from them her anxiety about Carrie's wedding. A helicopter went overhead just as her stepmother was telling her something about buying her outfit and her decision not to wear a hat but, instead, a fascinator. Sarah nodded and smiled and hoped she wasn't supposed to be sympathetic. Inside, she was dying with anxiety and knew if such a thing were actually possible, she'd be dead in minutes.

As she turned to the neighbour on her right, hoping to take her mind off her increasing panic, there was a tap on her shoulder. It was Hugo. In person.

'How on earth—'

'Come on. Say goodbye as quickly as you can. I've got a taxi waiting.'

'A taxi? Hugo . . .'

It was only after she left the tent that she realised she hadn't actually said goodbye to anyone. She'd glimpsed Lily waving merrily at her, and flapping her towards the door. When Sarah had turned Lily had kissed her hands to her and Sarah knew that one wedding at least would be all right.

She was about to ask Hugo how he'd got there, when she was ushered firmly into the back of a taxi.

Hugo got in next to her. 'Fast as you can, mate,' he said to the driver, who, engine already running, sped forward.

'It's not going to be any quicker to get there by taxi,' Sarah complained, 'and a whole lot more expensive. Although I must say, he has got you here very quickly. I wasn't expecting you for an hour at least.'

'Which would have been far too late and which is why we're not going by taxi.'

'What do you mean? This is a taxi!' Nerves were making her tetchy.

'Yes,' he said patiently, 'but it's taking us somewhere else.'

'Don't tell me there's an express train?' Her mind whirled around uselessly. Did this mean she could have got to Somerby, or at least the nearest town, in record time?

'Not a train, a helicopter.'

Chapter Forty-One

Up until that point in her life Sarah had always believed she would only go in a helicopter if she were on a sinking ship. Now she discovered that sinking ships could be metaphorical.

She closed her eyes as the taxi nipped round the back doubles to a playing field where a helicopter, hardly bigger than a dragonfly to Sarah's panic-stricken eyes, whirred impatiently.

'Keep to the front of the aircraft, out of the way of the rear rotor blade,' Hugo shouted into her ear.

Then he shoved her in the direction of the open door. She put her foot on the rail and scrambled in, her dress riding up horribly as she did so.

'Shove up,' Hugo commanded and she shuffled over to the second seat. He did up her seatbelt for her and handed her a headset. 'Put these on, then we can talk.'

Sarah put on her headset and, moments later, the helicopter rose into the air. Just for a second Sarah saw the ground get farther away and then she closed her eyes and gripped on to Hugo's hand with both of hers.

'Are you OK?' he asked her.

'I'll be fine once we're there,' she said, her eyes clamped shut.

'Not keen on flying?' asked the pilot.

'Not really,' Sarah managed. 'But I'll be fine.'

'We're really lucky Bob hung around for a few moments after he'd dropped off Carrie and Mandy. He's got to pick up some of their guests later,' said Hugo. 'I was able to nab him.'

'Mm,' said Sarah, knowing she should be enthusing about this stroke of luck but not able to do so at just that moment.

'Presumably you want to go straight to the hotel where Carrie's getting ready? We'll be there in about twenty minutes,' Hugo went on.

Sarah opened her eyes for a giddy-making second. 'Oh, that is good.' Then she closed them again.

'Carrie only arrived about half an hour ago. I think Elsa wanted to get cracking on the dress straightaway.'

'I should think Bron wanted to do her hair and make-up, too. I wonder if it was wrong of me to ask her to get involved?' Sarah was clinging on tight, her life and all her mistakes passing before her eyes behind her eyelids.

'She's done a brilliant job on the cakes, and helped with the flowers. And she is a hairdresser and make-up artist, isn't she?'

'Mm.'

'Well then.'

'And Elsa, those last-minute bridesmaids . . .'

'Sorted. She dressed them up at the house before taking the dress over to wait for Carrie at the hotel. Even the photographer is quite good.' This raised a faint smile from Sarah. 'So, you don't have to worry about anything except getting Carrie on side again.'

'That's quite bad enough,' she squeaked.

'Oh good,' said the pilot, 'it's all still clear for landing. There seem to be a good few paps there, but they know better than to get in the way of the blades.'

'They'll all think you're a celebrity,' said Hugo.

'If that's supposed to make me feel better, it doesn't.'

Hugo laughed.

Once Sarah had taken off her headset she became aware of how noisy the helicopter would have been without one.

She followed Hugo out of the door and he hurried her to the front of the helicopter. 'You go inside, I'll just have a word with Bob. Go and make your peace with Carrie.'

Sarah's last thought before she hurried into the hotel was that she must ask Hugo how much that had all cost.

The fact that she had arrived by helicopter and that the people on reception eventually remembered meeting her before, when she had checked out the hotel, meant she was ushered to Carrie's suite without too much fuss. She knocked on the door and Mandy opened it.

'Carrie!' Sarah was aware she had mud on her shoes, her fascinator was askew and she must have looked as if she'd been drinking. 'I am so sorry! How can I apologise enough? I was at my sister's wedding and I couldn't get away sooner.'

Carrie turned carefully towards her. She was wearing silk and lace cami-knickers, lace-topped white stockings and suspenders. Her hair was being divided into sections and some of it was in huge rollers. 'Your sister's wedding? Oh, honey! You had told me and I'd completely forgotten! On the same day as mine? What are the chances of that happening?'

Sarah shrugged and raised her palms in philosophical acceptance. 'Obviously better than any of us would have thought. Anyway, I'm so sorry . . .'

Mandy said, 'Here, have a glass of champagne, everything is cool here.' She smiled and Sarah knew that she was forgiven, but that from now on she needed to be fully in control. Nothing was going to mar this wedding, not if she was in charge. She took the glass that she offered and sipped gratefully. It was time to do what she did best.

'The security guys kept the press under control?' Sarah knew if this had gone wrong, Carrie's wedding day could have been ruined.

'Oh yes,' said Mandy. 'They knew what they were doing.'

'And your final dress fitting went well?' This was the second in the list of potential disasters.

'Yup,' said Carrie. 'Elsa did a great job. She's getting ready in the bathroom.'

Sarah chided herself for doubting Elsa.

Carrie went on, 'We all came over here – in two cars—'

'One for us and one for the dress,' said Mandy.

'Then I started to get ready,' said Carrie.

Sarah took another gulp of champagne, knowing it really should be water but needing it just at this moment. 'And the horse and carriage are here?'

'Ready and waiting,' said Mandy. 'We saw it as we came in. We thought Bron had taken the crimpers to the horse's mane, but apparently they always curl like that.'

'I think someone probably did something to it,' said Bron. 'But it did look beautiful.'

Elsa appeared from the bathroom and she and Sarah hugged. 'You got here!'

Sarah nodded. 'By helicopter. I was terrified, clung on to Hugo all the way.'

'He's been brilliant,' said Elsa.

'He's a really great guy,' said Carrie from the dressing table. 'He's taken lots of informal shots already. I'm glad we didn't get anyone else as well. He's so cool.'

Sarah nodded, draining her glass. He was indeed very cool. And very kind, and she was totally in love with him. She hadn't meant to fall in love, it had just crept up on her and despite her determination never to let her guard down ever again, she had. But it was no good; she could love him all she liked but he was engaged to someone else, even if that someone was wrong for him, and she just had to accept it and move on.

Everything looked perfect, thought Sarah as she walked through the house. She had already gone through the checklist with Fenella. Apart from the florist catastrophe, everything had gone to plan. The band had turned up and were looking extremely smart with a particularly glamorous lead singer. The caterers were so efficient they seemed to glide about on wheels, and no one had thrown a major tantrum. Now she was going to check every detail herself, down to the last service sheet.

She started at the chapel from the outside door end. The flowers were fantastic. No one with any amount of imported blooms could have done better than Sukie had. Sarah looked first at the arrangement by the font. Great swathes of bluey-grey rose foliage offset scarlet hips that backed an extravagant and sweeping arrangement that was like a wild hedgerow, although on closer inspection, Sarah spotted bought flowers in among the wilderness. It was perfect: high summer on a stand. There was another arrangement by the font and another by the altar. The arrangements at the pew ends were mostly trailing ivy, but looked romantic and definitely on purpose. Only someone with Sarah's experience would know that this was a trick to eke out the flowers.

From the chapel, she moved through to the house. The drawing room was still lovely, and the dining room, now filled with tables covered with sparkling glass and silver, was a wonderful setting for the cake and the double row of smaller, fake versions. She inspected the cake at close quarters and saw how perfect each little icing flower was, with its crystal centre. Bron definitely had a new career waiting for her if she wanted one.

The morning room, where people were to drink champagne until the call to dinner, shone. This was also where people not invited to the actual ceremony would gather until it was over. Several young men in elegant black uniforms were polishing glasses, prepared to serve champagne to all the guests as near simultaneously as possible.

Usually Sarah would have briefed them, but this time

she'd had to depend on Jess Allsop, the owner of the catering company, a woman she knew well and had worked with often. When Sarah gave the word, these men would spring into action and every guest would have a glass within seconds.

Sarah found Jess, smartly suited and calm, with Fenella. 'We were a bit worried you wouldn't make it,' said Fenella. 'Although we'd have been fine without you, Carrie really wanted you to be here.' Jess and Fenella exchanged friendly glances.

Sarah was pleased to see that everyone was getting on well and working as a team.

'And *Celeb* magazine have been looked after?' asked Sarah.

'There are place names on the pews. They've got two,' said Fenella. 'They took some shots earlier but I think they're going to use Hugo's. Should earn him a bit of pocket money.'

'Absolutely!' agreed Jess.

Upstairs Fenella and Rupert's room was looking tidy and welcoming. It was where Carrie would be remade-up after the ceremony and before the reception. She would change out of her wedding dress here too and, if she needed a break, she had somewhere to escape to. Someone, Elsa, Sarah suspected, had tidied it before taking Carrie's dress to the hotel.

'Has anyone seen the groom?' she asked Fenella.

'Rupert has. They're being kept well apart at the hotel. It was so brilliant you got here on time!'

'I couldn't have done it without the helicopter,' said Sarah and told Fenella the story.

Sarah waited at the door of the chapel, looking down the gentle curve of the hill to where the horse and carriage were coming up. She could see that Elsa's creation looked truly Faerie-Queen-like and the horse and carriage were the perfect vehicle for such an ethereal bride.

The security people had dealt with the paparazzi, presumably having let them get the agreed shots. Sarah didn't have to worry about anything now, except the ceremony and the reception.

Elsa and Bron had slipped into their places. They'd had a rush at the end and had barely had time to get into their own clothes. Elsa, Sarah noted, was wearing her ball gown, appropriate for an evening event. Sarah had meant to change out of the outfit she'd worn for Lily's wedding into something more formal, but it was too hot for confining garments and magic knickers. It had all been a frightful rush, but now she could focus. She knew that Hugo was somewhere about. They'd exchanged glances earlier and he'd given her a warm, encouraging smile. Just knowing he was around made her feel better, more confident.

The long-haired pony seemed to take for ever to come up the hill but Sarah realised it only seemed like that because she'd been rushing about so much. She could see Hugo now, taking photographs, naturally. She owed him a huge debt of gratitude. How could she repay him? Nothing she could think of doing seemed like half enough.

She looked back into the chapel and saw Carrie's handsome groom. He was chatting and laughing to his best man, far more confident than Dirk had looked. Sarah realised she recognised the best man and tried to remember what film or television programme she'd seen him in. It was a way of occupying her mind as the little horse clip-clopped its way up.

All the guests were pretty glamorous too. It was a small wedding, considering, but the spend per outfit would almost have covered the entire cost of Lily's budget affair.

She turned her mind back to that very different wedding. What were they getting up to now? Dancing, she hoped, to the CD the bride and groom had made together, marking the progression of their romance with the songs. She was so pleased that she'd been able to help her sister have her perfect day. Carrie was having a band later, for the dancing that was going to take place in the drawing room. Sarah had talked her out of having a string quartet playing during the meal as they would take up valuable space.

At last Carrie arrived. She was handed out of the carriage by her father, who was giving her away in the proper traditional manner Carrie had wanted. Her little bridesmaids were all ready. When Sarah heard Purcell's 'Trumpet Tune' for the second time that day she knew the end was in sight. In eight hours or so she could fall into bed.

Chapter Forty-Two

Elsa slipped into the back of the chapel, having arranged Carrie's dress for the final time before she set off up the aisle. She was very pleased with how it had turned out. The back, particularly, was a triumph. This was the part that people spent most time looking at, after all.

The crystal-studded corset and the stiffened georgette caught the light and glittered as if it had been sprinkled with diamonds. No theatrical costume could have looked more fairy-like or magical.

Even the little bridesmaids, whose dresses had been so last minute, looked like fairy servants behind their queen. No one would know the panic, the frantic sewing, the midnight hours that went into those costumes except a very few people, but, Elsa now knew, it had all been worth it.

She had spent the few minutes she had before Carrie appeared star-spotting. It was one way to pass the time, and she thought it might help her throw off the melancholy that had settled over her recently.

She'd heard nothing from Laurence for ages. He'd warned her he'd have very little time to call or text, and he was in the States anyway, so the time difference made things even more difficult. But she was a bit hurt. There were at least half a dozen ways a person could contact another person these days, not including carrier pigeon.

Had she made a mistake in sleeping with him? Was that why his texts had dwindled to nothing a matter of days afterwards? If she had, it was a lovely mistake, and she'd just have to be content with the memory of a wonderful night of passion with a caring, considerate, sexy man.

A little spark of excitement flickered, like light on Swarovski crystals, in her heart. Maybe he'd still be able to make it after all. Perhaps he was on his way at this very moment and unable to call her. The fact that he might turn up gave her that little hope.

Still, she thought, if he couldn't come, there were plenty of fit young men here, even if they were mostly accompanied by size zero, WAG-type starlets and unlikely to look at her in her Regency ball gown.

After the ceremony, and when the wedding supper was over, having checked Carrie's dress again after the bride'd been upstairs and had her lip-gloss reapplied, and her back and shoulders powdered and sprinkled with the merest dusting of iridescent make-up, Elsa looked around the room and caught Bron's eye. Bron, she knew, was worrying about the fact that her bed was still covered in glass from when the ladder went through it. There'd been no opportunity to do anything about it and while there would probably be somewhere spare for her to sleep, not knowing where that would be was depressing for her. As was the fact that James seemed to have disappeared.

'May I have the pleasure of this dance?' The best man, whom Elsa recognised as an American soap star, stood before her. He was smiling down at her with his perfect teeth practically twinkling.

It was a waltz: Carrie had wanted her reception to start with several traditional ballroom dances to show off her beautiful gown before it morphed into a more general free-for-all.

He was very good-looking, Elsa had to acknowledge, and although at one time she would have refused, there wasn't an adult bridesmaid he should have been dancing with and she could do waltzing now. She said yes. She smiled at him and allowed him to take her into his arms.

He was hopeless, she realised; as bad, if not worse, than she had been the very first time she had tried waltzing with Laurence. They went twice round the dance floor, which was not huge, and then he said, 'I'm sorry. I'm no good at this. Would you mind if we just did a slow dance instead?'

'What do you mean? Waltzing isn't terribly fast.'

He laughed at her teasingly. 'You're cute. I meant like this.' He took her hands and linked them behind his head and then put his arms round her waist. It was, she had to admit, much easier than trying to steer him round corners.

Nothing like being in the arms of an attractive man to chase away memories of another one, she thought as they circled the room. Not that this man really had chased away her thoughts of Laurence, but it was a distraction. At one time her dream scenario at an occasion like this would have been to find a good spot to watch it all from. But not now. Since being a substitute bridesmaid at Ashlyn's wedding, she had come on a lot. She now wanted to be part of the party, not just an onlooker.

For example, she pondered, as they plodded round in a small circle, would she have had the confidence to dance with him at all, to let him hold her close if it hadn't been for Ashlyn's wedding and all that followed it? She doubted it. Having her hair cut, Vanessa making her have her colours done, Laurence making her learn to waltz, had all given her confidence. So what if he'd decided it was a mistake, she told herself firmly, at least now she was a braver, more confident person. Having come to this conclusion she decided she should be bolder. She relaxed and smiled up at her partner and held his gaze as he smiled back.

'Excuse me!'

Someone tapped her on her shoulder and peeled her off her partner. It was Laurence.

'Excuse me,' he said again, to the man this time. 'But this is my girlfriend. I'm afraid I'm going to take her away.' Elsa's heart gave a little dance of pleasure.

'Hey, fella! Doesn't she have some say in the matter?' The young American film star was heavier than Laurence and seemed ready to fight for his woman.

'I'm afraid not. Come on, Elsa,' said Laurence. Then he took her hand and led her away.

'Laurence!' said Elsa, struggling to keep up with him. 'What are you doing here? I thought you couldn't come!'

He didn't stop until they were in a little pantry, miles away from the party. 'I know, I nearly didn't make it, but I just had to, whatever it took.'

'Why didn't you let me know?' she said. 'I haven't heard from you for so long. I thought . . .'

He looked suitably contrite. 'I'm so sorry I haven't been in touch. I was so busy. Then I lost my phone and the battery died on my laptop – couldn't get a spare where I was and all my telephone numbers were on it.'

'Oh.' That did cover most of the bases, apart from the carrier pigeon, of course.

He sighed deeply. 'I really am sorry. Anyway, I'm here now.'

She nodded.

'I had to get a taxi from the airport. Cost me an arm and a leg.'

'Oh dear.' She didn't know what else to say.

'Elsa, I haven't driven for over five hours to get here to listen to you saying "Oh", or if I'm lucky "Oh dear"!'

She twinkled up at him, thrilled to see him, standing there looking so handsome in his dinner jacket. Dear Laurence, he'd come back to her.

Then he took her in his arms and kissed her.

It took Elsa a few seconds to get into the kiss. At first their noses bumped and their teeth clashed but then it settled down into a stomach-weakening clinch that made

Elsa's head swim. She was glad he didn't let go when he stopped for breath or she might have fallen over.

'Goodness, Laurence,' she said breathlessly. 'That was quite a kiss.'

'I hope you know now how much I've missed you.'

'Well, I've got some idea.' She smiled, all warm inside.

'I know we hadn't really got that far in our relationship . . .' He paused.

'Did we have a relationship?'

'Well, friendship. But I couldn't wait any longer. And that gorilla would have had you if I hadn't stepped in.'

Elsa laughed. 'I don't think so. We were only dancing.'

'I know only too well what dancing can lead to!' said Laurence. 'That dancing teacher definitely fancied you.'

Elsa suddenly started to giggle. It was so lovely and funny and silly to be here with Laurence and him being jealous. 'Actually, I think the dancing teacher was gay.'

'If he was, he was thinking of changing his mind.'

'Idiot.' Then she went on, not wanting any awkwardness between them, 'When I didn't hear from you for such a long time I wondered if I'd made a mistake sleeping with you. We didn't know each other all that well. I thought maybe you'd lost all respect for me.'

'Oh Elsa! I could never do that.' He took her into his arms again for a long time.

As Elsa was sort of on duty, in case Carrie had a 'wardrobe malfunction', they drifted back up to the dancing. They met Sarah rubbing her foot in the doorway.

'Laurence!' she said, pleased to see him. 'You made it.'

'In the nick of time.' He glanced at Elsa and Elsa noticed a proprietorial gleam in his eye and it made her insides give a little skip of pleasure. 'She was just about to go off with the best man.'

'That's what I do at weddings,' Elsa explained. 'It's a golden rule.'

Laurence's hand found her waist and tickled her. 'Not any more it's not. From now on, it's bridegrooms only.'

'Bridegrooms?' asked Sarah, laughing and easing her foot back into her shoe. 'Not at any wedding I have anything to do with – it would ruin my business.'

'Not if the bridegroom was me,' said Laurence. 'I'm fed up with always being the best man, I want my moment in the sun.'

'You'll get a moment in the *Sun* if you're not careful. A few journalists have muscled their way in,' said Sarah. 'I'm just going to ask them to leave.'

Elsa laughed but uncertainly. She wasn't sure, but she might have been proposed to, in a very roundabout way.

'So,' said Laurence when he'd got them both fresh glasses of champagne, 'how would you like to be a bride?'

Elsa considered, still not sure if he was asking in a general way, or actually proposing. She decided to take it lightly. 'I don't think I would. I don't think I'd like being the centre of attention.'

'We could have a very quiet wedding, just family and a few friends . . .'

She bridled, a skill she didn't know she had. 'What's this "we" business? I thought we were discussing me being a bride!'

'If you're going to be a bride, I bagsy be the bridegroom.'

She shook her head reproachfully. 'You don't bagsy brides, as if they were a seat on a bus! You go down on one knee and propose—' She let out a small shriek. 'Don't you dare!'

'I won't go down on one knee if you don't want me to, but I would be very thrilled and happy if you'd agree to be—' He bent his knee.

'No!' She pushed at him, starting to laugh again. It was all so daft. 'We hardly know each other!'

'We know each other, in the Biblical sense, quite well.'

'Really, Laurence!'

402

'Really, Elsa!' He hesitated for a moment, and then the band struck up and the wonderful, poignant notes of 'Smoke Gets in Your Eyes' began, and the low, mellow tones of the singer started to float through the air.

He got up and took her hand, 'Come on, they're playing our song. Let's dance.'

She followed him to the dance floor. 'We haven't got a song, Laurence.'

'We will have from now on. From now on whenever we hear this we'll remember the night you nearly agreed to be my wife.'

Elsa chuckled. 'So will we have another song if ever I do agree?'

He snatched her into his arms. 'No. This one will have to do.'

Chapter Forty-Three

There was nothing like not knowing where you were going to lay your head that night for making you tired, thought Bron. She hadn't realised that being the make-up artist to the stars would be quite so exhausting. The trouble was, she'd been up before dawn for too many days prior to the actual wedding. Doing the cakes and a lot of flower-arranging meant she was tired before she started on her proper job.

She hadn't seen James for ages. He might have gone home. He might have felt that this was not his sort of party. Maybe she had lost her moment, for ever. Vanessa would be cross with them both. She suddenly felt sad. She'd just have to accept he saw her as a friend and be thankful at least for that. Bron wasn't sure it was her sort of party either, really. It was lovely to look at, beautiful people being beautiful all over the place. The cake had looked fabulous. Everyone had admired it. The caterers had taken Bron's details. It might be the start of a whole new career. When Sarah told her how much she was going to be paid for making it she realised there was more money in cake than in up-dos. She would have felt exhilarated if she hadn't been exhausted. The events of the last couple of months had finally caught up with her.

When the last lick of lip-gloss, the last brush of powder had been applied and Carrie and her new husband had been carried away, Bron decided to slip off. She was aware that lots of the people she knew, Rupert and Fenella, Elsa and Laurence – Elsa had looked so happy she was pleased for her friend despite the pang for herself – and probably Sarah, were going to kick back and relax. The wedding had been a huge success and they could now stop working and start partying. While Bron wanted to do this too, she wanted some sleep first.

She slipped away down to the kitchen and out of the back door. She thought about her bed, probably still strewn with broken glass and muttered to herself. Then she remembered the caravan. She could sleep there. She felt like someone in a desert on the way to the oasis – nothing was going to stop her getting her head down.

The caravan was occupied. James was sprawled across the double pull-out bed, sound asleep. There were other beds concealed somewhere, Bron knew, but she didn't want to crash about pulling down bunks or finding hidden mattresses. Too much like work and far too noisy. Carefully, she climbed over James so she was next to the bulkhead and lay down.

Those last few months of keeping to the edge of the bed with Roger have come in useful, she thought as she pulled the light cover that James had thrown off over herself. Then she slept.

She woke a little while later. James was still asleep. She raised herself on her elbow and watched him. His mouth was very slightly open and his shirt was half pulled out of his trousers, revealing a little triangle of flesh. She couldn't help herself. She wanted him.

She took a few deep breaths and then decided she was a modern woman – of many parts – and that she should take control of her destiny. Vanessa had implied as much. She put her hand on his shoulder. He was wearing a new shirt – she knew that because they'd discussed what he should wear for the wedding and he didn't have a decent shirt. She could feel the heat of his body through it.

Her courage increasing, she moved her hand to the buttons and pushed her fingers between them, finding his warm skin. She undid a button. He stirred slightly but didn't wake up so she undid another. When his whole torso was exposed she spent another few minutes admiring it. She had seen his chest before – and his well-muscled back – when he was working in his garden without his shirt. But she'd never had the opportunity to see it at such close quarters.

Her eye went to the hook of his trousers. He only had one suit, he'd told her, and it came from a charity shop. But it was a very good suit and he'd looked delightful in it. Now she wanted to see how delightful he'd look out of it. She couldn't seem to help herself.

She allowed her hand to drift down his chest to his stomach, but although she wanted to, she didn't let it go any lower.

Why didn't he wake up? She could make him, she supposed, but she didn't really want to do that. He might say, 'What on earth do you think you're doing?'

She sighed, suddenly feeling tired and despondent. She lay down again and then, without letting herself acknowledge what she was doing, she laid her head on his chest and put her hand just underneath it. Soothed by his warmth and his smell, her eyes closed and she fell asleep again.

She woke up a short time later in a panic. Why was her head on a man's chest? Who was he? She knew it wasn't Roger but it took her brain a few frantic seconds to remember where she was and what she'd done.

She froze in horror. What on earth had she been thinking of? She'd practically undressed him! She'd have to get away. If he found her there he'd think she was a total slapper! If she could only slide out of his bed and go back to the party, he need never know she'd been there. It would have been all right, she realised, if she hadn't undone his shirt. If she'd just had a nap next to him she could have just told him she needed somewhere to sleep.

Why oh why did she let her lust get the better of her?

Very carefully and slowly, she retracted her hand, but it had only moved an inch or so before it was gripped. Praying that James was still asleep and was only holding on from some reflex action, she tugged a bit harder. But she couldn't release herself. James was awake.

'Let me have my hand back!' she hissed.

'No. Why?'

He seemed perfectly relaxed about the situation, unlike Bron, who was beside herself with embarrassment. 'Because I want to get up and I obviously can't leave without my hand!'

'What was it doing there, anyway?' He was holding it more gently now. 'Your hand, I mean.'

'I . . . I was just having a nap – my bed is covered in glass if you remember – and must have put my hand on your chest in my sleep.' Reflex actions might be her best excuse.

He shook his head. 'Not buying it. Why is my shirt undone?'

'I have no idea!' Bron tugged at her hand again, longing to escape from this humiliation.

'Yes you have. You unbuttoned it!'

Bron was blushing too much to look at him. 'No! I didn't!'

James raised himself on one arm so he was now looking down at her. 'I know perfectly well that when I lay down my shirt was fully buttoned. I only intended to have a few moments' kip – I only kicked my shoes off at the last minute. You undid my buttons.'

There seemed to be nothing she could say to get her out of this dreadful situation. Her only relief was that she hadn't touched his trousers – although she had thought about it.

'You fancy me, don't you?' James went on relentlessly.

'No—'

'You may as well admit it. I caught you red-handed.'

She sighed. She could hardly deny it. 'OK, so hang me! I do – did – do fancy you a little bit. I'm a perfectly normal woman, after all—'

She didn't get to say any more for a while, which was probably just as well. He turned towards her and his mouth came down on hers and she accepted her fate as a total slapper. It felt very nice indeed.

Quite a bit later she said, 'You must fancy me too, then.'

James laughed. 'Of course I do, you ninny! Why would you doubt it?'

'Because you've never done anything about it! I kept sending you signals and you just didn't pick them up!'

James sighed now. 'Well, I wasn't sure. I really didn't want to make a mistake. I've been there before and it would have been so awkward for you if I was wrong. You'd have moved out of one bad relationship only to discover the man next door had a major crush on you.'

'That would have been quite a nice thought,' said Bron. 'Tell me, would you have ever made a move on me if I hadn't practically got into your bed?'

'Oh yes. Any time now I would have been asking you to dance and then kissing you.'

Bron sighed. What had just taken place was a little bit more than kissing. 'So why wait so long?'

'I only just found out for sure that you did really fancy me.'

'What? What do you mean?'

'Vanessa told me.'

Bron took the pillow and put it over her head. 'What?'

'When she told me that I had to go with you to this wedding she told me in no uncertain terms that you fancied me and that I'd be a fool not to snap you up. I think she thought I wouldn't work it out for myself '

'You didn't,' mumbled Bron, still under the pillow.

'Vanessa knew when I first came to work for her I'd just

broken up a long-term relationship. She probably thought she needed to help us along.'

Bron mumbled some more.

'Come out from under there.' He confiscated the pillow.

'I'm so embarrassed!'

'I really don't know why. By the way, Vanessa says, when we're ready to move in together, she'll let us have the flat above the old stables. Much more space for us, and she can rent out both our houses.'

'Oh, she really is the limit!' Bron laughed. 'Mind you, it's very kind of her to do that. Not that I'll be ready to move in with you for ages,' she added haughtily, trying to snatch back some pride.

'Why is that?'

James had a soft, low voice and he asked this question very close to her ear. Bron found herself sighing instead of blushing and there was no more conversation for a while.

Somehow they got themselves back to the party. Bron insisted. She was still blushing inside at her brazenness. She really didn't want her friends putting two and two together and working out what had gone on.

Of course, as soon as she saw Sarah she realised it would have been better to stay put. One glance from her put Sarah in full possession of all the facts.

'Oh Bron,' she said, kissing her cheek. 'And James! All loved-up – how wonderful!'

'Is it that obvious?' pleaded Bron.

''Fraid so.' Sarah kissed James too, and Bron wondered if she was beginning to lose her iron grip on events.

'I'm a very lucky man,' said James. 'Now, come and dance,' he said to Bron, and took her hand.

Chapter Forty-Four

Sarah was very pleased to see Bron and James looking so happy. While true love was definitely not something she'd experienced, she was coming round to the fact that it did work for others. Elsa and Laurence were waltzing round the ballroom looking like a couple on a greetings card. She sighed deeply and pushed Hugo out of her mind. At that very moment he appeared, almost as if she had conjured him up.

'Are you planning to work all night?' he asked. 'Carrie's gone; everything is fine. You could knock off now.'

'While there are still so many people here I feel I must hang around to help clear up.'

'Well, come and have a drink with me. I've taken a million pictures and I'm shattered.'

It was so unlike Hugo to sound tired that Sarah, weakened by her own fatigue and the temptation of putting her feet up, for a little while at least, agreed and she followed him until they reached the empty kitchen. Signs of the wedding were everywhere. Crockery that had unexpectedly been commandeered at the last minute – bedroom jugs that had been needed for water, wicker trugs for bread, almost anything that had been used for flowers – had found its way back to the kitchen and now littered every surface.

Automatically, Sarah went to the butler's sink and started to fill it.

'Don't you dare wash up, come and sit with me,' ordered Hugo. 'Here, have some of this. It's special.'

From behind a shelf of cookery books he produced a bottle. A couple of small glasses came from the same cache and he put both on the table.

'Is that Rupert's, or yours?' asked Sarah. She didn't want to accept Hugo's offer of a drink if it was really Rupert's. There was plenty of alcohol upstairs she wouldn't feel bad about drinking.

'It's mine. I put it here earlier for just this occasion.'

'Which is?' She pulled out a chair.

He didn't answer. He just smiled and poured a small amount of the drink into each glass. He handed her one. 'It's Armagnac. I brought it back from France a while ago.'

She sipped. It was delicious. Hugo pulled out a chair and sat opposite her, so their knees were almost touching. Sarah tried very hard to ignore the bolt of electricity and heat that went through her, and not just from the brandy. Her resistance was rapidly melting away. As Hugo set the bottle down Sarah noticed marks on the back of his hand. One of them had been bleeding. Without thinking she put down her glass and took hold of the damaged hand.

'You're hurt! How did this happen?' The moment the words were out she realised she knew how it had happened – the action of holding his hand was familiar. 'I did it, didn't I? Those are my nail marks – Hugo, I had no idea—'

He didn't wait for her apology. He put his free hand on her cheek and pulled her gently towards him and kissed her.

Sarah had been through a lot that day, her defences were wafer thin and his mouth on hers was more than enough to demolish them. She felt she could have sat at the table, kissing Hugo, tasting the brandy, feeling the contact between his tongue and hers for ever. The outside world faded away and she never wanted to move. Weeks of trying not to think about him, dream about him, about the kisses, telling herself he was no good for her, he was with someone else, dissolved. For the moment she could forget about Electra. For the moment, Hugo was hers.

Someone, one of the caterers possibly, came into the room, saw what was going on and apologised before backing out again.

'Come on,' said Hugo. 'We can't stay here.'

Sarah followed where he led, up the back stairs to a bedroom under the eaves. 'The servants' quarters,' he explained as they went. 'Which is why Rupert put me here.'

'Here' was a long low room right under the roof at the front of the house, on the opposite side to where she and Elsa were supposed to be sleeping, she briefly noted before she joined him in the room. The only light was from the long row of windows. In daylight the view would be spectacular. Hugo went to the bed and switched on the lamp beside it.

'There would have been a whole row of beds in here, for the female servants. Maybe they even slept two to a bed. It's going to make the most wonderful flat. Rupert and Fenella have got great plans for it.' He paused and turned towards her.

Sarah suddenly felt herself stiffen. 'Hugo, I can't do this,' she said.

She stopped in the doorway. She could appreciate the potential of the servants' quarters; she could see how much work needed doing, which was why a family friend, like Hugo, had been put here rather than anyone else, but she couldn't cross the threshold. Something, fear possibly, held her rooted to the spot.

'What can't you do?'

'I can't have sex with you, Hugo. My body wants to – or at least it did a few moments ago, but I can't cope with . . . just sex.'

'What makes you think it would be "just" anything?' He spoke softly, as if aware of how little it would take to send Sarah running back down the stairs.

'You're engaged to Electra. If you could make love to me while—'

'I'm not. I'm not engaged to Electra. In fact I never was. I've been trying to tell you . . .' He paused.

'Oh?' She couldn't keep the cynicism from her voice, although she tried hard to.

'Come and sit down. I can't talk to you while you're standing over there.'

She didn't move. He came towards her and took her hand and guided her out of the doorway. Then he shut the door. 'Nothing's going to happen here that we don't both want, but I need to tell you about Electra.' He led her over to the bed, which was the only place to sit, and before she could resist she found her knees giving way and she sat down.

'Electra and I have known each other all our lives. If there'd ever been any sexual spark between us we'd have been married by now.'

Sarah didn't speak. She felt trembly and confused. She didn't want to spoil the moment by saying something inappropriate.

'A couple of months ago – just after Ashlyn's wedding actually – I met Electra at some do or other. She was distraught. Because we're old friends I got her to tell me everything and it turned out she'd just been dumped. Worse than that for her, at least, seemed to be that she'd told everyone – she's got some very smug cousins – that she was about to get engaged. There was some sort of house party, with the cousins, that she was about to go to *sans* fiancé.' He sighed. 'We made a plan. I would pretend to be her fiancé – we didn't think we needed a ring or anything – until she'd had time to get over her real love and then she could break it off and go travelling or something.' He paused again, this time looking at Sarah with an intentness she found unnerving.

'I hadn't realised so many people had heard but I

413

couldn't say anything until Electra broke it off. It wasn't my decision.' He got up and paced the room. 'Anyway, I wouldn't have made the suggestion if you hadn't blown me off after I thought we were getting on so well that night.' He looked at her questioningly.

Sarah didn't need to be reminded of that night. She knew exactly what happened – what had nearly happened – after Ashlyn's wedding. Nor did she need to be reminded of her turning him down when he'd asked her out to dinner – a proper date: she'd made it perfectly clear she couldn't and didn't want a relationship with him.

Hugo went over to his overnight bag and rummaged inside. He produced another of the same sort of bottle and two stainless steel mugs.

She watched him pour more Armagnac, unable to say anything for a moment, taking in all that he had said.

He brought the mugs over and gave her one, sitting down beside her again.

'Do Fenella and Rupert know?' she finally managed.

'Yes, I've told them.' He smiled. 'Fen said thank God. She thinks we'd make a much better couple.'

Sarah blushed. 'You haven't told them – what I've been like?'

'No, don't worry . . . but I am confused. Why didn't you want to go out with me – not that I'm completely irresistible.' He grinned at her. 'But we did seem to be getting on well, and tonight . . . I've told you my story, what's yours? Why were you so casual with me after Ashlyn's wedding? And why are you so cynical about love?'

Sarah sipped her drink. Really, she wanted him to take her in his arms and kiss her until she forgot all about everything. Now she knew he wasn't another woman's man she could allow herself that pleasure. How had she ever doubted him? She'd brushed him aside, assuming he'd be like all the rest, like Bruce. But she knew she had to tell him about the past. She owed him that at least.

She took another sip, feeling a little calmer now. She swallowed, and began. 'Years ago I fell in love. I was at university. He was practically the first man I saw and I just fell. He was very sexy – sort of Hugh Grant-like, but more the part he played in *Bridget Jones*.' She smiled ruefully at Hugo who only nodded for her to continue. He was listening intently.

'I loved him so completely,' she went on. 'I gave him my virginity without even thinking about it. It was still Freshers' Week. We were together for nearly all our time at uni. I was devoted to him, and I thought he was to me. We planned our future together. Then one day I found him in bed with another woman. Looking back I think he wanted me to, to save him the trouble of dumping me. I should have seen the signs. He always was a moral coward. I knew that, even when I loved him, but I didn't care.'

Hugo took hold of her hand and held it gently. It was a touching gesture and Sarah almost flung herself into his arms but although she found it very hard to talk – these were painful memories – she forced herself on. 'He got married shortly afterwards, although they were both dreadfully young. I never heard from them again. Wouldn't have wanted to. He broke my heart.'

'Most of us get our hearts broken at some time or other, you know, it doesn't turn us all into monks and nuns,' said Hugo.

She smiled. 'I know, but . . .' She hesitated. 'It really hit me, hard.' She didn't want to go into the details, not tonight anyway. For now she just wanted Hugo to kiss her again. Somehow the pain of the past had evaporated. She'd been holding on to it for so long she hadn't realised it had just become a bad habit.

'The wedding was a shambles.' She smiled. 'I've never thought about it before, but I wonder if that's what turned me into a wedding planner? I thought it was my experience with events management and stuff, but maybe it was Bruce's wedding.'

Hugo was stroking her hand softly now. He seemed to have found some special spot that connected directly to her insides and caused them to melt. 'That's all over now – you can trust me. I'm not going to hurt you; I'd never hurt you.'

She heard someone sigh deeply and realised it was her and it was too late to stop Hugo hearing it. His hands went up her leg and found the top of her stocking. She always wore hold-ups if she knew it was likely to get hot, and now Hugo had discovered this fact.

'This is a surprisingly sexy secret you have, my love.'

'It's not supposed to be sexy!' she protested. 'It's cooler than tights. I mean – they are.' She decided to stop talking and just let herself be. She didn't stop him easing it down over her leg in a caressing, stroking movement. First one and then the other stocking was dropped on to the floor. The feeling of his hands on her legs was turning her stomach to water. Her breathing became audible and he gently pushed her back down on to the bed and lay down beside her.

'Maybe I've been a fool . . .'

She couldn't say any more because he was kissing her, and doing it so thoroughly, with such skill and purpose, she couldn't really think about being a fool any more. She couldn't think about anything except what his mouth was doing to hers and how that made her feel.

'Sit up,' he said after a lifetime, 'I need to unzip you.'

Sarah sat up and allowed him to unpeel the dress. The jacket that went with it had been left in the kitchen long since. She lay down again; a thought came into her mind, and suddenly she started to giggle.

'What's so funny?' Hugo asked, taking off his jacket.

'I just had a funny thought. It wouldn't be funny if I told you,' she said, giggling even more.

'What is it?' He was laughing with her but was also frustrated by not knowing why she was laughing so hard.

She took a breath. 'OK, I'll tell you,' she said, as he took off his shirt.

'What?'

'I'm just really glad I didn't wear my magic knickers.'

Laughing and loving and later, a bit of sleeping, took up most of the night. The next morning Sarah was caught in the kitchen wearing Hugo's shirt and her perfectly ordinary knickers. It was a bit embarrassing, but Fenella took it in her stride.

'Have you and Hugo got together at last? Brilliant! You're perfect for each other!'

Rupert arrived a few moments later. Sarah was seated and drinking tea.

'Hugo and Sarah have got it together!' said Fenella. 'Isn't that fab?'

'Gosh yes,' said Rupert. 'So does that mean you'll be getting married?'

Fortunately for Sarah, Hugo appeared at this moment. He was fresh from the shower and his hair was sticking up in spikes. If they'd been alone Sarah wouldn't have been able to resist him.

'Do you mind if I ask her first?' said Hugo. 'I realise you've got a vested interest in holding the reception, but really! Sarah? What do you think?'

Sarah started to laugh. 'The only wedding I'm remotely interested in is one where I don't have to organise a thing!'

'Suits me. I'll find the right moment and kidnap you. So, Rupert, Fenella, is there anything to eat? I'm bloody starving!'

'I can't imagine why,' said Fenella, giggling as she went to the fridge.

Sarah blushed furiously but, fortunately, no one noticed.

Epilogue

'Has everyone got a drink?' called Sarah from her kitchen. 'I'm bringing plates for the cake.'

'Oh do come on,' chivvied Elsa. 'We want to see these photos!'

'We promise not to get chocolate on them,' added Bron.

Sarah appeared carrying a loaded tray. 'OK, I'm here now.' She found space for the tray and Bron caught the champagne bottle that threatened to tip over as she did so.

'I thought we might need an extra bottle,' Sarah explained, seeing the surprised expressions of her companions. She raised her glass, saying, 'Cheers!' then picked up a large photograph album from where it had been propped against a chair and placed it on the table in front of them.

'It's been ages since we've all been together. In fact, not since the wedding,' said Bron having taken a large sip of champagne. 'Ooh, lovely fizz.'

'The fizz is left over from Carrie's wedding. She had a case sent to me,' said Sarah.

'Oh, she was lovely!' said Elsa, forgetting how long it had taken her star client to choose her fabrics, her design and the number of bridesmaids.

'She was,' agreed Sarah.

'But it must have been shattering for you, Sarah,' said Bron, 'with Lily's wedding on the same day.'

Sarah sighed. 'It was. I thought I'd sleep for ever afterwards.'

Elsa and Bron exchanged looks.

'Well,' said Elsa, fortified with more Pol Roger. 'You went to a very nice hotel for a few days. Are you saying you just slept?'

Sarah went pink. Although she and Hugo had been a couple for nearly a month now, she was still a bit embarrassed about how dreamy-eyed she was about it. 'Well, we did go for a few walks and things.'

It had been bliss. After Carrie's wedding, Hugo had put Sarah in his car and carried her off to a hotel he knew in a tiny fishing village on the Cornish coast. He'd taken her to buy clothes the afternoon they arrived. Her shopping choices had been limited: jeans, fishermen's smocks, stripy Breton tops, Guernseys and deck shoes – and a huge waterproof coat that they nicknamed The Tent, which now lived in Hugo's car. They had walked, eaten huge meals and slept but most importantly, they had made love. Sarah had never been so happy. Even tying up the odds and ends after Carrie's wedding, which had taken a bit of doing, made that break away from the world worthwhile. A gentle push from Elsa brought her back to the present and she opened the album.

'Goodness,' said Bron, after a few pages. 'If the gossip columnists got hold of these – although they are lovely – it would be terrible!'

'Well, *Celeb* would be a bit annoyed,' said Sarah. 'Look at you, Elsa.'

The picture was of Elsa, kneeling by the train of Carrie's dress, doing something to the hem. Carrie was turning back and smiling down, while Elsa looked up at her. One of the little bridesmaids was making a face in the background. It perfectly captured the pre-wedding scene.

'You should definitely have a copy for Laurence,' she said. 'You look gorgeous!'

'Well, I might,' said Elsa evasively.

'So, how's it going with you two? Are you living together yet?' prodded Bron.

'Just because you and James have shacked up together – quite early on in the relationship, if I may say so,' said Elsa, 'it doesn't mean that everyone has to. Laurence and I are still living in our separate homes.' Then she looked mischievous. 'We are looking for somewhere though. And he's job hunting. He's had to spend so much time away. And for him it's more a matter of choosing where to go rather than waiting to get offers.' Elsa was very proud of Laurence, but she hoped it didn't show too much. It didn't do to brag about these things.

'Oh that's brilliant,' said Bron. 'You'll love living together. Me and James decided there was no point in not sharing a roof when we shared everything else. I know I didn't live on my own very long, but I gave it a go.' Although neither of the other two were looking critical, she felt obliged to explain. 'He's so straightforward to live with. Really easy-going, and he makes me laugh.' She sighed deeply. 'We're so happy.'

'So it'll be babies next?' suggested Sarah.

'Well, maybe,' agreed Bron. 'Financially things will be tight, but neither of us wants to wait too long to start a family.'

'Ah!' said Elsa. 'Can I be an honorary aunt?'

'Until your own babies come along, of course,' said Bron generously. 'What about you and Hugo, Sarah?'

Sarah jumped. 'Oh we're not going to have babies just yet. Although we have talked about it,' she added with a smile.

'Before that – what about getting married?' said Elsa.

Sarah laughed, dreamily. 'Well, he's such a nag. He does ask me to marry him every day we're together, so I dare say I'll give in eventually.'

Bron and Elsa were delighted and clinked their glasses

together in a sort of alcoholic high five. 'Don't worry, we'll help you organise it.'

Sarah scowled at them as sternly as she could, given the fact that she was obviously very much in love.

'What about moving in together?' Bron took pity on her friend. 'That would be a start.'

'Well, location wise it's tricky. Hugo's got a lovely cottage in the country and a flat in town. I love them both but I'd like to stay around here.'

'So you're house hunting?' Elsa asked.

'Well, Hugo is. He keeps turning up with estate agent's details of completely unsuitable mansions.'

'Why are they unsuitable?' said Bron. 'What's wrong with them?'

'Too expensive. Just because he can afford to live in a small stately home, I can't.' She became aware of the other two's questioning glances. 'I want to pay my share.'

'Could he afford to buy the small stately home without help from you?' asked Elsa.

Sarah nodded, ruefully. 'He's loaded. If I'd known . . .'

'Well, thank goodness you didn't,' said Elsa. 'It took you long enough to realise he was in love with you – and you with him – without anything else coming between you! Let him buy the stately home and don't worry about it. Don't you think, Bron?'

'Absolutely. Don't let your pride come between you and your happiness any longer.' She grinned. 'I didn't.'

'But Hugo, of all people!' Sarah was struggling to be the old, efficient person she had been just a few weeks before.

'But Hugo's lovely,' said Bron and Elsa in chorus.

'I know, but the cynical old me tells me he's a Hugh Grant lookalike and I should know better.' She gave up the struggle. 'I don't though. I'm just so in love.'

'That's sweet,' said Elsa. 'And I don't know why you shouldn't be in love just because you're a wedding planner.' She paused. 'How's Lily?'

'Oh, very well. Her mother-in-law is now thrilled she's about to be a granny. She's all over Lily like a rash, buying equipment, telling Lily to put her feet up. Now they're married she's a changed woman. And they're a lovely couple.'

She turned another page of the album. 'Oh my goodness!' She nudged Bron who gave a little scream.

'It's the broken window and the glass all over my bed. When did Hugo have time to photograph that?'

'He was everywhere – ubiquitous I think the word is,' said Elsa. 'Oh, and there's the caravan.' She glanced at Bron. 'It looks really romantic, with all that ivy on it.'

'I'm surprised James didn't strip it all off for the floral arrangements,' Bron said. 'He must have missed it.'

'So how did you get him to make a move?' asked Elsa, not remotely interested in the ivy.

Bron looked embarrassed and then said playfully, 'Well – you know. I was so tired and after the fiasco with my bed and the broken glass I had nowhere to sleep except the caravan, so I went there. James was already asleep and the rest is history.'

'Not history I've heard,' said Elsa firmly. 'How do we get from "James was already asleep" to "the rest is history"? He's asleep. He can't be pouncing on you if he's unconscious.'

'OK, I admit it. It was me.' Bron was laughing and blushing at the same time. 'I lay down beside him – really just wanting a nap. But then when I woke up, he looked so gorgeous I just . . . undid a couple of buttons.' She sighed. 'He caught me at it. And if the rest isn't history, you can make it up!'

Everyone laughed and Sarah refilled their glasses. 'So, Elsa, tell us all the details about you and Laurence,' she said.

'I thought I had,' said Elsa, looking up at them from under her fringe. 'He's just lovely. My parents think he's perfect, which actually is a bit irritating, because whenever we go over for lunch he and Dad disappear into the bowels of the Morgan, leaving me and Mum with the washing-up.'

'Oh, I've so got that T-shirt,' said Bron with feeling.

Elsa grinned. 'But it's all right because Mum likes to be able to tell me how lucky I am for a few uninterrupted hours. Oh, and I've got a lovely new project – costumes for a very posh school's *Midsummer Night's Dream.'*

'Oh wow! But does that mean you won't have time for another wedding dress?' said Sarah. 'I'm meeting a new client next week.'

'Oh no, I can fit in a bride. The costumes aren't too fiddly, and I've got a couple of mums lined up to help.'

'I was hoping you'd say that. What a relief.' Sarah turned to Bron. 'And I'll be recommending my top hairdresser of course. I can't possibly do it all without my full team.' And she pointed to a picture of the three of them, arms linked, smiling happily at the camera.

'And what about the photographer?' Elsa teased.

'And the gardener?' threw in Bron before picking up the bottle and draining it into the three glasses.

They continued looking through the rest of the photographs, each chipping in with an appropriate comment every now and again.

On the last page, Sarah closed the album and reached for the second bottle of champagne, peeling off the foil in one expert move.

'I can't believe how much our lives have changed since Ashlyn's wedding. Sarah, for example,' said Bron, whilst her friend was distracted, 'has had a complete personality transplant since then.'

'No I haven't!' Sarah protested as she filled their glasses once more.

'Yes you have,' said Elsa. 'A couple of months ago you'd be making us all drink water.'

Sarah laughed. 'Well, *"to everything there is a season,"* or whatever the expression is. And this is the champagne season.' She raised her glass to join the others.

'Or even the wedding season,' said Elsa, 'or is that going too far?'

'Definitely too far,' said Sarah, 'but let's go there anyway!'